KU-167-085

The Web

Also by Jonathan Kellerman

WHEN THE BOUGH BREAKS

BLOOD TEST

OVER THE EDGE

THE BUTCHER'S THEATRE

SILENT PARTNER

TIME BOMB

PRIVATE EYES

DEVIL'S WALTZ

BAD LOVE

SELF-DEFENCE

The Web

JONATHAN
KELLERMAN

LITTLE, BROWN AND COMPANY

A *Little, Brown* Book

First published in Great Britain in 1995
by Little, Brown and Company

A CIP catalogue record for this book
is available from the British Library.

HARDBACK ISBN 0 316 91084 8
C FORMAT ISBN 0 316 87479 5

Typeset by Palimpsest Book Production Limited,
Polmont, Stirlingshire
Printed and bound in Great Britain by
Clays Ltd, St Ives plc

Little, Brown and Company (UK)
Brettenham House
Lancaster Place
London WC2E 7EN

To my daughter, Aliza.
Such pizzazz, such intellect,
flashing eyes and a smile that lights up the galaxy.
Wonderful things come in tiny packages.

The Web

1

The shark on the dock was no monster.

Four feet long, probably a low-lying reef scavenger. But its dead white eyes had retained their menace, and its jaws were jammed with needles that made it a prize for the two men with the bloody hands.

They were bare-chested Anglos baked brown, muscular yet flabby. One held the corpse by the gill slits while the other used the knife. Slime coated the gray wooden planks. Robin had been looking out over the bow as *The Madeleine* pulled in to harbor. She saw the butchery and turned away.

I kept my hand on Spike's leash.

He's a French bulldog, twenty-eight pounds of bat-eared, black-brindled muscle and a flat face that makes him a drowning risk. Trained as a pup to avoid water, he now despises it, and Robin and I had dreaded the six-hour cruise from Saipan. But he'd gotten his sea legs before we had, exploring the old yacht's teak deck, then falling asleep under the friendly Pacific sun.

His welfare during the trip had been our main concern. Six hours in a pet crate in the baggage hold during the flight from L.A. to Honolulu had left him shell-shocked. A pep talk and meatloaf had helped his recovery and he'd taken well to the condo where we'd stopped over for thirty hours. Then back on the plane for nearly eight more hours to Guam, an hour at the airport bumping shoulders with soldiers and sailors and minor government officials in guayaberas, and a forty-minute shuttle to Saipan. There Alwyn Brady had met us at the harbor and taken us, along with the bimonthly provisions, on the final leg of the trip to Aruk.

Brady had maneuvered the seventy-foot vessel through the keyhole and beyond the barrier reef. The yacht's rubber bumpers bounced gently off the pilings. Out at the remote edges, the water was deep blue, thinning to silvery green as it trickled over creamy sand. The green reminded me of something – Cadillac had offered the exact shade during the fifties. From above, the reef's ledges were coal-black, and small, brilliant fish flitted around them like nervous birds. A few coconut palms grew out of the empty beach. Dead husks dotted the silica like suspension points.

Another bump and Brady cut the engines. I looked past the dock at sharp, black peaks in the distance. Volcanic outcroppings that told the story of the island's origins. Closer in, soft brown slopes rose above small whitewashed houses and narrow roads that coiled like limp shoelaces. Off to the north a few clapboard stores and a single-pump filling station made up the island's business district. Tin roofs glinted in the afternoon light. The only sign I could make out read AUNTIE MAE'S TRADING POST. Above it was a rickety satellite dish.

Robin put her head on my shoulder.

One of Brady's deckhands, a thin, black-haired boy, tied the boat. 'This is it,' he said.

Brady came up a few seconds later, pushing his cap back and shouting at the crew to start unloading. Fiftyish, compact, and nearly as blunt faced as Spike, he was proud of his half-Irish, half-islander ancestry and talkative as an all-night disc jockey. Several times during the journey he'd turned the wheel over to one of the crewmen and come up on deck to lecture us on Yeats, Joyce, vitamins, navigation without instrumentation, sportfishing, the true depth of the Mariana Trench, geopolitics and island history. And Dr Moreland.

'A saint. Cleaned up the water supply, vaccinated the kids. Like that German fellow, Schweitzer. Only Dr Bill don't play the organ or no such foolishness. No time for nothing but his good work.'

Now Brady stretched and grinned up at the sun, displaying the few yellow teeth he had left.

'Gorgeous, isn't it? Bit of God's own giftwrap – go easy on that, Orson! *Fray*-gile. And get the doctor-and-missus gear out!'

He glanced at Spike.

'You know, doc, first time I saw that face I thought of a monkfish. But he's been a *sailor*, hasn't he? Starting to look like Errol Flynn.' He laughed. 'Too many hours on water, turn a sea cow into a mermaid – ah, here's your things – lay that *gently*, Orson, pretend it's your honeybunch. Stay there, folks, we'll unload it for you. Someone should be by any minute to pick you up – ah, talk about prophecy.'

He aimed his chin at a black Jeep coming down the center of the hillside. The vehicle stopped at the beach road, waited for a woman to pass, then headed straight for us, parking a few feet away from where the shark was being butchered. What remained of the fish was soft and pitiful.

The man with the knife was inspecting the teeth. In his late twenties, he had small features in a big, soft face, lifeless yellow hair that fell across his forehead, and arms embroidered with tattoos. Running his finger along the shark's gums, he passed the blade to his partner, a shorter man, slightly older, with heavy beard shadow, wild curly brassy hair, and matching coils of body fleece. Impassive, he began working on the dorsal fin.

Brady climbed out of the boat and stood on the dock. The water was flat and *The Madeleine* barely bobbed.

He helped Robin out and I scooped up Spike. Once on solid ground, the dog cocked his head, shook himself off, snorted, and began barking at the Jeep.

A man got out. Something dark and hairy sat on his shoulder.

Spike became livid, straining the leash. The hairy thing bared its teeth and pawed the air. Small monkey. The man seemed unperturbed. After shaking Brady's hand, he came over and reached for Robin's, then mine.

'Ben Romero. Welcome to Aruk.' Thirty to thirty-five, five six, one forty, he had a smooth bronze face and short, straight black hair side-parted precisely. Aviator glasses sat atop a delicate nose. His eyes were burnt almonds. He wore pressed blue cotton pants and a spotless white shirt that had somehow evaded the monkey's footprints.

The monkey was jabbering and pointing. 'Calm down, KiKo, it's just a dog.' Romero smiled. 'I think.'

'We're not sure, either,' said Robin.

Romero took the monkey off his shoulder and held it to his cheek, stroking its face. 'You like dogs, KiKo, right? What's his name?'

'Spike.'

'His name is *Spike*, KiKo. Dr Moreland told me he's heat sensitive so we've got a portable air conditioner for your suite. But I doubt you'll need it. January's one of our prettiest months. We get some rain bursts, but it stays about eighty.'

'It's lovely,' said Robin.

'Always is. On the leeward side. Let me get your stuff.'

Brady and his men brought our luggage to the Jeep. Romero and I loaded. When we finished, the monkey was standing on the ground petting Spike's head and chattering happily. Spike accepted the attention with a look of injured dignity.

'Good boy,' said Robin, kneeling beside him.

Laughter made us all turn. The shark butchers were looking our way. They winked and waved. The shorter one had his hands on his hip, the knife in his belt. Rosy-pink hands. He wiped them on his cutoffs and winked. The taller man laughed again.

Spike's bat ears stiffened and the monkey hissed. Romero put it back on his shoulder, frowning. 'Better get going. You must be bushed.'

We climbed into the Jeep, and Romero made a wide arc and headed back to the beach road. A wooden sign said Front Street. As we drove up the hill, I looked back. The ocean was all-encompassing and the island seemed very small. *The Madeleine*'s crew stood on the dock, and the men with the bloody hands were heading toward town, wheeling their bounty in a rusty barrow. All that was left of the shark was a stain.

2

'Let me give you a proper welcome,' said Romero. '*Ahuma na ahap* – that's old pidgin for "enjoy our home."'

He started up the same central road. Winding and unmarked, it was barely one vehicle wide and bordered by low walls of piled rock. The grade was steeper than it had appeared from the harbor and he played with the Jeep's gears in order to maintain traction. Each time the vehicle lurched, KiKo nattered and tightened his spidery grip on Romero's shirt. Spike's head was out the window, tilted up at the cloudless sky.

As we climbed, I looked back and caught a frontal view of the business district. Most of the buildings were closed, including the gas station. Romero sped past the small, white houses. Up close, the buildings looked shabbier, the stucco cracked, sometimes peeled to the paper, the tin roofs dented and pocked and mossy. Laundry hung on sagging lines. Naked and half-naked children played in the dirt. A few of the properties were fenced with chicken wire, most were open. Some looked unoccupied.

A couple of skinny dogs scrounged lazily in the dirt, ignoring Spike's bark.

This was U.S. territory but it could have been anywhere in the developing world. Some of the meanness was softened by vegetation – broad-leafed philodendrons, bromeliads, flowering coral trees, palms. Many of the structures were surrounded by greenery – whitewashed eggs in emerald nests.

'So how was your trip?' said Romero.

'Tiring but good,' said Robin. Her fingers were laced in mine and her brown eyes were wide. The air through the Jeep's open windows ruffled her curls, and her linen shirt billowed.

'Dr Bill wanted to greet you personally, but he just got called out. Some kids diving out on North Beach, stung by jellyfish.'

'Hope it's not serious.'

'Nah. But it does smart.'

'Is he the only doctor on the island?' I said.

'We run a clinic at the church. I'm an RN. Emergencies used to get flown over to Guam or Saipan till . . . anyway, the clinic does the trick for most of our problems. I'm on call for whenever I'm needed.'

'Have you lived here long?'

'Whole life except for Coast Guard and nursing school in Hawaii. Met my wife there. She's a Chinese girl. We have four kids.'

As we continued to climb, the shabby houses gave way to empty fields of red clay, and the harbor became tiny. But the volcanic peaks remained as distant, as if avoiding us.

To the right was a small grove of ash-colored trees with deeply corrugated trunks and sinuous, knobby branches that seemed to claw at the sky. Aerial roots dripped like melting wax from several boughs, digging their way back into the earth.

'Banyans?' I said.

'Yup. Strangler trees. They send those shoots up around anything unlucky enough to grow near them and squeeze the life out of it. Little hooks under the shoots – like Velcro, they just dig in. We don't want them but they grow like crazy in the jungle. Those are about ten years old. Some bird must have dropped seeds.'

'Where's the jungle?'

He laughed. 'Well, it's not really that. I mean, there're no wild animals or anything else for that matter except the stranglers.'

He pointed toward the mountaintops. 'Just east of the island's center. Dr Bill's place butts right up against it. On the other side is Stanton – the Navy base.' He shifted into low, got the Jeep over an especially steep rise, then coasted through big open wooden gates.

The road on the other side was freshly blacktopped. Four-story coco palms were set every ten feet. The piled rock was replaced by a hand-hewn, Japanese-style pine fence and rows of flame-orange clivia. Velvet lawns rolled away on all sides and I could make out the tops of the banyan forest, a remote gray fringe.

Then movement. A small herd of black-tailed deer grazing to the left. I pointed them out to Robin and she smiled and kissed my knuckles. A few seabirds hovered above us; otherwise the sky was inert.

A hundred more palms and we pulled into a huge, gravel courtyard shaded by red cedar, Aleppo pine, mango, and avocado. In the center, an algae-streaked limestone fountain spouted into a carved basin teeming with hyacinths. Behind it stood a massive two-story house, light-brown stucco with pine trim and balconies and a pagoda roof of shiny green tiles. Some of the edge tiles wore gargoyle faces.

Romero turned off the engine and KiKo scrambled off his shoulder, ran up wide stone steps, and began knocking on the front door.

Spike jumped out of the Jeep and followed, scratching at the wood with his forepaws.

Robin got out to restrain him.

'Don't worry,' said Romero. 'That's iron pine, hundreds of years old. The whole place is rock solid. The Japanese army built it in 1919, after the League of Nations took the territories away from

Germany and gave them to the emperor. This was their official headquarters.'

KiKo was swinging from the doorknob as Spike barked in encouragement. Romero said, 'Looks like they're already buddies. Don't worry about your stuff, I'll get it for you later.'

He pushed the door open with the monkey still holding on. It had been a long time since I'd left a door unlocked in L.A.

A round whitestone entry led to a big front room with waxed pine floors under Chinese rugs, high plaster walls, a carved teak ceiling, and lots of old, comfortable-looking furniture. Pastel watercolors on the walls. Potted orchids in porcelain jardinieres supplied richer hues. Archways on each side led to long hallways. In front of the right-hand passage was an awkward-looking, red-carpeted staircase with an oiled bannister, all right angles, no curves. It hooked its way up to the second-floor landing and continued out of view.

Straight ahead, a wall of picture windows framed a tourist-brochure vista of terraces and grasslands and the heartbreakingly blue ocean. The barrier reef was a tiny dark comma notched by the keyhole harbor, the western tip of the island a distinct knife point cutting into the lagoon. Most of Aruk Village was now concealed by treetops. The few houses I could see were sprinkled like sugar on the hillside.

'How many acres do you have here?'

'Seven hundred acres, give or take.'

Over a square mile. Big chunk of a seven-by-one-mile island.

'When Dr Bill bought it from the government, it was abandoned,' Romero said. 'He brought it back to life – can I get you something to drink?'

He returned with a tray of Coke cans, lime wedges, glasses, and a water bowl for Spike. Trailing him were two small women in floral housedresses and rubber thongs, one in her sixties, the other half that age. Both had broad, open faces. The older woman's was pitted.

'Dr Alexander Delaware and Ms Robin Castagna,' said Romero,

placing the tray on a bamboo end table and the water bowl on the floor.

Spike rushed over and began lapping. KiKo watched analytically, scratching his little head.

'This is Gladys Medina,' said Romero. 'Gourmet chef and executive housekeeper, and Cheryl, first daughter of Gladys and executive vice-housekeeper.'

'Please,' said Gladys, flipping a hand. 'We cook and clean. Nice to meet you.' She bowed and her daughter imitated her.

'False modesty,' said Romero, handing Robin her drink.

'What are you after, Benjamin? A ginger cookie? I didn't bake yet, so it won't do you any good. That's a very . . . cute dog. I ordered some food for him on the last boatload and it stayed dry.' She named the brand Spike was used to.

'Perfect,' said Robin. 'Thank you.'

'When KiKo eats here, it's in the service room. Maybe they want to keep each other company?'

Spike was belly down on the entry floor, jowls spreading on the stone, eyelids drooping.

'Looks like he needs to nap first,' said Romero.

'Whatever,' said Gladys. 'You need anything, you just come to the kitchen and let me know.' Both women left. Cheryl hadn't uttered a word.

'Gladys has been with Dr Bill since he left the Navy,' said Romero. 'She used to work for the base commander at Stanton as a cook, came down with scrub typhus and Dr Bill got her through it. While she recuperated, they fired her. So Dr Bill hired her. Her husband died a few years ago. Cheryl lives with her. She's a little slow.'

He led us upstairs. Our suite was in the center of the second-story landing. Sitting room with a small refrigerator, bedroom, and white-tiled bath. Old brown wool carpeting covered the floors. The walls were teak and plaster. Overstuffed floral-print furniture, more bamboo tables. The bathtub was ancient cast-iron and spotless with a marble shelf holding soaps and lotions and loofah sponges still in plastic wrap. Fly fans churned the air lazily in all three rooms. A faint insecticidal smell hung in the air.

The bed was a turn-of-the-century mahogany four-poster, made up with crisp, white linens and a yellow wilted-silk spread. On one nightstand was a frosted glass vase of cut amaryllis. A folded white card formed a miniature tent on the pillow.

Lots of windows, silk curtains pulled back. Lots of sky.

'Look at that view,' said Robin.

'The Japanese military governor wanted to be king of the mountain,' said Romero. 'The highest point on the island is actually that peak over there.' He pointed to the tallest of the black crags. 'But it's too close to the windward side. You've got your gales all year round and rotten humidity.'

He walked to a window. 'The Japanese figured the mountains gave them a natural barrier from an eastern land assault. The German governor built his house here, too, for the same reason. The Japanese tore it down. They were really into making the place Japanese. Brought in geishas, tea houses, baths, even a movie theater down where the Trading Post is now. The slave barracks were in that field we passed on the way up, where the accidental banyans are. When MacArthur attacked, the slaves came out of the barracks and turned against the Japanese. Between that and the bombing, two thousand Japanese died. Sometimes you still find old bones and skulls up along the hillside.'

He went into the bathroom and tried out the taps.

'You can drink the water. Dr Bill installed activated carbon filters on all the cisterns on the island and we take regular germ counts. Before that, cholera and typhus were big problems. You've still got to be careful about eating the local shellfish – marine toxins and rat lungworm disease. But fruits and vegetables are no problem. Anything here at the *house* is no problem, Dr Bill grows it all himself. In terms of outside stuff, the bar food at Slim's isn't much but the Chop Suey Palace is better than it sounds. At least my Mandarin wife doesn't mind it. Sometimes Jacqui, the owner, cooks up something interesting, like bird's nest soup, depending on what's available.'

'Is that where the shark's fin was headed?' I said.

'Pardon?'

'Those two guys down at the harbor. Was it for the restaurant?'

He pushed his glasses up his nose. 'Oh, them. No, I doubt it.'

A gray-haired, gray-bearded man brought up our bags. Romero introduced him as Carl Sleet and thanked him.

When he left, Romero said, 'Anything else I can do for you?'

'We seem to have everything.'

'Okay, then, here's your key. Dinner's at six. Dress comfortably.'

He exited. Spike had fallen asleep in the sitting room. Robin and I went into the bedroom and I closed the door on canine snores.

'Well,' she said, taking a deep breath and smiling.

I kissed her. She kissed back hard, then yawned in the middle of it and broke away, laughing.

'Me, too,' I said. 'Nap time?'

'After I clean up.' She rubbed her arms. 'I'm crusted with salt.'

'Ah, dill-pickle woman!' I grabbed her and licked her skin. She laughed, pushed me away, and began opening a carry-on.

I picked up the folded card on the bed. Inside was a handwritten note:

Home is the sailor, home from sea,
And the hunter home from the hill.

R. L. Stevenson

Please make my home yours.

WWM

'Robert Louis Stevenson,' said Robin. 'Maybe this will be our Treasure Island.'

'Wanna see my peg?'

As she laughed, I filled the bath. The water was crystalline, the towels brand-new, thick as fur.

When I returned, she was lying on top of the covers, naked, her hands behind her head, auburn hair spread on the pillow, nipples brown and stiff. I watched her belly rise and fall. Her smile. The oversized upper incisors I'd fallen for, years ago.

The windows were still wide open.

'Don't worry,' she said, softly. 'I checked and no one can see in – we're too high up.'

'God, you're beautiful.'

'I love you,' she said. 'This is going to be wonderful.'

3

A rasping noise woke me. Scratching at one of the screens. I sat up fast, saw it.

A small lizard, rubbing its foreclaws against the mesh.

I got out of bed and had a closer look.

It stayed there. Light brown body speckled with black. Skinny head and unmoving eyes.

It stared at me. I waved. Unimpressed, it scraped some more, finally scampered away.

Five p.m. I'd been out for two hours. Robin was still curled under the sheets.

Slipping into my pants, I tiptoed to the sitting room. Spike greeted me by panting and rolling over. I massaged his gut, refilled his water bowl, poured myself a tonic water on ice, and sat by the largest window. The sun was a big, red cherry, the ocean starting to silver.

I felt lucky to be alive, but disconnected – so far from everything familiar.

Rummaging in my briefcase I found Moreland's letter. Heavy white paper with a regal watermark. At the top in embossed black:

Aruk House, Aruk Island.

Dear Dr Delaware,

I am a physician who lives on the island of Aruk in the northern region of Micronesia. Nicknamed 'Knife Island' because of its oblong shape, Aruk is officially part of the Mariana Commonwealth and a self-governing U.S. territory, but relatively obscure and not listed in any guidebooks. I have lived here since 1961 and have found it a wonderful and fascinating place.

I chanced to come across an article you published in *The Journal of Child Development and Clinical Practice* on group trauma. Progressing to all your other published works, I find that you display a fine combination of scholarliness and common-sense thinking.

I say all this by way of making an interesting proposition.

Over the last three decades, in addition to conducting research in natural history and nutrition, I have accumulated an enormous amount of clinical data from my practice, some of it unique. Because the bulk of my time has been spent treating patients, I have not taken the time to properly organize this information.

As I grow older and closer to retirement, I realize that unless these data are brought to publication, a wealth of knowledge may be lost. Initially, my thought was to obtain the help of an anthropologist, but I decided that someone with clinical experience, preferably in a mental health field, would be better suited to the task. Your writing skills and orientation make me feel that you might be a compatible collaborator.

I'm sure, Dr Delaware, that this will seem odd, coming out of the blue, but I have given much thought to my offer. Though the pace of life on Aruk is probably a good deal slower than what you are used to, that in and of itself may have appeal for you. Would you be interested in helping me? By my estimate, the preliminary organization should take two, perhaps three months, at which point we could sit down and figure out if we've got a book, a monograph, or several journal articles. I would concentrate on the biological aspects, and I'd rely upon you for the psychological input. What I envision is a fifty-fifty collaboration with joint authorship.

I'm prepared to offer compensation of six thousand dollars per month, for four months, in addition to business-class transportation from the mainland and full room and board. There are no hotels on Aruk, but my own home is quite commodious and I'm sure you would find it pleasant. If you are married, I could accommodate your wife's transportation, though I could not offer her any paid work. If you have children, they could enroll in the local Catholic school, which is small but good, or I could arrange for private tutoring at a reasonable cost.

If this interests you, please write me or call collect at (670) 555–3334. There is no formal schedule, but I would like to get to work on this as soon as possible.

Thank you for your attention to this matter.

Sincerely,

Woodrow Wilson Moreland, M.D.

Slow pace of life; nothing in the letter indicated professional challenges, and any other time, I might have written back a polite refusal. I hadn't done long-term therapy for years, but forensic consultations kept me busy, and Robin's work as a builder of custom stringed instruments left her little free time for vacations, let alone a four-month idyll.

But we'd been talking, half jokingly, about escaping to a desert island.

A year ago a psychopath had burned down our home and tried to murder us. Eventually, we'd taken on the task of rebuilding, finding temporary lodgings at a beach rental on the far western end of Malibu.

After our general contractor flaked out on us, Robin began overseeing the project. Things went well before bogging down the way construction projects inevitably do. Our new home was still months from completion, and the double load finally proved too much for her. She hired a fellow luthier who'd developed a severe allergy to wood dust to oversee the final stages, and returned to her carving.

Then her right wrist gave out – severe tendinitis. The doctors said nothing would help unless she gave the joint a long hiatus. She grew depressed and did little but sit on the beach all day, insisting she was adjusting just fine.

To my surprise, she soon *was*, hurrying to the sand each morning, even when autumn brought biting winds and iron skies. Taking long, solitary walks to the tide pools, watching the pelicans hunt from a vantage point atop the rocky cove.

'I know, I know,' she finally said. 'I'm surprised, myself. But now I'm thinking I was silly for waiting this long.'

In November, the lease on our beach house expired and the owner informed us he was giving it to his failed-screenwriter son as an incentive to write.

Thirty-day notice to vacate.

Moreland's letter came soon after. I showed it to Robin, expecting her to laugh it off.

She said, 'Call me Robin. Crusoe.'

4

Something human woke her.

People arguing next door. A man and a woman, their words blunted by thick walls, but the tone unmistakable. Going at each other with that grinding relentlessness that said they'd had long practice.

Robin sat up, pushed her hair out of her face, and squinted.

The voices subsided, then resumed.

'What time is it, Alex?'

'Five-forty.'

She took a long breath. I sat down on the bed and held her. Her body was moist.

'Dinner in twenty minutes,' she said. 'The bath must be cold.'

'I'll run another.'

'When did you get up?'

'Five.' I told her about the lizard. 'So don't be alarmed if it happens again.'

'Was he cute?'

'Who says it was a he?'

'Girls don't peep through other people's windows.'

'Now that I think about it, he did seem to be ogling you.' I narrowed my eyes and flicked my tongue. 'Probably a lounge lizard.'

She laughed and got out of bed. Putting on a robe, she walked around, flexing her wrist.

'How does it feel?'

'Better, actually. All the warm air.'

'And doing nothing.'

'Yes,' she said. 'The power of positive nothing.'

She slipped into a sleeveless white dress that showed off her olive skin. As we headed for the stairs, someone said, '*Hello* there.'

A couple had emerged from next door. The woman was locking up. The man repeated his greeting.

Both were tall, in their forties, with short-sleeved, epauletted khaki ensembles. His looked well worn, but hers was right out of the box.

He had a red, peeling nose under thick-rimmed glasses and a long, graying beard that reached his breastbone. The hair on top was darker, thin, combed over. His vest pockets bulged. She was big busted and broad beamed, with brown hair pulled back from a round face.

They lumbered toward us, holding hands. Half an hour ago they'd been assaulting each other with words.

'Dr and Mrs Delaware, I presume?' His voice was low and grainy. Cocktail breath. Up close, his skin was freckled pemmican, the red nose due to shattered vessels, not sunburn.

'Robin Castagna and Alex Delaware,' I said.

'Jo Picker, Lyman Picker. *Dr* Jo Picker and Lyman Picker.'

The woman said, 'Actually, it's *Dr* Lyman Picker, too, but who cares about that nonsense.' She had a sub-alto voice. If the two of them had kids, they probably sounded like tugboat horns.

She gave Robin a wide, appraising smile. Light brown eyes, an even nose, lips just a little too thin. Her tan was as new as her getup, still pink around the edges.

'I've heard you're a craftswoman,' she said. 'Sounds fascinating.'

'We've been looking forward to meeting you,' said Picker. 'Round out the dinner table – make up for the host's absence.'

'Is the host absent often?' I said.

'All work, no play. When the man sleeps, I don't know. Are you vegetarians like him? We're not. My line of work, you eat what you can get or you starve to death.'

Knowing it was expected of me, I said, 'What line is that?'

'Epiphytology. Botany. Tropical spores.'

'Are you doing research with Dr Moreland?'

He gave a wet laugh. 'No, I rarely venture far from the equator. This is a cold weather jaunt for me.' He threw an arm around his wife's shoulder. 'Keeping the distaff side company. Dr Jo here is an esteemed meteorologist. Fluctuations in aerial currents. Uncle Sam's quite enamored, ergo grant money.'

Jo gave an uneasy smile. 'I study the wind. How was your trip?'

'Long but peaceful,' said Robin.

'Come over on the supply boat?' said Picker.

'Yes.'

'Out of Saipan or Rota?'

'Saipan.'

'Us, too. Damned tedious, give me a plane any day. Even the biggest ocean liner's a thumbnail in a swimming pool. Ridiculous, isn't it, big airfield over on Stanton and the Navy won't let anyone use it.'

'Dr Moreland wrote that the airport there was closed,' I said.

'Not when the Navy needs it. Damn boats.'

'Oh, it wasn't so bad, Ly,' said Jo. 'Remember the flying fish? It was lovely, actually.'

The four of us started toward the stairs.

'Typical government stupidity,' said Picker. 'All that land, no one using it – probably the result of some subcommittee. Wouldn't you say, dear? You understand the ways of the government.'

Jo's smile was tense. 'Wish I did.'

'Spend any time in Guam?' asked her husband. 'Read any of those tourist pamphlets they have everywhere? Developing the Pacific, making use of the native talent pool. So what does the military do to a place like this? Blocks off the one link between the base and the rest of the island.'

'What link is that?' I said.

'Southern coastal road. The leeward side is unapproachable from the north, sheer rock walls from the tip of North Beach up to those dead volcanoes, so the only other ways to get through are the southern beach road and through the banyan forest. Navy blockaded the road last year. Meaning no military contact with the village, no commerce. What little local economy there was got choked off.'

'What about through the forest?'

'The Japanese salted it with land mines.'

His wife moved out from under his arm. 'What kinds of things do you craft, Robin?'

'Musical instruments.'

'Ah . . . drums and such?'

'Guitars and mandolins.'

'Lyman plays the guitar.'

Picker scratched his beard. 'Took a guitar into the *hoyos* of central Ecuador – now *that* was a place – ocelots, tapir, kinkajou. Only indigenous thingies around here lack spines, and my bride despises spineless things, don't you?'

'He plays quite well,' said Jo.

'Regular Segovia.' Picker mimed a strum. 'Sitting around the campfire with the Auca Indians, trying to charm them so they'd lead me to a juicy trove of *Cordyceps militaris* – fungal parasite, grows on insect pupae, they eat it like popcorn. Humidity loosened the glue on the thing, woke up the next morning to a stack of soggy boards.' He laughed. 'Used the strings to strangle my supper that night, the rest for toothpicks.'

We reached the bottom of the stairs. Ben Romero was in the front room, KiKo on his shoulder. Picker eyed the animal. 'I've eaten them, too. Gamy. Can't housebreak them, did you know?'

'Evening, Ben,' said Jo. 'Alfresco, as usual?'

Ben nodded. 'Dr Bill will be a little late.'

'Surprise, surprise,' said Picker.

We walked through the right-hand hallway. Raw silk walls were hung with yet more pale watercolors. Nature scenes, well executed. The same signature on all of them: 'B. Moreland.' Another of the doctor's talents?

Ben led us through a big, yellow living room with a limestone fireplace, brocade couches, chinoiserie tables, Imari porcelain lamps with parchment shades. An oil portrait of a black-haired woman took up the space over the mantel. Her haughty beauty evoked Sargent.

The room opened to a wraparound terrace where a banquet table was covered with bright blue cloth. Bone china set for seven. Nascent light from hanging iron lanterns was swallowed by the still-bright evening.

The sun nudged the horizon, spilling crimson onto the skin of the water, a lovely wound. Down in the village tin roofs glinted through the treetops like tiny coins. The road leading up to the estate was a sleeping gray snake, its head resting at the big front gates. I thought of the slaves storming up from the barracks. Some Japanese general watching, helpless, knowing how it would end.

Lyman Picker touched his throat and winked at Ben.

'Bourbon,' Ben said in a tight voice. 'Straight up.'

'Excellent memory, friend.'

'And for you, Mrs Picker?'

'Just a soda, if it's no bother.'

'No bother at all.' Ben's jaws flexed. 'Ms Castagna? Dr Delaware?'

'Nothing, thanks,' I said.

Robin looked at me. 'Me, neither.'

'You're sure?'

'Positive.'

He left.

'Conscientious one, that,' said Picker.

Jo began examining the flatware. Robin and I walked to the pine railing. Picker followed us and leaned against the wood, elbows resting on the cap.

'So you're here to work with the old man. Sun and fun, maybe a publication or two. He's lucky to get you. You wouldn't find a serious scientist here.'

I laughed.

'No offense, man,' he said, as if offended. 'When I say serious, I mean us theoretical and oh-so-irrelevant types. Panhandlers with Ph.D.'s, rattling our beakers and praying stipends will drop in. This part of the globe, you want funding you don't study a place like this, you go for Melanesia, Polynesia. Big, fat, fertile islands, plenty of flora, fauna, agreeably colorful indigenous tribes, serious mythology for the folklore crowd.'

'Aruk doesn't have any of that?'

He coughed without covering his mouth. 'Micronesia, my friend, is two thousand dirt specks in three million square miles of water, most of them uninhabited bumps of coral. *This* bump's one of the most obscure. Did you know there were no people till the Spanish brought them over to grow sugar? The crop failed and the Spanish sailed away, leaving the workers to starve. Then came the Germans, who, for all their authoritarianism, hadn't a clue about colonizing. Sat around reading Goethe all day. Then the Japanese, trying the same damn sugar thing, slave labor.'

He laughed. 'So what was the payoff? MacArthur bombs them to hell and the slaves say payback time. Night of the long knives.' He drew a finger across his beard.

Jo came over. 'Is he regaling you with tales of his wideflung adventures?'

'No,' said Picker, grumpily. 'Reviewing local history.' He coughed again. 'Where's that drink?'

'Soon, Ly. So what led you to become a craftswoman, Robin?'

'I love music and working with my hands. Tell us about *your* research, Jo.'

'Nothing very exciting. I was sent to do a wind survey of several islands in the Mariana complex and Aruk's my last stop. We were renting a teeny place in town till Bill was kind enough to invite us up here. We're leaving in a week.'

'Don't make it sound like the weather service, girl,' said Picker. '*Defense* Department pays her bills. She's an important national asset. Marry an asset, get an all-expense vacation.'

He slapped his wife on the back, none too gently. She stiffened but smiled.

'Do you live in Washington?' said Robin.

'We have a town-house in Georgetown,' said Jo, 'but most of the time we're both gone.'

She recoiled. A lizard, just like the one I'd seen at the window, raced along the top of the railing. Her husband flicked a finger at it, laughing as it disappeared over the side.

'Still jittery?' he reproached her. 'I told you it's harmless. *Hemidactylus frenatus*. House gecko, semidomesticated. People feed them near the house, so they'll stick around and eat all the *buggies*.'

He wiggled his fingers in his wife's face. In grade school, he'd probably been a pigtail yanker.

She tried to smile. 'Well, I just can't get used to them doing pushups on my screen.'

'Squeamish,' Picker told us. 'Meaning I can't bring *my* work home.'

Jo colored beneath her tan.

The young housekeeper, Cheryl, came out with a tray. On it were the drinks the Pickers had ordered and mineral waters with lime for Robin and me.

'Retarded, that,' Picker said when she was gone. Tapping his temple. He raised his glass. 'To spineless things.'

Red light bounced off the ocean and bloodied his beard.

His wife looked the other way and sipped.

Robin drew me away to the opposite corner.

'Charming, huh?' I said.

'Alex, why were you so adamant about not ordering drinks?'

'Because Ben's teeth were clenched when Picker ordered his. He's a nurse, doesn't want to be thought of as a butler. Notice he sent Cheryl with the tray.'

'Oh,' she said. 'My psychologist.' She slipped her hand around my waist and lowered her head to my shoulder.

'Lovers' secrets?' Picker called out. His glass was empty.

'Let them *be*, Ly,' said Jo.

'Looks like they're *being* just fine.'

'Welcome to paradise,' I muttered.

Robin quelled a laugh. It came out sounding like a hiccup.

'Hitting the sauce, girl?' I whispered. 'Tsk, tsk. Damned self-indulgent.'

'Stop,' she said, biting her lip.

I leaned close. 'Great *fun* ahead, wench. Cooked flesh and spirits, and after dinner he'll *regale* us with tales of the giant-penised Matahuaxl tribe. Human tripods, they are. Very virile.'

She licked her lips and whispered back: 'Very, indeed. As they trip their way over the roots of the variegated crotchweed. 'Cause let's face it, when it comes to tribes, bigger *is* better.'

'Ah, love . . .' Picker called from across the terrace. 'Need another drinkie, I do.'

But he made no move to get one and neither did his wife. Welcome silence, then light footsteps sounded from behind. I turned and saw a lovely-looking blond woman walk toward us.

Late twenties or early thirties, she had a nipped waist, boyish hips, small breasts, long legs. She wore an apricot silk blouse and black crepe slacks. Blunt-cut hair ended at her shoulders, held in place by a black band. The honey tint looked real and her sculpted face had a scrubbed-clean look. Her features were fine and perfectly placed: soft, wide mouth, clean jaw, delicate ears. Blue eyes with a downward slant that made them look sad.

Except for her coloring, she could have been the woman in the oil portrait.

'Dr Delaware and Ms Castagna? I'm Pam, Dr Moreland's daughter.' Soft, musical, slightly reticent voice. She had a fetching smile but looked away as she extended her hand. I'd had patients with that tendency to avert; all had been painfully shy as children.

'Doctor *herself*,' Picker corrected. 'All these accomplished *femmes* and everyone's playing the modesty game.'

Pam Moreland gave him a pitying smile. 'Evening, Lyman. Jo. Sorry I'm late. Dad should be here shortly. If not, we'll start without him. Gladys has done a nice Chicken Kiev. Dad's vegetarian, but he tolerates us barbarians.'

She smiled beautifully but the eyes remained sad, and I wondered if physical structure completely explained it.

Picker said, 'Just gave our new chums a history lesson, Dr Daughter. Told them scientists shun this lovely bit of real estate because Margaret Mead showed the key to stardom is witch doctors, puberty rites, and bare-chested, dusky girls.' His eyes dropped to Pam's bodice.

'Interesting theory. Can I get you some coffee?'

'No thanks, my dear. But a refill of this wouldn't hurt.'

'Ly,' said Jo. She hadn't moved from her corner.

Picker kept his back to her. 'Yes, my love?'

'Come here and look at the sunset.'

He nibbled his mustache. 'The old distraction technique? Worried about my *liver*?'

'I just—'

He swiveled and faced her. 'If *Entamoeba histolytica* and *Fasciola hepatica* failed to do the trick, do you really think a little Wild *Turkey* will succeed, Josephine?'

Jo said nothing.

'Lived on metronodizole and bithionol for months,' Picker told Pam. 'Long overdue for a physical. Any referrals?'

'Not unless you're going to Philadelphia.'

'Ah, the city of brotherly love,' said Picker. 'Don't have a brother. Would I love him, if I did?'

Pondering that, he walked away.

'I *will* take that refill, Dr Pam,' he called over his shoulder.

'The man who came to dinner,' Pam said very softly. 'Excuse me.'

She returned with a quarter-full bottle of Wild Turkey, thrust it at the surprised Picker, and returned to us. 'Dad's sorry about not being able to greet you properly.'

'The jellyfish,' I said.

She nodded. Glance at a Lady Rolex. 'I guess we should get started.'

She seated Robin and me with a view of the sunset, the Pickers on the other end, herself in the middle. Two empty chairs remained and moments later Ben Romero came out and took one. He'd put on a tan cotton sportcoat.

'Usually I go home by six,' he said, unrolling his napkin, 'but my wife's having a card party, the baby's sleeping, and the older kids are farmed out.'

'Next time we'll have Claire up,' said Pam. 'She's a marvelous violinist. The kids, too.'

Ben laughed. 'That'll be real relaxing.'

'Your kids are great, Ben.'

The food came. Platters of it.

Watercress salad with avocado dressing, carrot puree, fricassee of wild mushrooms with walnuts and water chestnuts. Then the chicken, sizzling and moist.

A bottle of white burgundy remained untouched. Picker poured himself the rest of the bourbon. His wife looked the other way and ate energetically.

'Gladys didn't learn to cook like this at the base,' said Robin.

'Believe it or not, she did,' Pam said. 'The commander thought himself quite the gourmet. She's very creative, lucky for Dad.'

'Has he always been a vegetarian?'

'Since after the Korean War. The things he saw made him determined never to hurt anything again.'

Picker grunted.

'But he's always been tolerant,' said Pam. 'Had meat shipped over for me when I arrived.'

'You don't live here?' said Robin.

'No, I came last October. It was supposed to be a stopover on the way to a medical convention in Hong Kong.'

'What's your specialty?' I said.

'Internal medicine and public health. I work at the student health center at Temple U.' She paused. 'Actually, it was a combination work trip and breather. I just got divorced.'

She filled her water glass, shrugged.

'Did you grow up here?' asked Robin.

'Not really. Ready for dessert?'

Picker watched her walk away. 'Some fool in Philadelphia's missing out.'

Ben eyed him. 'Another bottle, Dr Picker?'

Picker stared back. 'No thank you, amigo. Better keep my wits. I'm flying tomorrow.'

Jo put down her fork. Picker grinned at her.

'Yes, darling, I've decided to go ahead.'

'Flying in what?' said Ben.

'Vintage craft, but well maintained. Man named Amalfi owns it.'

'Harry Amalfi? One of those crop dusters? They haven't flown in years.'

'They're quite serviceable, friend. I examined them myself. Been buzzing jungles for fifteen years and I'm going to buzz your poor excuse for one tomorrow morning, me and Dr

Missus. Take some aerial photographs, prove to the boys back at the institute that I've been here and that there was nothing to dig up.'

Jo's fingers were gathering tablecloth. 'Ly—'

Ben said, 'It's not a good idea, Dr Picker.'

Picker shot him a fierce smile. 'Your input is duly noted, friend.'

'The forest is Navy territory. You'll need official permission to fly over.'

'Wrong,' said Picker. 'Only the east end is Navy land. The western half is public land, never formally claimed by the Navy. Or so Dr Wife here tells me from her maps.'

'That's true, Ly,' said Jo, 'but it's still—'

'Zoom,' Picker spoke over her. 'Up and away – would you rather I remain bored to the point of brain death?'

'The entire forest is one mile wide,' said Ben. 'Once you're up there it's going to be pretty hard to keep track—'

'*Concerned* about me, amigo?' said Picker, with sudden harshness. He picked up the bourbon bottle, as if ready to break it. Put it down with exquisite care, and got up.

'Everyone so concerned about me. *Touching*.' His beard was littered with crumbs. 'Fonts of human *kindness* to my face, but behind my *back*: drunken *buffoon*.'

He shifted his attention to his wife, glaring and grinning simultaneously. 'Are you coming, *angel*?'

Her lip trembled. 'You know how I feel about small craft, Ly—'

'Not that. *Now*. Are you coming, *now*?'

Without taking his eyes off her, he picked up a piece of chicken and bit in. Chewing with his mouth open, he shot a hard, dark glance at Romero: 'It's a metaphor, friend.'

'What is?' said Ben.

'This place. All the other damn *bumps* in the ocean. Volcanoes ejaculating, then dropping dead. Conquerors arriving with high hopes only to slink away or die, the damned coral parasites taking over, everything sinking. Entropy.'

Jo put down her fork. 'Excuse us.'

Picker tossed the chicken onto a plate and took her arm roughly.

'Everything sinks,' he said, pulling her away.

5

Pam came back carrying a huge bowl of fruit and eyed the empty chairs.

'They left,' said Ben. 'They're renting one of Harry's crop dusters and buzzing the jungle tomorrow morning.'

'In one of those wrecks? Are they safe?'

'I tried to talk him out of it. He's a world-class explorer.' He arched his eyebrows.

She put the bowl down and sat. 'I'm afraid sometimes Dr Picker gets a little . . . difficult.'

'Nice of your father to put them up all this time,' I said.

She and Ben exchanged looks.

'They kind of invited themselves,' she said. 'Dad's a soft touch. Apparently, she's quite a prominent researcher.'

'What about him?'

'He works part-time for some wildlife organization with a shoestring budget. Studying some fungus or other. I get the feeling he's having trouble finding grant money. I guess it's difficult . . . Dad should be here any moment.'

She passed the bowl.

'Is it true,' I said. 'About the Navy cutting off contact with the village with a blockade?'

She nodded.

'Why?'

'It's the military,' said Ben. 'They live in their own little world.'

'Dad's working on it,' said Pam. 'Wrote to Senator Hoffman because the two of them go back a ways. And Hoffman knows Aruk from personal experience; he was Stanton's commander during the Korean War.'

'The gourmet?'

She nodded. 'He used to come up here with his wife, sit right on this terrace and play bridge.'

'Sounds like a good contact,' I said. The senator from Oregon had been discussed as a Presidential candidate.

Ben put his napkin down and stood. ''Scuse me, got to pick up the kids. Anything you need for tomorrow, Pam?'

'Just more disposable needles. And vaccine if it's running low.'

'Already there,' said Ben. 'I set up before dinner.'

He shook our hands and left quickly.

'He's terrific,' said Pam. 'Really knows what he's doing. He found KiKo on the docks, dying of infection, and nursed him back to health.' She smiled. 'KiKo's short for King Kong. He sleeps in a cradle in Ben's house.'

'Dr Picker said monkeys can't be housebroken.'

'I'm no primatologist, but sometimes I think animals are a lot more tractable than people.'

The sound of a car engine drew my eyes down toward the road. Darkness had set in, but a pair of headlights shone through.

'. . . one of the most levelheaded people you'll ever meet. Dad wouldn't mind if he went on to med school; the island could use a younger doctor. But the time commitment – he's got a big family to support.'

'In his letter to me,' I said, 'your father mentioned retirement.'

She smiled. 'I don't imagine he'll ever fully retire, but with three thousand people on this island, he could use some help. I've been pitching in, but . . .' She put her spoon down.

'You asked before if I grew up on Aruk and I said not really. I was born here but boarded out very young. Went to Temple for med school and stayed in Philadelphia. I kept thinking I should come back here, but I grew up a city girl, found out I *like* the city.'

'I know what you mean,' said Robin. 'Small towns are great in theory but they can be limiting.'

'Exactly. Aruk is wonderful; you guys will have a great time. But as a permanent place to live, it's – how shall I put this? At the risk of sounding elitist . . . it's just very *small*. And the water all around. You just can't go very far without being reminded of your insignificance.'

'We lived on the beach this last year,' said Robin. There were times the ocean made me feel downright invisible.'

'Precisely. Everywhere you turn, it's *there*. Sometimes I think of it as a big, blue slap in the face.'

She nibbled more fruit. 'And the pace. Cross the international dateline and for some reason everything moves *slow*-ly. I'm not the most patient person in the world.'

Gladys and Cheryl arrived with a rolling tray and coffee, cleared the dishes and poured.

Pam said, 'Everything was delicious, Gladys.'

'Tell your father to show up for dinner. He needs to take better care of himself.'

'I've been telling him that since I got here, Gladys.'

'And I've been ignoring it, mule that I am,' said a voice from the house.

A very tall, very homely man stood in the double doorway. Stooped, gaunt, clean-shaven, bald except for white dandelion puffs over his ears, he had a narrow, lipless mouth, a thick, fleshy nose and a long face bottoming in a misshapen, crinkled chin that made me think of a camel. His cheeks were hollow and limp, his eye sockets deep and pouched. Sad blue eyes – the only physical trait he'd passed on to his daughter.

He wore a cheap-looking white shirt over baggy brown pants, white socks, and sandals. His chest looked caved in, his arms long and ungainly and spotted by the sun, the flesh loose on thin bones. Plastic eyeglasses hung from a chain. His breast pocket drooped with pens, a doctor's penlight, a pair of sunglasses, a small white plastic ruler. He carried an old black leather medical bag.

As I stood, he waved and came forward in an ungainly, headfirst lope.

Not a camel. A flamingo.

Touching his lips to Pam's cheek, he said, 'Evening, kitten.'

'Hi, Dad.'

The narrow mouth widened a millimeter. 'Miss Castagna. A pleasure, dear.' He gave Robin's fingertips a brief, double-hand clasp, then took my hand, sighing, as if he'd been waiting a long time to do it.

'Dr Delaware.'

His hand was dry and limp, exerting feeble pressure, then slipping away like a windblown leaf.

'I'm bringing you dinner,' said Gladys. 'And don't tell me you grabbed a snack in the village.'

'I didn't,' said Moreland, putting his palms together. 'I promise, Gladys.'

He sat down and inspected his napkin before unfolding it. 'I trust you've been well taken care of. Any seasickness coming over?'

We shook our heads.

'Good. *Madeleine*'s a fine craft and Alwyn's the best of the supply captains. She used to belong to a sportsman from Hawaii. Runs fine on sails, but Alwyn upgraded the engines and he really makes good time. He babies that boat.'

'How many boats make the run?' I said.

'Three to six, depending on orders, circulating among the

smaller islands. On the average, we get one or two loads twice a month.'

'Must be expensive.'

'It does inflate the cost of goods.'

Cheryl returned with two plates piled high with everything we'd eaten but the chicken. Beans had been added to the rice. She set the food in front of Moreland and he smiled up at her.

'Thank you, dear. I hope your mother doesn't expect me to finish all this.'

Cheryl giggled and scurried off.

Moreland took a deep breath and raised a fork. 'How's your little bulldog faring?'

'Sleeping off the boat ride,' I said.

Robin said, 'Matter of fact, I'd better go check on him. Excuse me.'

I walked her to the stairway. When I got back, Moreland was looking at his food but hadn't touched it. Pam was sitting in place, not moving.

Moreland's eyes drifted up to the black sky. For a moment they seemed clouded. Then he blinked them clear. Pam was fiddling with her napkin ring.

'I think I'll take a walk,' she said, rising.

'Good night, kitten.'

'Nice to meet you, Dr Delaware.'

'Nice to meet you.'

Another exchange of pecks and she was gone. Moreland took a forkful of rice and chewed slowly, washing it down with water. 'I'm *very* happy to finally meet you.'

'Same here, doctor.'

'Call me Bill. May I call you Alex?'

'Of course.'

'How are your accommodations?'

'Great. Thanks for everything.'

'What did you think of my Stevenson quote?'

The question threw me. 'Nice touch. Great writer.'

'Home is the sailor,' he said. 'This is *my* home, and it's my pleasure to have you here. Stevenson never made it to the northern Marianas but he did have a feel for island life. Great thinker as well as a great writer. The great thinkers have much to offer . . . I have high hopes for our project, Alex. Who knows what patterns will emerge when we really get into the data.'

He put the fork down.

'As I mentioned, I'm particularly interested in mental health problems because they always pose the greatest puzzles. And I've seen some fascinating cases.'

He aimed the pouchy eyes at me. 'For example, years ago I encountered a case of – I suppose the closest label would be lycanthropy, but it really wasn't classical lycanthropy.'

'A wolf-man?'

'A cat-*woman*. Have you seen that?'

'During my training I saw schizophrenics with transitory animal hallucinations.'

'This was more than transitory. Thirty-year-old woman, attractive, sweet nature. Shortly after her thirty-first birthday, she began withdrawing from her family and wandering around staring at cats. Then she started chasing mice – rather uselessly. Mewing, licking herself, eating raw meat. That's what finally brought her to me: rampant intestinal parasites caused by her diet.'

'Was this a constant delusion?'

'More like a series of fits – acute spells, but they lasted longer and longer as time went on. By the time I saw her the periods between the fits weren't good, either. Appetite loss, poor concentration, bouts of weeping. Tell all that to a psychiatrist and he'd probably diagnose psychotic depression or a bipolar mood disorder. An anthropologist, on the other hand, would pounce on tribal rituals or a plant-induced religious hallucinosis. The problem is, there *are* no native hallucinogenic plants on Aruk nor any pre-Christian shamanic culture.'

He ate more rice but didn't seem to taste it. 'Interesting from a diagnostic standpoint, wouldn't you say?'

'Did the woman drink heavily?' I said.

'No. And her vitamin B intake was sufficient, so it wasn't an idiopathic Korsakoff's syndrome.'

'What about the parasites? Had they infiltrated her brain?'

'Good question. I wondered about that, too, but her symptoms made conducting even a gross neurological exam impossible. She'd gotten quite aggressive – snarling and biting and scratching to the point where her husband tied her up in her room. She'd become quite a burden.'

'Sounds brutal.'

He looked pained. 'In any event, the symptoms didn't conform to any parasitical disease I'd ever come across, and I was able to treat her intestinal problems quite easily. After she died, the husband refused an autopsy and I certified cause of death as heart attack.'

'How did she die?'

He put down his fork. 'She screamed out one night – a *cri du chat* – cat's cry. Louder than usual, so the husband went in to check. He found her lying on her bed, open-eyed, dead.'

'No evidence of any kind of poisoning?'

'My lab was rather primitive in those days, but I was able to test her blood for the obvious things and found nothing.'

'What was her relationship with her husband like?'

He stared at me. 'Is there any particular reason you ask that?'

'I'm a psychologist.'

He smiled.

'Also,' I said, 'you said she'd become a burden. And that he only went in because her cat's cry was louder. That implies he usually ignored her. It doesn't sound like marital devotion.'

He looked up and down the table, then past it, into the living room, as if making sure we were alone.

'Shortly after she died,' he said, 'her husband took up with another woman and moved off the island. Years later, I found out he'd been quite a Don Juan.' His eyes dropped to his plate. 'I suppose I'd better get through this or Gladys will have my head.'

Eating a few mouthfuls of vegetables, he said, 'I fibbed. Had some chow mein brought into the clinic. Sudden emergency, influx of jellyfish on North Beach.'

'Pam told me. How are the children?'

'Sore and covered with welts and totally unchastened . . . Any more thoughts on our catwoman?'

'Did she have a history of fainting or any other evidence of syncope?'

'A cardiac arrhythmia to explain the sudden death? None that I picked up. And no family history of heart disease. But the mode – sudden death. Her heart stopped so I called it heart disease.'

'Allergies? Anaphylaxis?'

He shook his head.

'No heavy drinking,' I said. 'What about drug abuse?'

'Her habits were clean, Alex. A lovely lady, really. Until the change.'

'How completely was she bound when she slept?'

'Hands and feet.'

'Pretty severe.'

'She was considered dangerous.'

'And she was tied up the night she died.'

'Yes.'

'Perhaps something frightened or upset her,' I said. 'To the point of heart failure.'

'Such as?'

'An especially severe hallucination. Or a nightmare.'

He didn't respond and I thought he looked angry.

'Or,' I said, 'something real.'

He closed his eyes.

'Maybe,' I continued, 'her Don Juan husband took up with another woman *before* she died.'

Slow nods; the eyes remained shut.

'Tied up at night,' I said. 'But the husband and the girlfriend were in the next room. Did they make love in front of her?'

The eyes opened. 'My, my. You are a remarkable young man.'

'Just guessing.'

Another long pause. 'As I said, it wasn't till years later that I found out about him, and only then because I treated a cousin of his who lived on another island and came to me to be treated for shingles. I gave him acyclovir and it reduced his pain. I suppose he felt he owed me something. So he told me the catwoman's husband had just died and had mentioned me on his deathbed. He'd been married three more times.'

'Any other mysterious deaths?'

'No, three divorces. All because he couldn't stop philandering. But as he lay eaten away by lung cancer, his chest completely ravaged, he confessed to tormenting his first wife. Right from the beginning. The day after the wedding, she saw him kill a cat that had gotten into their yard and eaten a chicken. He choked it to death, chopped its head off and tossed the carcass at her, laughing. She learned of his infidelities soon after. When she complained, he called her a bitch-cat and sent her to clean the chicken coop. It became a regular pattern whenever they'd fight. Years later her symptoms began. The more disturbed she became, the less he cared about hiding his affairs. During her final months, the other woman was actually living with them, ostensibly to clean house. The night she died, the husband and the girlfriend *were* making love noisily. The wife cried out in protest and they laughed at her. This went on for a while, then she entered her cat mode and began mewing. Then hissing. Then screaming.' He touched one cheek and the flesh bobbled. 'They came into her room and continued to . . . in front of her. She strained at her bonds, screaming. I'm sure her blood pressure was skyrocketing. Finally, she gave a last scream.'

He pushed his plate away.

'Deathbed confession,' he said. 'Guilt is a great motivator.'

'Infidelities,' I said. 'Catting around?'

He said nothing for several seconds. Then: 'I like that.' But he sounded anything but happy. 'So what are we talking about, diagnostically? Manic-depression marked by some sort of primitive feline identification? Or a full-blown schizophrenia?'

'Or a severe stress reaction. Was there any psychiatric history in the family at all?'

'Her mother was . . . morose.' He leaned in closer, bald pate shining like an ostrich egg. 'Dying like that. Was it due to fear? Shame? Can a person truly die of *frustration*? Or did she suffer from some physical irregularity that I wasn't clever enough to discover? That's what I mean about puzzles. We'll document the case.'

'Fascinating,' I said, thinking of the catwoman's agony.

'I've got many more, son. Many, many more.' A hand began to reach out. For a moment I thought he'd put it on mine, but it landed on the table and lay there, exhibiting a slight tremor.

'I'm so glad you're here to help me.'

'Glad to be here.'

A bark made us both turn. Robin returned with Spike on his leash.

Moreland brightened. 'Oh, look at *him*.'

He went over and crouched, hand out, palm down.

Spike panted and jumped, then nosed the old man's crotch.

'Oh, my,' said Moreland, laughing and standing. 'You're a *friendly* little fellow . . . Has he had his dinner?'

'He just finished,' said Robin, 'and we took a short walk.'

'Lovely,' Moreland said, absently. 'Do you two have any plans for tomorrow? If you're up to it, you might try snorkeling down on South Beach. The reefs are beautiful and the fish come right into the shallows, so you don't need tanks. I have an extra Jeep for you to use.'

Fishing in his pocket, he pulled out some keys and gave them to me.

'Thanks,' I said. 'When do you want to start working?'

He smiled. 'We already have.'

6

We walked back through the silk-papered gallery, Moreland moving stiffly despite long strides, Robin and I slowing down for him.

'I like your paintings,' I said.

He gave a puzzled look. 'Oh, those. They were done by my late wife.'

He made no further comment till we reached the entry hall and a door slammed upstairs from the vicinity of the Pickers' suite.

'I heard about Lyman's behavior at dinner,' he said, stopping. 'I apologize.'

'No big deal.'

'They'll only be here another week or so. She's just about completed whatever it is she came here to do. He has *nothing* to do, which is part of the problem. He's unhappy about the lack of exotic molds and repulsive plants.'

'He may still be hoping to find some,' I said. 'They're flying over the banyan forest tomorrow morning.'

Thin arms folded across his chest. 'Tomorrow?'

'That's what he said.'

'Flying in what?'

'A plane owned by a man named Harry Amalfi.'

'Good lord. Those are junk heaps. Harry bought them from surplus years ago, expecting me to hire him to dust crops. I decided to use only organic pest-control, tried to explain it to him. Even after I compensated him, he convinced himself I ruined him.'

'You paid him, anyway?' said Robin.

'I gave him something because he'd taken initiative. I suggested he use the money to open a car repair business. He and his son know how to do that. Instead, he spent every penny and hasn't taken any initiative since. There's no reason to go up in one of those rattletraps. What do they expect to see?'

'The forest.'

'There's nothing down there. The area is mostly Navy land, the rest public domain that would have been cleared long ago except that it's not safe. Land mines left by the Japanese. And who's going to fly them? Harry hasn't been up in years. *And* he drinks.'

'Picker has a pilot's license.'

He shook his head. 'I must have a talk with them. Those land mines are a real danger if he tries to land. I had barbed wire put up along the eastern wall of my property to make sure no one climbed over. I'd better go up there right now.'

'He may not be receptive,' I said.

'Oh . . . yes, you're probably right. Tomorrow morning, then . . . Now, in terms of your recreation here at the house, we don't get television reception but the radio in your room should be working. There's also a small library on the other side of the dining room.' He gave a little wave. 'Converted silver room. You may not find much of interest there. Mostly condensed books and biographies. There are many more books in your office, and mine. Periodicals come in with the provisions. If there's something specific you're interested in reading, I'll do my best to find it for you.'

He bent slowly and petted Spike. 'Well, I'll let you go now. Is there anything you need?'

Robin said, 'It's so pleasant out I thought we might walk some more.'

Moreland nodded happily. 'Have you noticed the sweetness in the air? I've planted for aroma. Frangipani, night-blooming jasmine, old roses, all sorts of things.'

'Picker said the soil isn't good,' I said.

'He's right about that. Any residues of volcanic ash have drifted into the jungle, and the rest of the island is too high in salt and silica. In some places, the dirt only goes down a couple of feet before you hit coral. With the exception of a few pines planted by the Japanese, this place was scrub when I bought it. I brought in boatloads of topsoil and amendments. It took years. It's turned out fairly well. Would you like to see – no, forgive me, I won't interrupt your walk.'

'We'd love to,' said Robin.

He blinked. 'I believe you're being kind to an old bore. But at my age, one takes what one gets – let's go, little doggy.'

Behind the house was a courtyard planted with privet-hedged rose gardens and precisely cut flower beds. Big conifers, some pruned in the spare, graceful Japanese style. Then, looser plantings of palm and fern and crushed rock walkways lined with low-growing lillies. Artfully placed spotlights allowed just enough illumination for safe passage. The botanic perfumes blended in strange combinations. Sometimes the result was cloying.

'It goes back a ways,' said Moreland, pointing to a wooden arbor at the rear of the lawn. To the side, high-voltage spots exposed a grass tennis court without a net, then more grass. Off to the left stood a group of flat-roofed buildings: one huge hangarlike structure and several smaller sheds. Moreland led us to them, saying, 'It's too dark to see, but I've got all sorts of things behind the arbor. Citrus, plum, peach, table grapes, bananas, vegetables. Feel free to go picking tomorrow. Everything's safe to eat.'

'Are you self-sufficient?' I said.

'For the most part. Meat and fish and dairy products, I buy for the staff and guests. I used to keep a goat herd for milk, but we didn't consume enough to justify it. As I wrote you, I conduct nutritional research. Sometimes there's surplus for the village.'

'Do people in the village grow anything?'

'A bit,' he said. 'It's not an agricultural culture.'

As we got closer to the outbuildings, he said, 'Those are my offices and labs and warehouses. Your office is the nearest bungalow, and I've set aside studio space for you, as well, Robin, right next door. A nice room with northern exposure and a skylight. My wife used to paint there. How's your wrist doing?'

'Better.'

He stopped again. 'May I?' Lifting her arm, he flexed the joint very gently. 'No crepitus. Good. Ice for acute inflammation and follow up with warmth for pain. Keep it relaxed and it should knit nicely. The southern lagoon stays very nice all year round. Swimming's a low-resistance exercise that will strengthen the muscles without unduly stressing the joint.'

Releasing her arm, he looked out into the darkness.

'I should, probably dig up some of that lawn. Ridiculously labor intensive and useless, but I grew up on a ranch and the smell of new grass brings me back to my childhood.'

'A ranch where?' I said.

'Sonoma, California. Father grew Santa Rose plums and pinot noir grapes.'

We continued walking.

'Do you see patients here?' I said.

'No, that's done at the clinic in town. The X-ray machine is there and it's a lot more convenient for the villagers.'

'So what kinds of labs do you have here?'

'Research. I have a long-standing interest in *alternative* pesticides – are either of you squeamish?'

'About what?' said Robin.

'Natural predation.' He blinked. 'Spineless creatures.'

'If they're crawling all over me, I am.'

He laughed. 'I certainly hope not, dear. If you're ever interested, I have some very interesting specimens.'

'You keep live specimens here?'

He turned to pat her shoulder. 'Under lock and key in that big building over there. I'm sorry, dear. I should have told you. Sometimes I forget how people get.'

'No, it's all right,' she said. 'When I was a kid I had a tarantula as a pet.'

'I didn't know that,' I said.

She laughed. 'Neither did my parents. A friend gave it to me when *her* mother made her get rid of it. I hid it in a shoebox in my closet for weeks. Then *my* mother discovered it. One of the more memorable episodes of my childhood.'

'I have tarantulas,' said Moreland. Excitement tinged his voice. 'They're really quite wonderful, once you get to know them.'

'Mine wasn't that big, maybe an inch long. I think it was from Italy.'

'Probably an Italian wolf spider. *Lycosa tarantula.* Here's something for *you*, Alex: the bite of the Italian wolf was once thought to cause madness – weeping and stumbling and dancing. That's how the tarantella dance got its name. Nonsense, of course. The little thing's harmless.'

'Wish you could have been there to convince my mother,' said Robin. 'She flushed it.'

Moreland winced. 'If you'd like to see another one, I can oblige.'

'Sure,' she said. 'If it's okay with you, Alex.'

I stared at her. Back home she called upon me to swat mosquitoes and flies.

'Love to see it,' I said. Mr Macho.

'I'm afraid you'd best leave *him* outside, though,' said Moreland, looking at Spike. 'Dogs are still basically wolves, and wolves are predators with all the hormonal secretions that entails. Little scurrying things may set off an aggressive response in him. I don't want to upset him. Or them.'

'Humans are predators, too,' I said.

'Most definitely,' said Moreland. 'But we seem to be naturally afraid of them, and they can deal with that.'

We tied Spike to a tree, gave him a cheese-flavored dog cracker, and told him we'd be back soon.

Moreland took us to the hangarlike building. The entrance was a gray metal door.

'The Japanese officers' bath house,' he said, releasing a key lock. 'They had herbal mudpits here, wet and dry steam, fresh and saltwater pools. The saltwater was brought up from the beach in trucks.'

He flipped a switch and light flooded a windowless room. White tile on all surfaces. Empty. Another gray door, closed. No lock.

'Careful, now,' he said. 'I have to keep the light dim. There are thirteen steps down.'

Opening the second door, he flicked one of a series of toggles and a weak, pale-blue haze stuttered to life.

'Thirteen steps,' he reiterated and he counted out loud as we followed him down a stone flight, grasping cold metal handrails.

The interior was much cooler than the main house. At the bottom was a sunken area, maybe sixty feet long. Concrete walls and floors. The floors were marked by several rectangles. Seams, where concrete had been poured to fill the baths.

Narrow windows so high they nearly touched the ceiling let in feeble dots of moonlight. Translucent wire glass. The blue light came from a few fluorescent bulbs mounted vertically on the walls. As my eyes got accustomed to the dimness, I made out another flight of stairs at the far end. A raised work space: desk and chair, storage cabinets, lab tables.

A wide aisle spined through the center of the sunken area. Metal ribs on both sides: ten rows of steel tables bolted to the concrete.

The tables housed dozens of ten-gallon aquariums covered by wire mesh lids. Some tanks were completely dark. Others glowed pink, gray, lavender, more blue.

Random spurts of sound from within: flutterings and scratchings, sudden stabs, the ping of something hard against glass.

The panic of attempted escape.

A strange mixture of smells filled my nose. Decayed vegetation, excreta, peat moss. Wet grain, boiled meat. Then something sweet – fruit on the verge of rot.

Robin's hand in mine was as cold as the handrails.

'Welcome,' said Moreland, 'to my little zoo.'

7

He led us past the first two rows and stopped at the third. 'Some sort of classification system would have been clever, but I know where everyone is and I'm the one who feeds them.'

Turning left, he stopped at a dark tank. Inside was a floor of mulch and leaves, above it a tangle of bare branches. Nothing else that I could see.

He pulled something out of his pocket and held it between his fingers. A pellet, not unlike Spike's kibble.

The wire lid was clamped; he loosened it and pushed, exposing a corner. Inserting two fingers, he dangled the pellet.

At first, nothing happened. Then, quicker than I believed possible, the mulch heaved, as if in the grip of a tiny earthquake, and something shot up.

A second later, the food was gone.

Robin pressed herself against me.

Moreland hadn't moved. Whatever had taken the pellet had disappeared.

'Australian garden wolf,' said Moreland, securing the top. 'Cousin of your Italian friend. Like *tarantula*, they burrow and wait.'

'Looks as if you know what it likes,' said Robin. I heard the difference in her voice, but a stranger might not have.

'What *she* likes – this one's quite the lady – is animal protein. Preferably in liquid form. Spiders always liquefy their food. I combine insects, worms, mice, whatever, and create a broth that I freeze and defrost. This is the same stuff, compressed and freeze-dried. I did it to see if they'd adapt to solids. Luckily, many of them did.'

He smiled. 'Strange avocation for a vegetarian, right? But what's the choice? She's my responsibility . . . Come with me, perhaps we can bring back some memories.'

He opened another aquarium at the end of the row, but this time he shoved his arm in, drew out something, and placed it on his forearm. One of the vertical bulbs was close enough to highlight its form on his pale flesh. A spider, dark, hairy, just over an inch long. It crawled slowly up toward his shoulder.

'Does this resemble what your mother found, dear?'

Robin licked her lips. 'Yes.'

'Her name is Gina.' To the spider, now at his collar: 'Good evening, señora.' Then to Robin: 'Would you like to hold her?'

'I guess.'

'A new friend, Gina.' As if understanding, the spider stopped. Moreland lifted it tenderly and placed it in Robin's palm.

It didn't budge, then it lifted its head and seemed to study her. Its mouth moved, an eerie lipsynch.

'You're cute, Gina.'

'We can send one to your mother,' I said. 'For old time's sake.'

She laughed and the spider stopped again. Then, moving with

mechanical precision, it walked to the edge of her palm and peered over the edge.

'Nothing down there but floor,' said Robin. 'Guess you'd like to go back to Daddy.'

Moreland removed it, stroked its belly, placed it back in its home, walked on.

Pulling out his doctors' penlight, he pointed out specimens.

Colorless spiders the size of ants. Spiders that *looked* like ants. A delicate green thing with translucent, lime-colored legs. A sticklike Australian *hygropoda*. ('Marvel of energy conservation. The slender build prevents it from overheating.') A huge-fanged arachnid whose brick-red carapace and lemon-yellow abdomen were so vivid they resembled costume jewelry. A Bornean jumper whose big black eyes and hairy face gave it the look of a wise old man.

'Look at this,' he said. 'I'm sure you've never seen a web like this.'

Pointing to a zigzag construction, like crimped paper.

'*Argiope*, an orb spinner. Custom-tailored to attract the bee it loves to eat. That central "X" reflects ultraviolet light in a manner that brings the bees to it. All webs are highly specific, with incredible tensile strength. Many use several types of silk; many are pigmented with an eye toward particular prey. Most are modified daily to adapt to varying circumstances. Some are used as mating beds. All in all, a beautiful deceit.'

His hands flew and his head bobbed. With each sentence, he grew more animated. I knew I was anthropomorphizing, but the creatures seemed excited, too. Emerging from the shadows to show themselves.

Not the panic I'd heard before. Smooth, almost leisurely motions. A dance of mutual interest?

'. . . why I concentrate on predators,' Moreland was saying. 'Why I'm so concerned with keeping them fit.'

A brilliant pink, crablike thing rested atop his bony hand. 'Of course, natural predation is nothing new. Back in nineteen twenty-five *levuana* moths threatened the entire coconut crop on

Fiji. Tachinid parasites were brought in and they did the job beautifully. The following year, a particularly voracious destructor scale was done in by the coccinellid beetle. And I'm sure you know gardeners have used ladybugs on aphids for years. I breed them to protect my citrus trees, as a matter of fact.' He pointed to an aquarium that seemed to be red carpeted. A finger against the glass made the carpet move. Thousands of miniature Volkswagens, a ladybug traffic jam. 'So simple, so practical. But the key is keeping them nutritionally robust.'

We moved further up the row and he stopped and breathed deeply. 'If it weren't for public prejudice, *this* beauty and her compatriots could be trained to clear homes of rats.'

Shining the penlight into a dark tank, he revealed something half covered by leaves.

It crawled out slowly and my stomach lurched.

Three inches wide and more than twice that length, legs as thick as pencils, hairs as coarse as boar bristle. It remained inert as the light washed over it. Then it opened its mouth wide – yawning? – and stroked the orifice with clawlike pincers.

As Moreland undid the mesh I found myself stepping back. In went his hand; another pellet dangled.

Unlike the Australian wolf, this one took the food lazily, almost coyly.

'This is Emma and she's spoiled.' One of the spider's legs nudged his finger, rubbing it. '*This* is the tarantula of B-movies, but she's really a *Grammostola*, from the Amazon. In her natural habitat, she eats small birds, lizards, mice, even venomous snakes, which she immobilizes, then crushes. Can you see the advantages for pest control?'

'Why doesn't she use her own venom?' I said.

'Most spider venom can't do harm except to very small prey. You can be sure spoiled Madame Emma wouldn't have the patience to wait for the toxin to take effect. Despite her apparent indolence, she's quite eager when she gets hungry. All wolves are; they got their name because they chase their prey down. I must confess they're my favorite. So bright. They quickly recognize individuals. And they respond to kindness. All tarantulae do. That's why your little *Lycosa* made such a good pet, Robin.'

Robin's eyes remained on the monster.

Moreland said, 'She likes you.'

'I sure hope so.'

'Oh yes, she definitely does. When she doesn't care for someone, she turns her head away – quite the debutante. Not that I bring people in here very often. They need their peace.'

He petted the huge spider, removed his hand, and covered the aquarium. 'Insects and arachnids are magnificent, structurally and functionally. I'm sure you've heard all the clichés about how they're competing with us, will eventually drive us to extinction. Nonsense. Some species become quite successful but many others are fragile and don't survive. For years entomologists have been trying to figure out what leads to success. The popular academic model is *Monomorium pharaonis* – the common ant. Many tenures have been granted on studies of what makes *Monomorium* tick. The conventional wisdom is that there are three important criteria: resistance to dehydration, cooperative colonies with multiple fertile queens, and the ability to relocate the colony quickly and efficiently. But there are insects with those exact traits who fail and others, like the carpenter ant, who've done quite well despite having none of them.'

He shrugged.

'A puzzle.'

He resumed the tour, pointing out walking stick bugs, mantises with serrated jaws, giant Madagascar hissing cockroaches topped with chitinous armor, dung beetles rolling their fetid treasures like giant medicine balls, stout, black carrion beetles ('Imagine what they could do to solve the landfill problems you've got over on the mainland'). Tank after tank of crawling, climbing, darting, crackling, slithering things.

'I stay away from butterflies and moths. Too short-lived and they need flying room to be truly happy. All my guests adapt well to close quarters and many of them achieve amazing longevity – my *Lycosa*'s ten years old, and some spiders live double or triple that amount . . . Am I boring you?'

'No,' said Robin. Her eyes were wide and it didn't seem like fear. 'They're all impressive, but Emma . . . her size.'

'Yes.' He walked quickly to a tank in the last row. Larger than the others, at least twenty gallons. Inside, several rocks formed a cave that shadowed a wood-chip floor.

'My brontosaurus,' he said. 'His ancestors probably *did* coexist with the dinosaurs.'

Pointing to what seemed to be an extension of the rock.

I stayed back, looking, steeling myself for another heart-stopping movement.

Nothing.

Then it was *there*. Without moving. Taking shape before my eyes:

What I'd thought to be a slab of rock was organic. Extending out of the cave.

Flat bodied, segmented. Like a braided brown leather whip.

Seven, eight inches long.

Legs on each segment.

Antennae as thick as cello strings.

Twitching antennae.

I moved further back, waiting for Moreland to play the pellet game.

He put his face up against the glass.

More slithered out of the cave.

At least a foot long. Spikes at the tail end quivered.

Moreland tapped the glass, and several pairs of feet pawed the air.

Then, a lunging motion, a sound like snapping fingers.

'What . . . is it?' said Robin.

'The giant centipede of East Asia. This one stowed away on one of the supply boats last year – Brady's as a matter of fact. I obtain a lot of my specimens that way.'

I thought of our ride on *The Madeleine*. Sleeping below deck, wearing only bathing trunks.

'He's significantly more venomous than most spiders,' he said. 'And I haven't named him yet. Haven't quite trained him to love me.'

'How venomous is significant?' I said.

'There's only one recorded fatality. A seven-year-old boy in the Philippines. The most common problem is secondary infection, gangrene. Limb loss can occur.'

'Have you ever been bitten?' I asked.

'Often.' he smiled. 'But only by human children who didn't wish to be vaccinated.'

'Very impressive,' I said, hoping we were through. But another pellet was between Moreland's fingers, and before I knew it another corner of mesh had been drawn back.

No dangling this time. He dropped the food into the centipede's cage from a one-foot height.

The animal ignored it.

Moreland said, 'Have it your way,' and refastened the top.

He headed up the central aisle and we were right behind him.

'That's it. I hope I haven't repulsed you.'

'So your nutritional research is about them,' I said.

'Primarily. They have much to teach us. I also study web patterns, various other things.'

'Fascinating,' said Robin.

I stared at her. She smiled from the corner of her mouth. Her hand had warmed. Her fingers began tickling my palm then dropped. Crawling down my inner wrist.

I tried to pull away but she held me fast. Full smile.

'I'm glad you feel that way, dear,' said Moreland. 'Some people are repelled. No telling.'

Later, in our suite, I tried to extract revenge by coming up behind her as she removed her makeup and lightly scratching her neck.

She squealed and shot to her feet, grabbing for me, and we ended up on the floor.

I got on top and tickled her some more. '*Fascinating?* All of a sudden I'm living with *Spiderwoman*? Shall we begin a new *hobby* when we get back?'

She laughed. 'First thing, let's learn the recipe for those pellets . . . Actually, it *was* fascinating, Alex. Though now that I'm out of there, it's starting to feel creepy again.'

'The *size* of some of them,' I said.

'It wasn't a typical evening, that's for sure.'

'What do you think of our host?'

'Mucho eccentric. But courtly. Sweet.'

'*Dear*?'

'I don't mind that from him. He's from another generation. And despite his age, he's still passionate. I like passion in a man.'

She freed an arm and ran it up mine. 'Coochie-coo!'

I pinioned her. 'Ah, my little *Lycosa*, *I* am passionate, *too*!'

She reached around. 'So it *seems*.'

I bared my teeth. 'Hold me and crush me, Arachnodella – *liquefy* me!'

'You scoff,' she said, 'but just think what I could do with six more hands.'

8

The next morning swim fins, snorkels, towels, and masks were waiting for us at the breakfast table.

'Jeep's out in front,' said Gladys.

We ate quickly and found the vehicle parked near the fountain. One of those bare-bones, canvas-top models that kids in Beverly Hills and San Marino favor when pretending to be rural. This one was the real thing: clouded plastic windows, rough white paint, no four-figure stereo system.

Just as I started the engine, the Pickers burst out of the house, waving.

'Hitch a ride into town?' Lyman called out. They were in khakis again, with bush hats. Binoculars hung around his neck and a big, yellow smile opened in his beard. 'Seeing as this used to be *our* borrowed vehicle, don't see how you can decently refuse.'

'Wouldn't think of it,' I said.

They climbed in the back.

'Thanks,' said Jo. Her eyes were bloodshot and her mouth looked tight.

From Robin's lap, Spike grumbled.

'Talk about brachycephaly,' said Picker. 'Is he able to breathe?'

'Apparently,' said Robin.

'Where would you like me to drop you?' I said.

'I'll direct you. Terrible shocks on this thing, so watch for potholes.'

I drove through the gates, the Jeep gliding on the fresh blacktop, speeding along the palm-lined road. Soon the ocean came into view, true-blue, unperturbed by breakers. As we neared the harbor, the water swooped toward us; driving toward it was like tumbling into a box of sapphires. I remembered Pam's comment about a big, blue slap in the face.

Picker said, 'Did you notice the rotary phones in the house? Thank God it's not two cans and a string.'

Robin put her hand on my leg and turned back to him, smiling. 'If you don't like it, why stay?'

'We do like it,' said Jo, quickly.

'Excellent question, Ms Craftsperson,' said her husband. 'If it were up to me, we would *not* be staying. If it were up to me we would not be staying within a thouand miles of this *isle*. But Dr Wife's research is urgent. Heard you saw the zoo-ette last night. Rich man's version of firefly in a jar. No systemization. Scientifically, it's a waste of time.'

Spike reared his head and stared. Picker tried to pet him but he backed away and curled up in Robin's lap again.

'Male dogs,' said Picker, 'always go for the *femmes*.'

'That's not true, Ly,' said his wife. 'When I was little we had a miniature schnauzer and he preferred my father.'

'Because, dearest, he'd met your *mother*.'

He didn't mind laughing by himself. 'Hormones. Dogs go after women, men go after bitches.'

He began humming. Spike growled.

'Not a music fan,' said Picker.

'On the contrary,' said Robin. 'He likes melody but sour notes drive him wild.'

At Front Street Picker said, 'Go right.'

I drove north, parallel to the waterfront. No boats were in dock and the gas station was still closed, a fuel-rationing schedule posted on the pump. A couple of children rode bikes up and down the waterfront, a woman pushed a baby stroller. Men sat with their feet in the water, and one lay stretched out on the dock, sleeping.

'Where's the airfield?'

'Just keep going.'

We passed the shops. A saltwater tang hung in the air; the temperature was a perfect eighty. The windows of Auntie Mae's Trading Post were filled with faded T-shirts and souvenirs and signs above the entrance advertising postal service and snacks and check-cashing. Next door was the Aruk Market – two open-air stalls of fruit and vegetables. A few women squeezed and bagged the merchandise. As we passed, a couple of them smiled.

The adjoining building was white and shuttered with a Budweiser sign long depleted of neon – SLIM'S ORCHID BAR. Skinny, ragged specimens slouched in front, long-necks in hand. The Chop Suey Palace facade was red with gold lettering, and stone Fu dogs guarded the door. Three outdoor tables were set up in front. A dark-haired man sat at one of them drinking a beer and pushing something around his plate with chopsticks. He looked up but didn't smile.

Next came more stores, all empty, some of the windows boarded, then a freshly whitewashed block structure with several cars parked in front and a sign claiming: MUNICIPAL CENTER. North Beach began as more barrier reef and palms, sand dunes spotted with clumps of white-flowered beach plum. To the right a paved road twisted up the hillside. The stucco houses at the top had been turned to vanilla fudge by the morning sun. I spotted a church steeple and a copper peak below it.

'Is that where the clinic is?'

'Yup,' said Picker. 'Keep going.'

No more outlets appeared as we continued to hug the island's upper shore. No keyhole harbor on the north side, and the water was a little more active. Scattered swimmers stroked lazily and sunbathers offered themselves like bits of cookie batter, but birds outnumbered the human population by far, droves of them searching the water's edge for breakfast.

Front Street ended at a six-slot parking area. To the east was a fifteen-foot wall of untrimmed bamboo. Hand-lettered signs read PRIVATE PROPERTY and < > DEAD END < > NO OUTLET.

Picker leaned forward and pointed over my shoulder at a break in the bamboo. 'In there.'

I turned up a dirt path so narrow that bamboo brushed the sides of the Jeep. A hundred-yard drive brought a house into view.

More Cape Cod than Tahiti, its splintering planks hadn't been white in a long time. The front porch was piled high with junk, and a stovepipe vent spouted from the tar roof.

The property was wide and flat, maybe fifteen acres of red dirt walled by bamboo. The tall plants along the rear border looked puny backed by two hundred feet of sheer black rock.

The western edge of the volcanic range. The mountains hurled shadows so dark and defined they resembled paint splotches.

A smaller house sat fifty feet behind the first. Same construction and condition with a strange-looking doorway – bright white gingerbread molding that didn't fit.

Between the two buildings rested half the fuselage of a propellor plane, its sheet-metal edges sliced cleanly. The rest of the acreage was a grimy sculpture garden peppered with more plane carcasses, heaps of parts, and a few craft left intact.

As I pulled up a man wearing only dirty denim cutoffs came out of the bigger house knuckling his eyes and shoving limp yellow hair out of his face. The younger of the shark butchers we'd seen yesterday.

Picker drew back the Jeep's plastic window flap. 'Where's your father, Skip?'

The man rubbed his eyes again. ''Side.' His voice was thick and hoarse and peevish.

'We're renting a plane from him this morning.'

Skip tried to digest that. Finally he said, 'Yeah.'

'Where's the takeoff strip, Ly?' said Jo.

'Anywhere we please; these aren't jumbo jets. Let's get going.'

The two of them climbed out of the Jeep, and Picker went up to Skip and began talking. Jo hung back, mouth still busy, hands plucking at her vest.

'Poor thing,' said Robin. 'She's scared.'

As I started to turn the Jeep around, another bare-chested man came out of the house. Flowered boxer shorts. The same wide face as Skip but thirty years older. Sloping shoulders and a monumental gut. What was left of his hair was tan-gray. A two-week beard coated a face made for suspicion.

He pointed at us and approached the Jeep.

'You the *doctor's* new guests?' Heavy voice, like his son, but not as sleepy. 'Amalfi.' His tiny blue eyes were bloodshot but alert, his nose so flat it was almost flush. The beard was patchy and ingrown. The skin it didn't cover was a ruin of mounds and puckers.

'What's that you got?'

'French bulldog.'

'Never saw nothing like that in France.'

Robin stroked Spike, and Harry Amalfi drew back his head. 'Having a good time, miss?'

'Very much so.'

'Doctor treating you good?'

She nodded.

'Well, don't count on it.' He licked a finger and held it to the wind. 'Wanna go up in the air, too?'

'No thanks.'

He laughed, started coughing, and spat on the ground. 'Nervous?'

'Maybe some other time.'

'Don't worry, miss, my planes are all greased and tuned. I'm the only way to fly around here.'

'Thanks for the offer,' I said, and completed the turn. Amalfi put his hands on his hips and watched us, hitching up his shorts. The Pickers had gone inside the house with Skip.

As I drove away, I looked back and got a closer look at the smaller house. The white molding around the door was a ring of sharks' jaws.

I got on Front Street and drove back toward South Beach. The man with the chopsticks was still in front of the Palace and this time he stood as we approached and waved his arms, as if hailing a cab.

I pulled over and he trotted to the curb. He was around forty, average height and narrow build, with black hair combed down over his forehead and a black mustache too thin to see from a distance. The rest of his face was sallow and smooth, nearly hairless. He wore wide, black Porsche sunglasses, a short-sleeved blue button-down shirt, seersucker pants, and topsiders. Back at his table was a stuffed Filofax next to a platter of noodles-and-something, and three empty Sapporos.

He said 'Tom Creedman' in a tone that said we should recognize the name. When we didn't, he smiled unhappily and clicked his tongue. 'L.A., right?'

'Right.'

'New York,' he said, pointing to his chest. 'Before that, D.C. Used to work in the news business.' He paused, then dropped the names of a TV network and two major newspapers.

'Ah,' I said, as if all was clear. His smile warmed up.

'Care to join me for a beer?'

I looked at Robin. She nodded.

We got out and went over to his table, Spike in tow. He looked at the dog but didn't say anything. Then he stuck his head in the restaurant's open door. 'Jacqui!'

A statuesque woman came out, dishcloth balled in one hand. Her long dark hair was thick and wavy, crowning a full-lipped, golden face. A few lines but young skin. Her age was hard to gauge – anywhere from twenty-five to forty-five.

'The new guests up at Knife Castle,' Creedman told her. 'A round for everyone.'

Jacqui smiled at us. 'Welcome to Aruk.'

'Something to eat?' said Creedman. 'I know it's early but I've found Chinese for breakfast a great pick-me-up. Probably all the soy sauce, gets that blood pressure up.'

'No thanks.'

'Okay,' said Creedman to Jacqui. 'Just beers.'

She left.

'Knife Castle?' said Robin.

'Local nickname for your lodgings. Didn't you know? The Japanese owned this island; Moreland's manse was their headquarters. They used the locals as slaves to do all the dirty work, imported more. Then MacArthur decided to take over everything from Hawaii to Tokyo and bombed the hell out of them. When the surviving Japanese soldiers were trying to entrench, the slaves grabbed any sharp thing they could find, left their barracks, and finished the job. Knife Island.'

I said, 'Dr Moreland said it was because of the shape.'

Creedman laughed.

'Sounds like you've done some research,' I said.

'Old habits.'

Jacqui brought the beers and he threw a dollar tip at her. She looked irritated and left quickly.

Creedman lifted a bottle but instead of drinking rubbed the top of his hand against the glass.

'What brings you here?' I said.

'Little wind-down from reality. Running with the Beltway movers and shakers too long.'

'You covered politics?'

'In all its sleazy splendor.' He raised his bottle. 'To island torpor.'

The beer was ice-cold and terrific.

Robin took my hand. Creedman stroked the bottle some more,

then the Filofax. 'I'm working on a book. Nonfiction novel – life-changes, isolation, internal revolution. The island mystique as it relates to the end-of-the-century zeitgeist.' He smiled. 'Can't really say more.'

'Sounds interesting,' I said.

'My publisher hopes so. Got them to pay me enough so they'll break their asses promoting.'

'Is Aruk your only subject or have you been to other islands?'

'Been traveling for over a year. Tahiti, Fiji, Tonga, the Marshalls, Guam, rest of the Marianas. Came here last year to start writing because the place is dead, no distractions.'

Taking a long swallow, he gave yet another closed-mouth laugh. 'So how long will you be here?'

'Probably a couple of months,' I said.

'What exactly are you here for?'

'Helping Dr Moreland organize his data.'

'Medical data?'

'Whatever he's got.'

'Any specific diseases you're looking at?'

'No, just a general overview.'

'For a book?'

'If there's a book in it.'

'You're a psychologist, right?'

'Right.'

'So he wants you to analyze his patients psychologically?'

'We're still discussing the specifics.'

He smiled. 'What's that, *your* version of no comment?'

I smiled back. 'My version of we're still discussing the specifics.'

He turned to Robin. 'And you, Robin? What's your project?'

'I'm on vacation.'

'Good for you.' He faced me again. 'Another beer?'

'No thanks.'

'Good stuff, isn't it? Most of the packaged goods that get over here are from Japan. Marked up two, three hundred percent – ultimate revenge.'

He drained his bottle and put it down. 'I'll have you guys over for dinner.'

'Where do you live?' I said.

'Just up there.' He tilted his head toward the hillside. 'Spent a few days up at Moreland's but couldn't take it. Too intense – he is something, isn't he?'

'He seems very dedicated.'

'Easy to be dedicated when you're loaded. Did you know his father was a big San Francisco investment honcho?'

I shook my head.

'*Big* bucks. Mega. Owned a brokerage house, some banks, ranchland all over wine country. Moreland's an only child, inherited the whole kit and k. How else could be keep that place going? Not that it's going to matter. Lost cause.'

'What is?' said Robin.

'Saving this place. I don't want to put a downer on your trip, but Aruk's on the way out. No natural resources, no industry. No industriousness. Talk about your slackers – look at that beach. They don't even have the energy to swim. The smart ones keep leaving. Only a matter of time before it looks like one of those cartoon desert islands, shipwrecked loser under a palm tree.'

'I hope not,' said Robin. 'It's so beautiful.'

Creedman inched closer to her. 'Maybe so, Robin, but let's face it, ebb and flow is part of the life rhythm – that's a theme of my book.'

'How much of the island's decline is due to the Navy's blocking the southern road?' I said.

'Have you been to Stanton?'

'No.'

'If that's a base, I'm a sea anemone. The only incoming flights are to feed and clothe the skeleton crew that runs the place. Letting a few sailors come into town to get drunk and laid doesn't create a viable economy.'

'What happens to Stanton after the island closes down?'

'Who knows? Maybe the Navy will sell the island. Or maybe they'll just let it sit here.'

'The base has no strategic value?'

'Not since the Cold War ended. Main thing is there's no constituency here. Seagulls don't vote.'

'So you don't think the Navy's intentionally shutting the island down?'

'Who told you that?'

'A guest up at the estate suggested it.'

'Dr Picker.' He chuckled. 'Kind of an asshole, isn't he? Couple more weeks in the sun, he'll be spotting Amelia Earhart skinnydipping in the lagoon with Judge Crater. Sure you don't want another?'

I shook my head.

'Actually,' said Robin, petting Spike, 'we were going to do some snorkeling.'

We stood and I tried to put money on the table.

'On me,' said Creedman. 'How often do I get to have an intelligent conversation. And your pooch is okay, too. Didn't pee on me.'

He walked us back to the Jeep.

'I like to cook. Have you up for dinner sometime.'

We got in the car. He leaned into Robin's window and took off his sunglasses. His eyes were small and very dark, scanning slowly.

'There was a good reason for blockading the south road,' he said. 'Public safety.'

'Disease control?' I said.

'If you consider murder a disease. It happened half a year ago. Local girl found on the beach, right where you're headed. Raped and mangled pretty badly. The details never came out. Moreland can give them to you – he did the autopsy. Villagers were sure the murderer was some sailor because that kind of thing just doesn't happen here, right? At least not since they massacred the Japanese.' He chuckled. 'Some of the young bloods worked themselves up and started hiking up to Stanton for a tête-à-tête with Captain Ewing. Navy guards stopped them, a little civil *unrest* resulted. Soon after, the Navy started building that blockade.'

He shrugged. 'Sorry to darken your day, but one thing I've learned: the only real escape is in your head.'

Putting his shades back on, he walked back to his table, scooped up his Filofax, and went inside the restaurant.

I started up the Jeep, shifted into first, and pulled away.

Just as I shifted into second, the sound hit – a giant paper bag being popped. Then a swirling black plume spiraled up from behind the volcano tips, rising high above them, inking the perfect sky.

9

Spike's neck was bow-tight. He growled and sniffed the air and began to bark. The people on the dock pointed up at the explosion.

Robin's hand was clamped around my wrist.

'Navy maneuvers?' I said.

'At a nonfunctional base?'

I reversed the jeep quickly. As I passed the Chop Suey Palace, Jacqui stepped out, still holding her dishtowel. Her curiosity and fear stayed in my head as I sped back to the airfield.

Harry Amalfi stood near his house, looking dazed. Studying the black smoke as if it bore a message.

We drove up right behind him and got out, but he didn't move. Shouts made all three of us pivot.

Skip Amalfi and the other shark carver were running toward us. The older man wore bathing trunks too long for his stocky legs. Harry Amalfi said, 'It's a good craft.'

'Was,' said Skip, Amalfi's companion. His voice was soft, his eyes rainwater gray, very close-set.

Skip said, 'Maybe he fucked up and flooded the engine or something, Dad.'

Amalfi turned back to the sky. The smoke was thinning and curling.

The other man shaded his eyes and looked upward too. 'Looks like it might have gone down right over Stanton.'

'Probably,' said Skip. 'Probably right on the fucking *tarmac*.'

His father started to say something, then shuffled back toward his front porch.

'Want me to call over there?' said Skip. 'See if it went down there?'

Amalfi didn't answer. Pulling a bandana out of his pocket, he wiped his face and kept trudging.

'Shit deal,' said Skip's companion. The gray eyes washed over Robin, then checked to see if I was watching. I was. He nodded.

'Major shit,' said Skip.

'He probably did flood it.'

Skip turned to us. 'Dumb fuck said he knew how to fly. Did he?'

'Just met him yesterday,' I said.

He shook his head disgustedly.

'Probably got it up there and flooded it first thing,' said the gray-eyed man, pushing his hand through wild, curly hair.

'His poor wife,' said Robin. 'She didn't want to go.'

'Asshole said he knew what he was doing,' said Skip. 'You guys come *back* here for something?'

We returned to the Jeep and I drove toward the bamboo thatch. Just as I was about to turn onto the dirt path, Jo Picker came running out, hatless, her big purse flopping against her thigh.

Her mouth was open and her eyes were wide and blank. She kept coming toward us and I jammed the brakes. Slapping her hands on the Jeep's hood, she stared at us through the windshield.

Robin jumped out and embraced her. Spike wanted to jump out but I restrained him. He hadn't relaxed since the explosion.

All that remained in the sky were gray wisps.

Jo said, 'No, oh God, no!' She struggled away from Robin and I saw her mouth contort.

Off in the distance, Skip and the gray-eyed man watched.

We finally got her in the Jeep and drove home. She cried softly till we got through the big, open gates and close to the house. Then: 'We had a – I was planning to *go*, but I got scared!'

Ben was already outside, KiKo on his shoulder, along with Gladys and a crew of men in work clothes. This close, I could still see hints of smoke. The noise would have been louder up here.

Jo had stopped crying and looked stunned. Robin helped ease her out of the Jeep, and she and Gladys walked her into the house.

Ben said, 'So it *was* him. I wasn't sure. He couldn't have been up long.'

'Not long at all.'

'Did you see the plane?'

'We saw a bunch of them when we dropped him off.'

'Junk,' he said. 'Whole thing was stupid. No point.'

'Amalfi's son said he might have come down on the base.'

'Or darn close to it. Forget about retrieving the body. 'Course, the alternative's dealing with the Navy. I'm not sure which is worse.'

He turned to the house. 'Why didn't she go up with him? Cold feet?'

I nodded.

'Well, she was the smart one,' he said. 'You try to tell people . . . Dr Bill talked to Picker this morning. Picker just got rude.'

'Does Dr Bill know yet?' said Robin.

He nodded. 'I called him at the clinic. He's on his way up.'

'My first thought was some sort of military maneuver,' I said. 'Does the Navy ever shoot anything in the air?'

'The only things that fly in and out of there are big transports. If one of those went down, you'd think the volcano had erupted.'

A white subcompact came barreling through the gates and stopped short, scattering gravel. POLICE was stenciled in blue on the door. Pam Moreland was in the front passenger seat. A man was driving.

They both got out. Pam looked frightened. The man was good-looking, in his late twenties and huge – six four, two fifty, with nose-tackle shoulders and enormous hands. His skin was bronze with islander features, but his hair was light brown and his eyes pale hazel.

He had on a short-sleeved sky-blue shirt and razor-creased blue pants over military lace-ups. A silver badge was pinned to the breast pocket, but he had no club or gun. Pam matched his stride.

'This is terrible,' she said.

The big man clasped Ben's hand. 'Hey,' he said in a deep voice.

Ben said, 'Hey, Dennis, some mess. Folks, meet Dennis Laurent, our chief of police.'

Laurent shook both our hands, noticed Spike and suppressed a smile. His gaze was intense.

'Anyone know how many people were in the plane?' he said.

'Just Lyman Picker,' I said. 'His wife started to go but changed her mind. She's in the house.'

He shook his head. 'Can't remember anything like this.'

'Never happened,' said Ben. 'Because no one goes up in Harry's heaps. You figure it crashed on Stanton?'

'Either there or right near the eastern border. I called Ewing, got put on hold. Finally his aide says he's busy, will get back to me.'

'Busy,' said Ben with scorn.

Laurent said, 'The wife's probably going to want details.' He put on mirrored sunglasses and looked around some more. 'Guess she's in no shape now.'

'She's in shock,' said Robin.

'Yeah,' said Laurent. 'Let me know if she wants to talk to me or if there's anything I can do for her. Weren't they supposed to be leaving soon?'

'In a week or so,' said Pam. 'She's just about finished her work.'

Laurent nodded. 'Weather research. She came into the station a couple of weeks ago with this little laptop computer, wanting to know if we kept storm records. I told her we really never got the big ones so we didn't. Any idea why her husband went up in the first place?'

'To take pictures of the jungle,' said Ben. 'Prove to his colleagues he'd been here.'

'He was a scientist, too, right?'

'Botanist.'

'So what was he looking at, the banyans?'

'He wasn't really working,' said Pam. 'Told us he was bored. Tagging along after her probably made him feel like a third foot. Maybe he just wanted to do some flying.'

Laurent digested that. 'Well, too bad he picked this time and place . . . Harry probably should have been closed down, but like you said, no one used him. I hope the wife doesn't think we're going to be able to do any big FAA-type investigation. If he went down in the jungle, we'll be lucky to get the body.'

He shook his head again. Pam had been standing close to him and she moved nearer. A downward flick of a hazel eye acknowledged her presence. Laurent put his hands in his pockets and stretched the fabric with his fists.

Then he looked at the Jeep, the diving gear still piled on the backseat. 'Someone snorkeling?'

'We were on our way when it happened,' said Robin.

'We were vaccinating,' said Pam.

'How'd the kids at the clinic react?' I said.

'They don't know exactly what happened yet,' she said. 'Some of them looked up when they heard the noise, but their minds were on their shots. We just kept the line going for a while and then broke for a snack.'

'How many shots did you get through?' said Ben.

'About half. We were going to finish this afternoon, but I guess not.'

'Planning to dive at South Beach lagoon?' Laurent asked us.

'Yes,' said Robin.

'It's beautiful there,' he said. 'Give it another go when you're ready. Life generally goes smoothly here.'

Pam walked him back to his car and stayed to talk after he got behind the wheel.

Ben called out KiKo's name, and the monkey and Spike followed us into the house. Cheryl was washing the front room's big windows and didn't turn to acknowledge us. Except for the hiss of the glass-cleaner spray, the interior was silent.

Robin said, 'I think I'll go up and see how Jo's doing.'

She hurried up the stairs.

'Something to drink?' Ben asked me.

'No, thanks. We had a couple of beers in town. A guy named Creedman was buying.'

'Oh?' He stared straight ahead. 'Where'd he snag you, front of the Palace?'

'Does he make a habit of snagging people there?'

'That's his spot. I figured he'd go for you, being outsiders and all that. He used to live here for a while.'

'He mentioned that.'

'Did he also mention he was asked to leave?'

'No. He said it was too intense an environment for him.'

'Intense? I guess you could say that.'

He turned and looked me in the eye. 'The thing you need to understand is that Dr Bill is the most hospitable person you'll ever meet. Anyone visits the island, they get an invite. That's how the Pickers ended up here, and after meeting them, you can see what a patient man Dr Bill is. Creedman was also extended hospitality.

He was up here for only three days when we found him snooping around.'

'Snooping where?'

'Dr Bill's office. I caught him red-handed. Not that there's anything to hide, but patient info's confidential. Except, of course, for something scientific like you and Dr Bill are doing. Some thanks for hospitality, huh?'

'Did he have an excuse?'

'Nope.' His jaw bunched the way it had when Picker had asked him to serve drinks, and he pushed his aviators up his nose. 'He tried to laugh it off. Said he was taking a walk and had just wandered in looking for something to read. Except the books were in the back room and he was in the front, so give me a break. I called him on it and he told me to screw myself. Then he complained to Dr Bill that I'd harassed him. Dr Bill might have tolerated the snooping, but he didn't appreciate Creedman badmouthing me. Did he badmouth us some more?'

'Not really,' I said. 'But he did say the reason the southern road was blockaded was because of a murder half a year ago. A local girl killed on the beach, and passions toward the Navy got high.'

'The guy makes like he's an ace reporter – probably told you he was a media hotshot, right? Truth is he was strictly small-time. And keep him away from Ms Castagna. He thinks he's God's gift to women.

'So I noticed. But she can handle herself.'

'My wife can, too, but he still annoyed her. Right after I kicked him out. Came up to her in the market, making small talk, offering to carry her bags. Real subtle.'

He shoved his glasses harder. 'Did you meet the owner of the Palace, a tall woman named Jacqui?'

I nodded.

'He came on to *her*, too, till he found out she was Chief Laurent's mother.'

'She looks way too young.'

'She's in her forties, had Dennis when she was a teenager. She and Dennis are good people. He was a couple of grades behind me. Jacqui's half islander, half Cauc, originally from Saipan. Dennis's dad was a French sea captain, used to run cargo boats between the bigger islands, died at sea just before Dennis was born. She raised him right. Anyway, do what you want, but in my humble opinion Creedman's someone to avoid. He just hangs out all day, acting superior.'

'He told us he was working on a book.'

'Maybe a book on beer.' His laugh was merciless.

'Speaking of unwanted attention,' I said, 'the guy who was working on the shark with Skip Amalfi seemed to notice Robin too. Any potential problems there?'

'That's Anders Haygood. He's a bit of a lowlife, but no problems with him so far. Came over a year ago, mostly keeps to himself. Lives in back of Harry's place.'

'Working for Harry?'

'Odd jobs now and then. Once in a while someone brings them an appliance to fix or a car to tune. Basically, he and Skip are beach bums and Harry's an old bum.'

He laughed. 'I'm some Chamber of Commerce, huh? By now you probably think Aruk's nothing but lowlife. But between Skip and Harry and Haygood and Creedman, you've just about exhausted the list. Everyone else is great. You'll end up having a great time.'

10

'He wasn't Mr Charm,' said Robin, 'but to go like that . . .'
We were up in the sitting room of our suite. No sounds came through the wall bordering Jo Picker's room.

'How's Jo?' I said.

'Wiped out. She decided to call his family. I left her trying to get a phone connection . . . I know it's trite, but one moment you're talking to someone, the next they're gone.'

She put her head on my chest and I traced her jawline.

'How're you doing?' I said.

'With what?'

'Vacation.'

She laughed. 'Is that what it is? No, I'm fine. Assuming we've used up all the bad vibes, nothing but sunshine and sweetness lies ahead.'

'Ben assures me we've exhausted the island's supply of miscreants.'

I told her about Creedman's snooping, his hitting on Jacqui and Claire Romero.

'I'm not surprised,' she said. 'When we were sitting there he put his hand on my knee.'

'What!'

'It's okay, honey, I handled it.'

'I didn't see a thing!'

'It happened right at the beginning, when Jacqui came out to take our order. You looked up for a second and he made his move. No big deal – I ended it.'

'How?'

'Pinched the top of his hand.' She grinned. 'Hard. With my nails.'

'He didn't react,' I said.

'Nope, just kept on talking and cooled the hand on his beer bottle.'

I remembered that. 'Bastard.'

'Forget it, Alex. I know the type. He won't try it again.'

'Someone else noticed you,' I said. 'At the airfield. Skip Amalfi's buddy, that wild-haired guy. Now that I think about it, both he and Skip were probably ogling you the minute we stepped off the boat.'

'Probably a woman shortage. Don't worry, I'll stick close to home. Work on my pinching.'

'Don't you think Creedman's behavior is pretty risky for a small place like this? You should have seen Ben's face when he talked about Creedman coming on to his wife.'

'Maybe that's his kick,' she said. 'That stupid thrill-of-the-hunt thing. Or maybe Aruk's such a peaceful place the locals are able to laugh him off as a fool.'

'It certainly doesn't seem to be high-crime. The police chief's unarmed.'

'I noticed that. Probably why everyone was so sure the murderer was a sailor.'

'Does the murder bother you?'

'I didn't love hearing about it, but one homicide a year is heaven compared to L.A., right?'

'According to Ben it wasn't the reason for the blockade.'

'What was?'

I thought back. 'He didn't say.'

'He's an interesting fellow,' she said.

'In what way?'

'Nice, but a bit . . . hard, don't you think? Like the way he reacted to the crash. Angry at Picker, no sympathy.'

'Picker gave him a hard time,' I said. 'But you're right, it was cold. Maybe it's his training as a nurse. Struggling to save people and then watching someone take what he thought was a stupid risk. Or maybe he's just one of those perfectionists incapable of suffering fools. He seems awfully meticulous. Proprietary about Moreland and Aruk, too. Now Moreland's getting old and Aruk's having problems, so he could be under stress.'

'Could be,' she said. 'Aruk's definitely having problems. All those businesses boarded up, and did you see the gas ration sign in town? How do you think people make a living?'

'In his letters, Moreland said fishing and some crafts. But I haven't seen much sign of either. Ben's educated, could live anywhere, so perhaps he stays here because of some special commitment.'

'Yes, it must be hard for him.' She snuggled closer. 'It *is* lovely, though. Look at those mountains.'

'Want to try diving tomorrow?'

'Maybe.' She closed her eyes.

'I'd like everything to go smoothly for you,' I said.

'Don't worry. I'll have a great time.'

'How's your wrist?'

She laughed. 'Much better. And I pledge to go to bed on time and drink my milk.'

'I know, I know.'

'It's okay, honey. You like to take care of me.'

'It's not just that. For some reason, after all these years, I still feel I need to court you.'

'I know that, too,' she said softly, and slipped her hand under my shirt.

The phone woke us up.

Moreland said, 'Oh . . . were you sleeping? I'm terribly sorry.'

'No problem,' I said. 'What's up?'

'Picker's accident – I just wanted to make sure you were all right.'

'It was a shock but we're fine.'

'I tried to warn him . . . I want to reassure you that it was a freak event. The last crash we had was in sixty-three, when a military transport went down over the water. *Nothing* since. I just feel terrible that your welcome has been interrupted by something like this.'

'Don't worry about it, Bill.'

'I dropped in on Mrs Picker, gave her some brandy. She's resting peacefully.'

'Good.'

'All right then, Alex. Sorry again for disturbing your rest.' He paused. 'We can start working whenever you're ready. Just give me a call downstairs.'

Robin sat up and yawned. 'Who is it?'

I covered the phone. 'Bill. Do you mind if I work a bit?'

She shook her head. 'I'm going to get up, too.'

'I've got some time right now,' I told Moreland.

'Well then,' he said, 'I could show you your office. Come down when you're ready. I'll be waiting.'

We found him sitting in an overstuffed chair near a picture window, drinking orange juice. His legs looked so thin they seemed to fold rather than cross. He wore the same type of plain white shirt. This time the baggy pants were gray. The chained glasses rested low on his nose. He stood, closed his book and put it down. Leather-bound copy of Flaubert's *L'Éducation sentimentale*.

'Have you read him, son?'

'Just *Madame Bovary*, years ago.'

'A great realistic novel,' he said. 'Flaubert was excoriated for *being* realistic.' Bending slowly, he petted Spike. 'I've set up a little run for this fellow, in a shaded area behind the rose garden. That is, if you feel comfortable leaving him alone.'

'Is there a problem with his coming along?'

'Not at all. No zoo this morning. Come, let me show you the smaller library.'

He led us through the dining room, pale blue with Chippendale furniture.

'We rarely dine here,' he said. 'We go outside whenever we can.'

The former silver room was on the other side of a mahogany door. He opened it halfway. Salmon moiré walls, two dark bookcases, carved moldings, crystal lamps. Dried flowers on the verge of disintegration sprouted from a huge *famille verte* vase.

He closed the door. 'As I said, you'll probably have little use for it.'

We continued through a waxed-pine breakfast room, yellow pantry, industrial kitchen, past wall-freezers and out the rear door, ending on one of the rock paths. The closest bungalow was the same light brown as the main house, the rooftiles replaced with asphalt shingles.

Inside the bungalow was a small, cool room paneled beautifully with red-gold koa and set up with an old but flawless walnut desk topped by a leather blotter, a sterling silver inkwell, and an electric typewriter.

Another ceiling fan, desultory rotations. On the opposite wall was a brown couch and matching armchair, some tables and lamps. A carved Japanese motif ran along the top of the paneling. Seashells and corals rested on high shelves. Below hung more of Mrs Moreland's watercolors.

Two small, open windows let in the breeze and offered a long view of the entry to the estate. The spray from the fountain sparkled like Tivoli lights. Between Spike's heavy breathing, more of that same narcotic silence.

'Very nice,' I said.

Behind the desk was a door that Moreland opened, revealing a much larger room with four walls of ceiling-high bookcases.

The floor was crowded with high stacks of cardboard cartons – brown columns rising nearly to the ceiling.

Hundreds of boxes, nearly filling the space, randomly separated by narrow aisles.

Moreland shrugged apologetically. 'As you can see, I've been waiting for you.'

I laughed, as much at his flamingo awkwardness as at the enormity of the task.

'It's shameful, Alex. I won't insult you by making excuses. I can't tell you how many times I've sat down to figure out some system of classification only to get overwhelmed and give up before I began.'

'Is it alphabetized?'

He rubbed one sandal against his shin, a curiously boyish gesture. 'After my first few years in practice, I tried to alphabetize them. Repeated the process every few years. But somewhat . . . haphazardly. All in all, there are probably a dozen or so independently alphabetized series.' He threw up his hands. 'Why pretend – it's virtually random. But at least my handwriting's not bad for a doctor.'

Robin grinned and I knew she was thinking of my scrawl.

'I don't expect miracles,' said Moreland. 'Skim, peruse, whatever, tell me if anything jumps out at you. I've always tried to include psychological and social data . . . Now permit me to show you your atelier, dear.'

The adjoining bungalow was identical, but the interior walls were painted white. More old but well-maintained furniture, a drafting table and stool, easels, a flat file. Disposable pallets still wrapped in plastic sat atop the file, along with trays of oil-paint tubes, acrylics, and watercolors. Ink bottles, pens, charcoal sticks, brushes in every shape and size. Everything brand-new. The price tag on a brush was from an artists' supply store in Honolulu.

Off to one side was a table full of shiny things.

'Shell,' said Moreland. 'Cowry, abalone, mother of pearl. Some hardwood remnants as well. And carving tools. I bought them from an old man whose specialties were USNC insignia and leaping dolphins. Back when there was a trinket business.'

Robin picked up a small handsaw. 'Good quality.'

'This was Barbara – my wife's special place. I know you're not carving right now, but Alex told me how gifted you were, so I thought you might like to . . .'

He trailed off and rubbed his hands together.

'I'd love to,' said Robin.

'Only when your hand permits, of course. It's too bad you didn't get a chance to swim.'

'We'll try again.'

'Good, good . . . Would you like to stay here and look around, dear? Or do you prefer to be there as Alex discovers how truly disordered I am?'

It was as gracious a way as any to ask for privacy.

'There's plenty here to keep me busy, Bill. Pick me up when you're done, Alex.'

'And you?' Moreland said to Spike.

'Watch,' I said. Walking to the door, I said, 'Come, Spike.' The dog ran immediately to Robin and flopped down at her feet.

Moreland laughed. 'Impeccable taste.'

When we were outside, he said, 'What a lovely girl. You're lucky – but I suppose you hear that all the time. It's nice to have someone in Barbara's studio after all these years.'

We began walking. 'How long has it been?'

'Thirty years this spring.'

A few steps later: 'She drowned. Not here. Hawaii. She'd gone there for a vacation. I was busy with patients. She went out for an early-morning dip on Waikiki Beach. She was a strong swimmer, but got caught up in a riptide.'

He stopped, fished in his pocket, drew out a battered eelskin wallet and extricated a small photo.

The black-haired woman from the mantel portrait, standing alone on a beach, wearing a black one-piece bathing suit. Hair shorter than in the painting, pinned back severely. She looked no older than thirty. Moreland would have been at least forty.

The snapshot was faded: gray sand, the sky an insipid aqua, the woman's flesh nearly dead-white. The ocean that had claimed her was a thin line of foam.

She had a beautiful figure and smiled prettily but her pose – legs together, arms at her side – had a tired, almost resigned quality.

Moreland blinked several times.

I gave him back the snapshot.

'Why don't we work our way downward,' he said, lifting a box from the top of an outer column, carrying it into the office, and placing it on the floor between the couch and the armchair.

The carton was taped shut. He cut the tape with a Swiss Army knife and pulled out several blue folders. Putting on his glasses, he read one.

'Of all things . . .'

Handing me the folder, he said, 'This one isn't from Aruk, but it was a case of mine.'

Inside were stiff, yellowed papers filled with elegant, indigo, fountain-penned writing that I recognized from the card he'd left on the bed. Forty-year-old medical records of a man named 'Samuel H.'

'You don't use full names?' I said.

'Generally, I do but this was . . . different.'

I read. Samuel H. had presented with gastric complaints and thyroid problems that Moreland had treated with synthetic hormones and words of reassurance for eleven months. A month later, several small benign nerve tumors were discovered and Moreland raised the possibility of travel to Guam for evaluation and surgery. Samuel H. was unsure, but before he could decide, his health deteriorated further: fatigue, bruising, hair loss, bleeding lips and gums. Blood tests showed a precipitous drop in red blood cells accompanied by a sharp rise in white cells. Leukemia. The patient 'expired' seven months later, Moreland signing the certificate and directing the remains to a mortuary in a place called Rongelap. I asked where that was.

'The Marshall Islands.'

'Isn't that clear across the Pacific?'

'I was stationed there after Korea. The Navy sent me all over the region.'

I closed the chart.

'Any thoughts?' he said.

'All those symptoms could be due to radiation poisoning. Is Rongelap near Bikini atoll?'

'So you know about Bikini.'

'Just in general terms,' I said. 'The government conducted nuclear tests there after World War II, the winds shifted and polluted some neighboring islands.'

'Twenty-three blasts,' he said. 'Between nineteen forty-six and nineteen fifty-eight. One hundred billion *dollars* worth of tests. The first few were A-bombs – dropped on old fleets captured from the Japanese. Then they got confident and started detonating things underwater. The big one was Bravo in fifty-four. The world's first hydrogen bomb, but your average American has never heard of it. Isn't that amazing?'

I nodded, not amazed at all.

'It broke the dawn with a seventy-five-thousand-foot mushroom cloud, son. The dust blanketed several of the atolls – Kongerik and Utirik and Rongelap. The children thought it was great fun, a new kind of rain. They played with the dust, tasted it.'

He got up, walked to the window and braced himself on the sill.

'Shifting winds,' he said. 'I believed that, too – I was a loyal officer. It wasn't till years later that the truth came out. The winds had been blowing east steadily for days before the test. Steadily and predictably. There *was* no surprise. The Air Force warned its own personnel so they could evacuate, but not the islanders. Human guinea pigs.'

His hands were balled.

'It didn't take long for the problems to emerge. Leukemias, lymphomas, thyroid disorders, autoimmune diseases. And, of course, birth defects: retardation, anencephaly, limbless babies – we called them "jellyfish."'

He sat down and gave a terrible laugh. 'We *compensated* the poor devils. Twenty-five thousand dollars a victim. Some government accountant's appraisal of the value of a life. One hundred and forty-eight checks totaling one million two hundred and thirty-seven thousand dollars. One hundred-thousandth the cost of the blasts.'

He sat back down and placed his hands on bony knees. His high forehead was as white and moist as a freshly boiled egg.

'I took part in the compensation program. Someone upstairs thought it a good use of my training. We did it at night, going from island to island in small motorboats. Pulling up to the shore, calling the people out with bullhorns, then handing them their checks and sailing off.'

He shook his head. 'Twenty-five thousand dollars per life. An actuarial triumph.' Removing his glasses, he rubbed his eyes. 'After I figured out what the blast had done, I put in for extended stay and tried to do what I could for the people. Which wasn't much . . . Samuel was a nice man. A very fine carpenter.'

'How'd the people react to being paid?' I said.

'The more perceptive among them were angry, frightened. But many were grateful. The United States extending a helping hand.'

He put his glasses back on.

'Well, let's crack another box. Hopefully something a bit more routine.'

'At least you tried to help them,' I said.

'Sticking around helped me more than them, son. Till then I thought medicine boiled down to diagnosis, dosage, and incision. Encountering my own impotence taught me it was much more. And less. You worked in pediatric oncology, you understand.'

'By the time I got involved, cancer was no longer a death sentence. I saw enough cures to keep me from feeling like an undertaker.'

'Yes,' he said. 'That's wonderful. Still, you saw the misery, too.

Your articles on pain control – scientific yet compassionate. I read them all. Read between the lines. It's one of the reasons I felt you were someone who would understand.'

'Understand what, Bill?'

'Why a crazy old man suddenly wants to organize his life.'

The other cases *were* routine and he seemed to tire. As I scanned the chart of a woman with diabetes, he said, 'I'll leave you alone. Don't try to do too much, enjoy the rest of the day.'

He stood and headed for the door.

'I wanted to ask you something, Bill.'

'Yes?'

'I met Tom Creedman in the village this morning. He mentioned something about a murder a half year ago and some social unrest that led to the blockade.'

He leaned against the jamb. 'What else did he have to say?'

'That was it. Ben told me he lived here, caused some problems.'

'Oh, indeed.'

I pointed to the rear storage room. 'Was that where Ben caught him snooping?'

'No,' he said. 'That was *my* office. Two bungalows down. Creedman claimed he'd wandered in and was on his way out when Ben found him. I might have let it pass, but he insulted Ben. That kind of thing isn't tolerated around here. I ordered him off the grounds. He delights in accentuating the negative about me and Aruk.'

'He called this place Knife Castle.'

'And probably told you that yarn about the slaves butchering every last Japanese.'

'It never happened?'

'Allied bombs killed the vast majority of the Japanese soldiers. Three days of constant bombardment. On the third night, the Americans radioed victory and some of the forced workers left the barracks and came up here to loot – understandable, after what they'd been put through. They encountered a few survivors and there was some hand-to-hand fighting. The Japanese were outnumbered. Mr Creedman calls himself a journalist, but he seems attracted to fiction – not that there's that much difference, nowadays, I suppose.'

'He also said that you did the autopsy on the murder victim. Do you agree with the theory that it was a sailor?'

He sucked in breath. 'I'm growing a bit concerned, Alex.'

'About what?'

'Picker's accident, and now this. You certainly can't be faulted for seeing Aruk as a terrible place, but it's not. Yes, the murder was terrible, but it was the first we'd had in many years. And the only one of its type I remember in over three decades.'

'What type is that?'

He pressed his hands together, clapped them silently and looked up at the ceiling fan, as if counting rotations.

Suddenly, he opened the door and stepped out. 'I'll be right back.'

11

The folder he returned with was brown with a white paper label.

ARUK POLICE

INVEST: D. LAURENT.

CASE NO. 00345

The first four pages were a typed report composed by the police chief in slightly clearer-than-usual cop prose.

The body of a twenty-four-year-old woman named AnneMarie Valdos had been found at three A.M. on South Beach by two crab fishermen, wedged between rocks overlooking a tide pool. The amount of blood indicated violence at the site.

Other fishermen had been at that exact spot at nine P.M., allowing Laurent to narrow the time the corpse had lain there.

During that period, birds and scavengers had done their work, but Laurent, referring to a conversation with 'Dr W. W. Moreland,

M.D.' had been able to distinguish the 'external shredding and mostly superficial laceration from multiple, deep knife wounds leading to exsanguination and death.'

The victim had lived on Aruk for two years, coming over from Saipan to work as a cocktail waitress at Slim's but losing that job after three months due to chronic intoxication and absenteeism. Her lodgings had been a rented room in the village and she was two months in arrears. She'd been known to socialize with Navy men. The only surviving relative was an alcoholic mother in Guam who had no money to travel or to pay for burial.

Questioning the villagers produced no witnesses or leads but did elicit the repeated claim that the viciousness of the crime proved the perpetrator was a sailor.

Laurent's final paragraph read: *'Investigating officer has repeatedly attempted to communicate with Captain E. Ewing, Commanding Officer of Stanton USN Base, for possible questioning of enlisted men re: this crime, but has been unable to make contact.'*

I started to turn the page.

'You might not want to,' said Moreland. 'Photographs.'

I thought about it and flipped anyway.

The shots weren't any worse than some of the ones Milo had shown me, which is to say they'd be additions to my nightmare file.

I moved past them to Moreland's report.

He'd been thorough, inspecting, dissecting, enumerating each wound.

At least fifty-three wounds, additional ones possibly obscured by scavenger bites.

The killing blow probably a neck slash.

Contrary to what Creedman had said, no sexual penetration.

All the cuts probably inflicted by the same weapon, a very sharp, unserrated blade.

The next page was written out in Moreland's elegant longhand:

Dennis: You may want to keep this private. WWM

Postmortem mutilation

A. The left leg has been severed completely at the patellar joint.

B. The left femur has been broken discretely in three places, with a considerable quantity of bone marrow removed.

C. A deep 26 cm. longitudinal upward slashing wound extends from the pubic region to the sternum.

D. Disembowelment has taken place, with the small and large intestines piled atop the chest region, obscuring both breasts. The breasts are intact. (Extensive crustaceal invasion of these tissues exists, as well.)

E. Both kidneys and the liver have been removed and are not present.

F. Decapitation has occurred between the third and fourth cervical vertebrae with the head left next to the left side of the body at a distance of 11 centimeters.

G. A deep, transverse wound of the neck is visible both above and below the decapitation line. Probable downward stroke from left ear across the neck indicates right-handed person slashing from the back. The trachea and jugular vein have been severed.

H. Significant enlargement of the foramen magnum has been accomplished, possibly with some kind of grasping/crushing instrument. Portions of the occipital skull have been shattered, probably by blunt force.

I. Both cerebral hemispheres have been removed, with the cerebellum and lower brain left intact.

I shut the file and took a slow breath, trying to settle my stomach.

'I'm sorry,' said Moreland, 'but I want you to see that I'm not concealing anything from you.'

'The killer was never caught?'

'Unfortunately not.'

'And the Navy man theory?'

He blinked and fidgeted with his glasses. 'In all the years I've lived here, the islanders have never engaged in serious violence, let alone this. I suppose it could have been one of the cargo boat deckhands, though I've come to know most of them and they're decent chaps. And Dennis did question them. Unlike the sailors.'

Remembering Laurent's remark about not having his call to Stanton returned, I said, 'He never got access to the base?'

'No, he didn't.'

'Why do you still have the file? Is the investigation ongoing?'

'Dennis thought I might come up with something if I studied it for a while. I haven't. Any suggestions?'

'It's not your typical sadistic murder,' I said. 'No rape – though Creedman said there was.'

'You see,' he said. 'The man has no credibility.'

'No positioning of the body, either. Mutilation, but of the head and the back and the legs, not the genitalia or the breasts. Then there's the multiple organ theft – coring out the femur to remove the marrow. It sounds ghoulish – almost ritualistic.'

He smiled sourly. 'The kind of thing some primitive *native* would do?'

'I was thinking more of a satanic rite . . . Were any satanic symbols left behind?'

'None that we found.'

'*Does* the killing bear the mark of some sort of ritual?'

He rubbed his bald head, took a thick, black fountain pen out of his pocket, uncapped it and inspected the nub.

'What do you know about cannibalism, Alex?'

'Mercifully little.'

'Conducting the autopsy brought to mind things I'd heard about when I was stationed in Melanesia back in the fifties.'

He put the pen back, uncrossed his leg, and rubbed a bony knee.

'The sad truth is, from an historical perspective, eating human flesh isn't a cultural aberration. On the contrary, it's culturally entrenched. And I don't mean just the so-called primitive continents. Old Teuton had its *menschenfresser*s; there's a grotto in Chavaux in France, on the banks of the Meuse, where archaeologists found heaps of hollowed-out human leg and arm bones – your early Gallic gourmets. The ancient Romans and Greeks and Egyptians consumed each other with glee, and certain Caledonian tribes wandered the Scottish countryside for centuries turning shepherds into two-legged supper.'

He started to sit back, then grimaced violently.

'Are you all right?' I said.

'Fine, fine.' He touched his neck. 'A crick – slept the wrong way . . . Where was I – ah, yes, patterns of anthropophagy. The most common motive, believe it or not, is *nutrition* – the quest for protein in marginal societies. However, when alternative sources are provided, sometimes the preference endures: "tender as dead man" was once high praise among the old tribes of Fiji. Cannibalism can also be a military tactic or part of a spiritual quest: ingesting one's own ancestors in order to incorporate their benevolent spirits. Or a combination of the two: eating the enemy's brain grants wisdom; his heart, courage; and so on. But despite all this diversity, there are fairly consistent procedural *patterns*: – decapitation, removal of vital organs, shattering the long bones for marrow. As the Bible says, "The blood is the soul."'

He tapped the file in his lap. Looked at me expectantly.

'You think this woman was killed to be eaten?' I said.

'What I'm saying is her wounds were consistent with classic cannibalistic practices. But there are also *in*consistencies: her heart, typically considered a delicacy, was left intact. Skulls are frequently taken as trophies and preserved, yet hers was left behind. I suppose both could be explained in terms of time pressure – the killer may have been forced to leave the beach before finishing the job. Or perhaps – and I think this is the best guess – he was just a psychopathic deviant *mimicking* some ancient rite.'

'Or someone who'd watched the wrong movie,' I said.

He nodded. 'The world we live in . . .'

Finishing the job.

I pictured the gentle waves of the lagoon, the arc of a long blade cutting the moonlight. 'What he did to her took quite a bit of time. What's your estimate?'

'At least an hour. The human femur's a sturdy thing. Can you imagine sitting there working at sawing it free?' He shook his head. 'Repulsive.'

'Why'd you suggest to Laurent that he not publicize the details?'

'Both as a means of concealing facts only the killer would know and in order to maintain public safety. Tempers were already running high, rumors spreading. Can you imagine what the notion of a cannibal sailor would have done?'

'So the villagers still don't know.'

'No one knows, other than you, Dennis, and myself.'

'And the murderer.'

He winced. 'I know I can trust you to keep it to yourself. I showed you the file because I value your opinion.'

'Cannibalism's not exactly my area of expertise.'

'But you have some understanding of human motivation – after all these years, I find people more and more perplexing. What could have *led* to this, Alex?'

'God only knows,' I said. 'You said the villagers aren't violent. What *about* the sailors? Any previous incidents of serious violence?'

'Brawls, fistfights, nothing worse.'

'So Creedman's story about locals storming the southern road was true?'

'Another exaggeration. No one *stormed*. A few of the younger men, fortified with beer, tried to reach the base to protest. The sentries turned them back and there was some shouting and shoving. But anyone who thinks the Navy would go to the expense of building that blockade two days later to keep out a handful of kids is naive. I spent enough time in the service to know that nothing moves that quickly in the military. The blockade must have been planned for months.'

'Why?'

He frowned. Hesitated. 'I'm afraid it may very well be the first stage in closing down the base.'

'Because it has no strategic value?'

'That's not the point. Aruk was *created* by colonial powers and the Navy's the current colonizer. To simply pull out is cruel.'

'How do the villagers make a living, now?'

'Small jobs and barter. And federal welfare checks.' He said it sadly, almost apologetic.

'The checks come on the supply boats?'

He nodded. 'I think we both know where that kind of thing leads. I've tried to get the people to develop some independence, but there's very little interest in farming and not enough natural resources for anything commercial. Even before the blockade, basic skills were already dropping, and most of the bright students left the island for high school and never returned. That's why I'm so glad people like Ben and Dennis choose to stay.'

'And now the blockade has sped up the decline.'

'Yes, but things don't need to be hopeless, son. One good trade project – a factory of some kind – would sustain Aruk. I've been trying to get various businesses to invest here, but when they learn of our transport problems they balk.'

'Pam said you've corresponded with Senator Hoffman.'

'Yes, I have.' He placed the murder file on the couch.

'Is there any history of tribal cannibalism on Aruk?' I said.

'No, because there's no pre-Christian culture of any kind. The first islanders were brought over by the Spanish in the fifteen-hundreds already converted to Catholicism.'

'A pre-Christian culture is necessary for cannibalism?'

'From my reading it's a virtual constant. Even the most recent documented cases seem to incorporate Christian and pre-Christian ideas. Are you familiar with the term "cargo cult"?'

'Vaguely. A sect that equates material goods with spiritual salvation.'

'A *spontaneous* sect spurred by a self-styled prophet. Cargo cults develop when native people have been converted to a Western religion but have held onto some of their old beliefs. The link between acquiring goods and receiving salvation occurs because basic missionary technique combines gifts with doctrine. The islander believes the missionary holds the key to eternal afterlife and that everything associated with him is sacred: white skin, Caucasian features, Western dress. The wonderful *kahgo*. The cults are rarer and rarer, but as late as the sixties there was a cult that worshiped Lyndon Johnson because someone got the notion *he* was the source of the cargo.'

'Correlation confused with causation,' I said. 'The same way all superstitions are learned. A tribe goes fishing the night of the full moon and brings in a record catch: the moon acquires magical properties. An actor wears a red shirt the night he gets rave reviews: the shirt becomes sacred.'

'Exactly. Groundless rituals provide comfort, but if the belief system is shaken up – the missionary leaves and the cargo stops – the islander may view it as the beginning of the apocalypse. Stick a charismatic prophet into the picture and – years ago I was sent to Pangia, in Southern Highlands Province, to survey infectious diseases. Fifty-five, right after the war. In the course of my research, I learned of a minor government clerk who suddenly quit his job and started reading the Bible aloud twenty hours a day in the village square. Handsome, intelligent young fellow. His association with the ruling class had lent additional status. A small group formed around him, and his delusions grew more florid. And bloody. He ended up slaughtering and eating his own infant son, sharing the meal with his followers in an attempt to bring in plane loads of goods. The morning of the murder he'd been preaching from Genesis. The story of Abraham binding Isaac for sacrifice.'

'Abraham never went through with it.'

'In his view that was because Abraham didn't merit true fulfilment. He, of course, was quite another story.'

Telling the story had turned him pale.

'I can still see his face. Smiling, tranquil.'

'Any similarities to this murder?'

'Several.'

'And some of the factors you've just mentioned are present here, too. Dependence upon the white man, then abandonment.'

'But still,' he said, bending forward, 'it doesn't make sense. Because other factors are absent.'

'No pre-Christian culture.'

'And absolutely no history of cults on Aruk!'

He rapped his knuckle against the file. 'I continue to insist that this hideousness was the work of a single, sick person.'

'Someone who'd read up on cannibalism and was trying to simulate a cult murder?'

'Perhaps. And most important, someone who's moved on.'

'Why do you say that?'

'Because it hasn't happened again.'

He was ashen. I lacked the heart for debate.

'For a while, son, I couldn't stop thinking that he'd simply gone off to do it somewhere else. But Dennis has been checking international reports for similar crimes in the region and none have come up. Now, what say we put aside this ghastly stuff and move on?'

12

For the next hour and a half, we were dispassionate scientists, discussing cases, suggesting different ways to organize the data.

Moreland looked at his watch. 'Feeding time for Emma and her friends. Thank you for a stimulating afternoon. It's not often I get to engage in collegial discussions.'

I thought of his daughter the physician, trained in public health. 'My pleasure, Bill.'

'It'll be dark soon, don't work too hard,' he said. He strode to the door. 'I didn't bring you over here to enslave you.'

Alone, I sat back and looked out the window at the fountain spitting jewels.

My mind's eye kept focusing on the photos of AnneMarie Valdos's murder scene.

White body on dark rock; the details Moreland and Laurent had witheld.

Probably what Creedman had been after when Ben caught him snooping: ace reporter comes to islands to find himself, finds a gore-fest instead, and phones his agent ('What a concept, Mel!').

Then he came up against Moreland and was cut off from the information and resented it.

Moreland had concealed the whole truth from his beloved islanders but offered them to me after a forty-eight-hour acquaintance.

Wanting input from me . . . about *human motivation*.

More worried about recurrence than he'd admitted?

Couching it in *collegiality* – a couple of guys with doctorates having a clubby chat about *two-legged supper*.

A brilliantly colored bird flew past the window. The sky was still a peacock blue I'd seen only on crayons.

I got up and headed for Robin's studio. What would I tell her?

By the time I reached the door, I'd decided on limited honesty: letting her know I'd discussed the murder with Moreland and that he believed it an isolated crime, but leaving out the details.

She wasn't there. Bits of shell were laid out neatly atop the flat file along with a billet of koa and two small chisels.

No dust. Wishful thinking.

I went looking for her, finally spotted her down by the fruit groves, a white butterfly flitting among the citrus trees, Spike a wiggly, dark shadow at her feet.

I jogged to her side, she put her arm in mine, and we walked together.

'So how did work go?' she said.

'Very scholarly. What'd you do?'

'Played around in the studio, but it was a little frustrating not being able to work, so Mr Handsome and I decided to stroll. The estate's wonderful, Alex. Huge. We made it all the way to the edge of the banyan jungle. Bill must have sunk a fortune into landscaping; there are some beautiful plantings along the way – herbs, wildflowers, a greenhouse, orchids growing on tree trunks. Even the walls are pretty. He's got different kinds of vines trailing down them. The only thing that spoils it is the barbed wire.'

She stopped to pick up an orange that had dropped, peeled it surgically as we continued.

'How much of the jungle can you see over the walls?'

'Treetops. And those aerial roots. There's a coolness that seems to make its way over. Not a breeze. Even milder. A subtle current. I'd take you there but Spikey didn't like it, kept pulling away.'

'Our little mine detector.'

'Or some kind of animal on the other side. I couldn't hear anything, but you know him.'

I bent and rubbed behind the dog's bat ears. His flat face looked up at me, comically grave.

'With those radar detectors, it's no wonder,' I said. 'Finally style and substance merge.'

She laughed. 'Umm, smell those orange blossoms? This is great, Alex.'

I kept my mouth shut.

We decided to dive the following morning and got up for an early breakfast. Jo Picker was already on the terrace dressed in a black T-shirt and loose pants, her hair tied back carelessly, sooty shadows under her eyes. She kept both hands on her coffee cup and stared down into it. The food on her plate was untouched.

When Robin touched her shoulder, she smiled weakly. Spike's licking her hand sparked another smile.

As we sat down, she said, 'Ly never liked dogs . . . too much maintenance.'

Her lips tightened, then trembled. She stood abruptly and marched into the house.

We left Spike in the run with KiKo and drove down to South Beach. As I turned off Front Street to park, I looked up the coastal road. The Navy blockade was at the top, a crude wall of grey concrete, at least twenty feet tall. It appeared to be crammed into the hillside. Warning signs applied generously. An extension of chain link and barbed wire snaked up the hill and continued into the brush.

The beach at that point was just a narrow spit and the wall cut across it and continued into the ocean, creating a damming effect. But the water was shallow and still, lapping weakly at the algae-stained base of the sea-barrier. Large chunks of coral were stacked nearby, desiccated and sunbaked: part of the reef had been shattered to accommodate the barrier.

I parked atop the widest section of beach. The sand was as smooth and white as a freshly made bed, the lagoon that same silvery green.

We collected our gear, and as I carried it to the shoreline, I noticed flat, smooth rocks above the tide pools.

The altar where AnneMarie Valdos had been sacrificed.

To what?

We stepped onto the sand. The temperature was holding as mild and steady as Moreland had promised. When I tested the lagoon with my foot, there was no chill, and when I eased in for a swim a soft warmth enveloped me.

'Perfect,' I called out to Robin.

We put on our fins and masks and snorkels, flipper-walked the shallows till the water reached our thighs, then knifed in and floated belly down on the surface of the pool. The reef took a long time to deepen, finally reaching eight feet as we neared the brown-red ring of coral that held back the ocean.

The coral colonies grew in wide, flat beds. Despite the lack of current, the reef's living rock seemed to dance, patches of tiny animals sharing space with bio-condos of sea urchins, chitons, feather duster worms, and gooseneck barnacles. Small, brilliant fish grazed, untroubled by our presence: electric-blue damsels, lemon-yellow tangs, confident gray-black French angels, shocking-pink basslets with the stern little faces of tax auditors.

Orange-and-white clownfish nested in the soft, stinging embrace of fluorescent sea anemones.

The bottom sand was fine, almost downy, spotted with shells and rocks and shreds of coral. The sunlight made its way down easily, dappling the ocean floor. We shattered the light with our shadows, causing some of the shells to move in reflexive panic.

Drifting in opposite directions, we explored separately for a while, then I heard Robin burble through her breathing tube and turned to see her pointing excitedly at the far end of the reef.

Something torpedo shaped was shooting between us, speeding across the lagoon. A small sea turtle, maybe a foot long, head down, legs compressed, skimming the top of the coral as it headed for bluer pastures.

I watched it disappear, then looked back at Robin, making the OK sign. She waved and I paddled to her, extending a hand. We bumped masks in a mock kiss, then swam together, thrilled and weightless, suspended like twins in a warm salty womb.

When we got back on the beach we were no longer alone.

Skip Amalfi and Anders Haygood had spread a horse blanket thirty feet from our clothes. Skip was lying on his back, eyes closed, belly surging and collapsing as he sucked on a cigarette and blew smoke. Haygood crouched nearby, hairy thighs thick as logs, tongue tip sticking out the corner of his mouth. Concentrating as he pulled the limbs off something huge and ugly.

The biggest crab I'd ever seen. Easily thirty inches from claw to claw, with a knobby, blue, spotted carapace and pincers the size of bear traps. My year for monster arthropods.

Haygood looked up at us and snapped a leg free, watched the juice drip out of it, then held it up and waved it.

'Ma'am. Sir.' Again, the gray eyes washed over Robin and I became aware of how she looked in her two-piece, hair dripping over smooth, bare shoulders, hips swelling above the low-cut bottom, the sharp, sweet contrast between bronze skin and white nylon.

She turned her back on them just as Skip sat up. Both men watched her trudge to our blanket. Walking in the sand made her sway more than she intended to.

'Big crab,' I said.

'Stoner,' said Haygood. 'Great eating – can I give you a couple of legs, sir?'

'No, thanks.'

'You're sure?'

'Forget it,' said Skip. 'Old man Moreland don't eat animals.'

'That's right,' said Haygood. 'Too bad. Stoners are great eating. This one liked coconuts – that's why it's blue. When they eat other things, they can be orange. I've seen them even bigger, but he's healthy.'

'Mean though,' said Skip. 'Bite your finger clear off. Best thing is throw 'em in the pot live – how was your swim?'

'Great.'

'See any octopus?'

'No, just a turtle.'

'Little one?'

I nodded.

'Last summer's hatch. They come in, lay at the breaker line, bury the eggs. The natives dig 'em up – makes a helluva omelet. The suckers that make it swim the hell out of here, but most of them get eaten too. Sometimes a real stupid one comes back. Musta been what you saw.'

'Checking out the old 'hood,' said Haygood, laughing. His teeth were widely spaced and white. The sun turned his body hair into dense copper wire.

'Octopus are smart,' said Skip. 'Those big eyes, you swear they're checking you out.' A glance Robin's way.

'Best omelet for my money is tern,' said Haygood. 'Lays pink eggs. First time people see it they freak out, think it's blood. But pink's the true color. Pink omelet.' He licked his lips. 'Salty – like duck.'

'You can have it, man,' said Skip. 'Too fuckin' gamy.'

Haygood smiled. 'Well, I go for the pink.'

Skip snickered.

'Shark's good eating, too,' said Haygood, 'but you have to soak the meat in acid or it tastes like piss – how long are you here for, doc?'

'Couple of months.'

'Like it?'

'It's beautiful.'

They looked at each other. Haygood snapped off another crab leg.

Skip said, 'Rich people would dig this place, right?'

'I guess anyone who likes swimming and relaxing would.'

'What about *you*? What kind of stuff do *you* dig?'

'All kinds of things.'

He dragged on his cigarette and flipped the butt onto the spotless sand. 'Me and my buddy Hay here wanna build a resort. But different. Grass huts, like a Club Med. Pay one price up front, get your food, drinks, the works. No TV or phones or video movies, just swimming and digging the beach, maybe we'll bring some girls over to put on a dance show or something.'

His eyes got hard. 'So what do you think?'

'Sounds good.'

'It does, huh?'

'Sure.'

He spat on the sand. 'I figure rich assholes from the mainland'd go for it in a big way, right? 'Cause otherwise, we'd hafta go for the Japanese tour groups like all the other islands do.' He put both hands in front of his face, hooked his upper teeth over his lower lip and flexed his thumbs.

'Take *pikcha*, crick crick.' He laughed.

Haygood smiled and examined the crab's legless body.

'Full of roe,' he said. 'A girl.'

'We wanna get *Americans*,' said Skip. 'This is America even though no one in America knows shit about this place.'

'Good luck.' I started to walk away.

'Wanna invest?' he called after me.

I was about to laugh, then I saw his face and stopped.

'I'm not really much of an investor.'

'Then maybe you should *start*, man. Get in early. Guys who invested in Hawaii after the war are wiping their asses with hundred dollar bills.'

He held out a palm, as if panhandling.

'Hey, the man came here to mellow out,' said Haygood. 'Give him a break.'

Skip flipped him a middle finger and his weak chin struggled for a jut. 'Shut the fuck up, man. I'm talking business, here.'

Haygood didn't speak but his wrists flexed and the crab's torso shattered wetly.

Skip tried to stare him down, but the older man ignored him.

'Think about it, man,' said Skip, passing some of the anger over to me. 'Talk to your lady; she looks pretty smart.'

Another glance Robin's way. She'd draped her shoulders with a towel and was sitting with her knees drawn up to her chest, looking out at the sea.

A voice to my back said, 'Gentlemen,' and Skip's dull eyes narrowed. Haygood wiped his hands with a T-shirt but his face didn't move.

I turned. Dennis Laurent stood on the sand in full mirrored sunglasses flashing white light. He looked vast. None of us had heard him approach.

He touched an eyebrow. 'Doctor. Got a nice stoner, there, Hay. Must be what, six seven pounds of meat?'

'Eight at least,' said Skip.

'Pull it off a coco?'

'Didn't have to,' said Haygood. 'Lazy one, sleeping over there.' He pointed to the tide pools.

'Nothing like an easy target,' said Laurent. 'I see you finally got in the water, doc. Nice?'

'Perfect.'

'Always is. Have a nice day, gentlemen.' He and I walked to Robin. His shoed feet were steady on the sand. Spotting the butt Skip had discarded, he picked it up and pocketed it.

'Those two give you any trouble?'

'No. Are they troublemakers?'

'Not generally, but they've got too much free time and one IQ between them, most of it Haygood's. Skip hit on you for his resort scheme, right?'

'Just before you arrived.'

'Club Skip. Ready to call your broker?'

'Got a cell phone?'

He laughed. 'Can't you just see Skip greeting a boatload of tourists – "Hey, welcome to fucking Aruk, man."'

'Chamber of commerce should hire him.'

'Yeah,' he said, 'if we had one – hello, Ms Castagna. How was the water?'

'Warm.'

'Always is. Something about the lack of water movement and the insulating properties of the coral. I'm happy to see you two finally enjoying yourselves. Finally got a callback from the Navy: just headed up to the estate to talk to Mrs Picker. They found the wreckage just inside Stanton. Nothing much left; they'll be shipping the remains back to the States, billing her later for the transport.'

'You're kidding.'

'Wish I was. Captain Ewing thinks he's being generous because the plane was trespassing on military property. He says he could have filed a complaint, fined Picker bigtime, and the estate would be financially responsible.'

'That's despicable,' said Robin.

Laurent flicked a speck of sand off his badge. 'Yup. How's Mrs Picker doing?'

'This morning she looked pretty exhausted.'

'I'd better leave out the part about the bill for now. Knowing the military – I'm an ex-Marine – they'll take two years just to finish the paperwork, if they even follow through. Trouble is, I'm not going to be able to get her the body. Even if Ewing was cooperative, there's no real mortuary here, just a couple of guys who dig graves for the cemetery behind the church, and no supply boat for another ten days or so. Without proper embalming it could get pretty ripe—'

He stopped himself. 'Sorry.'

'Why's Ewing so hostile?' I said.

He shrugged. 'Maybe it's his nature, maybe he doesn't like being here. He was involved in Skipjack – that Navy sex scandal in Virginia? Got exiled here because of it. But maybe that's just talk . . . Anyway, I'll just tell Mrs Picker the Navy's doing her a favor by shipping the body. Ewing asked me to get an address. She can have someone claim it in the states.'

He removed his shades and blew sand off the lenses. His light eyes took in the beach, the harbor. Lingering for a split second on the flat rocks above the tide pools. Or had I imagined it?

'Do you know if Dr Bill's up at the house?' he said.

'He wasn't at breakfast.'

'He's usually up way before breakfast. Goes to sleep late, too. Never met a man who needs less sleep, always moving, moving, moving. If you see him, tell him hi. Pam, too.'

13

As we got back in the Jeep, Skip and Haygood were walking along the shore, smoking and flicking ash into the water.

Robin said, 'Let's drive around a bit, explore some of the smaller roads.'

I turned the vehicle around and she looked up at the barricade.

'It's almost as if they wanted it to be ugly.'

'Moreland agrees with Picker that the Navy's shutting the island down gradually. I asked him how people live and he admitted the main source was welfare.'

'End of an era,' she said. 'That may be why he's so eager to document what he's done.'

I headed toward the bowed gray pilings of the dock. The open-air market was closed and the ration sign remained atop the gas pump.

'Did you talk about the murder?'

'A bit.'

'And?'

'Moreland and Dennis are assuming it's a one-shot, that the murderer's gone. Because he hasn't done it again in the region. So it could very well be a sailor who's transferred to another base.'

'Meaning he could be doing it in another region.'

'Dennis has been keeping an eye out for similar crimes and none have come up.'

We were nearing the Chop Suey Palace. Creedman was outside again, with a bottle and a mug. Looking straight ahead, I passed him and hung a sharp right onto the next road, passing more tumbledown houses and empty lots. Then a small, poorly tended patch of grass housing a World War Two cannon and a life-size statue of MacArthur shading his eyes. A wooden sign said VICTORY PARK, EST. 1945. The only obvious triumph was that of birds over bronze.

More shacks and lean-tos and dirt till the crest, where a narrow white church stood. I stopped. Two stories high, with a sharply pitched roof, fish-scale trim, and a badly tarnished copper steeple, the building canted to the right. The balusters of the front stair rail were intricately turned but flaking. The five-pace front yard was thick with high grass edged with leggy white petunias.

'Early Victorian,' said Robin. 'It's sunk a little on the foundation, but the design's nice.'

A display board staked in the lawn said OUR LADY OF THE HARBOR CATHOLIC CHURCH. VISITORS WELCOME. A few feet away a metal flagpole hosted Old Glory. The flag drooped in the motionless air.

Behind the church was more tall grass squared by a low picket fence. Rows of white crosses, stone and wooden grave markers. A few flashes of color. Floral wreaths, some so bright they had to be plastic.

Next door was a large aluminum Quonset hut labeled ARUK COMMUNITY CLINIC. The old black Jeep Ben had used to pick us up was parked near the door next to an even older MG roadster, once red, now faded to salmon. The emergency number on the door was that of Moreland's estate.

Just as I started to drive on, Pam came out, removing her stethoscope. She waved and I stopped again. Taking something out of the MG, she came over. Handful of plastic-wrapped lollipops.

'Hi. Snack?'

'No, thanks,' said Robin.

'Sure? They're sugarless.' Unwrapping a green pop, she put it in her mouth. 'So you guys got to swim. How was it?'

Robin told her about our dive. Through the open door I could see children, their small faces pinched with fright.

'They seemed okay about the crash,' said Pam, 'but still pretty nervous about their shots, so we decided to get it over with. Want to come in?'

We followed her into the hut and breathed in the sharp smell of alcohol. The floor was blue linoleum. Fiberboard partitions sectioned the interior into cubicles. Cartoon posters and nutritional charts nearly covered the walls, but the aluminum fought the attempt to cheer.

Fifteen or so children, all dark haired, none older than eight, were lined up in front of a long, folding table. Two chairs sat behind the table, the one on the right empty, the other occupied by Ben. To his left were steel trays of bandages, cotton swabs, disinfectant pads, disposable syringes, and small glass jars with rubber stoppers. A trash basket near his left foot brimmed with discarded needles and blood-specked pads.

He crooked his finger and a little girl in a pink T-shirt and red-and-white paisley shorts stepped forward. Her hair was waist long; her feet were in beach thongs. She was losing the struggle not to cry.

Ben unwrapped a pad, picked up a bottle, and jabbed the needle through the rubber cap with his left hand. Filling the syringe, he squirted it clear of air, took hold of the girl's arm and drew her closer. Cleaning her bicep swiftly, he tossed the pad in the basket, said something that made her look at him and flicked the needle at her arm, almost teasingly. The girl's mouth opened in pain and insult. The tears flowed. Some of the boys in line laughed, but none with enthusiasm. Then, the needle was out and Ben was bandaging her arm. The whole process had taken less than five seconds and he remained impassive.

The girl kept crying. Ben looked back at us. Pam rushed over and unwrapped a lollipop for the whimpering child. When the tears didn't stop, she cradled the girl.

Ben said, 'Next,' and crooked a finger. A small, chubby boy stepped into position and stared down at his arm. Dimpled fists drummed his thighs. Ben reached for a pad.

'All done, Angie,' said Pam, walking the girl to the door. You did great!' The child sniffed and sucked her lollipop and the white paper stick bobbed. 'These are some visitors from the mainland, honey. This is Angelina. She's seven and a half and very brave.'

'I'll say,' said Robin.

The girl wiped an eye.

'These people came all the way from California,' said Pam. 'Do you know where that is?'

Angelina mumbled around the sucker.

'What's that, sweetie?'

'Disn'land.'

'Right.' Pam tousled her hair and guided her outside, watching as she ran to the church.

By the time she returned, Ben had vaccinated two more children, working rapidly, as rhythmic as a machine. Pam stayed with us, comforting the children and seeing them off.

'School's still in session,' she said. 'They're in class for another hour.'

'Who teaches?' I said. 'The priest?'

'No, there is no priest. Father Marriot was called back last spring and Sister June just left for Guam – breast cancer. Claire – Ben's wife – was our substitute, but now she's the faculty. A couple of other mothers serve as part-time assistants.'

Another weeping child passed through.

'Guess I should do a few,' said Pam, 'but Ben's so good. I hate inflicting pain.'

Cheryl was sweeping the entry to the big house, but when we walked in she stopped.

'Dr Bill said give you this.' She handed me a scrap of yellow, lined paper. Moreland's writing:

Det. Milo Sturgis called 11 A.M., Aruk time.

West Hollywood exchange. Milo's home number.

'That's one in the morning, L.A. time,' said Robin. 'Wonder what it could be.'

'You know what a night owl he is. Probably something to do with the house and he's trying to catch us at a good time.'

Mention of the house tightened her face. She looked at her watch. 'It's two-thirty there, now. Should we wait?'

'If he was up an hour and a half ago, he probably still is.'

Cheryl stood there, as if trying to follow the conversation. When I turned to her, she blushed and began sweeping.

'Is it all right to use the phone for long distance?'

She looked puzzled. 'There's a phone in your room.'

'Is Dr Bill around?'

She thought. 'Yes.'

'Where?'

'In his lab.'

We went back to the run to pick up Spike. He and KiKo stopped their play immediately and he ran to Robin. The monkey shinnied up a low branch, then let go and landed feather light on my shoulder. A small dry hand cupped the back of my neck. He'd been shampooed recently – something with almonds. But his fur also gave off a faint hint of zoo.

We left with both animals. Robin said, 'I'd like to freshen up.'

'I'll go ask Moreland about using the phone.'

She turned back toward the house; KiKo jumped off and joined her and Spike. I walked down to the outbuildings and knocked on Moreland's office door.

He said, 'Come in,' but the door was locked and I had to wait for him to open it.

'Sorry,' he said. 'How was your swim?'

'Terrific.'

He was holding a pencil stub and looked distracted. His office was the same size as the one he'd given me, but with pale green walls and no furniture other than a cheap metal desk and chair. Papers, loose and bound, carpeted half the floor. The desk was blanketed too, though I did notice one high stack that had been squared neatly and placed in the center. Journal reprints. The top one, an article I'd written ten years ago on treating childhood phobias. My name underlined in red.

The door to the lab was open. Tables, beakers, flasks, test tubes in racks, a centrifuge, a balance scale, equipment I couldn't identify. Next to the scale was a tall jar full of the gray-brown pellets he'd used to feed the insects. A smaller container of some sort of brownish liquid sat beside it.

'So,' he said, taking off his glasses. His tone was strained; I'd interrupted something.

'I wanted to check if it was okay to use the phone for long distance.'

He laughed. 'Returning Detective Sturgis's call? Of course. There was no need to ask. Give him my best. He's a pleasant fellow.'

Robin sat there caressing her two hairy pals as I dialed. The phone rang twice and a cranky deep voice grunted, 'Sturgis.'

'Hi, it's me. Still up?'

'Alex.' Milo's voice lightened. I hadn't thought much about his missing us.

'Yeah, wide awake,' he said, reverting to a grumble. 'So how's Bali Hoo?'

'Sunny and clear. Want to hop over and join us?'

'I don't tan, I parboil.'

'Thought you were Black Irish.'

'That's temperament, not complexion. So you pretty much settled in?'

'Very nicely. Just got back from diving in a gorgeous coral reef.'

'Yo, Jacques. There really is a Garden of Eden, huh?'

'My fig leaf says yes. What are you doing up past your bedtime, sonny boy?'

'Working double shifts and building up the overtime. Reason I called is the guy who's handling your house has a couple of questions. Seems the crown and floor moldings Robin told him to order have been discontinued. He can get something similar, a little wider, or go for her exact specifications and have it custom milled. The difference is a couple of thou and he wants authorization. Also, the cost of your alarm is going to be a little higher than estimated. Something about having to connect up with a power line that's outside the basic contractual area. Probably another grand. It's never *below* estimate, is it? Anyway, ask the lovely Ms. C. what she wants to do, get back to me, and I'll forward the message.'

'I'll put her on right now.'

I handed over the receiver. Robin said, 'Hi!' and KiKo's eyes widened. As she began to speak the monkey stuck his head closer to the phone and began talking along in a wordless chittering singsong.

'What? Oh . . . no, it's a monkey, Milo . . . a *monkey.* As in barrel of . . . No, he hasn't replaced Spikey, we still love him . . . No, they're getting along fine, as a matter of fact . . . That's it in terms of mammals . . . What? . . . No, just some bugs . . . *Bugs*. Insects, spiders . . . tarantulas. Dr Moreland does research on them . . . What's up, detective?'

She talked to him about the construction, then ended with more small talk and returned the phone to me. 'I'm putting these guys outside again, then running a bath. Love it if you'd join me when you're through.'

She left.

'Bugs,' said Milo. 'Eden has bugs.'

'God created them, too. What day was it?'

'His bad-joke day. Exactly what kind of research does this guy do?'

'Nutrition. Predatory behavior.'

'He sounded a little spacey when I talked to him.'

'How so?'

'Taking the message, but somewhere else.'

'He thought you were a pleasant fellow.'

'That proves he was somewhere else.'

I laughed. 'What kind of things are you working on?'

'You really want to know?'

'Intensely.'

'Four armed robberies, one with hostages in a meat locker and a near fatality. One drive-by of a drug dealer slash rap artist that we probably won't solve, aw shucks, and the beauty that's been keeping me up late: sixteen-year-old girl out in the Palisades shot her father to death while he sat on the can. She claims long-time molestation, but the mother says no way and she's been divorced from the old man for years, no love lost. The kid has a history of naughty behavior, and Daddy had promised her a brand-new Range Rover for her birthday if she passed all her classes. She flunked, he said no go, and friends say she got mighty pissed.'

'Any evidence of molestation?'

'Nope, and friends say she was a big fan of those two little shits with shotguns from Beverly Hills. She's got dead eyes, Alex, so who knows what was done to her. But that's not my concern, right now. She retained a mouthy lawyer with dead Daddy's dough . . . but enough, Ishmael. You set sail to escape all this barbarism.'

'True,' I said, 'but allow me to raise your cynicism quotient even higher. Even Eden has its problems.'

I told him about AnneMarie Valdos's murder.

He didn't answer.

'You still there?'

'Cracking her bones to eat the marrow?'

'That's Moreland's hypothesis.'

'You go to Paradise and outdo me in the grossness department?'

'According to Moreland, cannibalism's pretty common across cultures. Ever come across it?'

'He an expert on that, too? Tell me, is there some huge guy stomping around the estate with a bad haircut and bolts in his neck? Marrow . . . no, thanks, dear, I'll pass on that breakfast steak and stick with the veggie plate.'

'Funny you should say that. Moreland's a vegetarian. His daughter says he saw things after the Korean War that made him never want to be cruel again.'

'How sensitive. And no, I haven't personally come across any bad guy gourmets. But there are a few years left to retirement, so now I've got something to live for.'

'How's Rick?'

'He says, changing the subject. Doing the workaholic thing as usual, night shift at the ER . . . *Marrow*? Why do I keep hearing jungle drums going *oonka loonka*? Come across any missionaries in a pot?'

'Not yet, and Moreland says not to worry. There's no history of cannibalism here. Both he and the chief of police see it as a sicko killer trying to look exotic. Local opinion pins it on a Navy man who moved on.'

'Moreland's a crime sleuth, too?'

'He's the only doctor on the island, so he handles all the forensics.'

'Cannibalism,' he said. 'Does Robin know about this?'

'She knows there was a homicide, but I haven't given her the details. I don't want to make too big of a deal about it. Other than that, there's been no serious crime here for years.'

'"Other than that, Mrs Lincoln, how was the play." Why a Navy man?'

'Because the locals aren't violent and the killer seems to be transitory.'

'Well,' he said, 'I was Joe Army, so you won't get any big debate from me. Okay, hang loose, don't eat anything you can't identify, and stay away from jokers with bones in their noses.'

'A creed to live by,' I said. 'Thanks for calling, and good luck on your cases.'

'Yeah . . . all bullshit aside, I'm really glad you guys got to do this. I know what last year was like for you.'

A phone rang in the distance and he grunted.

'Other line,' he said. 'More sludge. Sayonara and all that, and if you see a bearded French guy painting ladies in flowery mumus, buy up the canvases.'

14

Robin napped and I took a walk, crossing the rose garden and descending the sloping acres of lawn. Four men in drive-and-mows were working on the turf. The rotting-sugar smell of cut grass brought to mind childhood Sundays.

So had Victory Park, I realized. The war memorial in my Missouri hometown had been only slightly larger. Sunday meant my mother bundling my sister and me off to the park when my father chose to drink at home. Bologna sandwiches and apple juice, climbing the cannon, pretending to fire, Mother's sweet, forced smiles. When she died, Dad's drinking stopped, and so did the rest of his life.

Shaking off melancholy, I continued down to the fruit groves, stepping among fallen oranges and tangerines and a popcorn spray of citrus blossoms. The meadow Moreland had created out of wildflowers was brilliant. A collection of miniature conifers had been trimmed surgically and a boxwood knot garden was as intricate as any maze I'd encountered in graduate school. Then the greenhouses, every pane spotless, and trees full of orchids, the plants tucked into the folds and hollows of branches like hatchlings. I kept going till I spotted patches of granite and the brown, thorny fuzz of rusty barbed wire.

The eastern border. Plumbago and honeysuckle and wisteria covered most of the high stone walls, softening the wire but not hiding it.

On the other side, the banyan tops formed a greener-gray awning, aerial roots shooting through the canopy like the tentacles of a beast in pain. From what I could see, the tree trunks below were stout and kinked cruelly, whipsawing in a struggle for space.

For a second, the entire forest seemed to be moving, tumbling down on me, and I felt myself losing balance.

After I restored equilibrium, a tight spot remained at the base of my throat.

I looked up at the trees again.

Robin had mentioned a subtle coolness drifting over the walls, but all I felt was an internal chill.

I hiked along the border, listening for sounds from the other side but hearing nothing. When I stopped, the same illusion of movement recurred and I placed both hands on the stone and breathed in deeply.

Probably low blood sugar. I hadn't eaten since breakfast.

I headed back. When I got to the grove, I picked up an orange, peeled it, and finished it in three bites, letting the juice run down my chin the way I'd done as a child.

Back in my office, I tackled another carton of medical files. More routine; the only psychological diagnoses Moreland had noted were stress reactions to physical illnesses.

I pulled down another box and found myself growing bored till a folder at the bottom made me take notice.

On the front cover Moreland had drawn a large, red question mark.

The patient was a fifty-one-year-old laborer named Joseph

Cristobal, with no history of mental disorder, who began to experience visual hallucinations – 'white worms' and 'white worm people' – and symptoms of agitation and paranoia.

Moreland treated him with tranquilizers and noted that Cristobal did have 'a fondness for drink but is not an alcoholic.' The symptoms didn't abate.

Two weeks later Cristobal died suddenly in his sleep, the apparent victim of a heart attack. Moreland's autopsy revealed no brain pathology but did discover an occluded coronary artery.

Then the doctor's final remark in large, bold print, the same red color as the question mark: '*A. Tutalo?*'

I figured that for a bacterium or virus but the medical dictionary he'd provided me didn't list it.

A drug? No citation in the *Physicians' Desk Reference*.

I returned to the storage room, squeezed my way past the columns of boxes, and searched the bookshelves.

Natural history, archaeology, mathematics, mythology, history, chemistry, physics, even a collection of antique travelogues.

One complete case devoted to insects.

Another to plant pathology and toxicology, which I went through carefully.

No mention of *A. Tutalo.*

Finally, in a dark, musty corner, the medical books.

Nothing.

I thought of the catwoman. Moreland's telling me about the case moments after we'd met.

Now another case of spontaneous death.

I'd reviewed perhaps sixty files. Two out of sixty was three percent.

An emerging pattern?

Time for another collegial chat.

When I reached the house, I saw Jo Picker near the fountain, watching Dennis Laurent's police car drive away. Water dotted her hair and face. As I came up to her she wiped her cheek and looked at the moisture on her hand. The spray continued to hit her. Slowly she moved out of its arc.

'That policeman came over to tell me what's going on.'

She rubbed her eyes. Her new tan had been replaced by mourner's pallor. 'They say Ly landed on the base and they're shipping him back today . . . I should've expected it, working in Washington. But when it happens to you . . . I've been calling his family.'

One of her hands rolled tight.

'I didn't really chicken out,' she said. 'Though that would have been rational.'

She looked at me. I nodded.

'I probably *would've* been stupid enough to go up even though I had bad feelings about it. But this time . . . he got mad at me, called me a . . . I just said to heck with it and walked away.'

She moved her face nearer to mine. Close enough to kiss but there was nothing seductive about it.

'Even so, I still probably would've relented. But he wouldn't let up . . . as I was walking through that bamboo I heard the plane engine start up and almost ran back. But instead I kept going. To the beach. Found a nice spot on the rocks and sat down and stared at the ocean. I was feeling pretty relaxed when I heard it.'

Our noses were nearly touching. Her breath was stale.

'I miss him,' she said, as if finding it hard to believe. 'You're with someone for a long time . . . I told his mother she could bury him in New Jersey near his father. We never made any plans for that kind of thing – he was forty-eight. When I get back we'll have some kind of service.'

I nodded again.

She noticed a stain on her shirt and frowned. 'My ticket out of Guam isn't for another two weeks. I guess I should say that I can't wait to get back, but the truth is, what's waiting for me? I might as well stay and finish up my work.'

Wetting her finger with her tongue, she rubbed the stain. 'That sounds cold to you, doesn't it?'

'Whatever helps you through it.'

'My *work* helps me. Coming here's the final leg of a three-year study – why throw it away?'

She backed away and drew herself up. 'Enough blubbering. Back to the old laptop.'

It was just before five. I strolled to the rose garden and watched through the boughs of a pine tree as the men in the mowers painted broad stripes in the lawn. I thought about sudden death.

The catwoman. White worms.

AnneMarie Valdos killed to be eaten.

Routine medical cases collected during a thirty-year practice.

Some routine.

I was probably making too much of it. After all, *I'd* initiated the conversation about the Valdos murder.

Though it had been Moreland who'd brought over the autopsy photos, sparing no detail.

Maybe the old man had a strong stomach and assumed I did too.

He'd implied as much during the tour of the bug zoo.

Research on predators.

I recalled the animation with which he'd discussed the history of cannibalism.

Not exactly your simple country doctor.

Milo had thought him spacey. Joked about Frankenstein monsters.

Milo was a self-admitted sultan of cynicism, but he was also a trained detective, his hunches more often right than wrong . . .

Neurotic, Delaware. Bunked down in Eden, getting paid handsomely to do a dream job and you just can't cope.

I returned to the house but couldn't get the catwoman out of my mind.

Her ordeal. Bound to a chair while her husband made love to another woman. The final scream . . .

Such cruelty.

Maybe *that* was it.

Over the years, Moreland had seen too much cruelty.

Radiation poisoning, the hopeless deterioration of the Bikini islanders.

The catwoman. Joseph Cristobal. The cargo cult leader.

Absorbing the pain the way sensitive people often do.

Confronting his helplessness but able to forget about it during dark hours in the bug zoo. His lab. His own private paradise.

Now, watching Aruk deteriorate – nearing the end of his own life – his defenses had been shaken.

He needed to make sense of the cruelty.

Needed someone to share it with.

15

That night at dinner, there were five places set.

Jo was last to come down. She wore a white blouse and a dark skirt; her face looked fresh and her hair was shiny and combed out.

'Go on with the small talk.' She sat and unfolded her napkin. 'Grapefruit, one of my favorites.'

The talk hadn't been small: Moreland giving a detailed lecture on the history of colonization. He'd seemed to lose his train of thought a couple of times.

Now there was silence, as Jo peered at the serrated edge of her grapefruit spoon. She cut a section from the fruit, and the rest of us picked up our utensils.

Moreland reached for a roll and spread it with apple butter. He closed his eyes and chewed.

'Dad?' said Pam.

His eyes opened and he looked around the table, as if trying to locate the sound.

'Yes, dear?'

'You were talking about the Spanish.'

'Ah, yes, machismo's finest hour. What gave the *conquistadores* a unique approach was the combination of risk taking and a strong religious commitment. When you believe you have God on your side, anything's possible. Hormones *and* God are unbeatable.'

He nibbled on the roll. 'Then, of course, there was the easy funding: outright theft, in the name of heaven. Señor Columbus's journeys were funded with the plunder of the Inquisition.'

'Hormones, religion, and money,' said Pam very softly. 'That just about sums up the world, doesn't it.'

Moreland stared at her for a second. A worried parental stare that he ended abruptly by shifting his attention to his bread. 'In toto, a force to be reckoned with, the Spanish. They came to the Pacific in the sixteenth century, set about trying to do precisely what they'd done in—'

He stopped and looked across the terrace. Gladys had come out of the house.

'I'm not sure we're ready for the next course, dear.'

'There's a phone call, Dr Moreland.'

'A medical call?'

'No, sir.'

'Well, then, please take a message.'

'It's Captain Ewing, sir.'

Moreland's stooped frame jerked forward, then he straightened. 'How curious. Please excuse me.'

After he was gone, Pam said, 'This is the first we've heard from Ewing in months. I spoke to him once over the phone. What a sour man.'

I repeated what Dennis had told me about Ewing's being exiled for the sex scandal.

'Yes, I heard that, too.'

Jo said, 'He's crating and shipping Lyman like luggage.'

Pam paled. 'I'm sorry, Jo.'

Jo dabbed at her lips. 'Government is like junior high. Your status depends upon whom you're able to persecute.'

'Maybe Dad can work something out with them.'

'I doubt it,' said Jo. 'I think they shipped him already.'

'Your connections don't help?' said Robin.

'What connections?'

'Working at the Defense Department.'

Jo's bosom heaved and she let out a barklike laugh. '*Thousands* of people work at the Defense Department. It's not exactly as if I'm the Secretary of Defense.'

'I just thought—'

'I'm *nothing*,' said Jo. 'Lowly G-12 nerds don't count.'

She stabbed the grapefruit, turned the spoon, freeing the last bits of pulp.

More silence, heavier, oppressive. Geckos racing along the rail would have been welcome, but they were keeping a low profile tonight.

Pam said, 'Gladys made lamb. It looks great.'

Moreland came back out, a loping skeleton.

'An invitation. To all of us. Dinner at the base, tomorrow night. Casual formal. I shall wear a tie.'

That night, I awoke at two in the morning and was unable to fall back asleep. As I got out of bed Robin turned away from me. I slipped into some shorts and a shirt and she rolled back.

'Y'okay, honey?'

'Think I'll just get up for a while,' I whispered.

She managed to mumble, 'Restless?'

'A little.'

If her head was clear enough, she was thinking: *Some things never change.*

I bent and kissed her ear softly. 'Maybe I'll take a little walk.'

'. . . not too late.'

I covered her shoulders, pocketed the room key, and slipped out of the bedroom. As I passed Spike's crate, he snored a greeting.

'Nighty-night, handsome.'

My bare feet were silent on the landing carpet. The stairs were sturdy, not a creak.

Down in the entry, the stone floor was cool and welcome as summer lemonade. All the lights were off and the island silence saturated the house. I opened the front door and stepped outside.

The moon was ice-white and the sky pulsed with stars. Starlight frosted the trees and the fountain, turning the spatter to glycerine, giving life to the gargoyle roof tiles.

I walked to the gates. They were open and I looked down the long, sloping road, matte-black till it hit the onyx of the ocean.

Something moved along the grass at the road's edge.

Something else skittered in response.

I turned back, fully awake now. Maybe I'd look over a few more charts. I headed for my bungalow, then stopped when I heard a door shut.

Footsteps from the rear of the house. The back door, leading from the kitchen to the gravel paths.

Slow, deliberate footseps. They ceased. Continued.

Someone came out into the open and stood looking up at the sky.

Moreland's unmistakable silhouette.

Not wanting to talk to him or anyone else – I retreated into the shadows and watched as he descended the path, landing thirty feet in front of me.

Something clunked in his hand. A doctor's bag.

Same clothes he'd worn at dinner plus a shapeless cardigan sweater. He headed for the outbuildings, passed my bungalow, and continued past Robin's.

Stopping at his office.

At the door, he put the bag down, fumbled in his pocket, finally found the key but had some trouble inserting it in the lock. Starlight filtered through trees slashed his face diagonally, highlighting a cucumber of nose, the deep pouches columning his downturned mouth.

The door swung open. He picked up his bag and entered.

The door closed silently.

The lights went on, then off. The room stayed dark.

16

The following morning brought cooler air and cotton-swab clouds drifting from the east.

'Rain,' said Gladys, as she poured our coffee. 'Five or six days.'

The clouds were translucent and filmy, not a hint of moisture.

'They pick up the water as they go,' she said, offering the bread basket. 'Sucking it up from the ocean. Do you like whole wheat?'

'Sure.'

'Dr Bill does too, but a lotta people don't. One time he had me bake rolls for the kids at school. They didn't eat too many.'

She tugged the corner of the yellow tablecloth. We were the only ones at breakfast.

'Kids like the soft stuff. We used to get lots of white bread on the supply boats. Now, when we get anything, it's stale. Were you planning on swimming again?'

'Yes.'

'Well, don't be fooled by those clouds: be sure to put on sunscreen. You got the nice olive skin, ma'am, but the doctor here, with those pretty blue eyes, he could burn.'

Robin smiled. 'I'll take good care of him.'

'Men think they're tough, but they need to be taken care of. How about some nice fresh-squeezed juice?'

At the lagoon, the fish were quick learners, approaching for a handout but swimming away quickly when we had nothing to give them. Robin managed to get one large, latecoming, pink-and-yellow wrasse to nibble at her fingers. Then it too realized she was all show, and it shot away to a high mound of coral, where it snaked through a hole and disappeared.

She followed, head turning constantly, her eye for detail in full play. When she stopped, paddled in place, and waved me over, I joined her.

A tiny bald head floated in the crack. Chinless. Gray-brown skull. Oversized eyes bright with intelligence.

A baby octopus, legs as thin and flaccid as boiled spaghetti. It kept staring, finally retreated, slithering into a crevice, turning impossibly small.

We pressed closer.

It squirted ink in our faces.

I laughed, got water in my tube, and had to tread water to clear it. The surface of the water was a clean metal plate. The beach was empty.

I went under again, tagging along with a school of yellow surgeonfish, watching the bony, sharp protrusions under their pectoral fins pivot at the sense of threat, feeling the calmness of their blank, black stares.

Paradise.

We were back at the house by two. Jo's door was closed and an untouched lunch tray sat on the floor nearby. I imagined her tapping her keyboard in hopes of blunting her grief.

Studying the wind. Something too vast to control.

Moreland, on the other hand, delighted in manipulating nature's small variables. Had he once harbored grand plans for the island? Was his own grief what had kept him up last night, sitting in the dark?

I worked. No medical oddities, no gore, and the only untimely death I found was a young woman with ovarian cancer.

Another two cartons, more routine. Then the name of a drowning victim caught my eye.

Pierre Laurent, a twenty-four-year-old sailor lost in a squall near the Mariana Trench. The body had been returned to Aruk, and Moreland had certified the death, making note of the eighteen-year-old widow, four months pregnant with Aruk's future police chief.

Right below, Dennis's birth chart. A ten-pound baby, healthy.

Two more hours of tedium.

I liked that.

Just as I was heading for the back room to fetch yet another box, Ben knocked and came in. 'Base just called. Navy copter's picking you up in an hour on South Beach.'

'VIP treatment?'

'It's either that or they send down a big ship or rowboats.' He took in the clutter of my desk and I thought I saw disapproval. 'Need anything by way of supplies?'

'No thanks. Are you coming tonight?'

'Nope. One hour, you'll all be leaving from here together.'

He started to leave and I said, 'Hold on, I'll walk back with you.'

He shrugged and we left together.

'How're the vaccinations coming along?' I said.

'All finished till next year.'

'Tough job?'

'Not really. It's for their own good.'

'You had a real rhythm going, yesterday.'

'That's me,' he said. 'Natural rhythm.'

The taste in my mouth matched his expression. We walked in silence toward the big house.

As we neared the fountain, he said, 'Sorry, that was out of line. I'm not like that . . . What I mean is, race isn't a big thing to me.'

'Me neither; forget it.'

'Guess I'm bushed. The baby was up all night.'

'How old?'

'Six months.'

'Boy or girl?'

'Girl. All of them slept great except her. Sorry. I mean it.'

'No problem. Dr Bill said the dinner was formal casual. What does that mean, tux jacket and jeans?'

His smile was grateful. 'Who knows? Typical military, give out rules without explaining them. You serve any time?'

'No,' I said.

'After a month in the Guard I knew it wasn't for me, but no choice by then. I told them I was interested in medicine, so they put me in a hospital on Maui, pulling sea urchin spines out of toes. Never even hit the water. I love the ocean.'

'Do you dive?'

'Used to. Used to sail, too. Had an old catamaran that Dennis and I took out the few days a year we had enough wind. What with the kids, though, no time. And Dr Bill keeps me busy. No complaints – it's what I like.'

He gave another smile – full and warm. An old, dented gray Datsun station wagon was parked near the front steps of the house. A Chinese woman got out of it.

Tiny, with a bone-porcelain face under very short hair, she wore a red blouse tucked into blue jeans. Her eyes were huge. She smiled at me and gave Ben a sandwich wrapped in wax paper.

'Tuna,' he said, kissing her cheek. 'Excellent. Dr Delaware, this is my wife, Claire. Claire Chang Romero, Dr Alex Delaware.'

We exchanged greetings.

'Everything okay?' said Ben. 'We still on for hibachi dinner?'

‘After homework – addition practice for Cindy and composition for Ben Junior.’

He put his arm around her. He was a small man, but she made him look big. Walking her to the car, he held her door open. He looked happy. I left.

Casual formal for Robin was a long, sleeveless black dress with a mandarin collar and high slits on the side. Her hair was piled and mabe-pearl earrings glistened like small moons.

I put on the linen sportcoat she'd bought me for the trip, tropical wool slacks, blue shirt, maroon tie.

‘Spiffy,’ she said, patting my hair down.

Spike looked up at us with big eyes.

‘What?’ I said.

He began baying like a hound.

The give-me-attention-I'm-so-needy bit. Our dressing up was always a cue.

‘And the Oscar goes to,’ I said.

Robin said, ‘Poor *baby*!’ and bent down and mothered him for a while, then coaxed him into his crate with an extra-large biscuit and a kiss through the grill. He gave out a bass snort, then a whine.

‘What is it, Spikey?

‘Probably “I want my MTV,”’ I said. ‘His internal clock's telling him *The Grind*'s on in L.A.’

‘Aw,’ she said, still looking into the crate. ‘Sorry, baby. No TV, here. We're roughing it.’

She took my arm.

No TV, no daily newspaper. The mail irregular, packed on the biweekly supply boats.

Cut off from the world. So far, I was surprisingly content.

How would it suit me, long term?

How did it suit the people of Aruk? Moreland's letters had emphasized the isolation and insulation. Preparing us, but there'd been a bit of boast to it.

A man who hadn't switched from rotary phones.

Doing it his way, in the little world he'd built for himself. Breeding and feeding his bugs and his plants, dispensing altruism on his own schedule.

But what of everyone else on the island? They had to know other Pacific islanders lived differently: during our stopover on Guam, we'd had access to newsstands, twenty-four-hour cable, radio bands of music and talk. The travel brochures I'd picked up there showed similar access on Saipan and Rota and the larger Marianas.

The global village, and Aruk was on the outside looking in.

Maybe Spike wasn't the only one who missed his MTV.

Creedman had said Moreland was extremely wealthy, and Moreland had confirmed growing up on ranchland in California wine country.

Why didn't he use his money to improve communication? There was no computer in his office. Journals arrived in the unpredictable mail. How did he keep up with medical progress?

Did Dennis Laurent have a computer? Without one, how could he do his police tracking?

Was the failure to find a repeat of the beach murder the result of inadequate equipment, and was *that* why Moreland was still worried?

'Alex?' I felt a tug at my sleeve.

'What, hon?'

'You all right?'

'Sure.'

'I was talking to you and you spaced out.'

'Oh. Sorry. Maybe it's contagious.'

'What do you mean?'

'Moreland spaces out all the time. Maybe it's island fever or something. Too much mellow.'

'Or maybe you're both working too hard.'

'Snorkel all morning and read charts for a couple of hours? I can stand the pain.'

'It's all expenditure of energy, darling. And the air. It does sap you. I find myself wanting to vegetate.'

'My little brussel sprout,' I said, taking her hand. 'So it'll be a real vacation.'

'For you too, doc.'

'Absolutely.'

She laughed. 'Meaning what? The body rests but the mind races?'

I tapped my forehead. 'The mind makes a pit stop.'

'Somehow I don't think so.'

'No? Watch me tonight. Pinkies out, hmph hmph, how about them Dodgers?' I went limp and rolled my eyes.

'Maybe I should bring a snorkel, then. In case you nod off in the soup.'

17

Moreland was sitting in the Jeep when we got there. Wearing an ancient brown blazer and a tie the color of gutter water.

'We're waiting on Pam,' he said, looking preoccupied. He started the car and gave it gas, and a moment later the little red MG sped up and screeched to a halt. Pam jumped out, flushed and breathless.

'Sorry.' She ran into the house.

Moreland frowned and looked at his watch. The first hint of paternal disapproval I'd seen. I hadn't noticed any closeness, either.

He checked the watch again. An old Timex. Milo would have approved. 'You look lovely, dear,' he said to Robin. 'As soon as she's ready, we'll get going. Mrs Picker's not coming, understandably.'

A few minutes later, Pam sprinted out, perfectly composed in a blazing white trouser suit, her hair loose and shining, her cheeks flushed.

'Onward,' said Moreland. When she kissed his cheek he didn't acknowledge it.

He drove the way he walked, maneuvering the Jeep slowly and awkwardly down toward the harbor, veering close to the edge of the road as he pointed out plants and trees.

At the bottom of the road, he turned south. The sun had been subdued all day, and now it was retiring; the beach was oyster-gray, the water old nickel.

So quiet. I thought of AnneMarie Valdos sectioned like a side of meat on the flat rocks.

We got out and waited silently near the edge of the road.

'How long of a copter ride is it?' I said.

'Short,' said Moreland.

A scuffing sound came from the top of the coastal road.

A man emerged from the shadow of the barrier and came toward us.

Tom Creedman, waving. He wore a blue pinstripe suit, white button-down shirt, yellow paisley tie, tasseled loafers. His black hair was slicked down and his mustache smiled in harmony with his mouth.

Moreland's eyes were furious. 'Tom.'

'Bill. Hi, Moreland *fille*. Doctor-and-Robin.'

Insinuating himself into the middle of our group, he tightened the knot of his tie. 'Pretty nifty, personal aerial escort and all that.'

'Not much choice if they want us there,' said Moreland.

'Well,' said Creedman, 'we could swim. You're a strong swimmer, Pam. I saw you today, taking those waves on the North End with Chief Laurent.'

Moreland blinked hard and snapped his head toward the water.

'Maybe I should try it one day,' said Pam. 'What is it, a few knots? Do you swim, Tom?'

'Not if I can avoid it.' Creedman chuckled, fished a wood-tipped cigarillo out of his jacket, and lit it with a chrome lighter.

Sucking in deeply, he examined the lagoon with a flinty stare and blew smoke through his nose. Foreign correspondent on assignment. I waited for theme music.

'Funny, isn't it?' he said. 'After all the enforced segregation, they decide it's party time – at least for the white folk. I see Ben and Dennis weren't included. What do you think, Bill? Is brown skin a disqualifying factor?'

Moreland didn't answer.

Creedman turned to Robin and me. 'Maybe it's in *your* honor. Any Navy connections, Alex?'

'I played with a toy boat in the bathtub when I was five.'

'Ha,' said Creedman. 'Good line.'

Pam said, 'You don't swim, you don't sun. What do you do all day, Mr Creedman?'

'Live the good life, work on my book.'

'What exactly is it about?'

Creedman tapped his cigarillo and gave a Groucho leer. 'If I told you, it would kill the suspense.'

'Do you have a publisher?'

His smile flickered. 'The best.'

'When's it coming out?'

He drew a finger across his lips.

Pam smiled. 'That's top secret, too?'

'Has to be,' said Creedman, too quickly. The cigarillo tilted and he pulled it out. 'The publishing business is vulnerable to leaks. Information superhighway; the commodity is . . . ephemeral.'

'Meaning everyone's out to steal ideas?'

'Meaning billions are invested in the buying and selling of concepts and everyone's looking for the *golden* idea.'

'And you've found it on Aruk?'

Creedman smiled and smoked.

'It's not like that in medicine,' she said. 'Discover something important, you've got a moral obligation to publicize it.'

'How noble,' said Creedman. 'Then again, you doctors chose your field *because* you're noble.'

Moreland said, 'I think it's coming.' His finger was up but he was still facing the ocean.

I heard nothing but the waves and bird chirps. Moreland nodded. 'Yes, definitely.'

Seconds later, a deep tom-tom rumble sounded from the east, growing steadily louder.

A big, dark helicoper appeared over the bluffs, sighted directly over us, hovered, then lowered itself on the road like a giant locust.

Double rotors, bloated body. Sand sprayed and we dropped our heads and cupped our hands over our mouths.

The rotors slowed but didn't stop. A door opened and a drop-ladder snapped down.

Hands beckoned.

We trotted to the craft, eating sand, ears bursting, and climbed into a cabin walled with canvas and plastic and reeking of fuel. Moreland, Pam, and Creedman took the first passenger row and Robin and I settled behind them. Piles of gear and packed parachutes filled the rear storage area. A pair of Navy men sat up front. Half-drawn pleated curtains allowed us a partial view of the backs of their heads and a strip of green-lit panel.

The second officer looked back at us for a moment, then straight ahead. He pointed. The pilot did something and the copter shuddered and rose.

We headed out to sea, hooking southeast and following the coastline. High enough for me to make out the bladelike shape of the island. South Beach was the point of the dagger, our destination the hilt.

The blockade was no more than a paper cut from this height. The mountaintops were a black leather belt, the banyans obscured by burgeoning darkness and the ring of mountains. The copter veered sharply and the east end of the island slid into view.

Concrete shore and choppy water, no trees or sand or reefs. The windward harbor was a generous soupspoon indentation.

Natural port. Ships large enough to look significant from these heights were moored there. Some of them moved. Strong waves – I could see the froth, piling up against a massive seawall.

We turned north toward the base: empty stretches of black veined with gray, toy-block assemblages that had to be barracks, some larger buildings.

The copter descended and we touched down perfectly, the trip as brief as an amusement park ride, the blockade's cruel efficiency clearer than ever. The pilot cut the engine and exited without a word. The second officer waited till the rotors had quieted before releasing our door.

We got out and were hit by a blast of humid air, stale and chemically tainted.

'The windward side,' said Moreland. 'Nothing grows here.'

A sailor in a contraption that resembled an oversize golf cart drove us through a sentry post and past the barracks, storehouses, hangars, empty airstrips. Concrete fields crowded with planes and copters and disassembled craft made me think of Harry Amalfi's aerial junkyard. Some of the planes were antiques, others looked new. One sleek passenger jet, in particular, would have done a CEO proud.

The harbor was blocked from view by the seawall, a monstrous thing of the same raw construction as the blockade. Above it, an American flag whipped and snapped like a locker-room towel. I could hear the ocean charging angrily, hitting the concrete with the roar of a gladiator audience.

Looking toward the base's western border, I saw the area where Picker must have gone down. At least half a mile away. Twenty-foot chain-link fencing completed the banyan's prison. Creedman had said the base was run by a skeleton crew, and there were very few sailors on the ground – maybe two dozen, walking, watching.

The golf cart veered across a nearly empty parking lot, through a small drab garden, up to a colonial building, three stories high, white board and brick, green shutters.

HEADQUARTERS

CAPT. ELVIN S. EWING

Next door was a one-story building of the same design. The officer's club.

Inside the club was a long walnut hallway – deep red wool carpeting patterned with crossed sabers, brass fixtures. The paneling was lined with roiling seascapes and model ships in glass cases.

Another sailor took us to a waiting room decorated with photo blowups of fighter jets and club chairs. A sailor in dress uniform stood behind a host's lectern. Glass doors opened to a dining room: soft lighting, empty tables, the smell of canned vegetable soup and melted cheese.

The sailors saluted one another, and the first one left without breaking step.

'This way,' said the one behind the lectern. Young, with clipped hair and a soft face full of pimples. He took us to an unmarked door. A sign hanging from the knob said Captain Ewing had reserved the room.

Inside were one long table under a hammered-copper chandelier and twenty bright blue chairs. A portrait of the President wearing an uneasy smile greeted us from behind the head chair. Three walls of wood, one blocked by blue drapes.

A new sailor came and took our cocktail order. Two different men brought the drinks.

Creedman sipped his martini and licked his lips. 'Nice and dry. Why can't we get vermouth like this in the village, Bill?'

Moreland stared at his tomato juice and shrugged.

'I asked the Trading Post to get me something dry and Italian,' said Creedman. 'Took a month and what I ended up with was some swill from Malaysia.'

'Pity.'

'Go to any duty-free in the booniest outpost and they've got everything from Chivas to Stoli, so what's the big deal about filling an order here? It's almost as if they want to do it wrong.'

'Is that the theme of your book?' said Pam. 'Incompetent islanders?'

Creedman smiled at her over his drink. 'If you're that curious about my book, maybe you and I should get together and discuss it. That is, if you've got any energy after your swims.'

Moreland walked to the blue drapes and parted them.

'Same view,' he said. 'The airfield. Why they put a window here, I'll never know.'

'Maybe they like to see the planes take off, Dad,' said Pam.

Moreland shrugged again.

'How long did you and Mom live here?'

'Two years.'

Three men came in. Two wore officer's garb – the first fiftyish, tall and thickset, with rough red skin and steel glasses; the other even taller, ten years younger, with a long, swarthy, rubbery face and restless hands.

The man between them had on a beautiful featherweight gray serge suit that trimmed ten pounds from his two hundred. Six feet tall, heavy shouldered and narrow hipped, with a square face, bullish features, slit mouth, rancher's tan. His shirt was soft blue broadcloth with a pin collar, his foulard a silver and wine silk weave. His hair was bushy and black on top, the temples snow-white. The contrast was almost artificial, as dramatic in real life as on TV.

He looked like Hollywood's idea of a senator, but Hollywood had nothing to do with his becoming one, if newspapers and magazines could be believed.

The story was a good one: born to a young widow in a struggling Oregon logging camp, Nicholas Hoffman had been tutored at home till the age of fifteen, when he'd lied about his age and enlisted in the Navy. By the end of the Korean War, he was a decorated hero who gave the military another 15 years of distinguished service before entering the real estate business, making his first million by 40 and running successfully for the Senate at forty-three. His doctrine was the avoidance of extremes; someone dubbed him Mr Middle-of-the-Road and it stuck. Truc believers on both ends tried to use it against him. The voters ignored them, and Hoffman was well into his third term after a no-contest race.

'Bill!' he said, barging ahead of the officers and stretching out a meaty hand.

'Senator,' said Moreland, softly.

'Oh, Jesus!' roared Hoffman. 'Cut the crap! How *are* you, man?'

He grabbed Moreland's hand and pumped. Moreland remained expressionless. Hoffman turned to Pam. 'You must be Dr Moreland, Junior. Christ, last time I saw you, you were in diapers.' He let go of her father and touched her fingers briefly. 'You *are* a doctor?'

She nodded.

'Splendid.'

Creedman stuck out his hand and announced himself.

'Ah, the press,' said Hoffman. 'Captain Ewing told me you were here, so I said invite him, show him open government in action or he'll make something up. On assignment?'

'Writing a book.'

'On what?'

'Nonfiction novel.'

'Ah. Great.'

'What brings *you* here, Senator?'

'Fact-finding trip. Not one of those sun-and-fun junkets. Real work. Downsizing. Appraising military installations.'

Unbuttoning his jacket, he patted his middle. He had a small, hard paunch that tailoring had done a good job of camouflaging.

'And you must be the doctors from California.' He stuck out his hand. 'Nick Hoffman.'

'Dr Delaware's a psychologist,' said Robin. 'I build musical instruments.

'How nice . . .' He glanced at the table. 'Shall we, Captain?'

'Certainly, Senator,' said the red-faced officer. His voice was raspy. Neither he nor the swarthy man had budged during the introductions. 'You're at the head, sir.'

Hoffman strode quickly to his place and removed his jacket. The taller officer rushed to take it from him, but he'd already hung it on the back of the chair and sat down, removing his collar pin and loosening his tie.

'Drink, Senator?' the officer said.

'Iced tea, Walt. Thanks.'

The tall man left. The red-faced man remained in place near the door.

'Join us, Captain Ewing,' said Hoffman, motioning to one of the two empty chairs.

Ewing removed his hat and complied, leaving lots of space between his back and the chair.

'Can I assume everyone knows everyone, Elvin?' said Hoffman.

'I know everyone by name,' said Ewing. 'But we've never met.'

'Mr Creedman, Dr Pam Moreland, Dr and Mrs Delaware,' said Hoffman, 'Captain Elvin Ewing, base commander.'

Ewing put a finger to his eyeglasses. He looked as comfortable as a eunuch in a locker room.

The officer returned with Hoffman's tea. The glass was oversized and a mint sprig floated on top.

'Anything else, Senator?'

'No. Sit down, Walt.'

As he started to obey, Ewing said, 'Introduce yourself, lieutenant.'

'Lieutenant Zondervein,' said the tall man looking straight ahead.

'There,' said Hoffman. 'Now we're all friends.' Emptying most of the glass with one gulp, he picked out the mint sprig and chewed on a leaf.

'Are you traveling alone, Senator?' said Creedman.

Hoffman grinned at him. 'Just can't turn it off, can you? If you mean do I have an entourage no, just me. And yes, it's a leased government jet, but I rode along with the base supplies.'

The sleek craft I'd noticed.

'Actually,' continued Hoffman, 'there are three other leglislative luminaries assigned to this particular trip. Senators Bering, Petrucci, and Hammersmith. They're in Hawaii right now, arriving in Guam tomorrow, and I can't promise you they haven't been sunbathing.' Grinning. 'I decided to come early so I could revisit my old stomping grounds, see old friends. No, Mr Creedman, it didn't cost the taxpayers an extra penny, because my assignment is to assess facilities on several of the smaller Micronesian islands, including Aruk, and by coming alone I turned it into a cheap date.'

He finished the tea, crushed an ice cube, swallowed, and laughed. 'I got to sit up with the pilot. God, the instrumentation on these things. Might as well have been trying to play one of those damn computer games my grandkids are addicted to – did you know the average seven-year-old has more computer proficiency than his parents will ever achieve? Great eye-hand skills, too. Maybe we should train seven-year-olds to fly combat, Elvin.'

Ewing's smile was anemic.

'Let me get you a refill, Senator,' said Zondervein, starting to get up.

Hoffman said, 'No, thanks – anyone else?'

Creedman lifted his martini glass.

Lieutenant Zondervein took it and went to the door. 'I'll check on the first course.'

Hoffman unfolded his napkin and tucked it into his collar. 'Mafia style,' he said. 'But one wirephoto with grease spots on the tie and you learn. So what's on the menu, Elvin?'

'Chicken,' said Ewing.

'Does it bounce?'

'I hope not, sir.'

'Roast or fried?'

'Roast.'

'See that, Mr Creedman? Simple fare.'

He turned to Ewing. 'And for Dr Moreland?'

'Sir?'

Hoffman's lips maintained a smile but his eyes narrowed until they disappeared. 'Dr Moreland's a vegetarian, Captain. I believe I radioed you that from the plane.'

'Yes, sir. There are vegetables.'

'There are *vegetables*. Fresh ones?'

'I believe so, sir.'

'I hope so,' said Hoffman, too gently. 'Dr Moreland maintains a very healthy diet – or at least he used to. I assume that hasn't changed, Bill?'

'Anything's fine,' said Moreland.

'You were way ahead of your time, Bill. Eating right while the rest of us went merrily about, clogging our arteries. You look *great*. Been keeping up with the bridge?'

'No.'

'No? You had how many masters points – ten, fifteen?'

'Haven't played at all since you left, Nicholas.'

'Really.' Hoffman looked around. 'Bill was a great bridge player – photographic memory and you couldn't read his face. The rest of us were amateurs, but we did manage to put together some spirited matches, didn't we, Bill? You really quit? No more duplicate tournaments like the ones you used to play at the Saipan club?'

Another shake of Moreland's head.

'Anyone here play?' said Hoffman. 'Maybe we can get a game going after dinner.'

Silence.

'Oh, well . . . great game. Skill plus the luck of the draw. A lot more realistic than something like chess.'

Zondervein returned with Creedman's martini. Two sailors followed with a rolling cart of appetizers.

Honeydew melon wrapped in ham.

Hoffman said, 'Take the meat off Dr Moreland's.'

Zondervein rushed to obey.

The ham tasted like canned sausage. The melon was more starch than sugar.

Gladys had said Hoffman was a gourmet, but gourmand was more like it: he dug in enthusiastically, scraping honey-dew flesh down to bare rind and emptying his water glass three times.

'Dad's been writing to you,' said Pam. 'Did you receive his letters?'

'I did indeed,' said Hoffman. 'Two letters, right, Bill? Or did you send some I didn't get?'

'Just two.'

'Would you believe they just made their way to my desk? The filtering process. Actually only the second one got to me directly. Maybe the three times you wrote "personal" on the envelope did the trick. Anyway, I was tickled to receive it. Then I read the reference to your first letter and put out a search for it. Finally found it in some aide's office filed under "Ecology." You probably would have received a form letter in two or three months – where do you get the ham, Elvin? Not Smithwood or Parma, that's for sure.'

'It's through the general mess, sir,' said Ewing. 'As you instructed.'

Hoffman stared at him.

Ewing turned to Zondervein. 'Where's the ham from, Lieutenant?'

'I'm not sure, sir.'

'Find out ASAP. Before the senator leaves.'

'Yes, sir. I'll go to the kitchen right now—'

'No,' said Hoffman. 'Not important – see, Tom, we eat frugally when the public picks up the tab.'

'If you want great grub, Senator, come over to my house.'

'You cook, do you?'

'Love to cook. Got a great beef tournedos recipe.' Creedman smiled at Moreland. 'I'm into meat.'

'Get much meat on the island?' said Hoffman.

'I make do. It takes some creativity.'

'How about you, Pam? Do you like to cook?'

'Not particularly.'

'Only thing I can do is biscuits. Campside biscuits, recipe handed down from my great-grandmother – flour, baking soda, salt, sugar, bacon drippings.'

'How long will you be staying?' said Moreland.

'Just till tomorrow.'

'You've finished assessing Stanton?'

'The process began stateside.'

'Are you planning to close it down?'

Hoffman put down his fork and rubbed the rim of his plate. 'We're not at the decision stage, yet.'

'Meaning closure is likely.'

'I can't eliminate any possibilities, Bill.'

'If the base closes, what will happen to Aruk?'

'You're probably in a better position to say, Bill.'

'I probably am,' said Moreland. 'Do you remember what I wrote about the blockade of South Beach road?'

'Yes, I mentioned that to Captain Ewing.'

'Did Captain Ewing give you his reason?'

Hoffman looked at Ewing. 'Elvin?'

Ewing's red face was aflame. 'Security,' he rasped.

'Meaning?' said Moreland.

Ewing directed his answer at Hoffman. 'I'm not free to discuss it openly, sir.'

'The blockade was economic oppression, Nick,' said Moreland.

Hoffman cut free a white outer scrap of melon, stared at it, chewed, and swallowed.

'Sometimes things change, Bill,' he said softly.

'Sometimes they shouldn't, Nick. Sometimes under the guise of helping people we do terrible things.'

Hoffman squinted at Ewing again. 'Could you be a little more forthcoming for Dr Moreland, Elvin?'

Ewing swallowed. There'd been no food in his mouth. 'There was some local unrest. We appraised it given the data at hand, and the judgment was that it had the potential to escalate and pose a hazard to Navy security. Restricting contact between the men and the locals was deemed advisable in terms or risk management. The proper forms were sent to Pacific Command and approval was granted by Admiral Felton.'

'Gobbledygook,' said Moreland. 'A few kids got out of hand. I think the Navy can handle that without choking off the island's economy. We've exploited them all these years, it's immoral to simply yank out the rug.'

Ewing bit back comment and stared straight ahead.

'Bill,' said Hoffman, 'my memory is that *we* saved *them* from the Japanese. That doesn't make us exploiters.'

'Defeating the Japanese was in our national interest. Then we took over and imposed our laws. That makes the people our responsibility.'

Hoffman tapped his fork on his plate.

'With all due respect,' he said very softly, 'that sounds a little paternalistic.'

'It's *real*istic.'

Pam touched the top of his hand. He freed it and said: 'Local unrest makes it sound like some kind of uprising. It was nothing, Nick. Trivial.'

Ewing's lips were so tight they looked sutured.

'Shall I check on the second course, sir?' said Zondervein.

Ewing gave him a guillotine-blade nod.

'Actually, it's not quite that simple,' said Creedman. 'There was a murder. A girl raped and left cut up on the beach. The locals were sure a sailor had done it and were coming up here to protest.'

'Oh?' said Hoffman. 'Is there evidence a sailor was responsible?'

'None whatsoever, sir,' said Ewing, too loudly. 'They love rumors here. The locals got liquored up and tried to storm—'

'Don't make it sound like an insurgence,' said Moreland. 'The people had justification for their suspicions.'

'Oh?' said Hoffman.

'Surely you remember the people, Nick. How nonviolent they are. And the victim consorted with sailors.'

'Consorted.' Hoffman smiled, put his fingers together, and

looked over them. 'I knew the people thirty years ago, Bill. I don't believe Navy men tend to be murderers.'

Moreland stared at him.

Ewing was nearly scarlet. 'We were concerned about things getting out of hand. We still believe that concern was justified, given the facts and the hypotheticals. The order came from Pacific Command.'

'Nonsense,' said Moreland. 'The facts are that we're a colonial power and it's the same old pattern: islanders living at the pleasure of westerners only to be abandoned. It's a betrayal. Yet *another* example of abusing trust.'

Hoffman didn't move. Then he picked something out of his teeth and ate another ice cube.

'A betrayal,' repeated Moreland.

Hoffman seemed to be thinking about that. Finally, he said, 'You know that Aruk has a special place in my heart, Bill. After the war, I needed peace and beauty and something unspoiled.' To us: 'Anyone tells you there's anything glorious about war has his head jammed up his rectum so high he's been blinded. Right, Elvin?'

Ewing managed a nod.

'After the war I spent some of the best years of my life here. Remember how you and Barb and Dotty and I used to hike and swim, Bill? How we used to say that some places were better left untouched? Perhaps we were more prescient that we knew. Maybe sometimes nature has to run her course.'

'That's the point, Nicholas. Aruk *has* been touched. People's lives are at—'

'I know, I know. But the problem is one of population distribution. Allocation of increasingly sparse resources. I've seen too many ill-conceived projects that look good on paper but don't wash. Too many assumptions about the inevitable benefits of prosperity and autonomy. Look what happened to Nauru.'

'Nauru is hardly typical,' said Moreland.

'But it's instructive.' Hoffman turned to us. 'Any of you heard of Nauru? Tiny island, southeast of here, smack in the center of Micronesia. Ten square miles of guano – bird dirt. Two hundred years of hands-off colonization by the Brits and the Germans, then someone realizes the place is pure phosphate. The Brits and the Germans collaborate on mining, give the Nauruans nothing but flu and polio. World War Two comes along, the Japanese invade and send most of the Nauruans to Chuuk as forced laborers. After the war, *Australia* takes over and the native chiefs negotiate a sweet deal: big share of the fertilizer profits *plus* Australian welfare. In sixty-eight Australia grants full independence and the chiefs take over the Nauru Phosphate Corporation, which is exporting two million tons of gull poop a year. A *hundred* million dollars in income; per-capita income rises to twenty-thousand-plus. Comparable to an oil sheikdom. Cars, stereos, and junk food for the islanders. Along with a thirty-percent national rate of diabetes. Think of that – one in three. Highest in the world. No special hereditary factors, either. It's clearly all the junk food. Same for high blood pressure, coronary disease, gross obesity – I met an Australian senator who called it "land o' lard." Throw in serious alcoholism and car crashes, and you've got a life expectancy in the fifties. And to top it off, ninety percent of the phosphate is gone. A few more years and nothing'll be left but insulin bottles and beer cans. So much for unbridled prosperity.'

'Are you advocating the virtues of poverty, Nick?'

'No, Bill, but the world's changed, some people think we need to stop looking at ourselves as the universal nursemaid.'

'We're talking about *people*. A way of life—'

Creedman said, 'Whoa. You make it sound as though everything was hunky-dory before the Europeans came over and colonization spoiled everything, but my research tells me there were plenty of diseases in the primitive world and that the people who didn't die of them would probably have died of famine.'

I expected Moreland to turn on him, but he continued to stare at Hoffman.

Hoffman said, 'There is some truth to that, Bill. As a doctor you know that.'

'Diseases,' said Moreland, as if the word amused him. 'Yes, there were parasitic conditions, but nothing on the scale of the misery that was brought over.'

'Come on,' said Creedman. 'Let's get real. We're talking primitive tribes. Pagan rituals, no indoor plumbing—'

Moreland faced him slowly. 'Are you a waste-disposal expert in addition to all your other talents?'

Creedman said, 'My resear—'

'Did your *research* tell you that some of those primitive rituals *ensured* impeccable cleanliness? Practices such as reserving mornings for defecation and wading out to the ocean to relieve oneself?'

'That doesn't sound very hygien—'

Moreland's hands rose and his fingers sculpted air. 'It was fine! Until the civilized *conquerors* came along and told them they needed to dig holes in the ground. Do you know what that ushered in, Tom? An era of *filth*. Cholera, typhoid, salmonellosis, lungworm fever. Have you ever *seen* someone with cholera, Creedman?'

'I've—'

'Have you ever held a dehydrated child in your arms as she convulses in the throes of explosive *diarrhea*?'

The gnarled hands dropped and slapped down on the table.

'Research,' he muttered.

Creedman sucked his teeth. He'd gone white.

'I bow, doctor,' he said softly, 'to your superior knowledge of diarrhea.'

The door opened. Zondervein and three sailors, kitchen smells, more food.

'Well,' said Hoffman, exhaling. *'Bon appétit.'*

18

Other than Hoffman, no one ate much.

After his second dessert, he stood and ripped his napkin free. 'Come on, Bill, let's you and me catch up on old times. Nice to meet you all.'

A glance at Lieutenant Zondervein, who said, 'How about the rest of us head over to the rec room? There's a pool table and a big-screen TV.'

Outside in the hall, Ewing gave him a disgusted look. 'If you'll all excuse me.' He left swiftly.

'This way,' said Zondervein.

'Do you get cable?' Creedman asked.

'Sure,' said Zondervein. 'We get everything, have a satellite dish.'

'Excellent.'

'Isn't there a dish at the Trading Post?' I said.

Creedman laughed. 'Broke a year ago and no one's bothered to fix it. Does that tell you something about local initiative?'

* * *

Creedman and I played a couple of games of pool. He was good, but cheated anyway, moving the cue ball when he thought I wasn't looking.

The big-screen was tuned to CNN.

'News lite,' he said.

'Only thing I get from the news is depressed,' said Pam. She and Robin were sitting in chairs too big for them, looking bored. I caught Robin's eye. She waved and sipped her Coke.

A few minutes later, Zondervein brought Moreland back. He sagged with exhaustion.

Pam said, 'Dad?'

'Time to go.'

After we landed, Creedman walked away from us without a word. No one spoke during the ride back to the estate. When Moreland pulled up in front of the house it was nine-forty. 'I think I'll catch up on work. You all relax.' He patted Pam's arm. 'Have a good night, dear.'

'Maybe I'll go into town.'

'Oh?'

'I thought I might go for a night swim.'

He touched her arm again. Held on to it. 'That could be tricky, Pamela. Urchins, morays, you could run into trouble.'

'I'm sure Dennis can keep me out of trouble.'

He must have squeezed her arm because she winced.

'Dennis,' he said, just above a whisper, 'is engaged to a girl studying at the nursing school in Saipan.'

'Not anymore,' said Pam.

'Oh?'

'They broke up a few weeks ago.'

She touched his arm and he dropped it.

'A pity,' said Moreland. 'Nice girl. She would have been valuable to the island.' Fixing his eyes on his daughter: 'Dennis still is, dear. It would be best for all concerned if you didn't *distract* him.'

Turning on his heel, he walked down toward the bungalows.

Pam's mouth was wide open. She ran up to the house.

* * *

'Fun evening,' I said. We were up in our suite, sitting on the bed.

'The way he just acted,' said Robin. 'I know he's under stress, but . . .'

'Loves the natives but doesn't want them dating his daughter?'

'It sounded more like he was shielding Dennis from *her.*'

'It did. Maybe she's got an unfortunate history with men. The first time I saw her I noticed the sadness in her eyes.'

She smiled. 'Is that all you noticed?'

'Yes, she's good-looking but I don't find her sexy. There's something about her that sets up a clear boundary. I've seen it in patients: "I've been wounded. Stay away."'

'That obviously doesn't apply to Dennis.'

'The old man really lost it,' I said. 'Perfect capper to a charming dinner.'

She laughed. 'That base. Night of the uniformed dead. And Hoffman. Joe Slick.'

'Why do I get the feeling Hoffman's sole purpose for the dinner was the half hour he and Moreland spent alone?'

'Then why not just drop over here?'

'Maybe he wanted to be on his home turf, not Moreland's.'

'You make it sound like some sort of battle.'

'I can't help but think it was. The tension between them . . . as if the two of them have some issue that goes way back. At any rate, Moreland didn't get what he wanted for Aruk. Whatever that is.'

'What do you mean?'

'He puzzles me, Rob. Talks about helping the island, rejuvenating it. But if he's as rich as Creedman says, it seems to me there are things he could have already done. Like improve communication. Put some of his fortune into schooling, training. At the very least, more frequent shipping schedules. Instead, he pumps a fortune into his projects. Walled in here like some lord while the rest of the island molders. Maybe the islanders know that and that's why they're leaving. We certainly haven't seen any big show of civic pride. Not even a grass-roots movement to protest the barricade.'

She thought about that. 'Yes, he is very much the lord of the manor, isn't he? And maybe the islanders know something else: Hoffman's right about some places not being set up for development. Look at Aruk's geography. The leeward side has great weather but no harbor, the windward side has a natural harbor but rocks instead of soil. In between, you've got mountains and a banyan forest full of land mines. Nothing fits right. It's like a geographic joke. Maybe everyone gets it but Moreland.'

'And Skip and Haygood with their resort scheme. Which proves your point. Oh, well, looks like I signed on with Dr Quixote.'

She got up and rolled off her panty hose, frowning. 'It was so out of character, the way he just treated Pam. There doesn't seem to be much intimacy between them – which makes sense, with his being an absent father – but till tonight he's never been harsh.'

'He's the one who sent her to boarding school,' I said. 'And even with her M.D. he doesn't consider her a colleague. All in all, no candidate for father of the year.'

'Poor Pam. First time I saw her I thought, "homecoming queen." But you never know, do you?'

She unbuttoned her dress and stepped out of it. Folded it over a chair and touched her wrist.

'How does it feel?' I said.

'Excellent, actually. Are you working tomorrow?'

'Guess so.'

'Maybe I'll try to do something with those pieces of shell.'

She went into the bathroom. And screamed.

19

Three of them.

No, *four*!

Racing back and forth, light-panicked, on the white tile floor.

One scurried up the shower wall, pointed its antennae at us. Waved.

Robin was pressed into a corner, fighting another scream.

One crawled up the side of the tub, paused on the rim.

Lozenge shaped. Red-brown armored shell as long as my hand.

Six black legs.

The eyes, too damn smart.

It hissed.

They all began hissing.

Speeding toward us.

I pulled Robin out of the room and slammed the door behind us. Checked the space beneath the door. Tight fit, thank God.

My heart was hurtling. Sweat burst out of me and it leaked down in cold, itchy trails.

Robin's fingers bit into my back.

'Oh God, Alex! Oh God!'

I managed to say, 'It's okay, they can't get out.'

'Oh, God . . .' She gasped for breath. 'I walked in and something touched – my foot.'

She looked down at her toes and trembled.

I sat her down. She held onto my fingers, shaking.

'Easy,' I said, remembering the insect's face – stoic, intense.

'Get rid of them, honey. Please!'

'I will.'

'The light was off. I felt it before I saw it – how many were there?'

'I counted four.'

'It seemed like more.'

'I think four is all.'

'Oh, *God*.'

I held her tight. 'It's all right, they're confined.'

'Yucch,' she said. *'Yucch!'*

Spike was barking. When had he started?

'Maybe I should sic *him* on them.'

'No, no, I don't want him near them – they're disgusting. Just get them out of here, Alex! Call Moreland. I can take them in their cages, but please get them *out*!'

Gladys arrived first.

'Bugs?' she said.

'*Huge* ones,' said Robin. 'Where's Dr Bill?'

'Must be from the bug zoo. It never happened before.'

'Where *is* he, Gladys?'

'On his way. You poor thing. Where are they?'

I pointed to the bathroom.

She grimaced. 'Personally, I hate bugs. Nasty little things.'

'Little wouldn't be bad,' said Robin.

'Working here doesn't bother you?' I said.

'What, the zoo? I never go in there. No one goes in there but Dr Bill and Ben.'

'Well, something obviously comes out.'

'It never happened before,' she repeated.

Hissing from behind the door. I pictured the damn things chewing through the wood. Or escaping down the toilet and hiding in the pipes. Where the hell was Moreland?

'Did you see what they were?' said Gladys.

'They looked like giant cockroaches,' said Robin.

'Madagascar hissing cockroaches,' I said, suddenly remembering.

'Them I really hate,' said Gladys. 'Cockroaches in general. One of the things I like about Aruk is the dryness, we don't get roaches. Lots of bugs, period.'

'So we import them,' I mumbled.

'I keep my kitchen clean. Some of the other islands you've got bugs all over the place, got to spray all the time. Bugs bring disease – not Dr Bill's bugs, he keeps them real clean.'

'That's a comfort,' I said.

A knock sounded on the suite door and Moreland loped in carrying a large mahogany box with a brass handle and looking around.

'I don't see how . . . did you happen to notice what kind—'

'Madagascar hissing roaches,' I said.

'Oh . . . good. They can't seriously harm you.'

'They're in there.'

He advanced to the bathroom door.

'Careful,' said Robin. 'Don't let them out.'

'No problem, dear.' He turned the knob slowly and took something out of his pocket – a piece of chocolate cake that he compressed into a gummy ball. Spreading the door a crack, he tossed the bait, closed, waited.

A few seconds later, he opened the door again, peered through. Nodded, opened wider, slipped in.

'My new fudge loaf,' said Gladys.

Sounds came from inside the bathroom.

Moreland talking.

Soothingly.

He emerged moments later holding the mahogany box and giving the OK sign. Chocolate smears on his fingers. Crumbs on the floor.

Thumps from within the box.

Hiss.

'You're sure you got all of them?' said Robin.

'Yes, dear.'

'They didn't lay eggs or anything?'

He smiled at her. 'No, dear, everything's fine.'

It sounded patronizing and it got to me.

'Not really, Bill,' I said. 'How the hell did they get here in the first place?'

'I – don't know – I'm sorry. *Dreadfully* sorry. My apologies to both of you.'

'They're definitely from the insectarium?'

'Certainly, Aruk has no indig—'

'So how'd they get out?'

'I – suppose someone must have left the lid loose.'

'It's never happened before,' said Gladys.

'That's us,' I said. 'Trailblazers.'

Moreland tugged at his lower lip, rubbed his fleshy nose. Blinked. 'I suppose *I* must have left the lid off—'

'It's okay,' Robin said, squeezing my hand. 'It's over.'

'I'm *so* sorry, dear. Perhaps the scent of your dog food—'

'If it was food they were after,' I said, 'why didn't they head for the kitchen?'

'I keep my kitchen clean and shut up tight,' said Gladys. 'No flies, not even grain weevils.'

'Our door was locked,' I said, 'and the dog food's sealed in plastic bags. How did they get in, Bill?'

He went over to the door, opened and closed it a couple of times, kneeled and ran his hand over the threshold.

'There's some give to the carpet,' he said. They're very good at compressing themselves. I've seen them manage—'

'Spare the details,' I said. 'You probably knocked a year off our lives.'

'I'm terribly, terribly sorry.' He hung his head. The cockroaches bumped inside the box. Then the hissing began again. Louder . . .

'You did handle it perfectly,' he said. 'Locking them in. Thank you for not damaging them.'

'You're welcome,' I said. I'd turned phone solicitors down with a kinder tone.

Robin squeezed my hand again.

'It's okay, Bill,' she said. 'We're fine.'

Moreland said, 'An unforgivable laspse. I'm always so careful – I'll put double locks on the insectarium immediately. And door seals. We'll get working on it right now – Gladys, call Kamon and Carl Sleet, apologize for waking them up, and tell them I've got a job for them. Triple overtime pay. Tell Carl to bring the Swiss drill I gave him for Christmas.'

Gladys rushed out.

Moreland looked at the box and rubbed the oiled wood. 'Better be getting these fellows back.' He hurried to the door and nearly collided with Jo Picker as she padded in, wearing robe and slippers, rubbing her eyes.

'Is everything . . . okay?' Her voice was thick. She coughed to clear it.

'Just a little mishap,' said Moreland.

She frowned. Her eyes were unfocused.

'Took something . . . to sleep . . . did I hear someone scream?'

'I did,' said Robin. 'There were some bugs in the bathroom.'

'Bugs?'

The roaches hissed and her eyes widened.

'Go back to sleep, dear,' said Moreland, guiding her out. 'Everything's been taken care of. Everything's fine.'

When we were alone, we let Spike out and he raced around the room, circling. Sniffing near the bathroom before charging in head down.

'The dog food goes downstairs tomorrow,' said Robin.

Then she got up suddenly, pulled back the bedcovers, looked underndeath the box spring, and then stood. Smiling sheepishly.

'Just being careful,' she said.

'Are you going to be able to sleep?' I said.

'Hope so. How about you?'

'My heart's down to two hundred beats a minute.'

She sighed. Started laughing and couldn't stop.

I wanted to join in but couldn't manage more than a taut smile.

'Our little bit of New York,' she finally said. 'Manhattan tenement in our island hideaway.'

'Those things could *mug* New York roaches.'

'I know.' She put my hand on her breast. 'How many beats?'

'Hmm,' I said. 'Hard to tell. I need to count for a *long* time.'

More laughter. 'God, the way I shrieked. Like one of those horror movies.'

Her forehead was moist, curls sticking to it. I brushed them away, kissed her brow, the tip of her nose.

'So how long do we stay in bug-land?' I said.

'You want to leave?'

'Plane crash, unsolved murder, the zombie base, some fairly uncongenial people. Now this.'

'Don't leave on my account. I can't tell you I won't freak out if the same thing happens again, but I'm okay, now. Ms Adaptable. I pride myself on it.'

'Sure,' I said, 'but sometimes it's nice not having to adapt.'

'True . . . Maybe I'm nuts but I still like it here. Maybe it's my hand feeling better – a lot better, actually. Or even the fact that this may be our last chance to experience Aruk before the Navy turns it into a bomb yard or something. Even Bill – he's unique, Aruk is unique.'

She held my face and looked into my eyes. 'I guess what I'm saying, Alex, is I don't want to be back in L.A. next week, dealing with the house or some business hassle, and start thinking back with regrets.'

I didn't answer.

'Am I making sense, doctor?'

I touched my nose to hers. Curled my lip. Bared my teeth. Hissed.

She jumped up. Pounded my shoulder. '*Oh!* Maybe I should have Spike sleep in the bed and put *you* in the crate.'

Lights out.

A few self-conscious jokes about creepy-crawlies and she was sleeping.

I lay awake.

Trying to picture the roaches trekking all the way from the insectarium to our suite . . . marching in unison? The idea was cartoonish.

And even if the dog food *had* attracted them, why hadn't they stayed in the sitting room, near the bag?

Roaches were supposed to be smart, as bugs went. Why not head for an easier meal – the fruit from the orchard?

Instead, they'd taken a circuitous journey, scampering up the gravel paths, across the lawn, into the house somehow. Bypassing Gladys's kitchen. Up the stairs. Under our door.

All because of a sealed sack of kibble?

Despite Moreland's claim, the bathroom door seemed too snug to let them in or out. Had we left it open before leaving for dinner at the base?

Robin always left the bathroom door closed. Sometimes I didn't . . . Which of us had last used the lav?

Why hadn't they come running out when we arrived home? Or at least hissed in alarm?

An alternative scenario: they'd been placed in the bathroom and shut in.

Someone up to mischief during the dinner at Stanton. The house empty. Someone seizing the opportunity to send us a message: *Go away*.

But who and why?

Who had the opportunity?

Ben was the obvious choice, because he had access to the insectarium.

He'd said his evening was full, between fatherhood and a hibachi dinner with Claire.

Had he come back?

But why? Apart from the remark about natural rhythm, he'd shown no sign of hostility toward us. On the contrary. He'd gone out of his way to make us feel welcome.

Out of obligation to Moreland?

Were his own feelings something else?

I thought about it for a while, but it just didn't make sense.

Someone else on the staff?

Cheryl?

Too dull to be that calculating, and once again, what was her motive? Plus, she usually left after dinner, and no meal had been served tonight.

Gladys? Same lack of motive, and the idea of her purloining roaches seemed equally ludicrous.

There had to be at least a dozen groundskeepers and gardeners who came and went, but why would *they* resent us?

Unless the message had been meant for *Moreland.*

My surmise about his attitude of noblesse oblige and the resentment it might have generated in the villagers could be right on target.

The good doctor less than universally loved? His guests seen as colonial interlopers?

If so, it could be anyone.

Paranoia, Delaware. The guy had kept thousands of bugs for years, four had gotten out because he was old and absentminded and had forgotten to put a lid on tight.

Spacey, just as Milo had said.

Not a comforting thought, *considering* the thousands of bugs, but I supposed he'd be especially careful now.

I tried to empty my head and sleep. Thought of the way Jo Picker had come in: drowsy, asking if someone had screamed.

Robin's scream had sounded a full ten minutes before.

Why the delay?

The sleeping pill slowing her responses?

Or no need to hurry because she *knew*?

And *she'd* been alone upstairs all evening.

Paranoia run amok. What reason would a grieving widow have for malicious mischief?

She'd said she was squeamish about insects, had refused even to enter the bug zoo.

And there was no animosity between us. Robin had been especially kind to her . . . Even if she was a fiend, how could she have gained access to our room?

Her own room key – the lock similar to ours?

Or a simple pick. Most bedroom locks weren't designed for security. Ours back home could be popped with a screwdriver.

I lay there and listened for sounds through the wall.

Nothing.

What did I expect to hear, the click of her keyboard? Widow's wails?

I shifted position and the mattress rocked, but Robin didn't budge.

Teachers' voices from many years ago filtered through my brain.

Alexander is a very bright little boy, but he does tend to day-dream.

Is something wrong at home, Mrs Delaware? Alexander has seemed rather distracted lately.

A soft, liquid line of light oozed through a part in the curtains like golden paint freshly squeezed.

Playing on Robin's face.

She smiled in her sleep, curls dangling over one eye.

Take her example and *adapt.*

I relaxed my muscles consciously and deepened my breathing. Soon my chest loosened and I felt better.

Able to smile at the image of Moreland with his chocolate cake and schoolboy guilt.

My body felt heavy. Ready to sleep.

But it took a long time to fall under.

20

The next morning, the clouds were darker and moving closer, but still, remote.

We were ready to dive at ten. Spike was acting restless, so we decided to take him along. Needing something to shade him, we went to the kitchen and asked Gladys. She called Carl Sleet in from the rose garden, where he was pruning, and he trotted over carrying his shears. His gray work clothes, hair, and beard were specked with grass clippings, and his nails were filthy. He went to the outbuildings and came back with an old umbrella with a spiked post and a blue-and-white canvas shade that was slightly soiled.

'Want me to load it for you?'

'No, thanks. I can do it.'

'Put new locks on the bug house last night. Strong ones. Shouldn't be having any more problems.'

'Thanks.'

'Welcome. Got any fudge left, Gladys?'

'Here you go.' She gave him some and he returned to his work, eating.

Gladys walked us through the kitchen. 'Dr Bill feels awful about last night.'

'I'll let him know there are no hard feelings.'

'That would be . . . charitable – now you two have a good time.'

I pitched the umbrella on South Beach and realized we'd forgotten to bring drinks. Leaving Robin and Spike on the sand, I drove over to Auntie Mae's Trading Post. The same faded clothes were in the windows, which were fly-specked and cloudy. Inside, the place was barnlike, with wooden stalls lining a sawdust aisle and walls of raw board.

Most of the booths were empty and even those that were stocked weren't staffed. More clothing, cheap, out of date. Beach sandals, suntan lotion, and tourist kitsch – miniature thatched huts of bamboo and astroturf, plastic dancing girls, pouting tiki gods, coconuts carved into blowfish. The building smelled of cornmeal and seawater and a bit of backed-up bilge.

The only other human being was a young, plainfaced woman in a red tank top watching TV behind the counter of the third booth to the right. Her cash register was a scarred, black antique. Next to it were canisters of beef jerky and pickled eggs and a half-full bottle of Windex and a rag. The front case was filled with candy bars and chips – potato, corn, taro. On the rear wall were a swinging door and shelves holding sealed boxes of sweets. The television was mounted to the side wall that separated the stall from its neighbor, sharing space with a pay phone.

She noticed me but kept watching the screen. The image was fuzzy, streaked intermittently with bladelike flashes of white. A station from Guam. Long shot of a big room with polished wood walls, corporate logo of a hotel chain over a long banquet table.

Senator Nicholas Hoffman sat in the center behind a glass of water and a microphone. He wore a white-and-brown batik shirt and several brilliantly colored flower necklaces. The two white men flanking him were dressed the same way. One I recognized as a legislator from the Midwest; the other was cut from the same hair-tonicked, hungry-smile mold. Four other men, Asians, sat at the ends of the table.

Hoffman glanced at his notes, then looked up smiling. 'And so let me conclude by celebrating the fact that we all share a vision of a more viable and prosperous Micronesia, a multicultural Micronesia that moves swiftly and confidently into the next century.'

He smiled again and gave a small bow. Applause. The screen flickered, went gray, shut off. The young woman turned it back on. Commercial for Island Fever Restaurant #6: slack-key guitar theme song, pupu platters and flaming desserts, 'native beauties skilled in ancient dances for your entertainment pleasure.' A caricature of a chubby little man in a grass skirt rolling his hips and winking. *'C'mon, brudda!'*

The woman flicked the remote control. More black screen, then a ten-year-old sitcom. She watched as the credits rolled, then said, 'Can I help you?' Pleasant, almost childish voice. Twenty or so, with acne and short, wavy hair. No bra under the tank top. Not even close to pretty, but her smile was open and lovely.

'Something to drink, if you've got it.'

'I've got Coke and Sprite and beer in the back.'

'Two Cokes, two Sprites.' I noticed a couple of paperback books on the rear counter. 'Maybe something to read, too.'

She handed me the books. A Stephen King I'd read and a compact world atlas, both with curled covers.

'Any magazines?'

'Um, maybe under here.' She bent and stood. 'Nope. I'll check in back. You're the doctor staying with Dr Bill, right?'

'Alex Delaware.' I held out my hand and we shook. I noticed a diamond chip ring on the third finger.

'Bettina – Betty Aguilar.' She smiled shyly. 'Just got married.'

'Congratulations.'

'Thanks . . . he's a great man – Dr Bill. When I was a kid I had a bad whooping cough and he cured me. Hold on, lemme get you your drinks and see about magazines.'

She went through the swinging door.

So much for rampant island hostility to Moreland.

She came back with four cans and a stack of periodicals. 'This is all we've got. Pretty old. Sorry.'

'Is it hard to get current stuff?'

She shrugged. 'We get whatever comes over on the supply boats, usually it's a couple of issues late. *People* and *Playboy* and stuff like that goes fast – any of this interest you?'

Half-year-old issues of *Ladies Home Journal, Reader's Digest, Time, Newsweek, Fortune*, and at the bottom, several copies of a large glossy quarterly entitled *Island World.* Gorgeous smiling black-haired girls and sun-blushed tropical vistas.

The publications dates, three to five years old.

'Boy, those really *are* old,' said Betty. 'Found 'em under a box. They used to publish it out of Guam but I don't think they do anymore.'

I flipped through tables of contents. Mostly boosterism. Then a title caught my eye.

'I'll take them,' I said.

'Really? Gee, they're so old I wouldn't know what to charge you. Here, take 'em for free.'

'I'll be happy to pay.'

'It's okay,' she insisted. 'You're my best customer today and they're just taking up space. Want some munchies to go with your drinks?'

I bought two bags of kettle-boiled Maui potato chips and some jerky. As she took my money, her eyes drifted back to the TV. Another blackout. She switched the set on automatically, as if used to it.

'Bad reception?'

'The satellite keeps going in and out, depending on the weather and stuff.' She counted out change. 'I'm having a baby. Dr Bill's gonna deliver it. In six months.'

'Congratulations.'

'Yeah . . . we're excited. My husband and me. Here you go . . . After the baby's born we'll probably be moving away. My husband works construction and there's no work.'

'Nothing at all?'

'Not really. This here is the biggest building in town. A few years back Dr Bill was thinking of redoing it, but no one else really cared.'

'Dr Bill owns the Trading Post?'

She seemed surprised that I didn't know. 'Sure. He's real good about it, doesn't charge rent, just lets people order their own stuff and sell it outta the booths. There used to be more business here, when the Navy guys still came in. Now most of the stallkeepers don't come in unless someone calls to order. It's actually my mom's stall, but she's sick – bad heart. I've got time, waiting for my baby, so I take over for her and my husband delivers – most of our stuff's delivery.'

She touched her still-flat belly.

'My husband would like a boy, but I don't care as long as it's healthy.'

Laugh-track noise from the TV. She turned her head and smiled along with the electronic joy.

'Bye,' I said.

She waved absently.

When I got back to the beach, Robin's snorkel was a tiny white duck bobbing near the outer edge of the reef. Our blankets were spread, and Spike was leashed to the umbrella post, barking furiously.

The object of his wrath was Skip Amalfi, stark naked, peeing a high, arcing stream into the sand, several yards away. Anders Haygood stood next to him, in knee-length baggies, watching. Skip's bleached-bone buttocks said skinnydipping wasn't a habit. His green trunks lay next to him like a heap of wilted salad.

Spike barked louder. Skip laughed and aimed the stream closer to the dog, shaking with glee as Spike growled and spat drool.

Then the arc dribbled and died. Spike shook himself off theatrically, and moved closer to them.

I ran. Haygood saw me and said something to Skip, who stopped and turned, offering a full frontal view. I kept coming.

Grinning, Skip looked over his shoulder at Robin's snorkel. His urine trail was drying quickly, a brown snake sinking into the sand. Spike was pawing the blanket, finally moving enough of it to reach sand and scatter it.

Skip stretched and yawned and massaged his gut.

'Is that going to be the official welcome at your resort?' I said, smiling.

His face darkened, but he forced himself to smile back. 'Yeah, living naturally.'

'Better watch the ultraviolet radiation. It can lead to impotence.'

'Whu?'

'The sun.'

'Your hard-on,' said Haygood, amused. 'What the man's trying to tell you is bruise it and lose it. Watch the UV on your tool or you'll be hauling limp wiener.'

'Fuck you,' Skip told him, but he looked at me edgily.

'It's true,' I said. 'Too much UV to the genitals heats up the scrotal plexus and weakens the neurotestostinal reflex.'

'Boil it and spoil it,' said Haygood.

'Fuck you in the *ass*,' said Skip. Looking for his trunks.

Haygood lunged, grabbed them up, and began running down the beach. Stocky but fast.

Skip went after him, potbelly quivering, holding his crotch.

Spike was still drooling and breathing hard. I sat down and tried to calm him. Robin had moved into shallower waters. She stood, lifted her face mask, and waved. Then she saw the two men running and came out of the water.

'What was that all about?'

I told her.

'How rude.'

'He was probably hoping you'd come out and see him playing fireman.'

'Shucks, I missed it.' She squatted and petted Spike. 'Mama's all right, sweetie. Don't worry about those turkeys. It's gorgeous down there, Alex. Come on in.'

'Maybe later.'

'Is something wrong?'

'Let me just stick around for a while in case they return. Though I may have traumatized old Skip.'

I recounted my UV warning and she cracked up.

'You probably ruined what little sex life he's got.'

'Reverse therapy. My education is now fully validated.'

'Don't worry about them, Alex – dive with me. If they come back, we'll give Spike a run at them.'

'Spike can be drop-kicked by a twelve-year-old.'

'They don't know that. Tell them he's a neurotestostinal pit bull.'

We visited every crag in the reef side by side and emerged an hour later to an undisturbed beach. Spike slept noisily, under a cloud of sand flies. The drinks had warmed, but we poured them down our throats. Then Robin stretched out on a blanket and closed her eyes, and I picked up the spring 1988 issue of *Island World*.

The article that had caught my eye was on page 113, after come-hither tourist pieces on Pacific Rim archaeological sites, choice dive spots, restaurants and nightclubs.

'Bikini: A History of Shame.'

The author was a man named Micah Sanjay, formerly a civilian official of the Marshall Islands' U.S. military government, now a retired high school principal living in Chalan Kanoa, Saipan.

His story was identical to the one Moreland had told me: failure to evacuate the residents of Bikini and Majuro and the neighboring Marshall atolls. Clandestine nighttime boat rides doling out compensation.

The *exact* same story, down to the amount of money paid.

Sanjay wrote matter-of-factly but his anger came through. A Majuro native, he'd lost relatives to leukemia and lymphoma.

No greater anger than when recounting the payoff.

Sanjay and six other civil servants assigned the job.

Six names, none of them Moreland.

I reread the article, searching for any mention of the doctor. Nothing.

If the old man had never been part of the payoff, why had he lied about it?

Something else he said the first night resonated:

Guilt is a great motivator, Alex.

Feeling himself culpable for the blast? He'd been a Navy officer. Had he known about the winds?

Was it *guilt* that had transformed him from a trust-fund kid in dress whites to a would-be Schweitzer?

Coming to Aruk to *atone*?

Not that his lifestyle had suffered – living in a grand estate, indulging his passions.

Aruk, his fiefdom . . . but his daughter couldn't be permitted to fraternize with the locals.

Did he *want* the villagers isolated? So he could enjoy Aruk on his own terms – an idealized refuge for noble savages with good hygiene and clean water?

Maybe I was judging him unfairly – residual anger about the cockroaches.

But it did appear that he'd lied to me about the Marshalls' compensation program, and that bothered me.

I looked over at Robin's beautiful, prone body, gleaming in the sun. Spike slept too.

I was hunched, fingers tight on the magazine.

Maybe Moreland had indeed been in those boats. Another payoff team, not Sanjay's.

One way to find out: talk to the author.

Sanjay had worked for the government forty years ago, then as a school principal, meaning he was Moreland's age or close to it.

Still alive? Still on Saipan?

Robin rolled over. 'Umm, this sun is great.'

'Sure is,' I said. 'Hot, too, and the drinks are all gone. I'll bop over to the Trading Post and get us some more.'

21

I jogged this time, veering from the beach to the docks where Skip and Haygood sat dangling fishing poles. Haygood watched me. Skip kept his eyes on the water. He had his trunks on and a T shirt, the most clothes I'd seen him in.

Inside the Trading Post, Betty Aguilar was watching a game show and munching a Mars bar.

'Hi. Back so soon?'

'Couple of beers, two more Cokes.'

'You're *definitely* my best customer – hold on, I'll get them for you.'

'Does the pay phone work?'

'Usually, but if you want to call Dr Bill's place, I can let you use the one in back for free.'

'No, this is long distance.'

'Oh – do you need change?'

'I thought I'd use my calling card.'

'I think that'll work.' She went in back and I lifted the receiver.

Another rotary. It took a while to get a dial tone, a lot longer to work my way through several operators and finally obtain permission to use the card. Each successive connection was worse than the previous one, and by the time I reached Saipan Information, I was speaking through a hail of static and the echo of my own voice on one-second delay.

But Micah Sanjay was listed, and when I called his number an older-sounding man with a mild voice said, 'Yes?'

'Sorry to bother you, Mr Sanjay, but I'm a free-lance writer named Thomas Creedman, on temporary stopover in Aruk.'

'Uh-huh.'

'I just happened to come across your article in *Island World* on the nuclear testing in the Marshalls.'

'That was a long time ago.'

Unsure if he meant the disaster or the magazine piece, I pressed on. 'I thought it was very interesting and extremely well done.'

'Are you writing about Bikini, too?'

'I'm thinking about it, if I can get a fresh slant.'

'I tried to sell that article to some mainland magazines, but no one was interested.'

'Really?'

'People don't want to know, and those that do know want to forget.'

'Easier on the conscience.'

'You bet.' His voice had hardened.

'I think some of the most powerful scenes were your descriptions of the compensation process. Those nighttime boat rides.'

'Yes, that was tough. Sneaking around.'

'Were you and the six other men the entire compensation staff?'

'There were bosses who ordered it from behind a desk, but we did all the actual paying.'

'Do you remember the boss's names?'

'Admiral Haupt, Captain Ravenswood. Above them were people from Washington, I guess.'

'Are you still in touch with the other men on the team? If it would be possible for me to talk to them . . .'

'I'm not in touch but I know where they are. George Avuelas died a few years ago. Cancer, but I can't say for sure if it was related. The others are gone, too, except Bob Taratoa, and he lives in Seattle, has a boy there. But he had a stroke last year, so I'm not sure how much he could tell you.'

'So there's no one else still in the Marianas?'

'Nope, just me. Where'd you say you were from?'

'Aruk.'

'What is that, one of those small islands up north a bit from here?'

'That's it.'

'Anything to do there?'

'Sun and write.'

'Well, good luck.'

'There's a doctor who lives here named Moreland, says he was in the Navy when the tests went off. Says he treated some of the people who'd been exposed.'

'Moreland?'

'Woodrow Wilson Moreland.'

'Don't know him, but there were lots of doctors, some of them pretty good. But they couldn't do anything for the people even if they wanted to. Those bombs poisoned the air and the water, radioactivity got into the soil. No matter what they say, I'm convinced they'll never get the stuff out.'

As I left the post, I saw Jacqui Laurent and Dennis standing in front of the Chop Suey Palace. The mother was talking and the son was listening.

Scolding him. Being subtle about it – no hand gestures or raised voice – but her eyes flashed and the displeasure on her face was evident.

Dennis stood there and took it, his giant frame slightly bowed. She looked so young a casual observer might have thought it a lovers' spat.

She folded her hands over her chest and waited.

Dennis scuffed the ground. Nodded.

Similar look to the one Pam had worn after Moreland had reprimanded her.

Same issue?

Lord of the manor dropping in on one of his tenants this morning? Letting her know his displeasure about Dennis and Pam?

Dennis looked from side to side, saw me, and said something. Jacqui put a hand around his thick forearm and propelled him quickly inside.

Back at the estate, I sat through a lunch of broiled halibut and fresh vegetables, walked Robin and Spike down to the orchard, and headed for my office.

Moreland had left another folded card on my desk.

Alex:

Cannot locate catwoman file.

Spirits overwrought
Were making night do penance for a day
Spent in a round of strenuous idleness.
Wordsworth

A fitting quote for that case, don't you think?

Bill

I sat at my desk. *Night do penance . . . strenuous idleness.*

The philandering husband?

Always riddles.

As if he were playing with me.

Why had he lied to me about the payoff?

Time to talk.

*   *   *

The door to his office was unlocked, but he wasn't in there, and the lab door was closed. I went over to knock and, passing his desk, noticed the reprints of my journal articles fanned like playing cards. Next to some newspaper clippings.

Clippings about me.

My involvement in a mass child-abuse case years ago.

My consultation to a grade school terrorized by a sniper.

Accounts of court testimony in several murder cases.

My name highlighted in yellow.

Milo's, too.

I remembered the message he'd written about Milo's call: *Detective Sturgis*. Off the job Milo generally didn't identify himself by title.

Researching him, too?

Thick pile of clippings. On the bottom, a homicide trial. My testimony for the prosecution, debunking the phony insanity plea of a man who'd savaged a dozen women.

Moreland's notation in the margin: *Perfect!*

So I'd been selected for something other than 'a fine combination of scholarliness and common-sense thinking.'

Moreland, definitely worried about the cannibal killer.

Had he lured me here under false premises in order to pick my brain?

Dr Detective. What the hell did I have to offer?

Did he have reason to believe the murderer was still on Aruk?

A crash from inside the lab made me jump, and my hand brushed the clippings to the floor. I picked them up quickly and ran to the inner door.

Locked.

I knocked hard.

A groan from inside.

'Bill?'

Another groan.

'It's Alex. Are you all right?'

A few seconds later, the knob turned and Moreland stood there rubbing his forehead with one hand. The other was palm down, dripping blood. He looked stunned.

'Fell asleep,' he said. Behind him, on the lab table, were brightly colored boxes, plastic cartons. Test tubes on the floor, reduced to jagged glass.

'Your hand, Bill.'

He turned his hand palm up. Blood had pooled and was trickling down his wrist and narrowing to a single red line that wiggled the length of his scrawny forearm.

I led him to the sink and washed the wound. Clean gash, not deep enough to require stitching but still oozing steadily.

'Where's your first-aid kit?'

'Underneath.' Pointing drowsily to a lower cabinet.

I applied antibiotic ointment and a bandage.

'Fell asleep,' he repeated, shaking his head. The colored boxes contained dehydrated potatoes and wheat pilaf, precooked peas, lentils, rice mix.

'Nutritional research,' said Moreland, as if he owed me an explanation.

His attention shifted to the broken glass and he bent.

I reached out to restrain him. 'I'll take care of it.'

'Working late,' he said, weakly. He glanced at the bandaged hand, rubbed his mouth, licked his lips. 'Usually I do some of my best work after dark. Got a late start, making sure those locks got installed correctly. I'm still mortified about what happened.'

'Forget it.'

He stretched out a hand. We shook and I felt his tremor.

'I must have left the lid off and the door unlocked. Inexcusable. Must remember to check every detail.'

He began massaging his temples very rapidly.

'Headache?'

'Sleep deprivation,' he said. 'I should know better, at my age . . . Are you aware that most so-called civilizations are *chronically* sleep deprived?'

'Because of electricity?'

He nodded emphatically. 'Before electricity, people lit a candle or two, then went to bed. The sun was their alarm clock; they were tuned to a natural cadence. Nine, ten hours of sleep a day. It's a rare civilized man who gets eight.'

'Do the villagers sleep well?'

'What do you mean?'

'There's not much technology on the island. Lousy TV reception, less to keep them up.'

'TV', he said, 'is multiple-choice rubbish. However, if you miss it, I can arrange something.'

'No, thanks, but I wouldn't mind a newspaper now and then. Just to stay in touch with the world.'

'I'm sorry, son, can't help you there. We used to get papers more often when the Navy let us ship things on their supply planes, but now we depend upon the boats. Don't you find the radio news sufficient?'

'I noticed some American papers on your desk.'

He blinked. 'Those are old.'

'Research?'

Our eyes locked. His were clear and alert now.

'Yes, I use a clipping service in Guam. If you'd like I can have them bulk-order some periodicals for you. And if you'd like to watch TV, I can get you a portable set.'

'No, it's not necessary.'

'You're sure?'

'Hundred percent.'

'Please tell me if there's anything more you need by way of creature comforts. I want your stay to be enjoyable.'

He ran his tongue under his right cheek and frowned. 'Has it been – enjoyable? Excepting last night, of course.'

'We're having a fine time.'

'I hope so. One tries . . . to be a good host.' He smiled and shrugged. 'My apologies again about the hissers—'

'Let's really forget it, Bill.'

'You're very gracious . . . I suppose I've been living here by myself so long that the niceties of social discourse elude me.'

Staring at the floor again. Holding his bandaged hand with the other and getting that absent look in his eyes.

Then he snapped out of it, stood suddenly, and surveyed the lab. 'Back to work.'

'Don't you think you should rest?'

'No, no, I'm tiptop. By the way, what was it you came here for?'

What I'd *come* for were piercing questions about Samuel H. and radiation poisoning. Payoffs, half-truths, and subterfuge. What, if anything, his role had been forty years ago.

Now something else: why was my involvement in crime cases 'perfect'?

I said, 'Just wanted to know if there were any specific cases you wanted me to look over.'

'Oh, no, I wouldn't presume. As I told you at the outset, you have total freedom.'

'I wouldn't mind reviewing any other nuclear fallout cases you might have. Neuropsychological sequellae of radiation poisoning. I don't think anyone's studied it. It could be a great opportunity for us to produce a unique theoretical base.'

His head retracted an inch and he put a hand on the counter. 'Yes, it could.'

He began arranging boxes of dried food, peering at ingredients, straightening a test-tube rack. 'Unfortunately, Samuel's is the only radiation chart I took with me. Till I came across it, I didn't know it was there. Or perhaps I left it there unconsciously. Wanting a reminder.'

'Of what?'

'The terrible, terrible things people do under the guise of authority.'

'Yes,' I said, 'authority can be horribly corrupting.'

Short, hard nod. Another burdened look.

He stared at me, then turned away and held a testtube of brown liquid up to the light. His arm tremored.

'It would have been an interesting paper, Alex. Sorry I haven't any more data.'

'Speaking of authority,' I said, 'I was at the Trading Post this morning and happened to catch the tail end of Hoffman's press conference in Guam.'

'Really?' He inspected another tube.

'He was talking about his plan to develop Micronesia.'

'He made his fortune building shopping centers, so I'm not surprised. That and so-called managed forestry. His father was a lumberjack, but he's responsible for more timber clearing than his father could have ever imagined.'

'He has a reputation for being ecologically minded.'

'There are ways.'

'Of what?'

'Of getting one's way without fouling one's own nest. He chopped down rain forest in South America but supported national parks in Oregon and Idaho. So the ecology groups gave him an excellent rating. A fact he reminded me of last night. As if that excused it.'

'Excused what?'

'What he's doing here.'

'Letting Aruk die?'

He put down the test tube and glared at me. 'A loss of vigor doesn't imply the terminal state.'

'So you have hope for the island?'

His hands dropped to his sides again, skinny and rigid as ski poles. Blood had seeped under the bandage and crusted.

'I always have hope,' he said, barely moving his lips. 'Without hope, there's nothing.'

He lit a Bunsen burner and I returned to my office. Why hadn't I been more forthright?

The fall? His seeming fragility?

Falling. Forgetfulness. Tremors.

Sleep deprivation as he claimed, or was he just an old man in decline?

Declining along with his island.

His reaction to my suggestion that Aruk was dying had been

sharp. The same type of frosty anger he'd shown Pam last night. I wondered if he'd once been a harder, colder man.

Without hope, there's nothing.

Hope was fine, but what was he *doing* about it? The same question: why not take heroic measures to revive things, rather than put his energy into the nutritional needs of bugs?

Because he was running *out* of energy?

Needed a universe he could *control*?

Lord of the Roaches . . .

Where did I fit in?

22

I left to find Robin but she found me first, coming up the path with Spike, looking troubled.

'What's wrong?'

'Let's go inside.'

We returned to the office and sat on the couch.

'Oh, boy,' she said.

'What is it?'

'I took another walk. To the northeast corner of the estate where it curves away from the banyan forest. Actually, I followed Spike. He kept pulling me there.'

She pushed curls away from her eyes and rested her head on the back of the sofa.

'The stone walls continue all around, but as the road curves there's a very thick planting of avocado and mango that blocks the border. Hundreds of mature trees, you have to really squeeze to get through. Spike kept huffing, really yanking me. After a hundred feet or so I figured out why: someone was crying. I ran to see.'

She took my hand and squeezed it.

'It was Pam, Alex. Lying on a blanket between the trees. Picnic stuff with her, a thermos, sandwiches. Lying on her back, wearing a sundress . . . oh, boy.'

'What?'

'The straps were down and one hand was here.' She cupped her own left breast. 'Her eyes were closed; the other hand was up her dress. We just burst in on her—'

'Crying from pleasure?'

'No, no, I don't think so. More like emotional pain. She'd been . . . touching herself, and for some reason it had made her *miserable*. Tears were running down her cheeks. I tried to leave before she saw us, but Spike started barking and she opened her eyes. I was *mortified*. She sat up and adjusted her clothes, and meanwhile Spike's running straight to her, licking her face.'

'Our little protector.'

'Lord, lord.'

'Poor you.'

'Can you imagine, Alex? The size of this place, you'd figure you could find a private spot without Sherlock Bones sniffing you out.'

'Rotten luck,' I agreed. 'Though I guess a really private spot would have been in her room with the door closed. How'd she react?'

'A split second of shock, then calm, ladylike, as if I was a neighbor dropping by to borrow sugar. She invited me to sit down. I wanted to be anywhere *but* there, but what could I say? No, thanks, I'll just leave you to whatever dark and depressing sexual fantasies you were having, ta ta? Meanwhile, Spike's sniffing the sandwiches and drooling.'

'The boy knows his priorities.'

'Oh, yeah, the world stops for ham and cheese. Actually, having him there was a good distraction. She played with him for a while, fed him, and we were doing a pretty good job of pretending it never happened. Then all of a sudden she burst into tears and stuff just started *pouring* out – how rotten her marriage had been, what an ugly divorce . . . I felt like a sponge, soaking up her pain – I don't know how you've done it all these years. I didn't say a thing, but she just kept going. It was almost as if she was glad I'd found her.'

'Maybe she was.'

'Or being discovered lowered her defenses.'

'What was so rotten about her marriage?'

'Her husband was also a doctor, a vascular surgeon, couple of years younger. Very brilliant, very good-looking, the med center's most eligible bachelor. Love at first sight, whirlwind courtship, but sex with him was – she couldn't respond, so she faked it. It had never been a problem for her before; she figured it would work itself out. But it didn't and eventually he realized it. At first he didn't care, as long as he got his. Soon, though, it began to bother him. Affront to his manhood, he started pressuring her. Interrogating her. Then it became an obsession: if she didn't come, it wasn't real lovemaking. Eventually, they started avoiding each other and he started having affairs. Lots of affairs, not even trying to hide it. With both of them working in the same place, she felt she was a laughingstock.'

'She just sat there and told you all this?'

'It was more as if she was talking to herself, Alex. She asked him to go into counseling. He refused, saying it was her problem. So she went into therapy by herself, and eventually things just broke down between them completely and she filed for divorce. At first he was really rotten – humiliating her with cracks about her being frigid, telling her about all the girls he was going out with. But then he had a change of heart and wanted to reconcile. She turned him down; he kept calling her, begging for another chance. She said no and pressed on with the divorce. A month later he died in a freak accident. Working out in his home gym, bench-pressing. The barbell fell on his chest and crushed him to death.'

'And she feels guilty.'

'Extremely guilty. Even though she knows it's not rational.

Because she feels he really did still love her. She can't get rid of the idea that he was overdoing the weightlifting because he was stressed out over her. And to think the first time I saw her I thought she was the girl with everything.'

'The girl with nothing left,' I said. 'So she packs up and returns here. And finds another man. Did the flap over Dennis come up?'

'No. But it sure looks like you were right about her having man problems, so maybe that's what Bill *was* reacting to. He doesn't want her hurt again so soon.'

'Maybe. C'mere.' She climbed onto my lap and I held her close. 'Looks like you missed your true calling.'

'That's what I'm concerned about. It's *not* my calling. You always talk about patients saying too much, too quickly, then growing hostile.'

'Honey,' I said, 'you weren't probing, you just listened. And you have no professional responsibility—'

'I know, Alex, but I like her – basically she seems to be a sweet woman who's experienced some horrible things. She was only three when her mother died and Bill sent her away – farming her out to relatives and then boarding schools. She says she doesn't blame Bill, he was doing his best. But it's got to hurt. Is there anything more I should be doing for her?'

'If she seeks you out, listen, as long as it doesn't make you feel uncomfortable.'

'I don't want *her* to feel uncomfortable. We're all living together in close quarters.'

'This place,' I said, 'is starting to feel like Eden *after* the fall from grace.'

'No,' she said, smiling. 'No serpents, just bugs.'

'Maybe we *should* think about cutting our stay short, Rob—no, wait, hear me out. There are things bothering me that I haven't told you.'

She shifted position and stared up at me. 'Like what?'

'Maybe I'm being paranoid, but I can't get rid of the idea

that someone planted those roaches.' I told her my suspicions.

'But what would be the motive, Alex?'

'The only thing I can think of is that someone wants us out of here.'

'Who and why?'

'I don't know, but I'm pretty sure Bill hasn't been totally straight about his reasons for bringing me over, so there may be something going on that we're totally unaware of.'

I told her about Moreland's fall in the lab, my seeing the crime clippings on his desk, his knowledge of my friendship with Milo.

'You think he wants help with a crime?' she said. 'The murder on South Beach?'

'He says it's the only major crime they've had in a long time.'

'What could he want from you?'

'I don't know, but he did show me the record of the autopsy, and he claims no one else has seen it other than Dennis. Each time I talk to him I get the feeling he's holding back. Either he's building up his courage or making sure he can trust me. The question is, will I ever be able to trust him? Because he lied to me about something else.'

I recounted the case of Samuel H.'s radiation poisoning and my conversation with Micah Sanjay.

'That is odd,' she said. 'But maybe there's an explanation. Why don't you just come out and ask him?'

'I was on my way to do just that. But after he fell and started bleeding, I guess I felt sorry for him. I'll deal with it.'

'And then we leave?' She looked sad.

I said, 'There are also things about the murder I haven't told you. It was more than just a gory killing. There was organ theft. Evidence of cannibalism.'

She lost color. Got off my lap, walked to a teak wall, and traced the wood's grain with her finger. 'You thought I couldn't handle it?'

'I didn't think it was necessary to expose you to every disgusting detail.'

She didn't answer.

'I wasn't patronizing you, Rob. But this was supposed to be a vacation. Would hearing about marrow being sucked out of leg bones have done you any good?'

'You know,' she said, facing me, 'when Pam started unloading, it was tough at first, but then it felt good. The fact that she trusted me. Breaking my routine and finding out my *sympathies* have been awakened isn't a bad thing. I've started to realize how much I use work to escape people.'

'I've always considered you great with peop—'

'I'm talking about relating in depth, Alex. Especially to other women. You know, I've never done much of that, growing up so close to my dad, always trying to please him by doing boy stuff. You always say we're an odd couple – the guy dealing with feelings, the girl wielding power tools.'

I got up and stood next to her.

'Being here,' she said, 'away from the grind, even for these few days, has been a . . . learning experience. Don't worry, I'm not going to give it all up to be a therapist. Two shrinks in one house would be too much to bear. But helping people gratifies me.'

She threw her arms around me and pressed her face against my chest. 'Welcome to Robin's epiphany – all that said, we can leave early if you're uncomfortable here.'

'No, there's no emergency – I'm probably letting my imagination get out of control, as usual.'

She kissed my chin. 'I like your imagination.'

'So you're okay with cannibals on the beach?'

'Hardly. But it happened half a year ago, and as you said, sex killers don't just stop. So I figure he is gone.'

'You're a tough kid, Castagna.'

She laughed. 'Not really. First thing I did this afternoon was check my shoes for creepy-crawlies. And if something else happens, you may just see me swimming for Guam.'

'I'll be right behind you. Okay, if you're fine, I am – hey, you calmed me down. You can be *my* therapist.'

'Nope.'

'Why not?'

'Ethical considerations. I want to keep sleeping with you.'

23

I went back to Moreland's bungalow, locked now, and no one answered.

The next time I saw him was at the dinner table that evening. The bandage on his hand was fresh, and he acknowledged me with a smile. Pam stood in a corner of the terrace, hands at her sides. She wore a blood-red Chinese silk dress and red sandals. Her hair was pinned and a yellow orchid rested above her left ear. Forced festivity?

She turned and gave us a wave. Robin looked at me and when I nodded went over to her

I sat down next to Moreland.

'How's the hand?'

'Fine, thank you. Some juice? Mixed citrus, quite delicious.'

I took some. 'There's a case I'd like to discuss with you.'

'Oh?'

'A man named Joseph Cristobal, thirty-year-old file. He complained of visual hallucinations – white worms, white worm people

– and then he died in his sleep. You found a blocked coronary artery and gave the cause of death as heart failure. But you also noted an organism called *A. Tutalo*. I looked it up but couldn't find any mention of it.'

He rubbed his crinkled chin. 'Ah, yes, Joseph. He worked here, gardening. Looked healthy enough, but his arteries *were* a mess. Loved coconut, maybe that contributed. He never complained of any cardiac symptoms, but even if he had there wouldn't have been much I could have done. Today, of course, I'd refer him for an angiogram, possible bypass surgery. It's the humbling thing about medicine. Acceptable practice inevitably resembles medieval barbering.'

'What about *A. Tutalo*?'

He smiled. 'No, it's not an organism. It's . . . a bit more complicated than that, son – ah, one second.'

Jo had come out, Ben and Claire Romero right behind her. Moreland sprang up, touched Jo's hand briefly, then continued on and gave Claire a hug. Looking over his shoulder, he said, 'Shall we continue our discussion after dinner, Alex?'

Jo seemed different – eyes less burdened, voice lighter, almost giddy, praising the food every third bite, informing the table that Lyman's body had reached the States and been picked up by his family. Then, waving off condolences, she changed the subject to her research, pronouncing that everything was 'proceeding grandly.'

The sky turned deep blue, then black. The rainclouds were gray smudges. They hadn't moved much since morning.

When Jo stopped talking, Moreland strode to the railing where some geckos were racing. When he waved a piece of fruit, they stopped and stared at him; dinnertime was probably a cue. He hand-fed them, then returned to the table and delivered a discourse on interspecies bonding. Avoiding my eyes, I thought.

A bit of small talk followed before the conversation settled upon Claire Romero, the way it often does with a newcomer.

She was well-spoken, but very quiet. The Honolulu-born

daughter of two high school teachers, she'd played violin in college and in several chamber groups and had considered a professional career in music.

'Why didn't you?' said Jo, nibbling a croissant.

Claire smiled. 'Not enough talent.'

'Sometimes we're not our own best judges.'

'I am, Dr Picker.'

'She's the only one who feels that way,' said Ben. 'She was a child prodigy. I married her and took her away from it.'

Claire looked at her plate. 'Please, Ben—'

'You *are* immensely talented, dear,' said Moreland. 'And it's been so long since you played for us – last year, wasn't it? On my birthday, in fact. What a lovely night that was.'

'I've barely played since, Dr Bill.' She turned to Robin. 'Have you ever built a violin?'

'No, but I've thought of it. I have some old Alpine spruce and Tyrolean maple that would be perfect, but it's a little intimidating.'

'Why's that?' said Jo.

'Small scale, subtle gradations. I wouldn't want to ruin old wood.'

'Claire's got a terrific old fiddle,' said Ben. 'French – a Guersan. Over a hundred years old.' He winked. 'In *fact*, it just happens to be down in the car.'

Claire glared at him.

He smiled back with mock innocence.

She shook her head.

'Well, then,' said Moreland, clapping his hands. 'You must play for us.'

'I'm really rusty, Dr Bi—'

'I'm willing to assume the risk, dear.'

Claire stared at Ben.

'Please, dear. Just a piece or two.'

'I'm warning you, get out the earplugs.'

'Warning duly noted. Would it be possible to play the piece you did for us last year? The Vivaldi?'

Claire hesitated, glanced at Ben.

'I saw the case,' he said. 'Just lying there in the closet. It said, "Take me along."'

'If you're hearing voices, perhaps you should have a long talk with Dr Delaware.'

'Dear?' said Moreland, softly.

Claire shook her head. 'Sure, Dr Bill.'

She played wonderfully, but she looked tense. Mouth set, shoulders hunched, swaying in time with the music as she filled the terrace with a rich, brocade of melody. When she was through, we applauded and she said, 'Thanks for your tolerance. Now, I've really got to get going. Science projects due tomorrow.'

Moreland walked her and Ben out. Pam nibbled a slice of mango, distracted. Robin took my hand.

'She *is* good, Alex.'

'Fantastic,' I said. But I was thinking about *A. Tutalo*. The other things I'd ask Moreland when he returned.

He didn't.

When Robin said, 'Let's go upstairs,' I didn't argue.

The moment we closed our suite door we were embracing, and soon we were in bed, kissing deeply, merging hungrily.

Afterward, I sank into a molasses vat of dreamless sleep, a welcome brain-death.

That made waking up in the middle of the night so much more unsettling.

Sitting up, sweating.

Noises . . . my head was fogged and I struggled to make sense of what I was hearing:

Rapid pounding – footsteps out in the hall . . .

Someone running?

A tattoo of footsteps; more than one person.

Fast.

Panic . . .

Then shouts – angry, hurried – someone insisting, '*No!*'

Spike barked.

Robin sat up, hair in her face. She grabbed my arm.

A door slammed.

'Alex—'

More shouts.

Too far away to make out words.

'*No!*' Again.

A man's voice.

Moreland.

We got up, threw on robes, opened our door carefully.

The chandelier over the entry was on, whitening the landing. My eyes ached, struggling to stay open.

Moreland wasn't there, but Jo was, her broad back to us, hands atop the banister. A door down the hall opened and Pam came running out, wrapped in a silver kimono, her face paper-white. The door stayed open and I had my first look at her room: white satin bedding, peach-colored walls, cut flowers. At the end of the landing, her father's door remained closed.

But I heard him again. Down in the entry.

We hurried next to Jo. She didn't turn, kept looking.

At Moreland and Dennis Laurent. The police chief stood just inside the front door, in full uniform, hands on his hips. A holstered pistol on his belt.

Moreland faced him, hands clenched. He had on a long white nightshirt, soft slippers. His legs were varicosed stilts, his hands inches from the police chief's impassive face.

'*Impossible, Dennis! Insane!*'

Dennis held out a palm. Moreland came closer anyway.

'Listen to me, Dennis—'

'I'm just telling you what we—'

'I don't care *what* you found, it's impossible! How could *you* of all—'

'Take it easy. Let's just go one step at a time and I'll do what I—'

'What you can do is *end* it! Right *now*! Don't even entertain the possibility, and don't allow anyone *else* to. There's simply no *choice*, son.'

The policeman's eyes became black cuts. 'So you want me to—'

'You're the law, son. It's up to you to—'

'It's up to me to enforce the law—'

'Enforce it, but—'

'But not fully?'

'You know what I'm saying, Dennis. This must be—'

'Stop.' Dennis's bass voice hit a note at the bottom of his register. He stood even taller, bearing down on Moreland. Forced to look up, Moreland said, 'This is *psychotic*. After all you and—'

'I go with what I have,' said Dennis, 'and what I have looks bad. And it could get lots worse. I called the base and asked Ewing to keep his men under watch—'

'He took your call?'

'As a matter of fact, he did.'

'Congratulations,' said Moreland bitterly. 'You've finally arrived.'

'Doc, there's no reas—'

'There's no reason to continue this *insanity*!'

The police chief started to open the door. Moreland took hold of his arm. Dennis stared at Moreland's bony fingers until the old man let go.

'I've got things to do, doc. Stay here. Don't leave the estate.'

'How can you—'

'Like I said, I go with what I have.'

'And *I* said—'

'Stop wasting your breath.' Dennis made another attempt to leave, and once again Moreland reached for his arm. This time the big man shook him off and Moreland fell back.

Dennis caught him as Pam called out.

Dennis looked up at us.

'*Think*, son!' said Moreland. 'Does it make—'

'I'm not your damn *son*. And I don't need you to tell me what to think or how to do my job. Just stay up here till I tell you different.'

'That's house impris—'

'It's good *sense*. You're obviously not going to be of much help, so I'm calling over to Saipan and have them send me someone.'

'No,' said Moreland. 'I'll cooperate. I'm perfectly—'

'Forget it.'

'I'm the—'

'Not anymore,' said Dennis. 'Just stay here and don't cause problems.' Growling now. His enormous shoulders bunched.

He looked up at us again. Focused on Pam, then scanned the bannister from end to end, eyes darting like the geckos.

'What's going on?' I said.

He chewed his lip.

Moreland's head was down and he was holding it as if to keep it from falling off his neck.

Pam said, 'What's happened? What's happened, Dennis?'

Dennis seemed to consider an answer, then he looked back at Moreland, now leaning, face to the wall.

'A bad thing,' he said, putting one foot out the door. 'Daddy can tell you all about it.'

The door slammed and he was gone. Moreland remained in the entry, not moving. The chandelier turned his bald head metallic.

Pam rushed down to him and we followed.

'Dad?'

She put her arm around him. His color was bad. 'What is it, Dad?'

He mumbled something.

'What?'

Silence.

'Please, Daddy, tell me.'

He shook his head and muttered, 'As Dennis said. A bad thing.'

'What bad thing?'

More headshaking.

She guided him to an armchair in the front room. He sat reluctantly, remaining on the edge, one hand scratching a knobby knee, the other shielding most of his face. The visible part was the color of spoiled milk and his lips looked like slices of putty.

'What's going on, Daddy? Why was Dennis so rude to you?'

Moreland coughed. 'Doing his job . . .'

'A crime? There was a *crime*, Dad?'

Moreland dropped both hands in his lap. Defeat had stripped his face of structure; each wrinkle was as black and deep as freshly gouged sculptor's clay.

'Yes, a crime . . . murder.'

'Who was murdered, Dad?'

No answer.

'When?'

'Tonight.'

I said, 'Another—'

He cut me off with a hand-slash. 'A terrible murder.'

'Who?' said Jo.

'A young woman.'

'Where, Dad?'

'Victory Park.'

'Who was the victim?' pressed Jo.

Long pause. 'A girl named Betty Aguilar.'

Pam frowned. 'Do we know her?'

'Ida Aguilar's daughter. She works Ida's stall at the Trading Post. She came in for a checkup last week, I introduced you to her when—'

'My God,' I said. 'I just spoke to her today. She was three months pregnant.'

Robin said, 'Oh, no.' She was holding onto the sash of my robe, eyes belladonna-bright.

'Well, *that's* certainly dreadful,' said Jo. Not a trace of slur. Off the sleeping pills?

'Yes, yes,' said Moreland. 'Very dreadful, yes, yes, yes . . .' He grabbed for the chair's arm. Pam braced him.

'I'm so sorry, Daddy. Were you close to her?'

'I—' He began to cry and Pam tried to hold him, but he freed himself and looked over at the big dark windows. The sky was still deep blue, the clouds larger, lower.

'I *delivered* her,' he said. 'I was going to deliver her baby. She was doing so well with prenatal care – she used to smoke and . . .' He touched his mouth. 'She resolved to take good care of herself and stuck to it.'

'Any idea why she was killed?' said Jo.

Moreland stared at her. 'Why would I know that?'

'You knew her.'

Moreland turned away from her.

'Why does Dennis want you to stay up here?' I said.

'Not just me, all of us. We're all under house arrest.'

'Why, Daddy?' said Pam.

'Because . . . they – it's . . .' He listed forward then sat back heavily, both hands glued to the chair's arms. The fabric was a rose damask, silk, once expensive. Now I noticed the worn spots and the snags, a stitched-up tear, stains that could never be cleaned.

Moreland rubbed his temples the way he had after his fall in the lab. Then his neck. He winced and Pam put a finger under his chin and propped it. 'Why are we under house arrest, Daddy?'

He shuddered.

'Da—'

He reached up, removed her finger, held onto it. Shaking.

'Ben,' he said. 'They think *Ben* did it.'

24

He hid his face again.

Looking helpless, Pam left and returned with Gladys, who carried a bottle of brandy and glasses.

Seeing Moreland in that state frightened the housekeeper.

'Doctor Bill—'

'Please go back to bed,' said Pam. 'We'll need you in the morning.'

Gladys wrung her hands.

'Please, Gladys.'

Moreland said, 'I'm fine, Gladys,' in a voice that proved otherwise.

The old woman chewed her cheek and finally left.

'Brandy, Dad?'

He shook his head.

She filled a glass anyway and held it out to him.

He waved off the liquor but accepted some water. Pam took his pulse and felt his forehead.

'Warm,' she said. 'And you're sweating.'

'The room's hot,' he said. 'All the glass.'

The windows were open and scented air flowed through the screens. Chilly air. My hands were icy.

Pam wiped Moreland's brow. 'Let's get some fresh air, Dad.'

We moved to the terrace, Moreland offering no resistance as Pam put him at the head of the empty dining table.

'Here, have some more water.'

He sipped as the rest of us stood around. The sky was blue suede, the moon a slice of lemon rind. Droplets of light hit the ocean. I looked out over the railing, watching as lights switched on rapidly in the village.

I poured brandy all around.

Moreland's eyes were fixed and wide.

'Insane,' he said. 'How could they *think* it!'

'Do they have evidence?' said Jo.

'No!' said Moreland. 'They claim he – someone found him.'

'At the scene?' I said.

'Sleeping at the scene. Convenient, isn't it?'

'Who found him?' said Jo.

'A man from the village.'

'A credible man?' Something new in her voice – scientist's skepticism, an almost hostile curiosity.

'A man named Bernardo Rijks,' said Moreland. 'Chronic insomniac. Takes too many daytime naps.' He looked at the brandy. 'More water please, kitten.'

Pam filled a glass and he gulped it empty.

'Bernardo takes a walk late at night, has for years. Down from his home on Campion Way to the docks, along the waterfront, then back up. Sometimes he makes two or three circuits. Says the routine helps make him drowsy.'

'Where's Campion Way?' I said.

'The street where the church is,' said Pam. 'It's unmarked.'

'The street were Victory Park is.'

Moreland gave a start. 'Tonight when he passed the park he heard groans and thought there might be a problem. So he went to see.'

'What kind of problem?' I said.

'Drug overdose.'

'The park's a drug hangout?'

'Used to be,' he said angrily. 'When the sailors came into town. They'd drink themselves silly at Slim's or smoke marijuana on the beach, try to pick up local girls, then head for the park. Bernardo lives at the top of Campion. He used to call me to treat the stuporous boys.'

'Is he credible?' said Jo.

'He's a *fine* gentleman. The problem's not with him, it's—' Moreland ran his fingers through the white puffs at his temples. 'This is insane, just insane! Poor Ben.'

I felt Robin tense.

'What happened then?' said Jo. 'After this Bernardo went over to check the moaning?'

'He found . . .' Long pause. Moreland began breathing rapidly.

'Dad?' said Pam.

Inhaling and letting the air out, he said, 'The moaning was Ben. Lying there, next to . . . the foul scene. Bernardo ran to the nearest home, woke the people up – soon a crowd gathered. Among them Skip Amalfi, who pinned Ben down until Dennis got there.'

'Skip doesn't live nearby,' I said.

'He was down on the docks fishing and heard the commotion. Apparently he now fancies himself the great white leader, taking charge. He twisted Ben's arm and sat on top of him. Ben was no danger to anyone. He hadn't even regained consciousness.'

'Why was he unconscious?' I pressed.

Moreland studied his knees.

'Was *he* on drugs?' said Jo.

Moreland's head snapped up. 'They claim he was drunk.'

'Ben?' said Pam. 'He's as much a teetotaler as you, Dad.'

'Yes, he is . . .'

'Has he always been?' I said.

Moreland covered his eyes with a trembling hand. Touching his hair again, he twisted white strands. 'He's been completely sober for years.'

'How long ago did he have an alcohol problem?' I said.

'Very long ago.'

'In Hawaii?'

'No, no, before that.'

'He went to college in Hawaii. He had problems as a kid?'

'His problem emerged when he was in high school.'

'Teenage alcoholic?' said Pam, incredulous.

'Yes, dear,' said her father, with forced patience. 'It happens. He was vulnerable because of a difficult family situation. Both his parents were drinkers. His father was an *ugly* drunk. Died of cirrhosis at fifty-five. Lung cancer got his mother, though her liver was highly necrotic, as well. Stubborn woman. I set her up with oxygen tanks in her home to ease the final months. Ben was sixteen, but he became her full-time nurse. She used to yank off the mask, scream at him to get her cigarettes.'

'Poor genetics and environment,' pronounced Jo.

Moreland shot to his feet and staggered, shaking off help from Pam. 'Both of which he *overcame*, Dr Picker. After he was orphaned, I put him up here, exchanging work for room and board. He started as a caretaker, then I saw how bright he was and gave him more responsibility. He read through my entire medical library, brought his grades up, stopped drinking completely.'

Sadness had replaced Pam's surprise. Jealousy of his devotion to Ben or feeling left out because it was the first time she'd heard the story?

'Completely sober,' repeated Moreland. 'Incredible strength of character. That's why I financed the rest of his education. He's built a life for himself and Claire and the children . . . you saw him tonight. Was that the face of a psychopathic killer?'

No one answered.

'I tell you,' he said, slapping the tabletop, 'what they're claiming is *impossible*! The fact that it was a bottle of vodka near his hand proves it. He drank only beer. And I treated him with Antabuse, years ago. The taste of alcohol's made him ill ever since – he despises it.'

'What are you saying?' said Jo. 'Someone poured it down his throat?'

The coolness in her voice seemed to throw him off balance. 'I – I'm *saying* he has no tolerance – or desire for alcohol.'

'Then that's the only alternative I can see,' she said. 'Someone forced him to drink. But who would do that? And why?'

Moreland gritted his teeth. 'I don't *know*, Dr Picker. What I do know is Ben's nature.'

'How was Betty killed?' I said.

'She . . . it was . . . a stabbing.'

'Was Ben found with the weapon?'

'He wasn't holding it.'

'Was it found at the scene?'

'It was . . . embedded.'

'Embedded,' echoed Jo. 'Where?'

'In the poor girl's throat! Is it necessary to *know* these things?'

Robin was squeezing my hand convulsively.

'The whole thing is absurd!' said Moreland. 'They claim Ben was right next to her – *sleeping* with her, his arms around her, his head on her . . . what was left of her abdomen. That he'd be able to sleep with her after something like that is – *absurd!*'

Robin broke away and ran to the railing. I followed her and covered her shoulders with my arms, feeling her shivers as she stared up at the bright yellow moon.

Back at the table, Jo was saying, 'He *mutilated* her?'

'I don't want to continue this discussion, Dr Picker. The key is to help Ben.'

Robin wheeled around. 'What about Betty? What about helping her family?'

'Yes, yes, of course that's . . .'

'She was *pregnant*! What about her unborn child? Her husband, her parents?'

Moreland looked away.

'What *about* them, Bill?'

Moreland's lips trembled. 'Of course they deserve sympathy, dear. I *ache* for them. Betty was my patient – I *delivered* her, for God's sake!'

'Whooping cough,' I said.

'What's that?'

'I spoke with her yesterday. She told me you treated her for whooping cough when she was a kid. She considered you a hero.'

He slumped and sat back down. 'Dear God . . .'

No one talked. Brandy got poured. It burned a slow, cleansing trail down my gullet, the only sensation in an otherwise numb body. Everyone looked numb.

'Anyone know the time?' I said.

Pam shot the sleeve of her kimono. 'Just after four.'

'Rise and shine,' said Jo, softly. 'I still don't see why we're all locked up here.'

'For our own safety,' said Moreland. 'At least that's the theory.'

'Who's out to get us?'

'No one.'

'But Ben is closely identified with this place,' I said, 'so people may start talking.'

Moreland didn't answer.

Jo frowned. 'Staying cooped up just makes us sitting targets. You've got no security here – anyone can walk right in.'

'I've never *needed* security, Dr Picker.'

'Do you keep any weapons around?' she said.

'No! If you're concerned with your safety, I suggest you—'

'No problem,' said Jo. 'Personally, I'm fine. It's the only good thing that came out of losing Ly. When your worst fantasy comes true, you find out you can handle things.'

She got up and shuffled toward the living room, tightening the robe of her belt, big hips shifting like the pans of a balance scale.

When she was gone, Robin said, 'She's got a gun. A little pistol. I saw it in an open drawer of her nightstand.'

Moreland's mouth worked. 'I despise firearms.'

Pam said, 'Hopefully she won't shoot someone by accident. Is there any way you can get some rest now, Dad? You're going to be needing your strength.'

'I'll be fine, dear. Thank you for your . . . ministrations, but I believe I'll stay up for a while.' He leaned over as if to kiss her, but patted her shoulder instead. 'Hopefully when the sun comes up, cooler heads will prevail.'

'There are some things I'd like to discuss with you,' I said.

He stared at me.

'Things we never got to last night.'

'Yes, certainly. In the morning, right after I call Dennis—'

'I'm staying up, too. We can talk now.'

He fidgeted with the neckband of his nightshirt. 'Of course. What say we leave the terrace to the ladies and move to my office?'

I squeezed Robin's hand and she squeezed back and sat next to Pam, who looked baffled. But the two of them were already talking as Moreland and I left.

'What's so urgent?' he said, flicking the lights on in the bungalow. The newspaper clippings were gone from his desk. So were all his other papers; the wood surface gleamed.

'We never talked about A. Tutalo—'

'Surely you can see why that wouldn't be a priority at this time—'

'There are other things.'

'Such as?'

'Murder. Ben. What's really going on with Aruk.'

He said nothing for a while, then, 'That's quite an agenda.'

'We've got nowhere to go.'

'Very well.' He pointed crossly to the sofa and I sat, expecting him to settle in a facing chair. Instead, he went behind the desk, lowered himself with a grimace, opened a drawer, and began searching.

'You don't believe Ben could have done this,' he said. 'Do you?'

'I don't know Ben very well.'

He gave a small, tired smile. 'Psychologist's answer . . . Very well, I can't expect you to follow me blindly; you'll see, he'll be vindicated. The notion of his butchering Betty is beyond ridiculous – all right, trivial things first. 'A. Tutalo.' You couldn't find an organism by that name because it's not a germ, it's a fantasy. A local myth. The '*A*' stands for 'Aruk.' 'Aruk Tutalo.' An imaginary tribe of creatures who live in the forest. Goes back years. A myth. No one's believed it for a long time.'

'Except Cristobal.'

'Joseph hallucinated. That's not belief.'

'You convinced him he hadn't seen anything?'

Pause. 'He was a stubborn man.'

'Have there been other sightings?'

'None since I've lived here. As I said, it's a primitive idea.'

'Creatures from the forest,' I said. 'What do they look like?'

'Pale, soft, hideous. A shadow society, living under the forest. Nothing unique to Aruk; all cultures develop fantasies of fanciful, lustful creatures in order to project forbidden desires – animal *instincts*. The minotaurs, centaurs, and satyrs of ancient Greece. The Japanese have a saucer-headed anthro-creature called the *kappa* who lurks by forest streams, abducting children and pulling their intestines through their anuses. Witch's rituals use animal masks to hide the faces of participants, the Devil himself is often thought of as the Great Beast with goat feet and a serpentine tail. Wood-demons, anthro-bat vampiric creatures, werewolves, the yeti, Bigfoot, it's all the same. Psychological defense.'

'What about the catwoman—'

'No, no, that was something totally different.'

'A response to trauma.'

'A response to *cruelty*.'

'Worm people,' I said.

'There are no mammals native to Aruk – one uses what's at hand. 'Tutalo' is derived from an ancient island word of uncertain etymology: *tootali*, or wood-grub. From what I've gathered they're large, humanoid, with tentaclelike limbs, slack bodied but strong. And chalky *white*. I find that particularly interesting. Perhaps a covert indictment of colonizers: white creatures 'appearing' on the island and establishing brutal control.'

'Demonizing the oppressor?'

'Precisely.'

'Was Joseph Cristobal politically active?'

'On the contrary. A simple man. Illiterate. But fond of drink. I'm sure that had something to do with it. Today, your average villager would laugh at the notion of a Tutalo.'

'He was your gardener. Did he sight the Tutalo here?'

He licked his lips and nodded. 'He was working on the eastern walls, tying vines. Working overtime, everyone else had gone home. It was well after dark. Fatigue was probably a factor as well.'

'Where did he see the creature?'

'Making its way through the banyans. Waving its arms, then retreating. He didn't tell anyone right away. Too scared, he claimed, but I suspect he'd been drinking and didn't want to be thought of as a drunkard or old-fashioned.'

'So he suppressed the vision and began hallucinating at night?'

'It began as nightmares. He'd wake up screaming, see the Tutalo in his room.'

'Could the original sighting have taken place as he slept?' I said. 'Could he have dozed off on the job and made up the vision to cover up?'

'I wondered about that, but of course he denied it. I also wondered if he'd fallen off his ladder and hurt his head, but there were no bruises or swellings anywhere on his body.'

'Was he an alcoholic?'

'He wasn't a raving drunk but he did like his spirits.'

'Could the visions have been alcohol poisoning?'

'It's a possibility.'

'Bill, exactly how endemic is alcoholism on Aruk?'

He blinked and removed his glasses. 'In the past it was a serious problem. We've worked hard at education.'

'Who's we?'

'Ben and myself, which is why what's happened tonight is *madness*, Alex! You *must* help him!'

'What would you like me to do?'

'Speak to Dennis. Let him know Ben couldn't have done it, that he simply doesn't fit the profile of a psychopathic killer.'

'Why would Dennis listen to me?'

'I don't know that he would, but we must try everthing. Your training and experience will give you credibility. Dennis respects psychology, majored in it in junior college.'

'What profile don't you think Ben fits?'

'The FBI's two forms of lust-killer: he's neither the disorganized, low-intellect spree-murderer nor the calculating, sadistic psychopath.'

The FBI had earned a lot of TV time with patterns of serial killers obtained from interviews with psychopaths careless enough to get caught. But psychopaths lied for the fun of it, and profiles rarely if ever led to the discovery of a killer, occasionally confirming what police scutwork and luck had already accomplished. Profiles had been responsible for some serious fallacies: Serial killers never murdered across races. Till they did. Women couldn't be serial killers. Till they were.

People weren't computer chips. People had the uncanny ability to surprise.

But even if I'd had more faith in the orderly nature of evil, Ben wouldn't have been easily acquitted.

Right after Lyman Picker's death, Robin and I had discussed the hardness of his personality, and I recalled the cold, impersonal way he'd jabbed needles into the arms of the schoolchildren.

Family history of alcoholism.

Rough childhood, probably abuse from the 'ugly drunk' father.

A certain rigidity. Tight control.

Outwardly controlled men sometimes lost it when under the

influence of booze or drugs. A high percentage of serial killers committed their crimes buoyed by intoxication.

'I'll talk to him,' I said. 'But I doubt it'll do any good.'

'Talk to Ben, too. Try to make some sense of this. I'm shackled, son.'

'If I'm to succeed with Dennis, I need to be impartial, not Ben's advocate.'

He blinked some more. 'Yes, that makes sense. Dennis is rational and honest. If he responds to anything it'll be the rational approach.'

'Rational and honest,' I said, 'but you don't want him dating your daughter.'

It had slipped out like loose change.

He recoiled. Sank heavily into the desk chair. When he finally spoke, it was in a low, resigned voice:

'So you despise me.'

'No, Bill, but I can't say I understand you. The longer I stay here, the more inconsistent things seem.'

He smiled feebly. 'Do they?'

'Your love for the island and its people seems so strong. Yet you tongue-lash Pam for hanging around Dennis. Not that it's my business – you've devoted your life to Aruk and I'm just a visitor.'

He folded his arms across his chest and rubbed the sweat from his forehead.

'I know that this situation with Ben is terrible for you,' I said, 'but if I'm to stay here I need to know a few things.'

Looking away, he said, 'What else troubles you, son?'

'The fact that Aruk's so cut off from the outside world. That more of your energies haven't been spent opening it up. You say there's hope, but you don't *act* hopeful. I agree with you that TV's mostly garbage, but how can the people ever develop when their access to information is so limited? They can't even get mail on a regular basis. It's solitary confinement on a cultural level.'

His hands started to shake again and spots of color made his cheeks shine.

'Forget it,' I said.

'No, no, go on.'

'Do you want to respond to what I just said?'

'The people have books. There's a small library in the church.'

'When's the last time new books came in?'

He used a fingernail to scrape something off the desk top. 'What do you suggest?'

'More frequent shipping schedules. The leeward harbor's too narrow for big craft but couldn't the supply boats sail more often? And if the Navy won't allow planes to land on Stanton, why not build an airfield on the west side? If Amalfi won't cooperate, use some of your land.'

'And how is all this to be financed?'

'Your personal finances are none of my business, either, but I've heard you're very wealthy.'

'Who told you that?'

'Creedman.'

His laugh was shrill. 'Do you know what Creedman really does for a living?'

'He's not a journalist?'

'He's worked for a few minor papers, done some cable television work. But for the last several years he's written quarterly reports for corporations. His last client was Stasher-Layman. Have you heard of them?'

'No.'

'Big construction outfit, based in Texas. Builders of government housing and other tax-financed projects. They put up ticky-tack boxes, sell the management contract for high profits, and walk away. Instant slum. Creedman's scribblings for them made them sound like saints. If I hadn't thrown the reports out, I'd show them to you.'

'You researched him?'

'After we caught him snooping I thought it prudent.'

'Okay,' I said. 'So he's a corporate hack. Is he wrong about your wealth?'

He pulled on a long, pale finger till it cracked. Righted his glasses. Brushed nonexistent dust from the desk.

'I won't tell you I'm poor, but family fortunes recede unless the heirs are talented in business. I'm not. Which means I'm in no position to build airports or lease entire fleets of boats. I'm doing all I can.'

'Okay,' I said. 'Sorry for bringing it up, then.'

'No apology necessary. You're a passionate young man. Passionate but focused. It's rare when the two go hand in hand: "I may not hope from outward forms to win the passion and the life, whose fountains are within" – Coleridge said that. Another great thinker; even narcotics didn't still *his* genius . . . Your passion even comes through your scientific writing, son. *That's* why I asked you to join me.'

'And here I thought it was my experience with police cases.'

He sat back and let out another shrill laugh. 'Passionate *and* observant. Yes, your experience with criminal behavior was a bonus because to me it means you have a strict sense of right and wrong. I admire your sense of justice.'

'What does justice have to do with analyzing medical charts?'

'I was speaking in an abstract sense – doing things ethically.'

'Are you sure that's it?'

'What do you mean?'

'Has the cannibal murder remained on your mind, Bill? Have you been more worried about recurrence than you let on? Because if that's it, you're going to be disappointed. I've gotten involved in a few bloody things, mostly because of my friendship with Milo Sturgis. But he's the detective, not me.'

He took time to answer. Staring at his wife's watercolors. Twisting his fingers as if they were knitting needles.

'Worry's too strong a word, son. Let's just say the *possibility* of recurrence has remained in the back of my mind. AnneMarie's murder was my first real brush with this kind of thing, so I read up on it and learned that recurrence is the norm, not the exception. When I learned you had some experience with murder in addition to your scholarly achievements, I felt a great sense of . . . appropriateness.'

'How similar is Betty's murder to AnneMarie Valdos's?'

'Dennis claims there are . . . similarities.'

'Was Betty cannibalized?'

'Not . . .' He tapped the desk. The flutter of wings outside a window made us both start. Nightbirds or bats.

'Not yet,' he said. 'Nothing was missing. She was . . .' He shook his head. 'Decapitated and eviscerated, but nothing had been taken.'

'What about the long bones?'

'One leg was broken – hacked but not severed.'

'What kind of knife was used?'

He didn't reply.

'Bill?'

'Knives,' he said miserably. 'A set of surgical tools were found there.'

'Ben's?'

Headshake.

'Yours?'

'An old set I'd once owned.'

'Did you give it to Ben?'

'No. It was kept here – in the lab. In a drawer of this desk.'

'Where Ben had easy access.'

He nodded, almost crying. 'But you must believe me, Ben would never take anything without permission. Never! I know it sounds bad for him, but *please* believe me.'

'AnneMarie had a drinking problem,' I said. 'You implied Betty did too.'

'Did I?'

'Back in the house you said she used to smoke and . . . Then you trailed off and said she'd been taking excellent care of herself during her pregnancy.'

'The poor thing's dead. Why besmirch her memory?'

'Because it may be relevant. She's beyond hurt, Bill. Was she an alcoholic?'

'No, not an alcoholic. She was a . . . friendly girl. She smoked and drank a bit.'

'What does friendly have to do with it?'

'Friendly,' he said. 'To the sailors.'

'Like AnneMarie. One of those girls who went up to Victory Park. Was it common knowledge in the village?'

'I don't know *what's* common knowledge. I heard it from her mother.'

'Her mother complained about Betty's promiscuity?'

'Ida brought Betty in to be treated for a veneral infection.'

'Gonorrhea?'

He nodded.

'When?'

'A year ago. Before she became engaged. We kept it confidential from Mauricio – her boyfriend. Tested him, too, under a false pretense. Negative. Eventually they married.

'Maybe he found out anyway and reacted.'

'This? No, not Mauricio. What was done to her was beyond . . . no, no, impossible. Mauricio's not a . . . calculating sort. He'd never have thought to incriminate Ben.'

'Not smart enough?'

'He's simple. As was Betty.'

I remembered Betty's open manner and easy smile. Trusting me enough after meeting me to talk about herself. No bra under the tank top . . .

'Simple and trusting,' I said. 'A drinker, overly friendly with the boys. Sounds like a perfect victim. What was Ben's relationship with her?'

'They knew each other the way everyone on the island knows each other.'

'Did Ben know about her gonorrhea?'

He thought. 'I didn't discuss it with him.'

'But he could have found out – read it in the chart.'

'Ben was busy enough without sticking his nose where it didn't belong.'

'Maybe he came across it by accident. We both know you're not a compulsive filer.'

No answer. He got up and paced, twisting his fingers again, bobbing his neck.

I said, 'Learning that, he could have assumed she was easy.'

'I didn't record the diagnosis in my notes. I made sure to protect her.'

'What did you write?'

'Just that she had an infection that required penicillin.'

'Someone with Ben's medical sophistication could have figured it out, Bill. And what about the lab tests? Did you destroy the results?'

'I – don't believe so . . . but still it's not possible. Not Ben. Why are you *thinking* in these terms?'

'Because I have an open mind. If that upsets you, we can end the discussion.'

He gritted his teeth. 'This isn't the last time I'll be hearing these kinds of speculations. I might as well get used to it. Let's assume – for the sake of argument – that Ben did know she'd been infected. Why in the world would he murder her?'

'As I said, it could have led him to believe she was easy. One scenario is that they'd had a relationship for a while, or even that last night was a one-night stand. In either case, they went up to the park, got drunk, and things got out of hand.'

'That's ridiculous! You saw him with Claire tonight. He loves her, they've got so much going – the children.'

'Lots of psychopaths lead double lives.'

'No! Not Ben! And he's not a *psychopath*. He didn't kill AnneMarie and he didn't kill Betty!'

'Does he have an alibi for AnneMarie's murder?'

'He was never asked to present one. But I remember the way he reacted to the murder. Utterly *revolted*!'

'Did you tell him AnneMarie had been cannibalized?'

'No! Only Dennis and I knew. And now you.'

'But once again, Ben had access to the information. And Dennis knows AnneMarie's murder file is here. So even if Ben does develop an alibi for the first murder, Dennis may suspect he read up on the case and pulled a copycat. To disguise murdering Betty.'

'He's not a premeditated killer! This whole line of reasoning is spurious!'

'No one else knew about AnneMarie's wounds.'

'The killer knew – a killer who isn't Ben.'

'What about the fishermen who found AnneMarie's body?'

'Alonzo Rubino and Saul Saentz,' he said. 'They're even older than I. Saul's downright frail. And they didn't know the details.'

'Leaving only Ben, who might have.'

'You were at dinner tonight, son. Was that the demeanor of a cannibal butcher? Do you mean to tell me he drove Claire home, tucked her in bed, and left to commit murder?'

'He was in the park. What's his explanation for that?'

'Dennis hasn't interrogated him. Refuses to until there's an attorney present.'

'Ben's still free to offer an explanation. Has he?'

He paused. 'After Dennis and I had words, he was less than forthcoming.'

'When will Ben have an attorney?'

'Dennis has wired to Saipan for a court-appointed lawyer.'

'There are no lawyers on the island?'

'No. Until now that's been a plus.'

'How long will it take for the appointee to get over?'

'The next boat's due in five days. If the base allows a plane to land, it could be sooner.'

'Why would the base cooperate all of a sudden?'

'Because this is just what they want. Another nail in Aruk's coffin.' He made a fist and regarded it as if it belonged on someone else's arm. The fingers opened slowly. The bandage on his hand was soiled.

'Why is the Navy waging war on the island, Bill?'

'The Navy's a branch of the government, and the government wants to rid itself of responsibility. Ben's arrest is yet another reason to abandon ship: murderous savages. *Cannibals,* no less. And if the fiend who murdered AnneMarie was a Navy man, he's now off the hook, so Ewing's got a vested interest in having Ben prosecuted.'

'I thought you believed the killer had moved on.'

'Perhaps he left and returned. Corpsmen fly in and out all the time. A look at Navy flight records would be instructive, but try obtaining them. There's more than one kind of barricade, Alex.'

'You said Dennis never discovered any similar murders during the interim.'

'That's true. As far as it goes. But some of the places in the region – I've heard there's a restaurant in Bangkok that serves human flesh. Perhaps apocryphal, perhaps not. But there's no doubt things go on that we never hear about.'

He rubbed his head. 'Aruk has been abandoned, but I won't abandon Ben.'

'Does Senator Hoffman also have a vested interest in Aruk's decline?' I said.

'Most probably, strip away the veneer of political correctness and you've got a strip-mall builder.'

'In cahoots with someone like Creedman's employer – Stasher-Layman?'

'The thought has occurred to me.'

'Creedman's an advance man?'

'I've thought about that, too.'

'At dinner, Creedman and Hoffman acted as if they didn't know each other. But during the discussion of colonialism, Creedman rushed to defend Hoffman's point of view.'

'The *fool.*' He looked ready to spit. 'That *book* of his. No one's ever seen it and he won't be pinned down on details. Why else would Hoffman invite him to that abysmal dinner? Nicholas does nothing without a reason.'

'Have you found any connection between Hoffman and Stasher-Layman?'

'Not yet, but we mustn't get distracted. We must focus on Ben.'

'When Ben caught Creedman snooping, what was Creedman after?'

'I have no idea. There's nothing to hide.'

'What about the AnneMarie Valdos file? And not necessarily for nefarious reasons. Creedman's the one who told me about the murder. Said you did the autopsy, had the details. He sounded regretful. Maybe he smelled a good story.'

'No. As much as I'd like to attribute something malicious to him, he was snooping before AnneMarie's murder. Now let's—'

'One more thing: after you came back from speaking to Hoffman alone, you looked dejected. Why?'

'He refused to help Aruk.'

'Is that the only reason?'

'That's not enough?'

'I just wondered if there was some personal issue between the two of you.'

He sat straighter. Stood and smiled. 'Oh, there is. We dislike each other immensely. But that's ancient history, and I simply can't allow myself to be drawn into nostalgia. I acted stupidly with Dennis and now I'm persona non grata. But he may allow you to speak to Ben. Please call the police station tomorrow and ask his permission. If he grants it, use your professional skills to offer Ben psychological support. He's living a nightmare.'

He came around and rested a hand on my shoulder.

'Please, Alex.'

We hadn't gotten into his lie about being part of the Marshall Islands compensation, the nighttime boat rides. And he'd avoided explaining his reaction to Pam and Dennis's friendship. But the look in his eyes told me I'd taken things as far as I could tonight. Maybe there'd be another opportunity. Or maybe I'd be off Aruk before it mattered.

'All right,' I said. 'But let's get something straight: I'll give Ben the benefit of the doubt till the forensics come in. Unless I get into that cell and he tells me he murdered Betty – or AnneMarie. That happens, I'll march straight into Dennis's office and swear out a statement.'

He walked away from me and faced the wall. One of the watercolors was at eye level. Palms over the beach. Not unlike the one where Barbara Moreland had drowned.

Delicate strokes, washed-out hues. No people. A loneliness so intense . . .

'I accept your conditions,' he said. 'I'm glad to have you on my side.'

25

As we left for the house, he noticed a fat-petaled white flower and started to describe its pollination. 'Oh, shut up,' he told himself abruptly, and we continued in silence.

Inside, he gripped my hand. 'Thank you for your help.'

I watched him walk away quickly. Energized?

A man who studied *predation*.

Where had he come from the night I'd seen him with his doctor's bag? What had he been doing in the dark lab?

I'd phone the police station in the morning, but my first two calls would be to the airport at Saipan and the company that chartered the supply boats.

Upstairs, Spike's bark greeted me as I entered our suite. Robin wasn't back yet from talking with Pam. Four-fifty A.M. Someone else I might be able to reach.

The connection broke a few times before I finally got an international line. Wondering if anyone could listen in and deciding I didn't care, I told the desk officer at the West

L.A. station that I had urgent business with Detective Sturgis. He said, 'Yeah, I think he's here.'

A minute or so later, Milo barked his own name.

'Stanley? It's Livingstone.'

'Hey,' he said, 'buena afternuna – it's got to be what, five in the morning over there?'

'Just about.'

'What's up?'

'A bit of trouble.'

'Another cannibal?'

'As a matter of fact . . .'

'Shit, I was *kidding*. What the hell's going on?'

I told him about Betty's murder and everything else that had been on my mind.

'Jesus,' he said. 'After you told me about the first one, I got curious, so I played with the computers. Thankfully, cannibalism hasn't caught on big-time. Other than that Milwaukee moron only thing I came up with was a ten-year-old case, place called Wiggsburg, Maryland. Didn't sound that different from yours – neck slash, organ theft, legs cracked for the marrow – but they caught the bad guys, pair of eighteen-year-olds who decided Lucifer was their main man, he ordered them to carve up and dine on a local topless dancer.'

'Where are they now?'

'Jail, I assume. They were sentenced to life. Why?'

'There are two guys here who would have been around eighteen back then. They like to cut things up and they've been eyeing Robin.'

'But they're not suspects in the killing.'

'No, Ben does look good for it. But do you have the Maryland killers' names and descriptions, just to be thorough?'

'Got the fax right here . . . Wayne Lee Burke, Keith William Bonham, both caucs, brown and brown. Burke was six three, one seventy, Bonham five five, one fifty-two. Appendectomy—'

'I don't need any more, it doesn't match.'

'No big surprise. Things have gotten nuts but I don't see lads who suck out a young lady's bone marrow qualifying for early parole.'

'How far is Wiggsburg from Washington, D.C.?'

'About an hour's drive. Why?'

'There's another guy, here, D.C. background, also creepy.' I filled him in on Creedman.

'Sounds like a prince,' he said. 'Yeah, I've heard of Stasher-Layman 'cause they built public housing projects years ago in South Central, while I was riding a car at seventy-seventh Division. Bad plumbing, gang members hired to handle security. Immediate problems. They sold the management contract, then bailed. Had a deal to build a new jail, too, out in Antelope Valley, till the locals found out about their record, protested, and got it kaboshed. So what are they planning to build over there?'

'I don't know.'

'Not that it has anything to do with cannibals . . . so what's Dr Frankenstein's reaction to his protégé's predilection for intraspecies feasting?'

'Total denial. Ben was his project – rehabilitating a kid with a rotten background. Be interesting to know if that background includes any serious criminal activity Moreland didn't mention. If you've a mind to go back to the computer.'

'Sure, give me the particulars.'

'Benjamin Romero, I don't know if there's a middle name. He's thirty or so, born here, went to school in Hawaii and did Coast Guard duty there. Trained as a registered nurse.'

'I'll have a go at it. How's Robin handling all this?'

'She's a trooper but I want out. The next boats are due in around five days. If Chief Laurent allows us off the island, we'll be on one of them.'

'Why shouldn't he let you off?'

'Public opinion of Moreland and everything associated with

him isn't too high right now. We're all under informal house arrest.'

'Damned inconsiderate, not to say illegal. Want me to have a little cop-to-cop chat with him?'

'From what I saw tonight, that might make things worse. Moreland tried to influence him and he hardened his stance.'

'Maybe that's cause he's pissed at Moreland – "Not with my daughter, you don't."'

'Maybe, but I'll try to handle it myself first. If I have problems, believe me, you'll hear about it.'

'Okay . . . bugs and cannibals. Sounds almost as bad as Hollywood Boulevard.'

Feeling rancid, I showered. Robin returned as I was toweling off, and I summarized my talks with Moreland and Milo and told her I wanted to book us on the next boat out.

She said, 'It's too bad it had to end this way, but absolutely.' She sat down on the bed. 'What was that construction company?'

'Stasher-Layman.'

'I think Jo had something with their name on it in her room. Stack of computer printout – I assumed it was something to do with her research. The only reason it sticks in my mind is that when she saw me looking at it, she slid a book over it.'

'How sure are you it was Stasher Layman?'

'Very big Gothic initials – 'S-L,' then the name. I read it just before she covered it.'

An artist's eye.

'Jo and Creedman,' I said. 'Two people with D.C. connections. Two advance agents. I've had a weird feeling about her since the roaches. I didn't tell you because I thought I was just being paranoid, but I couldn't stop thinking that she was alone in the house that night. And the time lag between hearing your scream and coming in seemed odd. She excused it as drowsiness due to sleeping pills, but tonight she was out there before us, lucid as hell. Motive stumped me, but if she's doing dirty work for

Stasher-Layman and wants to get rid of distractions, that would serve nicely.'

'But then why not hide her gun, Alex? She kept it right out there on top of her suitcase, almost as if she wanted me to know she had it.'

'Maybe she did. Trying to intimidate you.'

'It didn't seem that way. There was absolutely no hostility between us. In fact, the more time I spent with her, the friendlier she got. As if I was helping her cope.'

And cope she had. Tranquilized widow to sharp-eyed interrogator in two days.

I said, 'She sure had an interest in the murder. Did you notice the way she was quizzing Moreland? That would also make sense if she's got an interest in Aruk's decline.'

'But if this company builds things, why would they want Aruk to decline?'

'Moreland said they build government projects. Milo's memory backs that up: low-income housing, prisons. Maybe they want the land cheap.'

'Low-income housing doesn't make sense,' she said, 'if the people are all leaving. But a prison might.'

'Yes, it might,' I said. 'No locals to protest. And what better place to dump felons than a remote island with no natural resources. It would be politically *beautiful*. Which is where Hoffman may fit in. What if Stasher-Layman paid him under the table to find a site and he chose Aruk because he remembered it from his days as base commander, knew there wasn't much of a constituency? If he embedded the prison, or whatever it is, in an extensive Pacific Rim revitalization – cash infusion for the bigger islands – who'd notice or mind? Other than Bill. But right now Bill's in a position to cause troubles for the deal because he owns so much of the island. Which could be the real reason Hoffman stopped over: making a final offer that Bill refused. So Hoffman pressured him, maybe threatened him with something.'

'Threatened him with what?'

'I don't know, but remember my feeling they had some issue between them that went way back? The first night I met Bill he said something about guilt being a great motivator. He could have done something years ago that he wants to forget. Something he's been trying to atone for all these years by being "the good doctor."'

She touched my arm. 'Alex, if he is holding up a giant deal he could be in serious danger. Do you think he's aware of what he's up against?'

'I don't know what he's aware of and what he chooses to deny. The man's a cipher and he's stubborn.'

'What about Pam? As his heir, she could also be in a treacherous position.'

'If she's his heir.'

'Why wouldn't she be?'

'Because she has no roots in Aruk, and Bill seems to view the *island* as his real child. He's excluded Pam from scientific discussion and just about everything else. You saw her surprise when he discussed Ben's family history. She's an outsider. So it wouldn't surprise me if he bequeathed his holdings to someone else. Someone with a strong commitment to Aruk.'

She stared at me. 'Ben?'

'In some ways he's Bill's *functional* son.'

'And being accused of murder gets *him* out of the way.'

'Sure, but nothing I've heard indicates he's not a murderer. In fact everything Bill told me just added to the picture of guilt: access to the weapon, Betty's medical records, and AnneMarie's autopsy file. And remember our discussion about his being a hard guy? No sympathy for Picker's crash. The way he vaccinated those children, mechanically. Add alcoholism and a rotten childhood and you've got a pretty good textbook history of a psychopath. Maybe even his outward devotion to Bill and the island is calculated. Maybe he's just after Bill's money.'

'Maybe . . . Yes, he is dispassionate. But he sat there

tonight at dinner with us, Alex, and I thought I saw a warmer side of him. As if Claire'd brought out something in him.'

'Could be acting. Psychopaths can turn it on at will.'

'You really think he could have been so lighthearted while planning to murder someone in a few hours? Planning to *mutilate* someone?'

'If he's a severe psychopath, he's got an extremely low level of anxiety. For all we know, sitting here listening to Claire play was part of the thrill.'

'Are you saying he killed both girls or just Betty?'

'It could go either way. AnneMarie could have been murdered by a sailor and Ben decided to do a copycat as a cover.'

'But why?'

'He and Betty could have been having an affair. Maybe the baby was his, he wanted out, permanently. When I talked to her, she seemed thrilled about the pregnancy; but who knows?'

'If he was so calculating, Alex, how'd he get caught so stupidly?'

'Screwing up's another psychopathic trait. Look at Bundy, escaping from Washington, where there's no death penalty, and murdering in Florida, where there is. Psychopaths walk a narrow line, all screwed up inside, constantly putting on a show. A psychiatrist named Cleckley labeled it perfectly: the mask of sanity. Eventually the mask falls off and shatters. Ben used booze to get rid of his.'

She shuddered. 'It's still hard to make sense of. I can see using alcohol to lower his inhibitions. But why stick around and get drunk *after* killing Betty?'

'It's possible he drank a little before meeting Betty, to take the edge off, had some more with Betty, killed her before the total effect set in, then boom. Bill said he'd always drunk beer. Vodka could have been too much to handle.'

'I guess so,' she said, rubbing her eyes. 'But he always seemed *decent.* I suppose I sound like one of those people who get interviewed on the news: he was such a quiet guy . . . well, at least the part about whose baby Betty was carrying can be tested. Who's doing the medical investigation?'

'Dennis is bringing a lawyer over from Saipan. I assume he'll call for a pathologist, too.'

She leaned against me heavily. 'What a horror.'

'How's Pam taking it?'

'At first she talked mostly about Bill – worried about him. Wanting to help, but feeling he pushes her away.'

'He does.'

'She's not ready to give up. She thinks she owes him.'

'For what?'

'Coming through for her during the divorce. She also talked more about herself. Said she'd had problems with men before her marriage – attracted to losers, guys who got rough with her, psychologically and physically. After the divorce she was so low she was having suicidal thoughts. Her therapist wanted to establish a support system, found out Bill was her only relative, and called him. To Pam's surprise, he flew out to Philadelphia, stayed with her, took care of her. Even apologized for sending her away. Said losing her mother had been too much to handle, he'd been overwhelmed, it had been a big mistake that he knew he could never make up for, but would she like to come back and give him another chance? But now that she's here . . .'

She looked at the clock. 'It's almost daybreak. Tell you one thing I've learned from all this. I could never be a therapist.'

'Most therapy cases aren't like this.'

'I know, but it's still not for me. I admire you.'

'It's a nasty job, but someone's got to do it.'

'I'm serious, honey.'

'Thank you. I admire you, too. And despite all that's happened, I have no regrets.'

'Me, neither.' She ran her fingers through my hair. 'In a few days when we're back in L.A., I'm going to remember being with you. Everything else good about this place. Frame it in my mind, like a picture.'

Psychic sculpting. I doubted I had the talent.

26

By ten A.M. the reservations were booked: back to Saipan in five days, LAX in a week. I'd try to find a good time to tell Moreland. If I didn't find one, I'd tell him anyway.

I phoned the Aruk police station. A man with a sibilant voice told me the chief was busy.

'When will he be free?'

'Who's this?'

'Dr Delaware. I'm staying at—'

'Knife Castle, yeah, I know. I'll give him your message.'

Robin was still sleeping and I went down to breakfast. Jo was there by herself, eating heartily.

'Morning,' she said. 'Get any sleep?'

'Not much.'

'It's something, isn't it? You come to an out-of-the-way place, think you're escaping big-city crime, and it runs after you like a mad dog.'

I buttered a piece of toast. 'True. Life can be a prison.

Sometimes, out-of-the-way places make the best prisons.'

She wiped her lips. 'I suppose that's one way of looking at it.'

'Sure,' I said. 'The isolation and poverty. For all we know there are all kinds of behavioral aberrations rampant.'

'Is that what you're looking for in your research?'

'I haven't gotten far enough to develop hypotheses. Looks like I won't; we're booked on the next boat out.'

'That so?' She placed a dollop of marmalade on a scone. The sun was behind her, crowning her with a rainbow aura.

'How long are you planning to stay?'

'Till I finish.'

'Wind research,' I said. 'What exactly are you looking at?'

'Currents. Patterns.'

'Ever hear of the Bikini atoll disaster? Atomic blast over in the Marshall Islands. Shifting winds showered the region with radioactive dust.'

'I've heard of it, but I study weather from a theoretical standpoint.' She nibbled the scone and gazed at the sky. 'There are wet winds coming, as a matter of fact. Lots of rain. Look.'

I followed her finger. The clouds had moved inland and I could see black patches behind the white fluff.

'When will the rain get here?'

'Next few days. It could delay your getting out. The boats won't sail if the winds are strong.'

'Are we talking winds or a storm?'

'Hard to say. The house probably won't fly away.'

'That's comforting.'

'It could be just rain, very little air movement. If the winds kick up, stay inside. You'll be fine.'

'The charter company didn't mention anything about delays.'

'They never do. They just cancel without warning.'

'Great.'

'It's a different way of life,' she said. 'People don't feel bound by the rules.'

'Sounds like Washington.'

She put the scone down and smiled, but held onto her butter knife. 'Washington has its own set of rules.'

'I'll bet. How long have you been working for the government?'

'Since I got out of grad school.' Her eyes returned to the clouds. 'As they get lower, they pick up moisture, then they turn jet-black and burst all at once. It's something to see.'

'You've been to the region before?'

She examined the cutting edge of the knife. 'No, but I've been other places with comparable patterns.' Another glance upward. 'It could come down in sheets. Only problem'll be if the cisterns fill too high for the filters to handle and the germ count rises.'

'I thought Bill had the water situation under control.'

'Not without access to the town he doesn't. But you heard Laurent. He's stuck here. All of us are. Guilt by association.'

'At least you've got your gun.'

She raised her eyebrows. Put the knife down and laughed. Pointing her finger at the coffeepot, she pulled an imaginary trigger.

'Crack shot?' I said.

'It was Ly's.'

'How'd he get it through baggage control?'

'He didn't. Bought it in Guam. He always traveled armed.'

'Exploring dangerous places?'

Filling her juice glass, she drank and looked at me over the rim. 'As you said, it's impossible to escape crime.'

'Actually, you said that. I said life could be a prison.'

'Ah. I stand corrected.' She put the glass down, snatched up the scone, bit off half, and chewed vigorously. 'It's incredible, being that close to a psychopathic killer. Ben seemed okay, maybe a little too *pukka sahib* with Bill, but nothing scary.' She shook her head. 'You never know what's inside someone's head. Or maybe *you* do.'

'Wish I did,' I said.

Dipping her hand into the pastry basket, she scooped up croissants, muffins, and rolls, and then broke off a cluster of grapes.

'Working lunch,' she said, standing. 'Good talking to you. Sorry you didn't have time to solve the mysteries of the island psyche.'

She headed for the doors to the house. When she got there, I said, 'Speaking of prisons, this place would make an especially good one, don't you think? U.S. territory, so there'd be no diplomatic problems. Remote, with no significant population to displace, and the ocean's a perfect security barrier.'

Her mouth got small. 'Like Devil's Island? Interesting idea.'

'And politically expedient. Ship the bad guys halfway around the world and forget about them. With the crime situation back home, I bet it would play great in Peoria.'

Crumbs trickled from her hand, dusting the stone floor. Squeezing the pastries. 'Are you thinking of going into the prison business?'

'No, just thinking out loud.'

'Oh,' she said. 'Well, you could take it one step further. When you get back home, write your congressman.'

Yet another folded card on my desk:

O let not Time deceive you,
You cannot conquer Time.

In the burrows of the Nightmare
Where Justice naked is,
Time watches from the shadow . . .

WH Auden

Below that: *A: Don't you think Einstein would agree? B.'*

What was he getting at now? The ultimate power of time . . . deceitful time . . . Einstein – time's relativity? The nightmare – death? Impending mortality?

An old man losing hope?

Making a typically oblique cry for help?

If so, I was in no mood to oblige.

I read a few more charts but couldn't concentrate. Returning to the house, I encountered Gladys coming out the front door.

'I'm glad I caught you, doctor. Dennis – Chief Laurent's on the phone.'

I picked it up in the front room. 'Dr Delaware.'

Dead air, then a click and background voices. The loudest was Dennis, giving orders.

I said, 'I'm here, Chief.'

'Oh – yeah. My man said you had something to tell me.'

'I was wondering if I could come into town to talk to Ben.'

Pause. 'Why?'

'Moral support. Dr Moreland asked me. I know it's a tall order—'

'No kidding.'

'Okay, I asked.'

'You don't want to do it?'

'I don't particularly want to mix in,' I said. 'Any idea when the rest of us will be allowed off the estate?'

'Soon as things quiet down.'

'Robin and I have reservations out in five days. Any problems with that?'

'No promises. No one's allowed off the island till we settle this.'

'Does that include the sailors on the base?'

He was silent. The noise in the background hadn't subsided.

'Actually,' he said, 'maybe you *should* come down to talk to him. He's acting nuts, and I don't want to be accused of not providing proper care, create any technicalities.'

'I'm not an M.D.'

'What are you?'

'Ph.D. psychologist.'

'Close enough. Check him over.'

'Pam's an M.D.'

'She's no head doctor. What, now that I want you, you're not interested?'

'Are you concerned about a suicide attempt?'

Another pause. 'Let's just say I don't like to see prisoners behave like this.'

'What's he doing?'

'Nothing. That's the point. Not moving or talking or eating. Even with his wife there. He wouldn't acknowledge her. I guess you'd call it catatonic.'

'Are his limbs waxy?'

'You mean soft?'

'If you position him, does he stay that way?'

'Haven't tried to move him – we don't want anyone claiming brutality. We just slide his food tray in and make sure he's got enough toilet paper. I'm bending over to protect his rights until his lawyer shows up.'

'When's that?'

'If Guam can free up a public defender and Stanton lets him fly in, hopefully in a couple of days – hold on.'

He barked more orders and returned to the line. 'Listen, you coming or not? If so, I'll send someone to pick you up and drive you back. If not, that's fine too.'

'Pick me up,' I said. 'When?'

'Soon as I can get someone over.'

'Thanks. See you then.'

'Don't thank me,' he said. 'I'm not doing it for your sake. Or his.'

He came himself, an hour later, emotions hidden behind mirrored shades, a shotgun clamped to the dash of the little police car.

As I walked out, he looked up at the gargoyle roof tiles and frowned, as if in imitation. I got in the car and he took off, speeding around the fountain and through the open gate, downshifting angrily and taking bumps hard. His head nearly touched the roof and he looked uncomfortable.

When we were out of sight of the estate, he said, 'I'll give you an hour, which is probably more than you need 'cause he's still playing statue.'

'Think he's faking?'

'You're the expert.' He grabbed the gearshift as we went around a sharp curve. His forearms were thick and brown, corded and veined and hairless. White crust flecked the corner of his mouth.

'He told me you two grew up together.'

Bitter smile. 'He was a couple of years older but we hung out. He was always small, I used to protect him.'

'Against who?'

'Kids making fun – his family was trash. He was too, didn't comb his hair, didn't like to bathe. Later, he changed so much you couldn't believe it.' He whipped his head toward the window, spat, returned his eyes to the road.

'After he moved in with Moreland?'

'Yeah. All of a sudden he got super-straight, studied all the time, preppy mail-order clothes, and Dr Bill bought him a catamaran. We used to go out sailing. I'd have a beer; he never touched it.'

'All that due to Moreland's influence?'

'Probably the military, too. We did that at the same time also. I was an MP in the Marines, he was Coast Guard. Then he got married, kids, all that good stuff. Probably decided it was a good idea to keep the straight life going.'

The next sentence came out a snarl: 'I *liked* the bastard.'

'Hard to reconcile that with what he did.'

He glanced at me and picked up speed. 'What're you trying to do? Put me on the couch? Dr Bill *tell* you to do that?'

'No. Sometimes I lapse into shoptalk.'

He shook his head and and put on more speed, turning the final dip to the harbor into a roller-coaster swoop.

The water enlarged as if at the hands of some celestial projectionist, blue, mottled platinum where the clouds hovered.

Laurent shoved the shift lever hard, yanked it back into neutral, gunned the engine, stopped so short I had to brace myself against the dash. My fingers landed inches from the shotgun and I saw his head swivel sharply. I put my hands in my lap and he chewed his cheek and stared out the windshield.

More people than usual on the waterfront, mostly men, milling around the docks and congregating in front of the Trading Post, which was closed. The only open establishment, in fact, was Slim's Bar, where a few more drinkers than usual loitered, smoked, and swigged from long-necks. I picked out Skip Amalfi's fair hair among the sea of black, then his father, hovering nervously at the back of the crowd.

Skip was animated, talking and gesturing and brushing hair out of his face. Some of the villagers nodded and gesticulated with their arms, slicing the air choppily, pointing up Front Street toward the road that led up to Victory Park.

Laurent put the car into gear and rolled down so fast I couldn't focus on anyone's face. Ignoring the stop sign on Front Street, he made a sharp right and raced toward the municipal center. The parking spaces facing the whitewashed building were all taken. Nosing behind a crumbling Toyota, he jerked the key out of the ignition, freed the shotgun, and got out carrying the weapon against his thigh. His size made it look like a toy.

Slamming the car door, he marched toward the center. Onlookers moved aside and I rode his wake, managing to get inside before the remarks to my back took form.

The front room was tiny, dingy, and hot, filled with the salty-fatty smell of canned soup. Nicked walls were covered with wanted posters, Interpol communiqués, lists of the latest federal regulations. Two desks, messy, with phones tilting on mounds of yet more paper. One held a hotplate.

The only spot of color was a tool company calendar over one of the workstations, starring a long-torsoed, pneumatic brunette in a red spandex bikini that could have been used for a handkerchief. A middle-aged deputy sat under sleek, tan thighs, writing and moving a toothpick around in his mouth. Skinny, he had a jutting stubbled chin and a sunken, lipless mouth. Lots of missing teeth. His hair was limp and graying, fringing unevenly over his collar. His uniform needed pressing but his engraved metal nameplate was shiny. *Ruiz*.

'Ed,' said Dennis. 'This is Dr Delaware, the psychologist from the castle.'

Ed pushed away from his desk and the legs of the folding chair groaned against the linoleum floor. The skin under his eyes was smudged. A pile of plastic-wrapped toothpicks was at his left hand. He lowered his head to the wastebasket and blew out the pick in his mouth, selected a new one, tore the plastic, rested the splinter on a ridge of bare gum, and laced his hands behind his head.

'Anything?' said Dennis.

'Uh-uh.' Ed manipulated the pick with his tongue and watched me.

'No action from the jokers at Slim's?'

'Nah, just big talk.' The sibilant voice. He touched the revolver in his belt with his left hand. I thought of something and filed it away.

'Why don't you take a walk up and down Front. Check things out.'

Ed shrugged and rose to a slumping five four. Pocketing more toothpicks, he ambled out the door.

Dennis said, 'You can sit in his chair.'

I took my place under Miss Redi-Lathe, and he settled half a buttock atop the other desk and folded his arms across his chest.

'Ed may not look like much to you, but he's reliable. Ex-Marine. In Vietnam he won enough medals to start a jewelry store.'

'Southpaw, too.'

He took off the mirrored glasses. His light eyes were clear and hard as bottle glass. 'So?'

'It reminded me that Ben's left-handed. I know because I saw him vaccinating the kids at the school. I read AnneMarie Valdos's file. Moreland said the killer was probably right-handed.'

'To me, "probably" means not for sure.'

I didn't answer.

Laurent's arms tightened and his biceps jumped. 'Moreland's no forensic pathologist.'

'He was good enough for the Valdos case.'

He chewed his cheek again and shot me a close-mouthed smile. 'Are you his rent-a-sherlock, supposed to raise doubts about my investigation?'

'The only thing he asked me to do was give Ben moral support. If my being here's a problem, take me back and I'll catch up on my sunbathing.'

Another bicep flex. Then the smile widened, flashing white. 'Look at that, I pissed you off. Thought shrinks didn't lose their tempers.'

'I came to Aruk to do some interesting work and get away from city life. Since I got here it's been nothing but weirdness, and now you're treating me like some kind of sleazeball. I'm not Moreland's surrogate and I don't enjoy being placed under house arrest. When those boats pull up, I plan to be on one.'

I stood.

He said, 'Take it easy, sit down. I'll make coffee.' Switching on the hotplate, he pulled packets of instant and creamer and styrofoam cups out of his desk.

'It ain't Beverly Hills café au lait. That okay?'

'Depends on what kind of conversation goes with it.'

Grinning, he went through a battered rear door. I heard water run and he returned with a metal coffeepot that he placed on the hotplate.

'You want to stand, suit yourself.'

I waited until the pot bubbled before sitting.

'Black or cream?'

'Black.'

'Tough guy.' Deep chuckle. 'No offense, just trying to take the tension off. Sorry if I rubbed you wrong before.'

'Let's just get through this.'

He fixed two cups, handed me one. Terrible, but the bitterness was what I needed.

'I know damn well Ben's a lefty,' he said. 'But all Moreland said in AnneMarie's case was that the killer was righthanded *if* she was grabbed from behind and done like this.' Tilting his head back, he exposed his Adam's apple and ran a hand along his throat. 'If she was cut from the front, it could have been a lefty.'

He shifted his weight.

'Yeah, I know what you're thinking. We dropped it before it was finished. But it's not like some big city, tons of money to follow every lead.'

'Hey,' I said, 'big-city cops don't always follow through. I watched thugs burn L.A. down while the police sat around waiting for instructions from brain-dead superiors.'

'You don't like cops?'

'My best friend is one – seriously.'

He stirred creamer into his cup and sipped with surprising delicacy. 'I've got a pathologist flying in. Looking at AnneMarie's file as well as Betty's. I don't know if she'll be able to make any determination about how Betty got cut, because her head was taken clean off. Maybe, though. I'm no expert.'

Shifting again, he got up and sat behind the other desk, propping his feet up.

'Does your gut tell you Ben's guilty?' I said.

'My gut? What the hell's that worth?'

'My friend's a homicide detective. His hunches have led him to some good places.'

'Well,' he said, 'good for him. I'm just one third of a dinky-shit three-man police force on a dinky-shit island. Ed's my main backup and my other deputy's older than him.'

'You probably never needed more.'

'Till now I didn't . . . Do I think Ben's guilty? It sure as hell looks like it, and he's not bothering to deny it. Only one who thinks otherwise is Dr Bill, with his usual . . .'

He shook his head.

'His usual singlemindedness?' I said.

He forced a smile. 'My word was "fanaticism." Don't get me wrong, I think he probably could have won a Nobel Prize for something if he'd put his mind to it. He's helped my mother and me plenty, giving her a free lease on the restaurant till things get better, paying for my schooling. I felt like a *shithead,* mouthing off to him last night. But you've got to understand, he's like a moray eel – gets hold of something and won't let go. What the hell does he want me to do? Let Ben walk on his say-so and watch the whole damn island explode?'

'Is the island near exploding?'

'Hotter than I've ever seen it – a lot worse than when AnneMarie got killed, and we had grumblings then.'

'The march up South Road?'

'No march, just a few kids shouting and waving sticks but look where it led. Now some people think they were fooled into believing a sailor did AnneMarie, and they're doubly pissed.'

'Fooled by Ben?'

'And Dr Bill. 'Cause Ben's seen as Dr Bill's boy. And even though people admire Dr Bill, they're also . . . nervous about him. You hear stories.'

'About what?'

'Mad scientist shit. Growing all this fruit and vegetables, bringing some into town, but rumor is he hoards it.'

'Is that true?'

'Who the hell knows? Guys who work the estate say he fools around with dehydration, nutritional research. But who cares? What's to stop anyone from growing their own stuff? My mother does. Dr Bill set her up years ago with soil and seeds, and she grows her own Chinese vegetables for the restaurant. But people get dependent, they like to piss and moan. Doesn't take much to get their tongues flapping. AnneMarie was a newcomer, no roots here, but everyone liked Betty.'

'Including the sailors.'

He turned toward me very slowly. 'Meaning?'

'Moreland said she'd socialized with them. As had AnneMarie.'

'Socialized . . . yeah, Betty liked to party before she got engaged, but for your own safety I wouldn't repeat that.'

'Any chance Betty and Ben had an affair?'

'Not that I heard, but who knows? But whatever Betty did, she was a nice kid. Didn't deserve to be ripped up like that.'

'I know. I spoke to her the morning before she died.'

He put his cup down. 'Where?'

'At the Trading Post. I bought drinks and magazines. She told me about her baby.'

He arced his feet off the desk and they hit the floor hard.

'Yeah, her mom said she loved the idea of having a baby.' Real pain clouded his eyes. 'Anyone who'd do that should have his nuts cut off and stuffed down his throat.'

The phone rang. He grabbed it. 'Yeah? No, not yet. No, not before his lawyer – I don't know.'

He slammed the phone down. 'That was Mr Creedman. Wants to do a story for the wire services.'

'Opportunity knocks,' I said.

'Meaning?'

'He's a writer. Now he's got a story.'

'What do you think of him?'

'Not much.'

'Me, neither. First day he got here, he hit on my mother. She straightened him out soon enough.'

He trained his eyes on me. He was a handsome man but I thought of a rhino, ready to charge.

'So tell me, doc, is Ben one of those guys, when you hear about his killing someone you say, "No way, couldn't be"?'

'I don't know him well enough to answer that.'

He laughed. 'Got my answer. Not that I've got any grudge against him. I've always admired him for the way he pulled himself up. I grew up without a father, but my mother's good enough for ten parents. Ben's mom was a dirty drunk and his dad was a real asshole, beat the hell out of him just for laughs. According to you guys, isn't that exactly the kind of thing that grows killers?'

'It helps,' I said. 'But there are plenty of abused kids who don't end up violent, and people from good homes who turn bad.'

'Sure,' he said, 'anything's possible. But we're talking odds. I took psychology, learned about early influences. Someone like Ben, I guess it's no surprise he cracked. I guess the big surprise is the time he had in between, acting normal.'

'In between what?'

Instead of answering, he finished his coffee. I'd barely touched mine and he noticed.

'Yeah, it's lousy – want some tea instead?'

'No, thanks.'

'The situation's really bad,' he said into his empty cup. 'Betty's family, Mauricio. Claire, her kids. Everyone thrown together, people can't escape each other.'

The phone rang again. He got rid of the caller with a couple of barks.

'Everyone wants to know everything.' He looked above me, at the bikini girl. 'I should take that down. Ed and Elijah like it, but it's disrespectful.'

He got up and came toward me. 'I've seen plenty, doctor, but never anything like what happened to those two women.'

'One thing you might want to know,' I said. 'After I read the Valdos file I called my detective friend. He ran a search for similar murders and came up with one, ten years old, in Maryland.'

'Why'd you ask him to look?'

'I didn't. He did it on his own.'

'Why?'

'He's a curious guy.'

'Checking out the island savages, huh? Yeah, I know about that one. Two satanists ate a working girl.' He shot out some details. 'My computer rarely works right, but I phone stuff in to the MPs on Guam and they hook into NCIC.'

'What do you think of the similarities?'

'I think satanic psychos have some sort of script.'

'Any evidence Ben was into satanism?'

'Nope.'

'Have you ever seen evidence of satanism on Aruk?'

'Not a trace, everyone's Catholic. But Ben was in Hawaii ten years ago – who knows what kind of shit he picked up?'

'Did he take any side trips to the mainland?'

'Like to Maryland? Good question. I'll look into it. For all I know, he killed girls in *Hawaii* and never got caught. For all I know, he was lucky the only thing they got him for was indecent exposure.'

The look on my face made him smile.

'That's what I meant by acting normal in between.'

'When?' I said.

'Ten years ago. He peeped in some lady's window with his pants down and his dick out. He was in the Guard and they handled it. Ninety days in the brig. That's how a lot of sex killers get started, isn't it? Watching and beating off, then moving on to the heavy stuff?'

'Sometimes.'

'*This* time.' He looked disgusted. 'Okay, have your hour with him. Give him his moral support.'

27

Behind the battered door was a warren of small, dim rooms and narrow corridors. At the back was a dented sheet-metal door bolted by a stout iron bar.

Laurent removed my watch and emptied my pockets, placed my belongings on a table along with his gun, then unlocked the bar, raised it, and pocketed the key. Pushing the door open, he let me pass, and I came up against grimy gray bars and the sulfur-stink of excreta.

A two-cell jail, a pair of three-pace cages, each with a cement floor, a grated, translucent window, a double bunk chained to the wall, a crusted hole with heel-rests for a toilet.

Thc ceilings were six and half feet high. Black mold grew in cracks and corners. The plaster had been scored by decades of fingernail calligraphy.

Laurent saw the revulsion on my face.

'Welcome to Istanbul West,' he said, with no satisfaction.

'Usually guys don't stay here for more than a few hours, sleeping off a drunk.'

The nearer cell was empty. Ben sat on the lower bunk of the other, chin in hand.

'Well, well, looks like we've had some movement,' said Laurent, loudly.

Ben didn't budge.

The keys jangled again and soon I was in the cell, locked in, and Laurent was outside saying, 'Trust me with your wallet and your watch, doc?'

I smiled. 'Do I have a choice?'

'Thanks for the vote of confidence. One hour.' Tapping his own watch. 'I'll leave the door open so you can shout.'

He left. Inside the cell, the stink was stronger, the heat almost unbearable.

I tried to find a place to stand that allowed me some distance from Ben, but the cramped space prevented it – so I contented myself with keeping maximum distance from the floor latrine as I scanned the graffiti. Names, dates, none of them recent. A large depiction of exaggerated female genitalia above the bunk. Sgraffito message: *Get me out of this hole!*

Ben didn't move. His eyes were unfocused.

'Hello,' I said softly. Though my five-ten height missed the ceiling by a few inches, I found myself hunching.

Silence. As complete as at the estate but not at all peaceful. After only seconds in here, my nerves screamed for some noise.

'Dr Bill sent me to see if there's anything I can do for you, Ben.'

He kept perfectly still, not even a blink, hair greasy, face streaked with sweat tracks. My armpits were already sodden.

'Ben?'

I took hold of his right arm and moved it from under his chin. Stiff and unyielding, as he resisted me.

No catatonia.

I let go. Repeated my greeting.

He continued to tune me out.

Three more attempts.

Five minutes passed.

'Okay,' I said. 'You're a political prisoner, giving the world the silent treatment as a protest against injustice.'

Still no response.

I waited some more. His cheeks were sunken – almost as hollow as Moreland's – and his eyes looked remote.

No eyeglasses. They'd been taken from him. Along with his shoelaces and belt and watch and anything else hard-edged. An angry boil had broken out on the back of his neck.

I kept staring at him, hoping my scrutiny would cause him to react. His nails were gnawed almost to the quick, one thumb bloody. Had he always been a biter? I'd never noticed. Or had Betty Aguilar resisted and snapped off some keratin? A clue he'd tried to conceal by chewing his other fingers?

I looked for nail bits on the floor. Nothing but inlaid dirt and scuffmarks, but they could have been tossed down the toilet hole. Big black ants single-filed under the bunk. After Moreland's zoo, they were laughable.

No scratches on his face and hands.

His color was bad, but he was unmarked.

'How well do you see without your glasses?'

Silence.

Slow count to one thousand.

'This isn't exactly the behaviour of an innocent man, Ben.'

Nothing.

'What about your family?' I said. 'Claire and the kids.'

No response.

'I know this has been a nightmare for you, but you're not helping yourself.'

Nothing.

'You're being a fool,' I said, loud as I could without attracting Dennis's attention. 'Pigheaded like Moreland, but sometimes it pays to think independently.'

Involuntary flinch.

Then back to stone-face.

'Sins of the father,' I went on. 'People are already making that connection.'

His lower lip twitched.

'Guilt by association,' I went on. 'That's why I had to come down here. Moreland's confined to the estate because Dennis is afraid of what people might do to him. We're all confined. It's gotten ugly.'

Silence.

'People are angry, Ben. It's only a matter of time before they start wondering about his being Dr Frankenstein, what he does in that lab. If maybe AnneMarie and Betty were *his* idea as well as yours.'

The lip dropped, then snapped shut.

I gave him a few more minutes, then came closer and spoke to his left ear.

'If you're really as loyal as you make out, tell me what happened. If you butchered Betty on your own, just admit it and let them know Moreland had nothing to do with it. If you have another story, tell it, too. You're not helping yourself or anyone else this way.'

Nothing.

'Unless Moreland *did* have something to do with it,' I said.

No movement.

'Maybe he did. All those late-night walks. God knows what he was up to. I saw him one night, two A.M., carrying his doctor's bag. Treating who? And those surgical tools were his.'

Another flinch. Stronger.

Flick of his head.

'What?' I said.

He clamped his mouth shut.

'He studies predators. Maybe his interest isn't limited to bugs.'

He blinked hard and fast. *Exactly* the way Moreland did when he was nervous.

'Is he in on it with you, Ben? Did he teach you – Aruk's own Dr Mengele?'

Half a headshake turned into a full one.

'Okay,' I said. 'So why clam up like this?'

Back to immobility.

'You want me to believe you did do it, alone. Okay, I'll buy it, for the moment. No surprise, I guess, given your family history.'

Silence.

'Your criminal history, too,' I added. 'Some sex killers start off as peepers. Some of them search for new ways to deal with their impotence. AnneMarie wasn't penetrated sexually, and I bet Betty wasn't, either.'

More blinking, as if to make up for lost time.

'Dennis told me about the Hawaii arrest. Soon everyone will know about it, including Claire and the kids. And Dr Bill. If he doesn't already.'

He let out hot, sour breath.

I forced myself to remain close.

'What else were you up to, back then? Ever travel to the mainland when you were in the Guard? See the sights – maybe Washington, D.C.?'

Blank look.

'Peeping Tom,' I said. 'Vivaldi on the terrace doesn't cancel it out. Whatever else you did over there will come out too, once they really start checking.'

No reaction.

'The reason I mentioned D.C. is it's not far from a place called Wiggsburg, Maryland.'

His eyes angled downward. Puzzled? Distressed? Then they were staring straight ahead, again, as unmoving as when I'd entered.

I was coated with sweat. Had become accustomed to the sulfur stench.

'The funny thing is, Ben, it's still hard for me to think of you that way. Despite the evidence. Do you actually like to *eat* people? Odd for someone raised by a vegetarian. Unless that's the *point*.'

He began breathing hard and fast.

'Is it your way of slapping Moreland in the face?'

He inhaled deeply, held his breath. His hands began curling and tightening, the knuckles almost glassy. I stepped back but kept talking:

'The brain, the liver. The bone marrow? How does something like that start? When did it start?'

He struggled to stay calm.

'Moreland taught you a lot about medicine. Did it include dissection?'

His chest swelled and his skin turned as gray as the cell floor.

Then he stopped.

Stilling his eyes.

Composing himself.

Another slow count. To two thousand.

I stood there watching him.

He pressed one hand against his breastbone.

His eyes, suddenly clear.

Not with insight.

Washed by tears.

He began shaking, flung his arms wide, as if welcoming crucifixion.

Staring at me.

I moved back further, my spine at the wall. Had I pushed it too far?

His arms fell.

Turning away, he whispered: 'Sorry.'

'For what, Ben?'

Long silence. 'Getting into this.'

'Getting into this?'

Slo-mo nod.

'Stupid,' he said, barely audible.

'What was?'

'Getting into this.'

'Killing Betty?'

'No,' he said, with sudden strength. He bent so low his brow touched his knees. The back of his neck was exposed, as if for the executioner's ax. The boil seemed to stare at me, a fiery cyclops eye.

'You didn't kill her?'

He shook his head and mumbled.

'What's that, Ben?'

'But . . .'

'But what?'

Silence.

'But what?'

Silence.

'But what, Ben?'

'No one will believe me.'

'Why?'

'You don't.'

'All I know are the facts that Dennis gave me. Unless you tell me different, why should I believe otherwise?'

'Dennis doesn't.'

'Why *should* he?'

He looked up, still bowed, face angled awkwardly. 'He knows me.'

'Then if you've got an alibi, give it to him.'

He straightened and returned his eyes to the wall.

Shaking his head.

'What is it?' I said.

'No alibi.'

'Then what's your story?'

More headshaking, then silence.

'What's your last memory before they found you with Betty?'

No answer.

'When did you start drinking last night?'

'I didn't.'

'But you were drunk when they found you.'

'They say.'

'You didn't drink but you were drunk?'

'I don't drink.'

'Since when?'

'A long time.'

'Since you cleaned up in high school?'

Hesitation. Nod.

'Were you drunk in Hawaii? The Peeping Tom bust?'

He started to cry again. Growled and stiffened and managed to hold it in check.

'What happened in Hawaii, Ben?'

'Nothing – it was a big . . . mistake.'

'You weren't peeping?'

Suddenly he laughed so heartily, it caused him to rock, rattling the bunk.

Taking hold of his cheeks, he tugged down and created a sad-clown face, horribly at odds with the laughter.

'Big mistake. Big, big, *big* mistake.'

After that, he stopped talking, fluctuating between long bouts of silence and incongruous laughter.

Some kind of breakdown?

Or faking it?

'I just don't understand it, Ben. You claim you didn't kill Betty, but you seem awfully comfortable being a suspect. Maybe it is something to do with Moreland. I'm going back to the estate to talk to *him.*'

I moved toward the cell door.

'You wouldn't understand,' he said.

'Try me.'

He shook his head.

'What's so damned profound that you can't part with it?' I said. 'The fact that you grew up low status and now you're being thought of as the scum of the earth again? Sure, it's a cruel irony, but what happened to those girls was a hell of a lot crueler, so forgive me if I don't shed tears.'

'I—' Shaking his head again.

'Everything comes round, Ben. Big insight. I'm a psychologist, I've heard it before.

'You – you're wasting your time. Dr Bill is. Best to cut me loose.'

'Why?'

'I – don't stand a chance. Because of who I am – what you just said. Scum family, scum child. Before Dr Bill took me in, they wanted to send me to reform school. I . . . used to do bad things.'

'Bad things?'

'That's why this makes sense to everyone. Dennis knows me, and *he* thinks I did it. When they brought me in, their faces – everyone's.'

He looked back at the wall. Put a finger to his mouth and tried to get a purchase on what remained of the cuticle.

'What about their faces?' I said.

The finger flew out. 'No! You're wasting your time! They *found* me there. *With* her. I know I wouldn't – couldn't have done it, but they *found* me. What can I say? I'm starting to think I . . .'

This time he let the tears come.

When his sobs subsided, I said, 'Have you ever done anything like this before?'

'No!'

'Did you kill AnneMarie Valdos?'

'No!'

'What about the Peeping Tom thing?'

'That was *stupid*! A bunch of us from the Guard were on weekend leave; we went to a club in Waikiki. Everyone was drinking and partying. Usually I had ginger ale, this time I thought I could . . . handle it. Had a beer. Stupid. *Stupid.* Then another . . . I'm a stupid asshole, okay? We tried to pick up some girls, couldn't, went to walk it off in some residential neighborhood. I had to take a . . . needed to urinate. Found a garage wall, behind some house. The window to the house was open. She heard. We got caught – I did. The others ran.'

He looked at me.

'That doesn't sound terrible,' I said. 'If that's really the way it happened.'

'It is. That's the only filthy thing I've ever done since . . . I reformed.'

'What was your relationship with Betty?'

'I knew her. Knew her family.'

'Did she have a reputation for fooling around?'

'I guess.'

'Did you fool around with her?'

'No!'

'No affair?'

'*No*! I *love* my wife – my life is *clean*!'

'Her baby wasn't yours?'

'I love my wife! My life is clean!'

'Repeating it won't make it so.'

He started to come toward me, stopped himself. 'It's true.'

'Did you know she had the clap?'

Surprise on his face. Genuine?

'I don't know about that. My life is clean.'

'So how'd you end up in the park with your head on Betty's entrails?'

'I – it's a . . . it's a crazy story, you'll never believe it.' Closing his eyes. 'Just go. Tell Dr Bill to forget about me. He's got important things to do.'

'You're pretty important to him.'

He shook his head violently.

'Tell me the story, Ben.'

The head kept shaking.

'Why not?'

He stopped. Another smile. Enigmatic. 'Too stupid. I couldn't even tell Claire – wouldn't believe it myself.'

'Try me. I'm used to strange stories.'

Silence.

'Keeping quiet just makes you look guilty, Ben.'

'Everything makes me look guilty,' he said. 'If you keep your mouth shut, you can't swallow flies.'

'Did Moreland tell you that? His quotations are usually a little more elegant.'

'No,' he said sharply. 'My . . . father.'

'What other words of wisdom did your father give you?'

Keeping his eyes closed, he tightened the lids.

Lying down on the bunk, face to the skimpy straw mattress.

'Okay,' I said. 'Maybe you should save it for your lawyer, anyway. Dennis has called for a public defender from Saipan. It'll take at least two days, maybe longer. Anything you want me to tell Moreland other than to abandon you?'

No movement.

I called out Dennis's name.

Deputy Ed Ruiz shuffled in and produced a key. 'Say anything?'

I didn't answer.

The toothless mouth creased in contempt. 'Figures. His old man never said anything either when we used to throw his ass in here. Just lie there, like he's doing. Like some damn piece of wood. Then, soon as the lights went out, he'd start having those drunk-dreams, screaming about things eating him alive.'

He put the key in the lock. 'When it got so loud we couldn't stand it, we'd hose him off and that would work for a while. Then he'd sleep again and go right back into those DTs. All night like that. Next morning, he'd be denying he did anything. Few days later, he'd be sauced up again, insult some woman or grab her, take a poke at some guy, and be back in here, the same damn thing all over.'

He came forward, pointing at Ben. 'Only difference is, Daddy used to sleep on the top bunk. We'd put him on the bottom, but he'd always find a way to get up there, no matter how drunk. Then, of course, he'd roll off in the middle of the night, fall on his ass, crack his head. But climb right back on top, the stupid shithead. *Stubborn*-stupid. Some people don't learn.'

He snickered and turned the key.

Behind me, Ben said, 'Hold on.'

28

Ruiz looked at him with disgust.

'Hey, killer.' Bracing one bony hand against the edge of the cell door. USMC tattoo across the top.

'How much time do I have left?' said Ben.

'The doctor here is ready to go.'

'I can wait,' I said. 'If he's got something to tell me.'

Ruiz mashed his lips and peered at his watch. 'Suit yourself. Eighteen minutes.'

He lingered near the door.

'We'll take all eighteen,' I said. He walked away, very slowly.

When I turned back to Ben, he was on his feet, next to the toilet hole, squeezing himself into a corner.

'This is the story,' he said in a dead voice. 'I don't care what you think of it, the only reason I'm telling you is so you'll pass it along to Dr Bill.'

'Okay.'

'Though you probably won't.'

'Why not?'

'You can't be trusted.'

'Why's that?'

'The way you talked about him before. He's a great man – you have no idea.'

'Hey,' I said. 'If you don't trust me to deliver the message, save it for your lawyer.'

'Lawyers can't be trusted, either.'

'The one in Hawaii didn't do well by you?'

'There was no trial in Hawaii,' he said. 'I pled guilty and the Guard gave me some brig time. They said it wouldn't go on my record. Obviously, they can't be trusted either.'

'Life's rough,' I said. 'I'm sure Betty's family thinks so too.'

He stared into the filthy pit.

I said, 'Sixteen minutes left.'

Without shifting position, he said, 'When we got home from dinner, Claire was upset with me. For pressuring her to play. She didn't show it, but that's the way she is. I shouldn't have done it.'

Wringing his hands.

'We had . . . a tiff. Mostly, she talked and I listened, then she went to bed and I stayed up, trying to read. To get rid of my anger. Sometimes that works for me . . . not that I'm angry a lot. And we don't have many tiffs. We get along great. I love her.'

Tears.

'What did you read?'

'Medical journals. Dr Bill gives me his when he's through. I like to educate myself.'

'Which journals?'

'New England Journal, Archives of Internal Medicine, Tropical Medicine Quarterly.'

'Do you remember any specific articles?'

'One on pyloric stenosis. Another on gallbladder disease.'

He rattled off more medical terminology, suddenly looking at ease.

'How long did you read?'

'Maybe an hour or two.'

'One hour or two? There's a big difference.'

'I – we got home around nine forty. The . . . tiff took maybe another ten minutes – mostly, it was cold silence. Then Claire was in bed by ten – so I guess a little over an hour. Maybe an hour and a half. Then the phone rang, some guy saying there was a medical emergency.'

'What time was this?'

'I don't know – when I'm not working I don't watch the clock. Bill taught me time was valuable, but when I'm home, not paying attention to time is my freedom.'

He looked at me in a new way. Childlike. Craving approval.

'I understand,' I said, thinking of the Auden poem Moreland had just left me.

O let not Time deceive you . . . burrows of the Nightmare . . . naked justice.

He scratched his cheek, then his chest. Gazed into the latrine as if he wanted to crawl in.

'It was probably eleven-thirty,' he said. 'Or around then.'

'Who called?'

'Some guy.'

'You don't know who?'

He shook his head.

'Small island like this,' I said, 'I'd think you'd know everyone.'

'At first I thought it was one of the gardeners at the estate, but it wasn't.'

'Which gardener?'

'Carl Sleet. But it wasn't. When I said "Carl" he didn't acknowledge, and this guy's voice was lower.'

'When you said "Carl" he didn't identify himself?'

'He was talking fast – very upset. And the connection was bad.'

'Like a long distance call?'

That surprised him. 'Why would anyone call me long distance? No, the worst calls are the local ones. The long distance ones if you get a satellite linkup, you're fine. But most of the island lines are old and corroded.'

'All right,' I said. 'Some guy you didn't recognize calls you sounding upset—'

'I've been wracking my brain to see if I could figure out who it was, but I can't.'

'Why was he upset?'

'He said there was an emergency, a heart attack on Campion Way, near the park, and they needed help.'

'He didn't say who had the heart attack?'

'No. It all happened very fast – as if he was panicked.'

'Why'd he call you instead of Moreland?'

'He said he had called Dr Bill and Dr Bill was on his way and told him to get me because I was closer to Campion. So I grabbed my stuff and went.'

'What stuff?'

'Crisis kit – paddles, epinephrine, other heart stimulants. I figured I'd start CPR till Dr Bill got there, then the two of us . . .'

'Then what happened?'

'I left the house—'

'Did Claire see you go?'

'No. I snu – left as quietly as possible. I didn't want to wake her or the kids.'

'Did she hear the phone ring?'

'I don't know . . . usually she doesn't. The phone's in the kitchen and there's no extension in the bedroom. We keep the ringer on low at night.'

'With no bedroom extension, how do you hear emergency calls?'

'I'm a light sleeper and we usually leave the bedroom door open. Tonight it was shut – Claire shut it 'cause she was mad. When it rang, I ran over and picked up on the first ring.'

Meaning no one could verify the call or the time frame.

'So you left with your medical kit,' I said.

'Yes.'

'Did you walk or drive?'

'Drove. I got to the park maybe five minutes after the call.'

'Close to midnight.'

'Must have been. It was really dark, there are no streetlights on the island except for Front Street. At first I couldn't see anything, was worried I'd run over the patient, so I parked and walked. As I got closer I saw someone lying by the side of the road.'

'Just one person? What about the caller?'

'No one else. I assumed whoever had called it in had chickened out. And I figured it would take another few minutes for Dr Bill to get there, so I went over, opening my kit, ready to start, and someone grabbed me.'

'Grabbed you how?'

'Like this.' Hooking his left arm around his neck, he did a rough imitation of a police chokehold.

'A left arm?'

'Uh – no, it came from this side.' Reversing the hold. 'I guess it was the right – I can't be sure. It was so sudden and I blacked out. Next thing I remember is Dennis's face staring down at me, looking really weird. *Angry*. Other people, all of them staring down at me, my head feels as if it's about to explode and my neck's stiff and I think something happened to me and they're there to rescue *me*. But their faces – their eyes are hard. Then someone I can't see calls me "killer." And they're all looking at me the way they used to look at me when I was – the way they did – before I *changed*.'

I waited a while before saying, 'Anything else?'

'That's it . . . great story, huh?'

'The one thing you can say for it is, if you killed her, it sure wasn't premeditated. If it had been, you'd have prepared something useful.'

His smile was rueful. 'Yeah, great planner. So what do I do?'

'Tell your lawyer the story and see what he says.'

'You'll tell Dr Bill? It's important to me – his knowing I'm innocent.'

'I'll tell him.'

'Thank you.'

I heard footsteps.

'Anything else I can do for you, Ben?'

He bit his lip. 'Have Dr Bill tell Claire I'm sorry. For pressuring her to play . . . for everything.'

'Do you want to see her?'

'No. Not like this – ask her to tell the kids something. That I'm away on a trip.' Once more, tears welled.

Ed Ruiz opened the metal door. 'Time's up.'

On the way back to the office he said, 'Have fun?'

'A real blast,' I said. 'Next time, I bring streamers and funny hats.'

He let me in. Dennis was at his desk. He put the phone down, looking annoyed.

'Time well spent?' he asked me.

I shrugged.

'Well, the screws are already turning. Dr Bill doing his thing.'

'What thing is that?'

'I just got a call from Oahu. Landau, Kawasaki and Bolt. High-powered law firm, senior partner's some motormouth named Alfred Landau. Flying over in a couple of days – scratch the public defender.'

'Flying into Stanton?'

'Nope, into Saipan by chartered jet, then a private yacht's taking him the rest of the way. If it can't fit into the keyhole harbor, I'm sure they'll find a way of getting him to shore.' He drummed the phone receiver. 'Must be nice to be rich. Let me take you back.'

As we stepped outside, Tom Creedman intercepted us. He was wearing a white polo shirt, white shorts, and tennis shoes. All that was missing was a racquet. Instead, he carried a thin black attaché case in one hand, a pocket tape recorder in the other. The crowd on the waterfront had dispersed somewhat. A few stragglers remained on the south end. Among them were Skip Amalfi and Anders Haygood. Skip pointing to the spot where AnneMarie Valdos had been found.

'Going to Wimbledon, Tom?' said Laurent.

'Yeah, me and the queen – got a minute, Dennis?'

'Not even half of one – come on, doctor.'

Creedman blocked me. 'See the suspect, Dr Delaware?'

'Let's go,' said Dennis, moving to his car.

Creedman didn't budge. 'Care for some coffee, Dr Delaware?'

'Sure,' I said.

Surprising both of them.

'Great,' said Creedman. 'Let's boogie.'

'I'm taking him back,' said Dennis. 'For his safety.'

'I'll take him back, Dennis.'

'No way—'

'I'll take the risk,' I said.

'It's not your risk to assume,' said Dennis.

'No?' I said. 'What law are you invoking to restrict my movement?'

He hesitated for a beat. 'Material witness.'

'To what?'

'You spoke to him.'

'With your permission. Let's call Mr Landau and see what he has to say about it.'

Dennis's huge shoulders spread even wider. He touched his belt, looked up and down Front Street.

'Fine,' he said savagely. 'You're on your own.'

Creedman and I walked past Campion Way to the next unmarked load. Past angry stares and mutters.

'Ooh,' he said. 'The natives are restless.'

'You're pretty relaxed about it.'

'Why not? I have nothing to do with good ol' Dr Bill. On the contrary, the fact that he evicted me works in my favor.'

He grinned, then continued, 'You, on the other hand, need to watch your back. But I'm here to stand up for you, buddy.' Unzipping the attaché, he peeled back a flap and revealed a chunky chrome automatic.

'Sixteen shots,' he said gaily. 'I'm sure that'll do the trick in the event of civil unrest. Very few of the natives own arms. Safe place and all that.'

'Do you usually carry?'

'Only during periods of stress.'

'Bring it over with you?'

'Bought it in Guam, bargain price. Owned by an Army lieutenant who ran up some debts. Took beautiful care of it.'

He zipped the case. 'I'm just up the hill.'

'Pretty close to the murder scene.'

'Not close enough.'

'What do you mean?'

'By the time I got there the crowd was thick – no chance to get close. I would have liked a close look at Mr Romero's face right after they caught him. Editors like that kind of immediacy. The emptiness in a psychopath's eyes.'

'I'm sure you can make something up.'

His smile died. 'That's not very kind, Alex.'

I winked.

His round face stayed angry, even after he restored the smile. 'But I understand. The cognitive dissonance must be painful for you. Coming here expecting Pleasure Island and getting Auschwitz. Did Ben have anything exculpatory to say?'

'Nothing an editor would be interested in.'

'What a sicko,' he continued. 'Cutting them up, then *eating* them.'

'Ever see that kind of thing before?'

The road had taken on a steeper slant, and though he kept up an athletic pace his breathing got louder. 'See what?'

'Cannibalism.'

'On other islands? No.'

'I meant back in the States, when you were on the crime beat.'

'Did I say I was ever on the crime beat?'

'I think you did. The first time we met.'

'I think I didn't. Not my meat – pardon the joke. No, Alex, I did politics. Dog eat *dog*.' He laughed. 'Have *you* seen it before?'

I shook my head.

'First time for everything,' he said.

We progressed up the hill, passing small houses, children, dogs, cats. Women with frightened eyes drew the children closer as we neared. Window shades lowered suddenly.

'Tsk, tsk,' he said. 'Paradise lost.'

29

His house was at the top, where the street dead-ended, a pale blue cottage with a full ocean view, hugged by pink oleander and yellow hibiscus. A Volkswagen bug sat at the end of a shattered-stone driveway. Much of the surrounding property was overrun by ivy and flowering vines. The nearest house was a hundred feet away, separated by a splintering wooden fence.

Inside was a different story: freshly painted white walls, black leather couches, oriental rugs that made the vinyl floor look better than it was, limited-edition posters, teak and lacquer furniture. In the closet-kitchen next to the dining area, a cast-iron ceiling rack bore expensive copper pots. German cutlery in a wooden case adorned a counter. All the appliances were European and they looked brand-new.

'Let me fix you a drink,' said Creedman, heading for a portable brass-and-glass bar.

'Just a Coke.'

He poured the soda and fixed a double scotch for himself. Johnny Black. Ice from a small, chrome-faced Swedish freezer.

I looked around. The main space was an office – living room. Computer and printer, thousand-watt battery pack, brass reflector telescope, stereo set, CD rack, German twenty-inch TV hooked up to a beefy cable that ran up through the ceiling.

'Had a dish,' he said, 'but a wind blew it down.'

'Looks like you've settled in for the long run.'

'I like to live well. Lime with that?'

'Sure.'

He brought the drinks and we sat down. The ocean was framed beautifully through a wide window.

'Best revenge,' he said, sipping. 'Living well.'

'Revenge against who?'

'Whoever deserves it.' He took a long, slow swallow and emptied his glass. Sucking in an ice cube, he moved it around his mouth.

'So what can I do for you?' I said.

'Nothing, Alex. Just trying to be friendly. Fellow ugly Americans, and all that. Too bad we didn't get much time together before you left.'

'Who said I'm leaving?'

He smiled. 'Aren't you?'

'Eventually. How about you?'

'I've got no schedule – one advantage of freelancing.'

'Sounds nice.'

'It is.'

We drank and he emptied his glass. 'Can I get you another one?'

'No, thanks.'

'Don't mind if I do.'

He poured himself a taller scotch and returned.

'It's really something, isn't it, this bloodfest. Guess I am on the crime beat now. Back in D.C. it never appealed to me because the vast majority of criminals were total shit-for-brains. The police and the prosecutors were no rocket scientists, either.'

'Are politicians smart?'

'Some of them.' He laughed. 'A few.'

'Nicholas Hoffman?'

He took a long, slow sip. 'Smart enough, from what I hear. So when are you packing out?'

'I'm not sure yet, Tom.'

'So what happens to your project with Moreland?'

'There isn't much of a project.'

'What was it all about, anyway?'

'Reviewing his files to see if we could find themes.'

'Themes?'

'Patterns of disease.'

'Mental disease?'

'All kinds.'

'That's it?'

'That's as far as it got.'

'And if you found patterns, then what?'

'We'd write it up for a medical journal. Maybe a book of our own. How's your own book going?'

'Great.'

'Going to add a chapter on the murders?'

'You better believe it . . . So how's Robin?'

'Fine.'

'Doggy okay, too?'

'Great.'

'Any chance Moreland put Ben up to killing those girls?'

I exaggerated my surprise. 'Why would he?'

He put the drink down, uncrossed his legs, scooted forward. 'Let's face it, Alex, the guy's strange.'

'He's a little different.'

'Like Norman Bates was different. That place – those bugs. And what the hell does he do all day in that lab? It sure ain't medicine, 'cause Ben handles most of the medical situations – or at least he used to. Till Pam came over. So what's the old guy up to all day?'

'I don't know.'

'Come on, you've been working with him.'

'In separate buildings.'

'What's he hiding?'

'I don't know that he's hiding anything.'

His mustache turned down. The black line was as flat as a grease-pencil scrawl, but he smoothed it anyway.

'He probably told you about the hassle Ben gave me. Probably made me out to be a thief.'

'He said you were looking for something. Were you?'

'Sure. Reporter's instincts. Because the minute I got to that place I started having a strange feeling.'

'About what?'

'Just general weirdness. And obviously I was right. All that do-gooding and his best boy's a serial killer. People are pissed, Alex. If you care about that pretty lady and that cute little pooch, you'll head back to lala land pronto.'

His voice had stayed low and even, but his eyes were holes burnt in linen.

'That sounds almost like a warning, Tom.'

'Word to the wise, Alex. Strategic assessment based upon the data at hand.'

I smiled. 'And *that* sounds kind of corporate. Almost like a quarterly report.'

He reached for the scotch. Missed, groped, got hold of it, drank. When he lowered the glass, his lower lip was wet and shiny. 'Guess I'd better be taking you back to Weird Castle.'

'Guess so.'

We left the house and he walked ahead of me and got into the VW. The engine squealed but it wouldn't turn over.

'Damn,' he said, without a trace of regret. 'Battery must have gone dead. I'd call Harry or Skip for a jump, but they're back in town with everyone else.'

'I'll walk.' I started down the road.

'I feel terrible,' he called after me. When I looked over my shoulder he was smiling.

* * *

The clouds had moved directly over the shoreline, and the air was warm and sticky.

I encountered no one on my way to the harbor, but a stray yellow mutt with a gray muzzle heeled for a while, then ran off as I reached Front Street. A group of young men standing near the intersection watched me over their cigarettes, grumbling as I passed and ignoring my 'good morning.'

Dennis's police car was still parked in front of the municipal center. He wouldn't want to play taxi.

I'd accepted Creedman's invitation in order to check him out. He'd wanted me there for the same reason.

Pumping me and warning me off.

Then stranding me.

His decor said someone was paying him well. His reaction to my crack about quarterly reports said it was probably Stasher-Layman.

Had it been a mistake to let him know I was onto that? No matter, I'd be gone soon.

I walked along the docks, ignoring stares. The municipal center's door opened and Dennis came out, followed by three small men, one middle-aged, the others in their twenties. They all wore thin shirts and jeans and talked wildly as Dennis tried to appease them.

The middle-aged man stamped a foot, waved a fist, and shouted. Dennis said something and the fist waved again. The man pointed and touched his heart. Dennis put a hand on his shoulder. The man shook it off angrily.

People started to move in from the street.

Dennis glared and they dispersed, very slowly.

The older man stamped and touched his heart again. One of the younger men turned and I got a look at his face: plain, round, acned.

Unmistakable resemblance to Betty Aguilar.

Dennis ushered them back inside and I continued south. I hadn't gone far before I heard footsteps behind me. A quick look back: some of the youths I'd passed at the intersection. Four of them, hands in pockets, advancing quickly.

I stopped, looked at them blankly and when that didn't stop them, tried to stare them down.

They kept coming.

I crossed the street, ending up in front of the Trading Post. The structure was sealed with yellow crime-scene tape. Some things were the same everywhere.

Slim's Bar was closed now too, but several beer swillers loitered in the gravel bed that served as the tavern's parking lot.

The four men behind me hesitated, then jogged across.

I reversed direction and headed back toward the center.

The youths picked up speed. One of them had something in his hand. A short wooden club – like a cop's billy, but sawn-off.

I ran.

They did too. Their mouths were open and their eyes were fixed.

The police station wasn't far, but the hangers-on at Slim's could be a problem.

As I got closer, they closed rank, forming a human wall.

Skip Amalfi among them, flushed, his lips pursed in an attempted belch. Anders Haygood, next to him, stolid and sober, the gray eyes amused.

The boys to my back shouted something.

The Slim's crowd moved forward.

Caught in the middle.

More shouts, loud murmuring, then someone's voice above it all: *'Idiots!'*

Jacqui Laurent had burst through the Slim's crowd. Taller than most of the men, she wore a grease-specked apron over her flowered dress and was waving something.

Big cast-iron frypan.

One of the Slim's crowd said something.

She cut him off: 'Shut up, you *moron*! What do you think you're *doing*?'

The four young men were close enough for me to hear their panting.

I whipped around.

The one with the club came forward, making small circles with the weapon. He had a feather beard and long hair. Some of his shirt buttons were missing, exposing a hairless chest.

Jacqui was at my side. *'Ignacio!'*

She grabbed for the club. Ignacio held on. She tugged.

Someone laughed.

She curled her lip. '*Big* shots. Big *heroes*. Ganging up on an innocent guy.'

'Who says he's innocent?' said one of the Slim's crowd. 'He lives up *there*.'

'*Yeah*.'

'*Yeah motherfu—*'

'So?' said Jacqui. 'So *what*?'

'So he's . . .'

'What?'

'A—'

'*What, Henry?* So he's a guest up at the castle? So what does that mean? That we act like animals?'

'*Someone's* been acting like an animal,' said Skip, 'and it ain't—'

'You *shut up* – look who's *talking*.'

Skip's nostrils opened. 'Hey—'

'Hey, *yourself*. Shut up and *listen*. *You're* an animal – and that animal's a *pig*.'

Skip moved forward. Haygood held him back, thick arms taut.

'Come on, big man,' said Jacqui, jerking the club. 'You going to *attack* me? A woman with a *frypan*? *That* how you get your jollies? Or is *peeing* at women your only thing?'

Skip's chinless face paled and he struggled in Haygood's grip.

Haygood said something and Skip made the sound of a hungry kid refused supper.

'*Big* shot,' said Jacqui. 'Big shot with your *bladder*. Every time a woman goes on the beach you follow her and pee near her blanket. Like a dog marking. Very brave.'

Skip lunged. Haygood restrained him, and some of the other men joined in holding him back.

'Easy, man,' said one of them.

'Come on,' said Jacqui, suddenly wresting the billy from Ignacio's grip and waving it along with the skillet. '*Go* at me, Skip. You like to get tough with women, right? Maybe *you* had something to do with Betty, tough guy.'

Skip snarled and Haygood did something to his shoulder that made his face go limp.

'Like a dog,' said Jacqui. 'Following every new woman around, peeing – you think that's funny?'

She ran her eyes over the other men: 'Any of *you* think that's funny? Peeing on the beach near a woman's blanket? Did it happen to any of your sisters? Or your mamas? 'Cause he did it to me when he first came over – remember that, Skip?'

Back to the others: '*That* your idea of brave, boys? Peeing on women and beating up on innocent men?'

Silence.

'*Big tough macho-men.* Gang up on a guest – what's his crime? Visiting? How do you think this island will ever get anywhere, you treat people like this?'

The men avoided her eyes.

Skip was rubbing his shoulder. Haygood turned him around and tried to move him away. Skip shoved Haygood's arm away but walked.

Jacqui stared at the Slim's crowd until it began to fall apart. Soon no one was left but the four youths who'd stalked me. The one named Ignacio stared at the billy in Jacqui's hand. She pointed the frypan at them.

'You should be ashamed of yourselves. I have a good mind to tell your mothers.'

One of the youths started to smirk.

'Think that's *funny*, Duane? I'll tell *your* mama *first*.'

'Go ahea—'

'Want me to? Really, Duane? First I'll tell her about what I saw on North Beach.'

Duane's mouth slammed shut. The other boys stared at him.

'Yeah, so?' he said.

'Yeah, so.' Jacqui tapped a firm thigh with the skillet. 'You really want me to do that, Duane?'

'Whu—?' said one of the other boys, giggling. 'Whud you do, Duane?'

'Nuthin'.'

'Sure *was* nothing,' said Jacqui, and Duane's nose twitched.

'Ah, fuck,' he said. 'Let's get the fuck out of here.'

'Good idea,' said Jacqui. 'All of you – scoot.'

They slunk away, the other boys surrounding Duane as he cursed them. When they were well past the center, Jacqui faced me.

'What did you think you were doing?'

'Walking home.'

'It's not a good time to play tourist.'

'I see that.'

She inspected the billy. Frowned and replaced it in her pocket. 'Walking all the way back to the castle?'

'My ride didn't come through.'

She gave me a puzzled look.

I told her about Creedman.

'What'd you want with *him*?'

'He invited me.'

Her expression said I was a cretin.

'Come on, I'll get Dennis or a deputy to drive you.'

'Dennis already offered,' I said. 'I turned him down, so I doubt he'll want to.'

She scraped something off the bottom of the frypan. Hefted the utensil as if considering braining me.

'Men,' she said. 'Why does everything have to be a contest? Come on, we'll go ask him again. He'll do it. He's been raised on the Fifth Commandment.'

Her fingers prodded the small of my back. Strong. Her skin was creamy and unlined, her body big and strong. She'd been eighteen when she'd given birth to Dennis, but even up close she could pass for his sister.

'Come on,' she said, 'I can't be here forever.'

She walked very fast, swinging the pan in a semicircle, big breasts heaving, mouth slightly parted.

I said, 'What did you see that boy Duane do on North Beach?'

She grinned.

'Never really saw him. *Heard* him.' Chuckle. 'Fooling around with his girlfriend.'

'Is that unusual?'

'Not for North Beach. Kids go there all the time.'

Avoiding South Beach because of the murder?

'So what was the big threat?' I pressed.

She laughed, high and girlish. It relaxed her face and made her seem even younger. Shifting closer to me, she said, 'The big *threat*, Dr Delaware, was that the boy was no *good* at it. His girlfriend was not very happy with him.'

More laughter as her hip nudged mine. 'You know, wham bam, thank you ma'am?'

'Ah,' I said.

'Ah.' She smiled, tightening the arc of the pan and scraping her flank. Her apron ruggled and her dress blew up, revealing brown leg. 'Ah.'

30

She went into the center first. I stuck my head in, saw Dennis huddled with Betty's family, and backed out quickly.

I waited next to the police car, keeping my eyes on the street. Quiet had settled over the waterfront. The rain clouds seemed to sag.

Deputy Ed Ruiz came out a few moments later and said, 'Let's go.'

The ride to the estate was silent. He stopped in front of the big gates. 'This far enough?'

'Thanks.' I got out.

'When you leaving Aruk?'

'Soon as the boats come in.'

He stuck his head out of the car. 'Listen, I've got nothing against Dr Bill. He helped my daughter out of a real bad situation a few years ago. Scraped herself on some coral, got this infection, we thought she'd lose the leg till he saved it.'

His toothless mouth folded inward.

'I'll forward your regards,' I said.

'But things change, you know? Not everyone's down on him. Some people know him better than others.'

'The ones he's helped directly?'

'Yeah. But others, they *don't* know.' He let the wheel spin back. 'Ben did those girls and you know it.'

'Let's say he did. What does Dr Bill have to do with it?'

Silence.

'You think he's somehow involved?'

He didn't answer.

'But people are saying he is?'

'People talk.'

'Maybe,' I said, 'someone wants Dr Bill to leave, and this is a golden chance to get rid of him.'

'Why?'

'Because he owns too much of the island.'

'That's the *point*,' he said angrily. 'He owns *too* damn much. Nothing much to go around and each year it's less. People get tired of wanting. Those that want, start thinking about those that got.'

Gladys was running a manual carpet sweeper over the second-floor landing, looking tired but moving quickly. As I approached the door to my suite, she put a finger to her lips.

'Robin's napping,' she whispered. 'That's why I'm using this instead of the Hoover.'

'Thanks for telling me,' I whispered back.

'Can I fix you some lunch?'

'No, thanks. Is Dr Bill around?'

'Somewhere. Claire came by to see him, brought KiKo for us to take care of. I've got him in a cage in the laundry room. Claire had the children with her – poor little things, so scared. Robin let them play with Spike.'

She looked ready to cry. 'Dennis promised to have someone watch them. So who does he send? Elijah Moon, everyone calls him Moojah. He's supposed to be a police deputy, but he's my age, got a belly out to here. What good can a fat old man do?'

I started down the stairs, then stopped.

'Gladys?'

'Yes, doctor?'

'You cooked for Senator Hoffman when he was the base commander?'

'I was head cook, sailors working under me.' She frowned.

'Tough job?'

'He liked his food fancy. All sauced up, always had to be something new. We used to send over for that really expensive beef from Japan – cows that do nothing all day but sit around and eat rice.'

'Kobe beef.'

'Right. And vegetables you never heard of and oysters and all kinds of expensive seafood. Nothing local, mind you. Had his crabs shipped from Oregon – Dungeness crabs. New England lobster. Philippine scallops. He was always clipping recipes out of magazines and sending them over to me. "Try this, Gladys." Why do you ask?'

'I was just curious what kind of relationship he and Dr Bill had. The night we had dinner at the base, they talked privately and Dr Bill was really upset afterwards.'

'I know,' she said. 'The next day he didn't eat a thing for breakfast or lunch. And him so thin in the first place.'

'Any idea why?'

'No. But he never liked Hoffman.' Her eyes misted. 'I don't believe Ben did anything, sir.'

'The people down in the village do.'

'Then they're stupid.'

'For all Dr Bill's accomplished, there's a lot of resentment toward him.'

She gripped the sweeper and the soft flesh of her arms quivered. 'Ungrateful *welfare* bums! Dr Bill tried to get them to work, but they don't want to know about that, do they? Did you know he offered free leases on the Trading Post and hardly anyone was interested?

Even those that rented stalls hardly showed up except to cash those *welfare* checks. Government keeps sending those checks, why should anyone bother? The nerve, to resent him!'

Anger had pulled her voice out of a whisper. She slapped her hand over her mouth.

'What with Ben's troubles, it's too bad about Dr Bill and Hoffman,' I said. 'It would be good to have friends in high positions.'

'Lot of good he'd do,' she said. 'That one was always for himself. Used to come up here and eat Dr Bill's food and cheat at cards. Illegal bridge signals, can you believe that? He was no gentleman, doctor.'

'Did Dr Bill know he cheated?'

'Of course, that's how I know! He used to joke about it with me, saying, "Nicholas thinks he's fooling me, Gladys." I told him it was terrible, he should put an end to it. He laughed, said it wasn't important.'

'Cheating at bridge,' I said. 'So Hoffman's wife went along with it.'

'No, she – it was—' She colored. 'What a thing! Shameful! Half the time Hoffman invited himself. Played tennis and sunned, ordered food from the kitchen, like I was still working for him. Like *everything* here was his.' The hand clamped over her lips again. This time, she blushed behind it.

'Everything?' I said.

'You know, a big shot – used to having things his way. I'll tell you something else, Dr Delaware: the man was heartless. Back when I was still his cook, a plane full of sailors went down – men and their wives and children, returning to the States.' She dipped a hand.

The crash Moreland had mentioned after Picker's accident. Nineteen sixty-three.

'All those people,' she said. 'A tragedy. So what did Hoffman do? That evening, he sends over a crate of scallops on ice and orders me to fix him coquille St Jacques.'

She resumed sweeping. 'Miss Castagna said you'll be leaving

soon. I'm sorry. From the way you treat Miss Castagna I can tell you're a gentleman. And we need more kindness.'

'On Aruk?'

'In the whole world, doctor. But Aruk would be a good place to start.'

I was surprised to find Moreland in my office, slumped in an armchair, reading a pathology journal. He looked like a skeleton coated with wax.

Putting down the magazine, he sat up sharply. 'How's Ben?'

I summarized my time in the cell.

He said nothing. The journal's table of contents was on the front cover and he'd circled an article. 'Bloodstain evidence.'

'Defense research?' I said.

'Someone called him on an emergency? Someone who sounded like Carl?'

'That's what he said.'

His fingers looked frail as sparrow's feet. They cracked as he flexed them. 'Meaning you don't believe him?'

'Meaning it's not much of a story, Bill.'

A long time passed.

'Doesn't that indicate to you,' he said, 'that he's innocent? Surely someone as intelligent as Ben could concoct a *first*-rate story if his object was to get away with something.'

'He's intelligent but he's also highly troubled,' I said. 'Drink was once a problem for him, and he obviously reacts strongly to it now. And he's got at least one prior sexual offense. Indecent exposure in Haw—'

'I know about that,' he said. 'That was nonsense. I took care of that for him.'

I let the non sequitur stand.

He said, 'So even after speaking with him you judge him guilty.'

'Things look bad for him, but I try not to judge.'

'Yes, yes, of course. You're a *psychologist*.'

'Last time we spoke, that was why you wanted me to see him, Bill.'

He picked up the journal, rolled it, hefted it. Blinking.

'Forgive me, son. I'm on edge – you're certainly entitled to your opinion, though I wish you felt differently.'

'I'd love to change my opinion, Bill. If you've got information, I'm listening. More important, communicate it to the lawyer you hired.'

He bent low in the chair.

'Maybe you've done all you can do for the time being,' I said. 'Maybe you should start looking after your own interests. Down in the village there's a lot of hostility toward you.'

'Alfred Landau is the best,' he said, softly. His firm handled Barbara's will, after she died . . . She was a wealthy woman. What she left me enabled me to buy up more parcels of land. Alfred was . . . most helpful.'

'Did he handle Ben's arrest in Hawaii, too?'

'Minimally. That was a military affair. I made a few calls, used my former rank.'

He stood. 'You're absolutely right. I'd better call Alfred now.'

'You're not concerned about what I just told you? The anger down in the village?'

'It will pass.'

I told him about the near confrontation with the four boys and how Jacqui had stepped in.

'I'm sorry it came to that. Thank God you weren't harmed.'

'But *you're* not out of harm's way, Bill. Betty's family is enraged. Lots of idle talk's circulating about you.'

That seemed to genuinely perplex him.

'You're a have among have-nots, Bill.'

'I've always shared.'

'Despite that, you're still lord of the manor. And the serfs aren't doing well.'

'I – it's hardly the feudal system—'

'Isn't it?' I said. 'Betty's murder is the spark that lit tinders, but it's obvious to me after just a few days here that things were heating up well before.'

He shook his head. 'The people are good.'

'But their lives are falling apart, Bill. Their entire society is shutting down – when's the last time the gas station pumps worked?'

'I've put in for a shipment.'

'You own that, too?'

'And I ration my personal vehicles the same way I do theirs. They know that—'

They also know how you live, and measure it against their own existence. More people leave than stay. Betty and her *husband* were planning to leave. Perfect climate for provocateurs, and you've got some: Skip Amalfi's been having fun whipping up the crowd. And I wouldn't be surprised if Tom Creedman starts to take a more active role. I was up at his place after visiting Ben, and he—'

'You didn't tell him anything, I hope.' His eyes were bright with alarm.

'No,' I said, trying to hold onto my patience. 'He asked, but I played dumb.'

'Asked about what?'

'If Ben had told me anything significant; what you and I were working on. He also clearly wanted to convince me to leave, which makes sense if he's working for Stasher-Layman and they want to control Aruk. Have you seen the interior of his house?'

He shook his head.

'Rooms full of brand-new furniture, computer equipment, expensive appliances.'

'Yes, I remember he received a large shipment shortly after he arrived. Right after I asked him to leave here.'

'Meaning he'd planned all along to settle down in his own place, came up here to snoop. What was he looking for, Bill?'

'I told you I don't know.'

'Not a clue?'

'None.' Taking hold of the journal, he rolled it again and let it unfurl.

'Jo Picker has something to do with Stasher-Layman, too.'

That nearly lifted him off the sofa. 'What – how do you know?'

'Robin saw their literature in her room. She's another one from Washington and she was here alone the night the roaches ended up in our room.'

'I – we've already established that was my fault. Leaving the cage open.'

'Do you actually remember leaving it open?'

That absent look came into his eyes. 'No, but . . . I . . . you really believe she could be working for them, too?'

'I think it's likely, and I'm bringing it up to warn you. Because you'll be dealing with her after I'm gone. Which is what I came to tell you: Robin and I are leaving on the next boat.'

He took hold of the chair. It slid forward and he lost his footing. I shot up and got hold of him just before he tumbled.

'Clumsy oaf,' he said, jerking away and pulling at his shirt as if trying to rip it off. 'Clumsy goddamned old *fool*.'

It was the first time I'd heard him swear. I managed to sit him back down.

'Pardon my language – the next boat is when, a week?'

'Five days.'

'Ah . . . well,' he said in a clogged voice, 'you must do what you feel is best. There's a time for everything.'

'Time is important to you,' I said.

He stared at me.

'Ben told me that. It made me think of your last note. The Auden poem – time's deceit. Your question about Einstein. What exactly were you getting at?'

He looked up at the ceiling. 'What do you think it meant?'

'To take time seriously but to understand that it's relative? What kind of deceit were you referring to?'

More of the absent look. Then: 'Einstein . . . in his own way, he was a magician, wouldn't you say? Turning the universe on its end, as if reality was one big illusion. Forcing us all to look at reality in a new way.'

'Unencumbered by time.'

'Unencumbered by prior *assumptions*.'

He lowered his gaze and met mine.

'And you want me to do that, Bill?'

'What I want really doesn't matter, does it, son?'

'A new way,' I said. 'Being skeptical about reality?'

'Reality is . . . to a good extent what we *want* it to be.'

He got up, inhaled, stretched and cracked more joints.

'The great thinkers,' I said.

'Always something to learn from them,' he answered, as if we were reciting responsively.

'I still don't understand the note, Bill.'

He came up to me, moving into my personal space the way he had with Dennis. A big, clumsy, intrusive bird. I felt as if I was about to be pecked and had to control myself from retreating.

'The note,' he said. 'Actually, you did very well with the note, son. *Bon voyage*.'

31

The rain came just before Milo called.

Robin and I were reading in bed when I felt the air turn suddenly heavy and saw the sky crack.

The windows were open and a burnt smell drifted through the screen. For one knife-stab moment, I thought of fire, but as I looked out, the water began dropping.

Panes of plate glass, filming the view. The burnt smell turned sweet – gardenias and old roses and cloves. Spike began barking and circling and the room got dimmer and warmer. I shut the windows, blocking out some but not all of the sound.

Robin got up and stared through a now filmy pane.

The phone rang.

'How's everything?' said Milo.

'Bad and getting worse.' I told him about my experiences in the village. 'But we're booked for home.'

'Smart move. You can always stop over in Hawaii for a real vacation.'

'Maybe,' I said, but I knew we'd be jetting back to L.A. as quickly as possible.

'Robin there? Got some house stuff to tell her.'

I handed over the phone and Robin listened. Her smile told me things were going well.

When I got back on, he said, 'Now *your* stuff, though now that you're leaving, who cares?'

'Tell me anyway.'

'First of all, both Maryland cannibals are still locked up. The asshole who only cut the victim is eligible for parole but has been refused. The asshole who cut *and* dined isn't going anywhere. Thank God it wasn't an L.A. jury, right? L.A. jury couldn't convict Adolf Hitler. What's that sound? Static on your end?'

'Rain,' I said. 'Think of a shower on high and triple it.'

'Typhoon?'

'No, just rain. Supposedly they don't get typhoons here.'

'Supposedly they didn't get crime, either.'

I moved closer to the window. Only the tops of the trees were visible through the downpour. Above the rain clouds, the sky was milk-white and peaceful.

'Nope, no wind. Just lots of water. I hope it lets up in time for the boats to come get us.'

'Daylight come and you wanna go home, huh? Well, when you hear the rest, you'll wish it were sooner. Guess who covered the cannibal case for a local rag?'

'Creedman.'

'Didn't even have to look for him, his name was right there on the articles. Then someone else took over mid-case and that made me a little curious, so I dug deeper. No one at the paper remembers Creedman specifically, but I found out there'd been some hassle with the local police around the same time he got pulled off the story: officers leaking information to his paper and others for money. A bunch of cops got fired.'

'Did reporters get fired, too?'

'Couldn't find that out, but it's a good bet. Anyway, Creedman's next gig of record was at a D.C. cable station, some kind of business show, but he only lasted three months before getting hired by Stasher-Layman Construction's D.C. office. Communications officer. The company issued a press release describing major balance-sheet problems. Their stock went way down and the owners bought it all up and went private. Next year profits went way, way higher.'

'Manipulation?'

'Maybe the owners are just a couple of lucky guys. And maybe lawyers go to heaven.'

'Who are the owners?'

'Two brothers from Oregon, inherited it from their daddy, moved to Texas. Big liberals on paper – funding ecology research, humane solutions to crime.'

'Oregon,' I said. 'Hoffman's constituents. Was he part of the buyout?'

'If he was, it didn't hit the news, but they did contribute big to his last reelection.'

'How big?'

'Three hundred thou – what they call soft money, gets around the spending limits. Seeing as Hoffman didn't have to put out much – he was a shoo-in – that's very sweet. So it wouldn't surprise me if he's backing them on some island project. He chairs a committee that considers big federal development grants, has the power to let things through or hold them up. But I can't find anything smelly.'

'The cops who got fired,' I said. 'Were the leaks directly related to the cannibal murder?'

'I had trouble getting details. The press doesn't believe in full disclosure when it comes to the press. But the firings took place right after the arrest.'

'Did you get any names of fired cops?'

I heard paper rustling. 'White, Tagg, Johnson, Haygood, Ceru—'

'Anders Haygood?'

'That's what it says.'

'He lives here. One of the guys who likes to cut things up. His buddy's been whipping the crowd up against Ben. Likes to pee when women are watching.'

'Wonderful.'

'So he and Creedman got booted at the same time – they know each other. Ten to one they're both on Stasher-Layman's payroll. Same for my next-door neighbor. She claims to be a botanist, but both she and Creedman are carrying guns that they picked up in Guam.'

'Jesus, Alex. Just sit tight till the boat comes in. Don't try to find out any more.'

'All right,' I said. 'But now I'm starting to think Moreland *could* be right about Ben being innocent. Not that he's got much of a story.'

'"I wuz framed"?'

'Ten points for the detective.'

'It's always "I wuz framed" unless it's "I blacked out" or "He started it."'

'Ben's two for three, claims he was choked out, the rest is blank.'

'Brilliant.'

I told him the rest of Ben's account.

'Beyond lame,' he said. 'Needs a four-prong walker. You know, Alex, a *real* bad smell's coming though the line. Even with Creedman and Haygood in cahoots over some development deal, that doesn't get Benjy off the hook – hell, for all you know *he's* on Stasher's payroll, too. You watch your back.'

'What should I do about the info on Creedman and Haygood?'

'Nothing. If the lawyer Moreland hired is really so sharp, let *him* do something with it. I'll tell him, not you. Name?'

'Alfred Landau. Honolulu.'

'When's he getting over there?'

'Two or three days.'

'Perfect timing. I'll wait till you've left.'

'Meanwhile Ben sits there rotting?'

'Ben ain't going anywhere no matter what anyone says or does. They found him *lying* on the goddamn body.'

'Convenient, isn't it?'

'Or stupid,' he said. 'But that just makes it typical. I had an idiot last month carjacked and killed some citizen, then drove the car for a couple of days before taking it to the dealer to complain about the fucking brakes. Funny, except the citizen's just as dead. Don't deal with it, Alex. I'll call Landau as soon as you're off the island. And don't feel bad about Ben. From what you're telling me, that jail cell may well be the safest place for him right now.'

'I'm not sure of that. We're not talking maximum security, just a hole at the back of the building. The victim's family visited the police station today. I saw the look in their eyes. It wouldn't take much of a mob to pull him out.'

'Sorry about that, but where else can he go? How's security at the estate?'

'Nonexistent.'

'Just stay *put*, Alex. Stay in your goddamn room – pretend it's a second honeymoon and you don't even *want* to come out.'

'Okay.'

'You definitely have your passage booked?'

'Definitely.' If the storm didn't stall things.

'See you soon. Enough of this paradise shit.'

Cheryl brought dinner up to our room and we picked at it. Darkness made its entrance virtually unnoticed. The rain got stronger, relentless, slapping the sides of the house.

But still warm. No lightning. The air was flat, deenergized.

As I sat there and did nothing, time's edges melted.

Time . . . *Einstein a magician . . . bending reality*.

Relativity – Moreland, a *moral* relativist?

Trying to *excuse* himself for something?

'Guilt's a great motivator.'

All these years – all his accomplishments – propelled by a troubled conscience?

Milo was right. It wasn't my battle.

Robin smiled from across the room. I'd told her what Milo had learned and she'd said, 'So it's good we're leaving.'

She was curled up now with some old magazines that had come with the suite. Spike snored at her feet. Peaceful scene, damned domestic. Pretending was fun.

I pointed to a wet window. 'Listen to it.'

She let her hand drop to Spike's head. 'It was a dark and stormy night.'

I laughed, went over, and kissed her hair.

She put the *Vogue* on her lap and reached up to stroke my face. 'This isn't so bad, huh? When you get down to it, making the best of a bad situation is the heart of creativity.'

She teased my tongue with hers. Our mouths collided. All the electricity, here.

We were slow-dancing toward the bed, fumbling with buttons, when the knocks on the door added thunder.

32

Pam's voice on the other side: 'Is anyone in there?'
We opened the door.

'Is Dad with you?' She stood, dripping, in a khaki raincoat drenched black, face shiny-wet under a snarl of run makeup.

'No,' said Robin.

'I can't find him anywhere! All the cars are here, but he isn't. We were supposed to get together an hour ago.'

'Maybe Dennis or one of the deputies picked him up,' I said.

'No, I called Dennis. Dad's not in town. I've searched all the outbuildings and every square inch of the house except your room and Jo's.'

She hurried next-door. Jo answered her knock quickly. She had on a bathrobe but looked wide awake.

'Is Dad with you?'

'No.'

'Have you seen him at all this evening?'

'Sorry. Been in all day – touch of the stomach bug.' She placed a hand on her abdomen. Her hair was combed out and her color was still good. When she noticed me studying her, she stared back hard.

'Oh God,' said Pam. 'This weather. What if he's outside and fell?'

'Older people do tend to spill,' said Jo. 'I'll help you look.' She went inside and returned wearing a tentlike transparent slicker over a black shirt and black jeans, matching hat, rubber boots.

'When's the last time you saw him?' she said. I followed her eyes down to the entry. Water had pooled there. Gladys and Cheryl were standing next to it, looking helpless.

'Around five,' said Pam. 'He was in his office, said he just had a little work, would be in soon. We were supposed to have dinner together at seven and it's already eight-thirty.'

'I spoke to him just before that,' I said, thinking of Moreland's tumble in the lab.

'Hmm,' said Jo. 'Well, I'm sorry, haven't noticed a thing. Been out of commission since noon.'

'Bad stomach,' I said.

She gave me another challenging look. 'Could he have gone off the grounds?'

'No,' said Pam, wringing her hands. 'He must be out there – Gladys, get me a flashlight. A big powerful one.'

She started for the stairs.

'Let's look for him in a group,' I said. 'Is anyone else here?'

'No, Dad sent the staff home early so they wouldn't get caught in the rain.' To the maids: 'Did anyone stay behind?'

Gladys shook her head. Cheryl watched her mother, then imitated the gesture. Her usual stoicism was replaced by a rabbity restlessness: sniffing, rubbing her fingers together, tapping a foot.

A sharp glance from Gladys stilled her.

'Okay,' said Jo, 'let's do it logically—'

'Did you check the insectarium?' I said.

'I tried to get in,' said Pam, 'but couldn't. The new locks – do *you* have the keys, Alex?'

'No.'

'The lights were out and I pounded hard on the door, no answer.'

'Doesn't he work in the dark sometimes?' said Jo. 'Doesn't he keep things dark for the bugs?'

'I guess so,' said Pam. Panic stretched her sad eyes. 'You're right, he could *be* in there, couldn't he? What if he's lying there hurt? Gladys, any idea where we can find a duplicate key?'

'I checked all the ones on the rack, ma'am, and it's not there.'

Cheryl grunted, then lowered her head.

Gladys turned to her. 'What?'

'Nothing, momma.'

'Do *you* know where Dr Bill is, Cheryl?'

'Uh-uh.'

'Have you seen him?'

'Just in the morning.'

'When?'

'Before lunchtime.'

'Did he say anything to you about going somewhere tonight?'

'No, momma.'

Gladys lifted her daughter's chin. 'Cheryl?'

'Nothin,' momma. I was in the kitchen. Cleaning the oven. Then I made lemonade. You said it had too much sugar, remember?'

Gladys's face tightened with irritation, then resignation set in. 'Yes, I remember, Cher.'

'Damn, damn,' said Pam. 'You're sure about the keys on the rack.'

'Yes, ma'am.'

'He probably forgot. As usual.'

'He gave it to Ben,' said Cheryl. 'I saw it. Shiny.'

'Lot of good that does,' said Pam. 'All right, I'm going back over to the insectarium and try to get in through one of those windows.'

'The windows are high,' said Jo. 'You'll need a ladder.'

'Gladys?' said Pam. Her voice was so tight the word was a squeak.

'In the garage, ma'am. I'll go get it.'

'I'll come with you,' said Jo. 'I can hold the ladder or climb it myself.'

'You're sick,' I said. 'Let me.'

She closed her door and positioned herself between Pam and me. 'I'm fine. It was just a twenty-four-hour thing.'

'Still—'

'No problem,' she said firmly. 'You probably don't have rainclothes, right? I do. Come on, let's not waste any more time.'

She and Pam hurried down, picked up Gladys, and headed toward the kitchen.

Cheryl remained alone in the entry. Fidgeting again. Looking everywhere but up at us.

Then right up at us.

At me.

'What is it, Cheryl?' I said.

'Um . . . can I get you something? Lemonade – no, too sweet . . . coffee?'

'No, thanks.'

She nodded as if expecting the answer. Kept bobbing her head.

'Is everything okay, Cheryl?' said Robin.

The young woman jumped. Forced herself to stand still.

Robin went down to her. 'What's the matter, hon?'

Cheryl kept looking up at me.

'It's pretty scary,' I said. 'Dr Bill disappearing like this.'

She began rubbing her thighs, over and over. I followed Robin down.

'What is it, Cheryl?' said Robin.

Cheryl looked at her guiltily. Turned to me. One hand kept rubbing her leg. The other patted a pocket.

'I need *you*,' she said, on the verge of tears.

I looked at Robin and she went to the far end of the front room. The rain was beating out a two-two rhythm, smearing the picture windows.

Cheryl's rubbing had intensified and her face was compressed with anxiety.

Sweating.

Conflict.

Then I remembered that Moreland had used her to deliver Milo's phone message.

'Did Dr Bill give you something for me, Cheryl?'

Running her eyes in all directions, she took a folded white card out of her pants pocket and thrust it at me. Stapled shut on all four corners.

I started to pull it open.

'*No!* He said it's for *secret*!'

'Okay, I'll look at it in secret.' I palmed the card. She started to leave, but I held her back.

'When did Dr Bill give it to you?'

'This morning.'

'To deliver tonight?'

'If he didn't come to the kitchen.'

'If he didn't come to the kitchen by a certain time?'

She looked confused.

'Why would he come to the kitchen, Cheryl?'

'Tea. I fix the tea.'

'You fix tea for him every night at a special time?'

'*No!*' Distraught, she tried to pull loose again. Staring at my pocket, as if expecting the paper to burst through.

'Gotta go!

'One second. Tell me what he told you.'

'*Give* it to you.'

'If he didn't want tea.'

Nod.

'When do you usually make him tea?'

'When he *tells* me.'

She started to whimper. Looked down at my hand on her arm.

I let go. 'Okay, thanks, Cheryl.'

Instead of running off, she held back. 'Don't tell momma?'

Moreland's trusty courier. He'd figured her limited intelligence would keep her on track, eliminate moral dilemmas.

Wrong.

'All right,' I said.

'Momma will be *mad*.'

'I won't tell her, Cheryl. I promise. Go on now, you did the right thing.'

She hurried away and I took the card to Robin. It was too dark to read and I didn't want to put on the lights. Hurrying back up to our suite, I popped the staples.

Moreland's familiar handwriting:

DISR. 184: 18

'What?' said Robin. 'A library catalogue number?'

'Some kind of reference – probably a volume or page number. He's been leaving cards since we got here. Quotes from great writers and thinkers: Stevenson, Auden, Einstein – the last one was something about time and justice. The only great thinker I can come up with who matches "DISR" is Disraeli. Did you notice a book by him up here?'

'No, only magazines. Maybe there's an article on Disraeli.'

'Architectural Digest?,' I said. 'House and Garden?'

'Sometimes they run features on ancestral homes of famous people.'

She divided the magazines and we started scanning tables of contents.

'French *Vogue*,' I muttered. 'Yeah, that'll be it. What Disraeli wore when addressing parliament. Now available at Armani Boutique. What the hell's he getting at? Even at his darkest hour the old coot's playing games.'

She discarded an *Elle*, started scrutinizing a *Town and Country*.

'Using poor Cheryl as a messenger,' I said. 'If he had something to tell me, why couldn't he just come out and say it?'

'Maybe he feels it's too dangerous.'

'Or maybe he's just going off the deep end.' I picked up a six-year-old *Esquire*. 'Everything he does is calculated. I feel like a character in a play. *His* script. Even this disappearance. Middle of the night, so damned *theatrical*.'

'You think he faked it?'

'Who knows what goes on in that big, bald head? I sympathize with the fact that his life's falling apart, but the logical thing would have been to beef up security and wait until Ben's lawyer arrives. Instead, he lets the staff go home early and puts his daughter through this.'

Rain hit the window so hard it shook the casement.

I ran my finger down another contents page, tossed it. 'Why choose *me* to play Clue with?'

'He obviously trusts you.'

'Lucky me. It makes no sense, Rob. He knows we're leaving. I told him this afternoon. Unless in his own nutty way he thinks this'll keep us here.'

'Maybe that or something else spurred him to action. But he could also be in real trouble. Knew he was in danger and left a message for you because you're the only one he's got left.'

'What kind of trouble?'

'Someone could have gotten in here and abducted him.'

'Or he fell, like he did in the lab.'

'Yes,' she said. 'I've noticed he loses his balance a lot. And the absentmindedness. Maybe he's sick, Alex.'

'Or just an old man pushing himself too hard.'

'Either way, his being out there on a night like this isn't a pleasant thought.'

The rain kept sloshing. Spike listened, tense and fascinated.

We finished the magazines. Nothing on Disraeli.

'There are books in your office,' she said. 'In back, where the files are.'

'But they're not categorized,' I said. 'Thousands of volumes, no system. Not too efficient if he's really trying to tell me something.'

'Then what about that library off the dining room?' she said. 'The one he told us wouldn't interest us. Maybe he said that because he was hiding something.'

'A book on or by Disraeli? What is this, Nancy Drew and Joe Hardy's blind date?'

'Let's at least check. What could it hurt, Alex? All we've got is time.'

We went downstairs again. The house was a scramble of streaks and shadows, hidden angles and blind corners, ripe with charged air.

We passed through the front room and the dining room. The library door was closed but unlocked.

Once inside, I turned on a crystal lamp. Dim light; the salmon moiré walls looked brown and the dark furniture muddy.

Very few books. Maybe a hundred volumes housed in the pair of cases.

Unlike the big library, this one *was* alphabetized: fiction to the left, nonfiction to the right, the former mostly *Reader's Digest* condensed editions of best-sellers, the latter art books and biographies.

I found the Disraeli quickly: an old British edition of a novel called *Tancred*. Inside was a rose-pink, lace-edged bookplate that said *EX LIBRIS: Barbara Steehoven Moreland*. The name inscribed in a calligraphic hand, much more elegant than Moreland's.

I turned hurriedly to page 184.

No distinguishing marks or messages.

Nothing noteworthy about line eighteen or word eighteen or letter eighteen.

Nothing noteworthy about anything in the book.

I read the page again, then a third time, handed it to Robin.

She scanned it and gave it back. 'So maybe "DISR" stands for something else. Could it be something medical?'

Shrugging, I flipped through the book again. No inscriptions anywhere. The pages were yellowed but crisp at the edges, as if never handled.

I put it back, pulled out another volume at random. *Gone With the Wind*. Then *Forever Amber*. A couple of Irving Wallaces. All with Barbara Moreland's bookplate.

'Her room,' said Robin. 'So he probably thinks of the big one as his. Leaving something there makes more sense – it's right behind your office. Maybe he pulled something out and left it for you.'

'This isn't exactly strolling weather.'

She wagged a finger at me. 'And someone forgot to bring his *rain* slicker!'

'Unlike the always-prepared Dr *Picker*. Wonder if she packed her little gun under that giant condom. I should have insisted on going with her and Pam. Maybe I should go over to the bug zoo and see what the two of them are up to.'

'No,' she said. 'If Jo *is* armed, I don't want you out there in the dark. What if she mistakes you for an intruder?'

'Or pretends to.'

'You really suspect her?'

'At the very least she's working for Stasher-Layman.'

She frowned. 'And Pam's out there with her – let's go see if Bill left anything for you.'

'Two targets in the dark? Forget it.' I buttoned my shirt at the neck and raised the collar. 'You go back and lock yourself in the room, and I'll dash over. I'll circle around from the back and avoid the bug house.'

She grabbed my arm. 'No way are you leaving me alone. Waiting for you to return will drive me batty.'

'I'll be quick. If I don't find anything in ten minutes, I'll forget about it.'

'No.'

'You'll get drenched.'

'We'll get drenched together.'

'Let's just forget the whole thing, Rob. If Moreland wanted to send a message, he should have used Western Union.'

'Alex, please. You know if I wasn't here, you'd be running to that bungalow.'

'I don't know that at all.'

'Come on.'

'The point is you *are* here. Let me go in and out or forget about it, Nancy.'

'Please, Alex. What if he's in danger and our not helping leads to tragedy?'

'There's already been plenty of tragedy, and what can Disraeli have to do with helping him?'

'I don't know. But like you said, he's got reasons for everything. He may play games, but they're serious ones. Come on, let's make a quick run for it.'

'You'll catch a cold, young lady.'

'On the contrary. It's a warm rain – think of it as showering together. You always like that.'

We were soaked immediately. I held her arm, and rain-blinded and slick-footed, concentrated on staying on the paths.

No worries about the gravel-crunch; the downpour blocked it out.

Vertical swimming; new Olympic event.

The downpour felt oily as it rolled off our skin.

Slow going till I spotted the yellow light over my office door. I stopped, looked around. No one in sight, but an army could have been hiding, and I knew if Moreland was out there it would be nearly impossible to find him before morning.

I glanced toward the insectarium. Lights still off. Pam and Jo hadn't gotten in.

The rain chopped our necks and our backs. Deep-tissue

massage. I tapped Robin's shoulder and the two of us made a dash for the bungalow. The door was unlocked, as I'd left it. I got Robin inside, then myself, and flipped on the weakest light in the room – a glass-shaded desk lamp.

Water flooded the hardwood floor. Our clothes clung like leotards and we sounded like squeegees when we moved.

Books and journals on my desk.

Piles of them that hadn't been there this afternoon.

Medical texts. But nothing by or about Disraeli.

No references beginning 'DISR.'

Then I found it, hefty and blue, on the bottom of the stack.

The Oxford Dictionary of Quotations.

I flipped to page 184. Samples of the wisdom of Benjamin Disraeli.

Line 18:

'Justice is truth in action.'

All that for this? The crazy old bastard.

Robin read the quote out loud.

I tried to recall the Auden quote . . . *naked justice, justice is truth.*

Wanting me do something to ensure justice?

But what?

Suddenly I felt tired and useless. Dropping a sodden sleeve onto the desk, I started to close the book, then noticed a tiny handwritten arrow on the bottom of page 185.

Pointing to the right.

Instruction to turn the page?

I did.

A notation in Moreland's handwriting parallel to the spine. I rotated the book:

214: 2

That turned out to be the wisdom of Gustave Flaubert.

Two quotations.

One about growing beards, the other demeaning the value of books.

More games . . . Moreland had been reading Flaubert the day he'd shown me the office. *L'Éducation sentimentale*. In the original French. Sorry, Dr Bill, I took Latin in high school . . . tapping the book, I felt something hard under the righthand leaf.

Ten pages down. Wedged into the spine and taped to the paper.

A key. Brass, shiny new.

I removed it. Underneath was another handwritten inscription, the letters so tiny I could barely make them out:

Thank you for persisting.
Gustave's girl will be assisting.

'Gustave's girl?' said Robin.

'Gustave Flaubert,' I said. 'The girl who comes to my mind is Madame Bovary. I told Bill I'd read the book years ago.'

'Meaning what?'

'I thought Madame Bovary was married to a doctor, got bored, had affairs, ruined her life, ate poison, and died.'

'A doctor's wife? Barbara? Is he trying to tell us she committed suicide?'

'He told me she drowned, but maybe. But why bring that up, now?'

'Could that be what he feels guilty about?'

'Sure, but it still doesn't make sense, making such a big deal about that now.'

I tried to reel the book's plot through my mind.

Then the truth came at me nastily and unexpectedly, like a drunk driver.

'No, not his wife,' I said. I shut the book.

Stomach turning.

‘What is it, Alex?’

‘Another Emma,’ I said, ‘is going to help us. A girl with eight legs.’

33

'Something hidden near her cage?' said Robin. 'Or in it?'

'He may have hidden it in the bug zoo to keep it from Jo. She claimed to be queasy about bugs, and this afternoon I told him my suspicions of her.'

'She's there right now.'

'Holding the ladder for Pam. Be interesting to see if she actually goes in.'

'What could he be hiding?'

'Something to do with either the murders or Stasher-Layman's plan. Ben's arrest made him realize things are bad and he has to play whatever cards he's got.'

The door opened suddenly and Jo and Pam sloshed in. I closed the book of quotations and tried to look casual. Dropped the shiny key into my pocket as the two women wiped the water from their eyes.

Pam shook her head despondently.

Jo fixed her gaze on me and shut the door. 'What are you folks doing out?'

'We wanted to help,' said Robin. 'Started looking around the grounds, but it got to be too much so we ducked in. Any luck at the insectarium?'

Pam shook her head miserably.

Jo scanned the room. 'The windows are bolted shut and layered with wire mesh. I managed to break the glass with the flashlight, but the wire wouldn't bend, so all I could do was shine it around and look in as best I could. Far as I could see, he's not there.'

'He didn't answer my shouts,' said Pam. 'We got a pretty good look.'

'Can't break the door, either,' said Jo. 'Three locks, plate steel and the hinges are inside.'

She removed her hat. Rain had gotten underneath and her hair was limp.

'I'm going back out,' said Pam.

'Reconsider,' Jo told her. 'Even if he is out there, with this kind of limited visibility, I don't see how you'd spot him.'

'I don't care.'

As she rushed for the door, Jo stared at me. 'What about you?'

'We'll stay here for a while, then return to the house. Let us know if you find him.'

Pam left. Jo put her hat back on.

'Are you armed?' I said.

'Excuse me?'

'Are you carrying your gun?'

She smiled. 'No. Weather like this, it could flood. Why? Think I need protection?'

'Anyone could be out there. The hostility down in the village . . . the rain'll probably keep people away, but who knows? We're all pretty vulnerable traipsing around.'

'So?' said Jo.

'So we need to be careful.'

'Fine, I'll be careful.' She threw the door open and was gone.

* * *

I opened the door a crack and watched as she melted into the downpour.

'Why'd you do that?' said Robin when I closed it.

'To let her know I was on to her. Maybe it'll prevent her from trying something, maybe not.'

We stood there, then I cracked the door again and looked outside. Nothing, no one. For what that was worth.

'Now what?' said Robin.

'Now we either go back to our room and wait till daylight or you go back and wait and I use the key and see what Gustave's girl can do for us.'

She shook her head. 'Third option: we both go visit Emma.'

'Not again.'

'I'm the one who had the pet tarantula.'

'That's some qualification.'

'What's yours?'

'I'm nuts.'

She touched my arm. 'Think about it, Alex: where would you rather I be? With you, or alone with Jo next door? There's no reason for her to think we have any way of getting in there. It's the last place she'll look for us, especially if she really is bug-phobic.'

'Nancy,' I said. 'Nancy, Nancy, Nancy.'

'Am I wrong? He's a strange old man, Alex, but in a crazy way he's left a logical trail. Maybe we should see the rest of it, Mr *Hardy*.'

I checked again twice. Waited. Checked again. Finally we snuck out.

Staying out of the path-lights as much as we could, we took a tortuously slow, route to the big building. Stopping several times to make sure we weren't being followed.

The rain kept battering us. I was so wet I forgot about it.

There, finally.

The three new locks were dead bolts.

The key fit all of them.

One final look around.

I pushed the steel door and we slipped in.

It closed on total darkness – the windowless anteroom.

Safe to turn on the light.

The space was exactly as I recalled: empty, the white tiles spotless.

And dry.

No one had entered recently.

We squeezed out our clothes. I shut off the lights and pushed open the door to the main room.

Cold metal handrails.

Robin's hand even colder.

A softer darkness in the zoo, speckled by pale-blue dots in some of the aquariums.

Muted moonlight struggled through the two windows Jo and Pam had broken. Each was dead center of the long walls, the glass punched out but the wire mesh remaining. Water shot through on both sides, making a whooshing noise, hitting the sill, and running down to the concrete floor, collecting in shiny blots.

Something else shiny – window shards, sharp and ragged as ice chips.

We waited, giving our eyes time to adjust.

The same rotten produce odor. Peat moss, overrripe fruit.

Steps down. Thirteen, Moreland had said.

I took in the central aisle, rows of tables on each side, the work space at the far end where he concocted insect delicacies.

Movement from some of the tanks, but again, the rain overpowered the sounds.

Thirteen steps. He'd said it twice, then counted each one out loud.

Making a point? Knowing this night would eventually come and preparing us for a descent in the dark?

I took Robin's hand. What I could see of her expression was resolute. Step number one.

*   *   *

Now I could hear it. Scurrying and slithering as we got closer to the tanks.

Even as we searched for Moreland, I knew we wouldn't find him. He had something else in mind.

Welcome to my little zoo.

Gustave's girl will be assisting . . .

The little glass houses were dark, and identical. Where was the tarantula . . . On the left side, toward the back.

As I tried to pinpoint the spot, Robin guided me to it.

The cage was dark, the mulch floor still.

Nothing on the table nearby.

Maybe Moreland had removed the creature and left something in its place.

I stooped and looked through the glass.

Nothing for a moment. Maybe I'd misunderstood. I started to hope – Emma shot up out of the moss and leaves, and I fell back.

Eight bristly legs drummed the glass frantically.

The spider's body segments pulsed.

Half a foot of body.

Slow, confident movements.

She's spoiled . . . eats small birds, lizards . . . immobilizes . . . crushes.

'Good evening, Emma,' I said.

She kept stroking, then scooted back down and sat in the mulch. Light from a neighboring tank hit her eyes and turned them to black currants.

Focused black currants.

Looking at Robin.

Robin put her face up against the glass. The spider's lipless mouth compressed, then formed an oval, as if pushing out a sound.

Robin tickled the glass with one fingertip.

The spider watched.

Robin made a move for the top lid and I held her wrist.

The spider shot up again.

'It's okay, Alex.'

'No way.'

'Don't worry. He said she wasn't venomous.'

'He *said* she wasn't venomous enough to kill *prey*, so she *crushes.*'

'I'm not worried – I have a good feeling about her.'

'Women's intuition?'

'What's wrong with that?'

'I just don't think this is the time to test theory.'

'Why you and not me?'

'Who says it has to be anyone?'

'Why would Bill put us in danger?'

'His being reasonable isn't something I'd take to the bank.'

'Don't worry.'

'But your hand—'

'My hand's fine. Though you're starting to hurt my wrist.'

I let go and before I could stop her, she nudged the lid back half an inch and was dangling her fingers in the tank – that damned dexterity.

The spider watched but didn't move.

I cursed to myself and kept still. Sweat mixed with the rain on my skin. I itched.

The spider pulsed faster.

Robin's entire hand was in the tank now, hanging limply. The spider caressed its own mouth again.

'Enough. Pull it out.'

Her face expressionless, Robin let her fingers come to rest near the spider's abdomen.

Touching tentatively, then with greater confidence.

Stroking.

The tarantula turned languidly, spreading to accept the caresses.

Nudging up against Robin's undulating fingers.

Covering them.

Encompassing Robin's hand.

Robin let the animal rest there for several moments, then slowly lifted her hand out of the aquarium.

Wearing the spider like a grotesque hairy glove.

Bending her knees, she placed her palm flat on the table. The spider extended one leg, then another. Stretching again . . . testing the surface. Peering back toward its home, it walked off the hand. Then back on.

Nosing Robin's fingertips.

Robin smiled. 'Hey, fuzzy one. You feel a little like Spike.'

As if encouraged, the spider continued up Robin's forearm and came to rest on her upper sleeve, its weight pulling down at the fabric.

'My, Emma, you've been eating well.'

The spider curled around Robin's bicep, hugging the arm, then inched forward, like a steeplejack scaling a pole.

Coming to a stop on Robin's shoulder.

Nuzzling the side of Robin's neck.

Stopping right near the jugular. All the while, Robin talked and stroked.

'See, Alex, we're buddies. Why don't you see if there's anything in the tank?'

I started to put my hand in, then stopped – was there another one in there? *Mr* Emma?

Oh hell, hadn't I read somewhere that the females were the tough ones? Removing the glass lid completely, I peered down, saw nothing, and plunged in. My hand groped leaves and soil and branches. Then something hard and grainy – lava rock.

Something underneath. Paper.

I pulled it out. Another folded card.

Too dark to read. I found a tank whose blue light was strong enough.

Impressive though Emma may be at first sight,
Everything's relative – size as well as time.

Relative.

Something bigger than the tarantula?

My eyes drifted to the last row of tanks.

One aquarium, larger than the others.

Twice as large.

A big piece of slate resting atop the lid.

What lived there was *twice* Emma's length.

My brontosaurus . . . significantly more venomous.

Over a foot of flat-bodied leather whip. Spiked-tail, antennae as thick as linguini.

Scores of legs . . . I remembered how the front ones had pawed the air furiously as we approached.

The flat, cold hostility.

I haven't quite trained it to love me.

Sadistic old bastard.

Robin was reading over my shoulder, Emma still resting on hers.

'Oh,' she said.

Before she could get brave again, I ran to the back of the zoo.

The centipede was just where it had been the first time, half out of its cave, the rear quarters concealed.

It saw me before I got there, antennae twitching like electrified cables.

All the front legs pawing this time.

Battling the air.

Everything's relative.

Including my willingness to go along with his little game.

I was about to leave when I noticed another difference about the large aquarium.

The entire tank was raised off the table.

Resting on something. More pieces of slate.

When I'd seen it a few nights ago, it had sat flush.

I ran my hand along the surface of the table. Dust and chips.

Moreland remodeling.

Creating a miniature crawlspace – it looked just wide enough to accommodate my hand.

As I extended my arm, the centipede coiled. As my fingers touched the edge of the slate platform, the creature attacked the glass. A cracking sound made me jump back.

The pane was intact, but I could swear I heard the glass hum.

Robin behind me now.

I tried again, and once more the monster lunged.

Kept lunging.

Using its knobby head to butt the glass while snapping its body into foot-long curlicues.

Something oily oozed down the glass.

Like that rattler-in-a-jar game in old Westerns; I knew I was safe, but each blow sent a jolt to my heart.

Robin made a small, high, wordless sound. I turned to see the spider doing pushups on her shoulder.

Jammed my hand under the slate and kept it there.

The centipede kept hurling itself. More cracking sounds. More venomous exudate.

Then something coarse and throaty I could have sworn was a growl came from inside the aquarium, rising above the rain.

I groped hyperactively. Touched something waxy and yanked back.

The centipede stopped attacking.

Tired, finally?

It glared and started again.

Crack, crack, crack . . . I was back in. The waxy thing felt inert, but God knew . . . *predators* . . . pull it out. Stuck.

Crack.

Right angles . . . more paper? Thicker than the card.

The centipede continued to tantrum and secrete.

I clawed the wax thing, got a purchase with my nails and pulled hard enough to feel it in my shoulder.

The wax thing slipped out of reach and I fell back, kept my balance, and crouched, eye to eye with the centipede.

Separated from its maniacal thrusts by a quarter inch of glass that trembled with each impact.

Its primitive face dead as rock. Then an infusion of rage turned it nearly human.

Human like a death-row resident.

The tank rocked.

I found the corner of the wax thing again, pinched, clawed, scraped . . . *crack* . . . missed, tried again – it moved, then resisted.

Stuck to the tabletop? Taped. The *bastard*.

Hooking a nail under the tape, I tugged upward, felt it give.

One more yank and the damned thing came out.

Thick wad of waxy paper, the edges crumbling between my fingers as I stepped away as fast as I could.

Robin followed me. So did Emma's black eyes.

Crack, crack . . . the beast reared up against the lid, trying to force it off. Noble in its own way, I supposed. A hundred-legged Atlas, fighting for liberation. I could *smell* its fury, bitter, steaming, hormonally charged.

Another push. The slate atop the lid bounced and I worried it would break the glass.

Spotting a flowerpot at the end of the aisle, filled with dirt, I used it for ballast.

The centipede continued lunging. The entire front of the aquarium was filmy with slime.

Crack.

'Nighty-night, you prick.'

Taking Robin by the hand, I hurried back to the front of the insectarium, stopping at a spot where the light through one of the broken windows was strongest. Then I realized Emma was still with us – why had I ever worried about *her*?

Everything's relative . . . time, too.

Moreland's point: nothing was what it seemed . . . I unfolded the wax paper. More pieces flaked off.

Dry. Old. Dark paper – black or deep blue, oversized, scored with light lines.

Blueprints.

Squares and circles, semicircles and rectangles. Symbols I couldn't understand.

Lines tipped with arrow points. Directional angles?

An aerial layout. The rectangles and squares were probably buildings.

The largest structure on the south side. Nearby a round thing – water waves within.

The front fountain.

The main house.

Oriented, I located the insectarium with its thirteen steps and central spine, lots of small rectangles angling off like vertebrae.

The baths . . .

I found my office, Moreland's, the other outbuildings.

To the east, a mass of overlapping amorphous shapes that had to be treetops. The edges of the banyan forest.

A map of the estate's center.

But what did he want me to *see*?

The longer I studied the sheet, the more confusing it got. Networks of lines, as dense as the streets on an urban map. Shapes that had no meaning.

Words.

In Japanese.

34

'The original construction plans,' said Robin. 'Can you make any sense of it?'

She took the blueprints and studied them. All those months at the jobsite in L.A. reading plans . . .

She traced lines, came to a stop.

'Maybe this?'

Guiding my hand to a rough spot – a pimpling of the paper, like Braille.

'Pinhole,' I said.

'Right in the center of this building here – his office. And look at this leading out of the office.' She ran her finger along a solid line that continued off the paper.

Due east. Out of his bungalow, through the neighboring buildings, past the border of the property, straight into the banyans.

'A tunnel?' I said.

'Or some kind of underground power cable,' she said,

flipping the sheet and examining the back. 'This *has* to be it.'

A circle had been drawn around the pinhole.

'A tunnel under his office,' I said. 'That explains the night I saw him go in there and turn the lights off. He went underground.'

She nodded. 'He's got a secret hiding place, and he's inviting us to sec it.'

She lifted Emma from her shoulder, talked soothingly to the spider, and stroked its belly. Eight limbs relaxed and stayed that way as the animal was returned to its home. Pausing a moment, Robin smiled.

'Nothing like new friends,' I said.

'Careful or I'll take her home with us.'

I folded the blueprints, tucked them in my waistband under my jacket, and we edged out of the insectarium.

The rain had lightened a bit and I could make out the shapes of shrubs and trees.

Nothing two-legged . . . then I heard something from behind and froze. Scraping – a tree branch rubbing against something.

We pressed ourselves against the wall and waited.

No human movement.

Moreland's bungalow was just a short walk under swaying trees. Off in the distance the main house was visible – lights on. Pam and Jo back?

We made a run for it.

The door was unlocked, probably from Pam's initial search. Or had Moreland left it that way for us?

Double-sided key lock. Once inside, I tried to bolt it with the key to my office and when that didn't fit, the new one. No go. We'd have to leave it open, too.

And the lights off.

The door to the lab was closed. Moreland's desk was

clear as it had been this afternoon, except for a single shiny object.

His penlight.

Robin took it and we crouched behind the desk and, shielded by wood, spread the blueprints on the floor. She shined the light on the plans. The ink had run. Our hands were indigo.

'Yes,' she said, 'definitely from behind there.' Pointing to the lab door.

She gave an uneasy smile.

'What is it?'

'All of a sudden I have visions of something disgusting on the other side.'

'I was just there, and there was nothing but test tubes and food samples. Nutritional research.'

'Or,' she said, 'he's feeding something.'

The lab looked untouched. Keeping the penlight low, Robin walked around, pausing to consult the blueprints, then resuming.

Finally, she stopped in the center of the room and stared, puzzled, at a black-topped lab table with a cabinet below.

'Whatever's down there would have to start here.'

A rack full of empty test tubes and an empty beaker sat on the counter. I placed the glassware on a nearby bench, then pushed the table. It didn't budge.

Wheels at each corner, but they weren't functional.

No sink, so no plumbing.

But attached, somehow, to the floor.

I opened the cabinet below as Robin aimed the penlight. Nothing but boxes of paper towels. Removing them revealed a metal rod running the height of the rear wall.

Springs, a handle.

I pulled down, encountered some resistance, then the rod lowered into place with a click.

The table shifted, rolled, and Robin was able to push it away easily.

Underneath was more concrete floor. A five by two rectangle. Etched. Deep seams.

A concrete trapdoor?

But no handle.

I stepped down on a corner of the rectangle, pressed and removed my foot, testing it. The slab rocked a fraction of an inch, then popped back into place, giving off a deep resonant sound, like a huge spinning top.

'Maybe it needs more weight,' said Robin. 'Let's do it together.'

'No. If Moreland can move it by himself, I can too. I don't want to trigger it too hard and have it slam up in our faces.'

I toed another corner. A bit more give, the slab bounced back again.

Pressure on the third corner caused it to yield further and I caught a view of the slab's side, at least half a foot thick. More metal underneath – some kind of pulley system.

Moving to the fourth corner, I felt myself being lifted and jumped off.

The slab rocked hard, stopped, then began rotating, very slowly. Barely making a full arc before continuing until it was perpendicular with the floor.

It came to a halt, shaking the floor. I tried to move it; locked into place.

Rectangular opening, four feet by two.

Dark, but not black – distant illumination from below.

I got down on my belly and peered down. Concrete steps, similar to those in the insectarium. Thirteen again, but these were striped with green.

Astroturf.

Leading to grayness.

'Guess this is why they call spies "moles",' I said.

Robin's smile was a faint courtesy. She brushed wet curls away from her face and took a deep breath.

Stepped toward the opening.

I blocked her and went in first.

The tunnel was seven feet high and not much wider, tubular walls of reinforced concrete, trowel seams marked by steel studs. The light I'd seen from above came from a caged mining fixture wired to the ceiling forty paces in the distance.

The astroturf lay over dirt, ending at the beginning of a single railroad track that bisected the tube.

Narrow track with polished pine ties. Too small for a train. Probably designed for a handcar, but none was in sight.

No rain sounds. I touched the ground. The soil was hardpacked and dry. Perfect seal.

Rapping the walls produced no tone either. The concrete had to be yards thick.

I told Robin to wait and returned to the tunnel's mouth. The slab loomed like a gigantic stiff lip. From down here the lab was a black hole.

I climbed the stairs, tested the slab a second time. Just as immobile – set into place by a mass of gears and counterweights, responsive to a special series of pressures.

Probably a safety feature installed by the Japanese army to prevent crushed fingers or accidental imprisonment. Probably some way to close it safely from below, but I didn't know it and we had no choice but to leave the entry exposed.

Maybe the best thing was to get out of here and wait till morning.

I climbed back down to Robin and offered her the choice.

'We've come this far, Alex. Let's at least follow it for a while and see where it leads.'

'If it extends past the property line, we'll be under the banyans. Land mines.'

'If there are mines.'

'You have doubts?' I said.

'If you wanted to hide something, what better way to discourage intruders than a rumor like that?'

'You want to test that hypothesis.'

'He's down here.' She gazed into the tunnel. 'He clearly wants us there too. Why would he want to hurt us?'

'He wants *me*,' I said. 'He brought me *over* for this.'

'Whatever, it's important to him. Look at all the precautions he took.'

'Cryptic messages. Voices of wise ones . . . bugs – he's like a big kid playing games.'

'Hide and seek,' she said. 'Maybe I'm way off but I don't think he's a bad man, Alex. Just a secretive one.'

I thought of Moreland and Hoffman and their wives playing bridge on the terrace. Hoffman cheating. Moreland never letting on.

'All right,' I said. 'Let's play.'

We walked along the tracks, passing under the glow of the caged light and slipping into darkness. A hundred paces later, the glint of an identical fixture came into view. Then another.

The monotony became pleasant – the *tunnel* was more pleasant than I'd imagined: warm, dry, silent. No bugs.

'What do you think it was, originally?' said Robin. 'An escape route for the Japanese?'

'Or some kind of supply channel.'

We reached the second light and were nearly out of its glow when we saw something against the wall.

Cardboard boxes. Scores of them, piled neatly in columns. Just like the case files in the storeroom.

Confidential files? Was this what Moreland wanted me to see?

I pulled down a box. The flaps were folded closed but unsealed.

Inside, zip-locked plastic bags.

Dried fruit and vegetables.

I tried another carton. More food.

A third contained pharmaceutical samples and bottles of pills – antibiotics, antifungals, vitamins, minerals, dietary supplements.

Then bottles of something clear – tonic water. The antimalarial properties of quinine.

Another carton. More dried fruit. Gatorade.

'Dr Bill's secret stash,' I said. 'He grows stuff in his garden, preserves it, and brings it down here. Maybe we're dealing with a survivalist. The question is, what's his Armageddon?'

Robin shook her head and fished out canned goods from another box. Beef stew, chicken and rice.

'So much for vegetarianism,' I said.

She looked sad. 'Maybe Armageddon's the destruction of the island. Could be he's planning to stay underground.'

'Under the forest,' I said. 'Protected by those mines, real or phony. It's pretty nuts, but there are bunkers full of folks just like that all over the States. The problem is, they also tend toward hair-trigger paranoia. A lust for the big battle.'

'That doesn't seem like Bill.'

'Why? Because he says he despises weapons? Everything the man's said or done is suspect – including his altruism. Aruk imports food at two, three times the usual cost. Bill helps out with occasional handouts but stockpiles all this stuff for himself. If he's been planning to go under for a while, that would explain why he hasn't been more aggressive promoting business for the island. Maybe he's given up on Aruk – on reality. Maybe he's concentrating on creating his own little subterranean world. Came up with the idea after finding the blueprints somewhere in the house. Eventually, he discovered the tunnel: instant caveman.'

She took something else out of the box. A foil packet with a white label.

'"Freeze-Dried Combat Meal,"' she read aloud. '"Segment B: reconstituted carrots, beets, peas, lima and string beans, soya protein' . . . then a whole bunch of vitamins . . . United States Navy issue . . . oh, boy.'

'What?'

'The date.'

Tiny numbers at the bottom of the label. February 1963.

'Sixty-three was his last year in the Navy,' I said. 'He bought the estate that year – he's been doing this for thirty years.'

'Poor man,' she said.

'He's obviously quite content. Damned proud of what he's accomplished.'

'Why do you say that?'

'Because now he wants to show it off.'

Six more ceiling lights, two more large caches of food and medicine.

We kept walking, automatically, like soldiers, drained of further conjecture, tracks and ties slipping past hypnotically.

My watch said we'd been underground nearly half an hour, but it felt both longer and briefer.

Time's deceit.

Another caged bulb.

Then a patch of green just beyond.

Another astroturf strip.

Another flight of stairs, fifty yards ahead.

Thirteen steps up to a metal door.

No handles or locks. I pushed, expecting ponderous weight, another tricky leverage system. It opened so easily I had to stop myself from falling forward.

On the other side was an upsloping concrete ramp lit by a weak bulb.

We climbed till we came to yet another door.

Metal grillwork – radiating circles of iron crisscrossed by spokes. Beyond it total darkness.

I knocked and pushed but this one didn't give. Then my brain put the grill design in context.

A web. What had Moreland called webs – *a beautiful deceit.*

Enough.

I turned to head back down the ramp.

Saw the first door closing behind us, rushed to catch it and failed.

It slammed shut, refused to yield.

Trapped in the ramp.

Ensnared.

Moreland's thin face appeared in my head. Long, loose limbs, fleshy snout, pouchy eyes, loping walk – arachnid walk.

Not a camel or a flamingo.

Predators . . .

Robin put her hand to her mouth. I stopped breathing; panic became a tight necktie.

Then light appeared behind the web, letting in a draft of very cool air.

The same chill I'd felt coming over the walls from the banyan forest.

The webbed door swung open. I saw walls of hewn stone, then blackness.

A cave.

The choice was to stay there and risk another entrapment or step through and take our chances with whatever was on the other end.

I stepped through.

A hand settled lightly on my shoulder.

I spun around. 'Damn you, Bill!'

But the eyes that stared back weren't Moreland's.

Dark slits – at least, the left one was. Its mate was a wide-open, milky-white crescent, drooping heavily, tugging at a ragged lid.

No iris. The white was shot through with capillaries.

The face around the orb was white, too.

The eyes lower than mine, set into an elliptical, neckless head that rested on meager, sloping shoulders.

Misshapen and hairless except for three patches of colorless down.

Ridges of skin in place of ears.

A mouth opened. Less than a dozen teeth, some of them no more than yellow buds. Framing them was a pouchlike, puckered aperture: no lower lip, the upper one thick, cracked, liverish – a smile? Why wasn't I screaming?

I smiled back. The hand so light on my shoulder . . . an inch of downy skin separated the mouth from a nose that was two black holes under a nub of pink-white flesh, twisted like a pig's tail.

Wens and scabs, keloid tracks, and crater scars danced across the face, a moonscape in closeup. A sharp smell fumed from the skin. Familiar smell . . . hospital corridors – antibiotic ointment.

The hand on my shoulder sat so delicately, I barely felt it.

I looked at it.

Four stumpy, broad-tipped fingers, the thumb clubbish and spatulate, no nail on the index finger. More of that soft, downy hair. Dimpled knuckles.

The wrist thin and frail, laced with baby-blue veins and scabbed heavily, disappearing into the cuff of a white shirt.

Clean, white oxford button-down.

Khaki trousers cinched tight around a thin waist, the cuffs rolled thick.

A man, I supposed . . . protruding from under the cuffs, brown loafers that looked new.

A boy-sized man – five feet tall if that, maybe eighty pounds.

'Hhh,' he said. *'Hhhii.'*

Whispery rasp. I'd heard voices like that before: burn victims, the larynx and vocal cords seared, learning to talk from the gut.

The pouch-mouth stayed open, as if struggling for speech. More medicinal smell – mouthwash. The single eye watched my face. The pouch twisted upward in what might have been a smile.

'Hi,' I said.

The eye studied me some more. Blinked – winked? No eyebrows, but the skin above the sockets creased into deep dual crescents that simulated brows.

Neckless, chinless, that congealed-fat complexion. But soft . . . I thought of the baby octopus in the lagoon.

The hand slid off my shoulder, slowly, gracefully.

The mouth closed and pouted – sad?

Had I done something wrong?
I tried smiling again.
The arm hung loosely.
Very loose. An invertebrate grace.
Fingers curling in ways that normal fingers couldn't.
Serpentine – no, even a snake had more firmness.
White and flaccid –
Wormlike.

35

He scratched a thigh, a cuff rode up, and I saw something shiny atop a loafer. Brand-new penny.

He saw something behind me and his head lowered shyly.

'Hi,' I heard Robin say.

Then I saw something behind *him*.

Another man emerging from the shadows, even smaller, so severely hunchbacked his head seemed to protrude from his chest.

Red-and-black plaid button-down, blue jeans, high-top sneakers.

Two good eyes. One ear. The eyes soft.

Innocent.

Curling a finger, he turned his back on us and stepped further into the cave.

The first man's forehead creased again and he followed.

We tagged along, tripping and stumbling as our feet snagged on bits of rock.

The little soft men had no trouble at all.

Gradually, the cave turned from black to charcoal to dove-gray to gold as we stepped out into a huge, domed cavern lit by several more of the caged fixtures.

Rock formations too blunt to be stalagmites rose from the floor. A bank of refrigerators filled one wall. Ten of them, smallish, a random assortment of colors and brands. Avocado. Gold. Hues fashionable thirty years ago. The wires met at a junction box attached to a thick black cable that ran behind a crag and out of the room.

In the center of the cavern were two wooden picnic tables and a dozen chairs. Shag area rugs were scattered over a spotless stone floor. A whirring, humming noise came from behind the junction box – a generator.

The rain slightly audible, now. A tinkle. But everything was dry.

Moreland came in and sat at the head of the table, behind a large bowl of fresh fruit. He wore his usual white shirt and his bald head looked oiled. His hands took hold of a grapefruit.

Four more small, soft people filed in and sat around him. Two wore cotton dresses and had finer features. Women. The others were dressed in plaid shirts and jeans or khakis.

One of the men had no eyes at all, just tight drums of shiny skin stretched across the sockets. One of the women was especially tiny, no larger than a seven-year-old.

They looked at us, then back at Moreland, their ruined faces even whiter in the full light.

Place settings before each of them. Fruit and biscuits and vitamin pills. Glasses of bright orange and green and red liquid. Gatorade. Empty bottles were grouped in the center of the table, along with plates full of rinds and pits and cores.

The two men who'd brought us stood with their hands folded.

Moreland said, 'Thank you, Jimmy. Thank you, Eddie.'

Rolling the grapefruit away, he motioned. The men took their places at the table.

Some of the others began to murmur. Deformed hands trembled.

Moreland said, 'It's all right. They're good.'

Runny eyes settled upon us, once again. The blind man waved his hands and clapped.

'Alex,' said Moreland. 'Robin.'

'Bill,' I answered, numbly.

'I'm sorry to put you through such a rigamarole, son – and I didn't know *you'd* be coming, dear. Are you all right?'

Robin nodded absently, but her eyes were elsewhere.

The tiny woman had engaged her visually. She had on a child's pink party dress with white lace trim. A white metal bracelet circled a withered forearm. A child's curious eyes.

Robin smiled at her and hugged herself.

The woman licked the place where her lips should have been and kept staring.

The others noticed her concentration and trembled some more. The generator kept up its song. I took in details: framed travel posters on the walls – Antigua, Rome, London, Madrid, the Vatican. The temples at Angkor Wat. Jerusalem, Cairo.

More cartons of food lined up neatly across from the refrigerators. Portable cabinets and closets, a couple of dollies.

So many refrigerators because they had to be small enough to fit down the hatch. I pictured Moreland wheeling them through the tunnel. Now I knew where he'd gone that night with his black bag. Where he'd gone so many nights, all these years, barely sleeping, working to the point of exhaustion. The fall in the lab . . .

A sink in the corner was hooked up to a tank of purified water. Gallon bottles stood nearby.

No stove or oven – because of poor ventilation?

No, the air was cool and fresh, and the rain sound was faint but clear, so there had to be some kind of shaft leading up to the forest.

No fire because the smoke would be a giveaway.

No microwave, either – probably because Moreland had doubts about the safety. Worries about people who'd already been damaged.

His lie about being part of the nuclear coverup a partial truth?

Lots of partial truths; right from the beginning he'd swaddled the truth in falsehood.

Events that had happened but in other places, other times.

Einstein would approve . . . it's all relative . . . time's deceit.

Everything a symbol or metaphor.

The other quotes . . . all for the sake of justice?

Testing me.

I looked at the scarred faces huddled around him.

White, wormlike.

Joseph Cristobal, tying vines to the eastern walls, hadn't hallucinated thirty years ago.

Three decades of hiding puncuated by only one mishap?

One of them going stir-crazy, emerging aboveground and heading toward the stone walls?

Cristobal sees, is gripped by fright.

Moreland diagnoses hallucinations.

Lying to Cristobal . . . for justice's sake.

Soon after, Cristobal gives one last scream and dies.

Just like the catwoman . . . what had *she* seen?

'Please,' said Moreland. 'Sit down. They're gentle. They're the gentlest people I know.'

We squeezed out our soaked clothes and took our places around the table as Moreland announced our names. Some of them seemed to be paying attention. Others remained impassive.

He cut fruit for them and reminded them to drink.

They obeyed.

No one spoke.

After a while, he said, 'Finished? Good. Now please wipe your faces – very good. Now please clear your plates and go into the game room to have some fun.'

One by one they stood and filed out, slipping behind the refrigerators and disappearing around a rock wall.

Moreland rubbed his eyes. 'I knew you'd manage to find me.'

'With Emma's help,' I said.

'Yes, she's a dear . . .'

'Time's deceit. Including the deceit you used to bring me over. You've been leading up to this since the first day I got here, haven't you?'

He blinked repeatedly.

'Why now?' I said.

'Because things have come to a head.'

'Pam's up there looking for you, scared to death.'

'I know – I'll tell her . . . soon. I'm sick, probably dying. Nervous system deterioration. Neck and head pain, things go blank . . . out of focus. I forget more and more, lose equilibrium . . . remember my tumble in the lab?'

'Maybe that was just lack of sleep.'

He shook his head. 'No, no, even when I *want* to sleep it rarely comes. My concentration . . . wanders. It may be Alzheimer's or something very similar. I refuse to put myself through the indignities of diagnosis. Will you help me before there's nothing left of me?'

'Help you how?'

'Documentation – this must be recorded for perpetuity. And taking care of them – we must figure out something so they'll be cared for after I'm gone.'

He stretched his arms out. 'You've got the training, son. And the character – commitment to justice.'

'Mr Disraeli's justice? Truth in action?'

'Exactly . . . there is *no* truth without action.'

'The great thinkers,' I said.

His eyes dulled and he threw back his head and stared at the cavern's ceiling. 'Once upon a time I thought *I* might develop into a significant thinker – shameless youthful arrogance. I loved music, science, literature, yearned to be a Renaissance man.' He laughed. '*Medieval* man would be more like it. Always mediocre, occasionally evil.'

He ruminated some more, snapped back to the present, licking his lips and staring at us.

Robin hadn't stopped glancing around the room. Her eyes were huge.

'Truth *is* relative, Alex. A truth that hurts innocents and causes injustice is no truth at all, and an evasive action that's rooted in compassion and leads to mercy can be justified – can you see that?'

'Did the second nuclear tests take place near Aruk? Because I know you lied about Bikini. If so, how was the government able to conceal them?'

'No,' he said. 'That's not it at all.'

Standing, he walked around the table. Stared at the boxes against the wall.

'Nothing you do is accidental,' I said. 'You told me about the nuclear blast and Samuel H. for a reason. You held on to Samuel's file for a reason. "Guilt's a great motivator." What are you atoning for, Bill?'

Putting his hands behind his back, he laced his fingers.

Long arms. Spidery arms.

'I *was* in the Marshalls during the blast,' he said. 'Perhaps that's why I'm dying.' Looking down. 'Now have I lied?'

'You didn't participate in the payoffs. I know. I spoke to a man who did.'

'True,' he said.

'So what's the point? What were the blasts a metaphor for—'

'Yes,' he said. 'Exactly. A metaphor.'

He sat back down. Retrieved the grapefruit. Rolled it.

'Injections, son.'

'Medical injections?'

Long slow nod. 'We'll never know exactly what they used, but my guess is some combination of toxic mutagens, radioactive isotopes, perhaps cytotoxic viruses. Things the military was experimenting with for decades.'

'Who's *they*?'

He jerked forward, bony chest pressing against the table edge.

'*Me. I* put the needle in their arms. When I was chief medical officer at Stanton. I was told it was a vaccination research program – confidential, voluntary – and that as chief medical officer, I was responsible for carrying it out. Trial doses of live and killed viruses and bacteria and spirochetes developed in Washington for civil defense in the event of nuclear war. The ostensible goal was to develop a single supervaccine against virtually every infectious disease. The "paradise needle" they called it. They claimed to have gotten it down to a series of four shots. Provided me experimental data. Pilot studies done at other bases. All false.'

He took hold of the white puffs over his ears. Compared to the soft people, his hair was luxuriant.

'Hoffman,' he said. 'He gave me the data. Brought the vials and the hypodermics to my office, personally. The patient list. Seventy-eight people – twenty families from the base. Sailors, their wives and children. He told me they'd agreed to participate secretly in return for special pay and privileges. Safe study, but classified because of the strategic value of such a powerful medical tool. It was imperative the Russians never get hold of it. Military people could be trusted to be obedient. And they were. Showing up for their injections right on time, rolling up their sleeves without complaint. The children were afraid, of course, but their parents held them still and told them it was for their own good.'

He pulled at his hair again and strands came loose.

'When exactly did this happen?' I said.

'The winter of sixty-three. I was six months from discharge, had fallen in love with Aruk. Barbara and I decided to buy some property and build a house on the water. She wanted to paint the sea. She told Hoffman, and he informed us the Navy was planning to sell the estate. It wasn't waterfront, but it was magnificent. He'd make sure we got priority, a bargain price.'

'In return for conducting the vaccination program secretly.'

'He never stated it as a quid pro quo, but he got the message across and I was eager to receive it. Blissful, stupid ignorance until a month after the injections, when one of the women who'd been pregnant gave birth prematurely to a limbless, anencephalic stillborn baby? At that point, I really didn't suspect anything. Those things happen. But I felt we should be doing some monitoring.'

'Pregnant women were included in the experiment?'

He looked down at the table. 'I had doubts about that from the beginning, was reassured by Hoffman. When I reported the stillbirth, he insisted the paradise needle was safe – the data proved it was.'

He bent low, talking to the table: 'That baby . . . no brain, limp as a jellyfish. It reminded me of things I'd seen on the Marshalls. Then one of the children got sick. A four-year-old. Lymphoma. From perfect health to terminally ill nearly overnight.'

He raised his head. His eyes had filled with tears.

'Next came a sailor. Grossly enlarged thyroid and neurofibromas, then rapid conversion to anaplastic carcinoma – it's a rare tumor, you generally only see it in old people. A week later he had myelogenous leukemia as well. The rapidity was astonishing. I started to think more about the nuclear tests in the Marshalls. I knew the symptoms of poisoning.'

'Why'd you tell me you were part of the payoff?'

'Couching my own guilt . . . actually, I was *asked* by my superior to participate, but managed to get out of it. The idea of placing a monetary value on human life was repulsive. In the end, the people who did participate were clerks and such. I'm not sure they had a clear notion of the damage.'

Craving confession for years, wanting some sort of absolution from me.

But not trusting me enough to go all the way. Instead, he'd used me the way a defensive patient uses a brand-new therapist: dropping hints, exploiting nuance and symbol, embedding facts in layers of deceit.

'I suppose,' he said, sounding puzzled, 'I was hoping this

moment would arrive eventually. That you'd be someone I could . . . communicate with.'

His eyes begged for acceptance.

My tongue felt frozen.

'I'm sorry for lying to you, son, but I'd do it all over again if it meant getting to this point. Everything in its time – everything has a time and place. Life may seem random, but patterns emanate. Like a child tossing stones in a pond. The waves form predictably. Something sets off events, they acquire a rhythm of their own . . . Time is a like a dog chasing its tail – more finite than we can imagine, yet infinite.'

He wiped his eyes and bit back more tears.

I took Robin's hand. 'After the other illnesses did you go back to Hoffman?'

'Of course. And I expected him to become alarmed, take some action. Instead, he *smiled*. Thirty years old but he had an evil old man's smile. A *filthy* little smile. Sipping a martini. I said, "Perhaps you don't understand, Nick: something we did to these people is making them deathly ill – *killing* them." He patted me on the back, told me not to worry, people got sick all the time.'

He gave a sudden, hateful look.

'A baby without a brain,' he said. 'A toddler with end-stage cancer, that poor sailor with an old person's disease, but he could have been dismissing a case of the sniffles. He said he was sure it had nothing to do with the vaccines, they'd been tested comprehensively. Then he smiled again. The same smile he gave when he cheated at cards and thought he was getting away with it. Wanting me to understand that he'd *known* all along.

'I'd planned to conduct an autopsy on the baby the next day, decided to do it right then. But when I got to the base mortuary, the body was gone. All the records were gone, too, and the sailor who'd been my assistant had been replaced by a new man – from Hoffman's staff. I stormed back to Hoffman and demanded to know what was going on. He said the baby's parents had requested a quick burial, so he'd granted compassionate leave and flown them to Guam the previous night. I went over to the flight tower to see if any planes had left. None had for seventy-two hours. When I got back to my office, Hoffman was there. He took me for a walk around the base and began talking about the estate. It seemed all of a sudden some other buyers had surfaced, but he'd managed to keep my name at the top of the list *and* to lower the price. It was all I could do not to rip out his throat.'

He put on his glasses.

'Instead,' he said. The word tapered off. He put a hand on his chest and inhaled several times. '*Instead*, I thanked him and smiled back. Invited the bastard and his wife to my quarters the next night for bridge. Now that I knew what he was capable of, I felt I needed to protect Barbara. And Pam – she was only a baby herself. But on the sly, I began checking the others who'd been injected. Most looked fine, but a few of the adults weren't feeling well – vague malaise, low-grade fevers. Then some of the children began spiking *high* fevers.'

He dug a nail into his temple. 'There I was, the kindly doctor, reassuring them. Dispensing analgesics and ordering them to drink as much as they could in the hope some of the toxins would be flushed out. But unable to tell them the *truth* – what good would it have done? What curse is worse than knowing your own death is near? Then *another* child died suddenly of a brain seizure. Another family supposedly flown out overnight, and this time Hoffman informed me my involvement with the paradise needle was terminated, I was to attend to all base personnel *except* the vaccinated families. *New* doctors had arrived for them, three whitecoats from Washington. When I protested, Hoffman ordered me to begin a new project: reviewing twenty years of medical files and writing a detailed report. Busy-work.'

'Sounds familiar.'

He smiled weakly. 'Yes, I'm a horrid sneak; being direct has always been difficult for me. I used to rationalize it as the result of growing up an only child in a very big house. One wanders about alone, acquires a taste for games and intrigue. But perhaps it's just a character flaw.'

'What happened to the rest of the vaccinated patients?' said Robin.

'More were growing ill, and rumors had finally gotten out on the base about some kind of mysterious epidemic. Too much to keep secret, so the doctors from Washington issued an official memo: an unknown island organism had infiltrated Stanton, and strict quarantine was imposed. The sick people were all isolated in the infirmary, and quarantine signs were nailed to the doors. Understandably, everyone gave the place a wide berth. Then I heard a rumor that all the vaccinated families would be shipped back to the Walter Reed Hospital in Washington for evaluation and treatment. I had a pretty good idea what that meant.'

He pulled down on his cheeks.

'I sneaked over to the infirmary one night after midnight. One attendant was on guard at the front door, smoking, not taking the job seriously. Which was typical of the base. Nothing ever happened here. Everyone had a slipshod attitude. I managed to sneak in through a rear door, using a skeleton key I'd lifted from Hoffman's office. The smug bastard hadn't even bothered to put on a new lock.'

Reaching out, he grabbed the grapefruit, clawing so hard juice flowed through his fingers.

'Some of them,' he said, softly, 'were already dead. Lying in cots . . . unconscious, rotting. Others were on the verge of losing consciousness. Sloughed skin was everywhere . . . limbs . . . the room stank of gangrene.'

He began crying, tried to stop, then to hide it. It took a while before he resumed, and then, in a whisper.

'Bed after bed, crammed together like open coffins . . . I could still recognize a few of their faces. No attempt was being made to treat them – no food or medication or I.V. lines. They were being *stored*.'

The grapefruit, a mess of pulp and rind.

'The last ward was the worst: dozens of dead children. Then, a miracle: some of the babies were still alive and looking relatively healthy. Dermal lesions, malnutrition, but conscious and breathing well – their little eyes *followed* me as I stood over their layettes . . . I counted. Nine.'

He stood again and circled the room unsteadily.

'I still don't understand it. Perhaps the relatively low dosage had protected them, or something in their newborn immune systems. Or maybe there is a God.'

Wringing his hands, he walked to the refrigerators and faced a copper-colored Kenmore.

'Sometimes it's good to be a sneak. I got them out. Four the first time, five the second. Swaddled in blankets so their cries would be muffled, but it wasn't necessary. They *couldn't* cry. All that came out was *croaking*.'

Facing us.

'The vaccine, you see, had burned their vocal cords.'

He picked up his pace, stalking an invisible victim.

'I had no place to take them but the forest. Thank God it was winter. Winter here is kind, warm temperatures, dry. I'd discovered the caves hiking. Had always liked caves.' Smile. 'Secretive places. Used to spelunk when I was at Stanford, did a senior thesis on bats . . . I didn't think anyone else knew of them, and there was nowhere else to go.'

'What about the land mines?' I said.

He smiled. 'The Japanese had plans to lay mines, but they never quite got around to it.'

'The night of the knives?'

He nodded.

'You spread the rumor?' I said.

'I planted the seed. When it comes to rumors, there's never a shortage of gardeners . . . where was I? . . . I placed them in a cave. Not this one, I didn't know about this one. Or the tunnel. Once they were secreted, I checked them over, cleared them up, gave them water and electrolytes, returned to the infirmary, disassembled their layettes, scattering the parts in the hope they wouldn't be missed. And they weren't. The entire place was a charnel house, corpses and dying people had slid onto the floor, lying on top of one another, body fluids dripping. I'll never forget the sound. Even now, when it drizzles . . .'

His face took on that absent look and for a moment I thought he'd slip somewhere else. But he started talking again, louder:

'Then, a complication: one of the adults had survived, too. A man. As I was finishing with the layettes he came in, reaching for me, *falling* on me. I nearly died of fright – he was . . . putrid. I knew who he was. Aircraft mechanic, huge fellow, enormously strong. Perhaps that's why the symptoms hadn't take him over as rapidly. Which isn't to say he wasn't gravely ill. His skin was pure white – as if bleached, one arm gone, no teeth, no hair. But able to stagger. He hadn't been a good man. A bully, really, with a vicious temper. I'd patched up men he'd beaten. I was worried he'd have enough strength to somehow set off an alarm, so I dragged him out too. It nearly killed me. Even starved, he must have weighed a hundred and eighty pounds. It took so long to get him across the base, I was sure some sentry would see me. But I finally made it.

'I put him in another cave, away from the babies, and tended to him as best I could. He was shaking with chills, skin starting to slough. Trying to talk and growing enraged at his inability . . . He kept looking at the stump where his arm had been and screaming – a silent scream. *Rabid* anger. His eyes were wild. Even in that condition, he frightened me. But I calculated it would only be hours.'

Lurching toward a chair, he sat.

'I was wrong. He lasted five days, fluctuating between stupor and agitation. He'd actually get up and lurch around the cave, injuring himself horribly but remaining on his feet. His premorbid strength must have been superhuman. It was on the fifth day that he managed to escape. I'd been at the base, got back that night and he wasn't there. At first I panicked, thinking someone had discovered everything, but the babies were still in their cave. I finally found him lying under one of the banyans, semiconscious. I dragged him back. He died two hours later.'

'But not before Joseph Cristobal saw him,' I said.

He nodded. 'The next day, Gladys came to my office and told me about Joe. One of the other workers at the estate had told her Joe had a fit, claimed to have seen some kind of forest devil.'

'A Tutalo.'

'No,' he smiled. 'I made that up, too. *Tootali* is the old word for "grub," but there's no myth.'

'Planting the seed,' I said. 'So Joe's story wasn't taken seriously?'

'Joe had always been odd. Withdrawn, talked to himself, especially when he drank. What concerned me were his chest pains. They sounded suspiciously like angina, but with anxiety, it was hard to know. As it turned out, his arteries *were* in terrible shape. There was nothing I could have done.'

'You're saying the sighting had nothing to do with his death?'

'Perhaps,' he said, 'his condition was complicated by fright.'

'Did you let him go on believing there *were* monsters?'

He blinked. 'When I tried to discuss it with him, he covered his ears. Very stubborn man. Very rigid ideation – not schizophrenic, but perhaps schizoid?'

I didn't answer.

'What should I have done, son? Told him he'd really seen something and endanger the babies? *They* were my priority. Every spare moment was spent with them. Checking on them, bringing blankets, food, medicine. Holding them in my arms . . . Despite everything I did, two of them got progressively worse. But every night that passed without one of them dying was a victory. Barbara kept asking me what was wrong. Each night I left her . . . a light dose of sleeping medicine in her bedside water helped . . . shuttling back and forth, never knowing what I'd find when I got there. Do you understand?'

'Yes,' I said, 'but all these years, they haven't come above-ground?'

'Not unsupervised they haven't. They need to stay out of the sunlight – extreme photosensitivity. Similar to what you see in some porphyric patients, but they have no porphyria and I've never been able to diagnose, never been able to find out what they were gi – where was I?'

Looking baffled.

'Shuttling back and forth,' said Robin.

'Ah, yes – after a week or so it finally got to me. I fell asleep at my desk, only to be shaken awake by a loud roar. I knew the sound well: a large plane taking off. Seconds later, there was a tremendous explosion. A Navy transport had gone down over the ocean. Something about the fuel tanks.'

The 1963 crash. Hoffman ordering Gladys to prepare coquille St Jacques that night. Celebrating . . .

'With the quarantined patients on board,' I said. 'Eliminating any witnesses.'

'The doctors from Washington, as well,' said Moreland. 'Plus three sailors who'd guarded the infirmary assigned as flight attendants, and two medics.'

'My God,' said Robin.

'The patients would have died anyway,' said Moreland. 'Most probably *were* dead when they loaded them on – an airborne hearse. But the doctors and the medics and the flight crew were sacrifices – all in the name of God and country, eh?'

'Why weren't you eliminated?' said Robin.

He put his hands together and studied the table.

'I've thought about that many times. I suppose it was because I bought myself some insurance. The day of the crash, I invited Hoffman over for drinks in my quarters. No wives, just us fellas in our snappy dress whites, veddy dry martinis – back then I was still indulging. As he picked pimiento out of his olive, I told him I knew exactly what he'd done and had made a detailed written record that I'd filed somewhere very safe with instructions to make it public if anything happened to me or any member of my family. That I was willing to forget the whole thing and move on if he was.'

'He bought that?'

'It was a theatrical little stunt, I got the idea from one of those stupid detective shows Barbara used to watch. But apparently, it did the trick. He smiled and said, "Bill, your imagination's been working overtime. Pour me another one." Then he drank up and left. For months I slept with a gun under my pillow – dreadful thing, I still hate them. But he never moved against me. The way I see it, he decided to deal because he believed me and felt it was the easy way out. Evil people have little trouble believing everyone else lacks integrity. The next day, a sailor delivered a sealed envelope to my quarters: discharge papers, three months early, and the deed to the estate. *Excellent* price, including all the furniture. The Navy moved us in, and we were provided with a year of free electricity and water. The pretense continued. Even our *bridge* games continued.'

'Along with his cheating,' I said.

'His cheating *and* my pretending not to know. That's as apt a metaphor for civilization as any, isn't it?'

He gave an unsettling laugh.

'Meanwhile, my real life continued at night, and any other time I could get away without attracting too much notice. I hadn't discovered the tunnel yet, and I hid a ladder so I could climb the wall. The two babies who'd deteriorated passed away, as did another. The first was a little girl named Emma – hers was the only name I actually knew, because I'd treated her as a newborn for herniated umbilicus. Her father had made jokes about how she'd look in a bikini and I told him that should be his biggest problem . . .'

He looked ready to cry again, managed to blink it away.

'She died of malnutrition. I buried her and conducted a funeral service as best I could. A month later, a second little girl left me. Bone marrow disease. Then a little boy, from pneumonia that wouldn't respond to antibiotics. The other six survived. You've just met them.'

'What's their health status?' I said. 'Physically and mentally?'

'None of them have normal intelligence, and they have no speech. I taught myself the rudiments of IQ testing, administered the nonverbal components of the Wechsler tests and the Leiter. They seem to fall in the fifty-to-sixty range, though Jimmy and

Eddy are a bit brighter. Their nervous systems are grossly abnormal: seizures, motor imbalance, sensory deficits, altered reflexes. Poor muscle tone, even when I can get them to exercise. Then there's the photosensitivity – the slightest bit of UV exposure eats up their skin. Even living down here hasn't managed to protect them completely. You saw their eyes, ears, fingers. Extensive fibrosing, probably something autoimmune – the actual process isn't unlike leprosy. They're not in danger of imminent wasting, but the erosion continues steadily. They're sterile – a blessing, I suppose. Not much libido, either. *That's* made my life easier.'

'I still don't see how you've managed to keep them down here all these years.'

'At first it was difficult, son. I had to . . . confine them. Now it's not a serious problem. They may not be normal, but they've learned what the sun does to them. Half an hour outside and they're in pain for days. I've made every effort to provide them with as rich a life as possible. Here, let me show you.'

He took us to an adjoining room, slightly smaller than the dining area. Beanbag chairs and homemade cases full of toys and picture books. A phonograph connected to a battery pack. Next to it, a stack of old 45s. The top one: Burl Ives singing children's songs. 'Jimmy Crack Corn' . . . A model train set in disarray on the shag carpet. Some of the soft people sat on the floor fooling with the tracks. Others reclined on the chairs, fingering dolls.

They greeted him with smiles and raspy cries. He went to each of them, whispered in their ears, hugged and patted and tickled.

When he turned to leave, one of them – the larger woman – took hold of his hand and tugged.

He pulled back. She resisted.

Giggles all around. A familiar game.

Finally, Moreland tickled her under the arm and she gave a silent, wide-mouthed laugh and let go, tumbling backward. Moreland caught her, kissed the top of her head, pulled a Barbie doll out of the case and gave it to her.

'Look, Suzy: *Movie* Star Barbie. Look at this beautiful, fancy *dress*.'

The woman turned the figurine, suddenly engrossed. Her features were saurine but her eyes were warm.

'Be right back, kids,' said Moreland.

We left the room and walked down a narrow stone passage.

'How often do you come down here?' I asked.

'Optimally, two to five times a day. Less frequent than that and things get out of hand.' His thin shoulders sagged.

'It sounds impossible,' said Robin.

'It's . . . a challenge. But I keep my other obligations to a minimum.'

Virtually no sleep.

No wife.

Sending his own daughter away as a toddler.

Allowing the island to decay . . . his one recreation the insects. A small world he could control.

Studying predators in order to forget about victims.

We came to a third room: six portable chemical toilets and two sinks attached to large water tanks outfitted with sterilization kits. A cloth partition halved the space. Three latrines and one basin on each side. Cutouts of men pasted on the stalls to the left, women to the right.

A strong wave of disinfectant.

Moreland said, 'I've toilet trained each of them. It took some time, but they're quite dependable now.'

Next were the sleeping quarters – three smaller caves, each with two beds. More books and toys. Piles of dirty clothes on the floor.

'We still have a ways to go on neatness.'

'Who does their laundry?' said Robin.

'We handwash, everything's cotton. They enjoy laundry time, I've turned it into a game. The clothes are old but good. Brooks Brothers and similar quality, brought in years ago on several boatloads. I couldn't order too much at a time, didn't want to attract attention . . . Come, come, there's more.'

He led us back into the passageway. It narrowed and we had to turn sideways. At the end was another webbed door. He saw me looking at it.

'Japanese ironwork. Beautiful, isn't it?'

On the other side was an exit ramp, descending steeply, its terminus out of view. The door was fastened with an enormous lock.

The soft people confined forever.

Moreland produced a key, rammed it into the lock, pushed the door open, and the three of us walked to the bottom of the ramp.

'Sometimes, when it's very dark and I can be sure they'll behave themselves, I take them up to the forest for nighttime picnics. Moonlight is kind to them. They love their picnic time. Mentally they're children, but their bodies are aging prematurely. Arthritis, bursitis, scoliosis, osteoporosis, cataracts. One of the boys has developed significant atherosclerosis. I treat him with anticoagulants, but it's a bit tricky because he bruises so easily.'

He stopped. Stared at us.

'I've learned more about medicine than I ever believed possible.'

'Do you have any idea of their life expectancy?' said Robin.

Moreland shrugged. 'It's difficult to say. They're deteriorating, but they've survived so many crises, who knows? With good care, all or most of them will probably outlive me.'

He leaned against the wall. 'And that is the issue. That's why I must arrange something for them.'

'Why haven't you gone public and gotten them care?' she said.

'What would that accomplish, dear? Subjecting them to the scrutiny of scientists and *doctors*? Scientists condemned them to this life. How long would they last out in the monstrosity we call the real world? No, I couldn't allow that to happen.'

'But surely they—'

'They'd wither and die, dear,' said Moreland, straining for patience.

He reached for the open door and took hold of one of the bars. 'What they need is *continuity*. A transfer of care.'

His eyes moved from Robin to me. Studying. Waiting.

I could hear music from the game room. A scratchy record. *Lou, Lou, Skip to My Lou.*

He said, 'I want you to be their guardians once I'm gone.'

'I'm not a physician,' I said. As if that was the only reason.

'I can teach you what you need to know. It's not that difficult, believe me. I've been composing a manual . . .'

'You just pointed out how tricky it—'

'You can *learn,* son. You're a smart man.'

Raising his voice. When I didn't answer, he turned to Robin.

'Bill,' she said.

'Hear me out,' he said. 'Don't close your minds. Please.'

'But why me?' I said. 'Give me the real answer, this time.'

'I already have – your dedication to—'

'You don't even *know* me.'

'I know enough. I've *studied* you! And now that I've met Robin, I'm even more convinced. With two people, sharing the challenge, it would be—'

'How did you really find me, Bill?'

'Coincidence. Or fate. Choose your nomenclature. I was in Hawaii taking care of some legal matters with Al Landau. My hotel delivered the daily paper. Despite my aversion to what passes for news, I skimmed it. The usual corruption and distortions, then I came across an article about a case in California. A little girl in a hospital, poisoned to simulate illness. You helped bring the matter to resolution. References were made to other cases you'd been involved in – abused children, murders, various outrages. You sounded like an interesting fellow. I researched you and learned you were a serious scholar.'

'Bill—'

'Please, son, listen: intellectual vigor and humanity don't always go together. One can be an A student but a D person. And you have *drive*. I need someone with *drive.* And *you*, dear. You're his soulmate in every way.'

I tried to find words. The look on his face said no language existed that would work.

'Mind you, I'm not proposing a one-way deal. Care for my kids properly, and the entire estate and all my other property holdings on Aruk will be yours, in addition to excellent real estate in Hawaii and California, securities, a bit of cash. What I told you about my family fortune dwindling was true, but it's still substantial. Of course, I'll have to give a generous inheritance to Pam as well as some stipends to trusted individuals, but the rest would be yours. Once the kids are all gone. You can see why I need someone with integrity. Someone who wouldn't kill them to get to the money. I now trust you – both of you. When your duties are through, you'll be wealthy and free to enjoy your wealth in any way that pleases you.'

Robin said, 'Pam's a doctor. Why don't you want her to take over?'

He shook his head so vigorously his glasses fell off his nose.

Retrieving them, he said, 'Pam's a wonderful girl, but not equipped. She has . . . vulnerabilities. My fault. I don't deserve the title "father." She needs to get out in the world. To find someone who values her – the kind of relationship you two have. But you *will* have assistance. From Ben.'

'Ben knows?'

'I let him into my confidence five years ago. The kids have come to adore him. He's been a tremendous help, taking shifts as my strength ebbs.'

'You don't want him to take over?' said Robin.

'I considered it, but he has his own family. My kids need full-time parents.'

Single-minded, isolated parents. As he'd been after Barbara died and Pam was sent away.

What he wanted was *philosophical cloning.* I felt stunned and sick.

'Ben will continue to pitch in,' he said. 'Between the three of you the task is do-able.'

'Ben's in no position to help anyone,' I said.

'He will be once we get past this nonsense. Al Landau's brilliant, especially when defending an innocent man. *Please*. Accept my offer. I've taken you into my confidence. I'm at the mercy of your good graces.'

He picked up Robin's hand and held it in both of his.

'A woman's touch,' he said. 'It would be so good for them.'

Smiling. 'Now you know everything.'

'Do we?' I said.

He let go of her hand. 'What's the problem, son?'

'The written report you threatened Hoffman with. Does it exist?'

'Of course.'

'Where is it?'

He blinked hard. 'In a safe place. If we progress, you'll know the precise location.'

'And you want us to believe it's the only reason he let you live all these years.'

He thumbed his chest and smiled. 'I'm here, am I not?'

'I think there's more, Bill. I think Hoffman's always known you wouldn't expose him because he's got something on *you*.'

The smile evaporated. He took a step up the ramp and ran his hand over the rough stone wall.

'My guess is the two of you are locked together,' I went on. 'Like rams, with tangled horns. Hoffman can't move in and destroy Aruk overnight because you might expose him. But he's still able to grind the island down gradually because he's younger than you, confident he'll survive you and eventually have his way. And I'll bet controlling Aruk's important to him on two levels: the money from the development project, *and* he wants to erase what he did thirty years ago from his mind.'

'No, no, you're giving him way too much credit. He's got no conscience. He simply wants to exploit for profit.' He turned around suddenly. 'You have no idea what he has in mind for Aruk.'

'A penal colony like Devil's Island?'

His mouth stayed open and he managed to work it into another smile. 'Very good. How did you figure it out?'

'He's in with Stasher-Layman, and in addition to instant slums they build prisons. Aruk's location is perfect. The dregs of society shipped and warehoused far, far away, with nowhere to escape.'

'Very good,' he repeated. 'Very, very good. The bastard told me the details that night at dinner. He wants to call it "Paradise Island." Clever, eh? But there's more: the waters surrounding Aruk will be used to sink other dregs: barrels of radioactive waste. He's confident of receiving environmental clearance because of Aruk's obscurity and because once the economy shuts down completely and the island's depopulated, there'll be no one to protest.'

'Nuclear dumpsite,' I said. 'Perfect complement to the prison: toxic water's another escape deterrent. If Hoffman pulls it off, he manages to fight crime and pollution on the mainland and pocket big cash payoffs from Stasher-Layman. Cute.'

'"Cute" is not an adjective I'd apply to him.'

Different music drifted from the game room. A woman singing, *This old man, he plays two . . .*

'When did you first suspect he was involved?'

'When the Navy started treating us differently. Ewing's predecessor was no saint but he was civil. Ewing has the demeanor of an assassin – did you know he was sent here as punishment for lewd behavior? Tied a woman down and took photographs . . . . From the moment I met him, I knew he'd been sent to punish *Aruk*. And that Hoffman had to be behind it. Who else even knew about the place? I wrote to him, he never answered. Then Ben caught Creedman snooping in my files and I asked Al Landau to do some research. He learned the skunk had worked for Stasher-Layman and what they were all about. But I had no idea it was a dumpsite till Hoffman bragged about it after dinner. Apologizing for not answering, he'd been *so* busy. Then that same *smile*.'

'Were your letters threatening?' I said.

'Poo! Give me credit, son. I was discreet. Nuances, not threats.'

'Nuances that he ignored.'

'He said he hadn't wanted to put anything in writing. That's why he'd come personally.'

'Why'd he invite all of us to dinner?'

'For cover. But you notice that he got me alone. That's when he boasted and made his offer.'

'To buy you out?'

'At a laughable price. I refused and reminded him of my little diary.'

'What did he say?'

'He simply smiled.'

'If he's worried about the diary, why can't you get him to stop the project?'

'I – we negotiated. He pointed out that stopping completely would be impractical. Things have gone too far. To reverse what's already been done would call attention to Aruk.'

'And you agreed to consider it because of the kids.'

'Exactly! Though the bastard thinks it's my own lifestyle I don't want jeopardized.' He grimaced. 'You're right, he and I are stalemated: he doesn't want publicity and neither do I. My only goal is to let my kids live out their lives in peace – how long do they *really* have? Five years, maybe six or seven. Hoffman's project will take years to complete even under the best of circumstances – you know the government. So hopefully, he and I can achieve some sort of compromise. I'll sell off token bits of land to the government, take my time, delay things without seeming unduly obdurate.'

'The Trading Post, and your other waterfront holdings.'

He nodded. 'And the money will be set aside for you two.'

'A compromise,' I said. 'As you both let Aruk die.'

He sighed. 'Aruk's been good to me, but I'm an old man and I know my limitations. Priorities must be set. What I've demanded from Hoffman was to slow things *down*.'

'Did he agree?'

'He didn't refuse.'

'The man coldbloodedly murdered six dozen people. Why would he give in to you?'

'Because of my insurance.'

'I still don't understand why, if you can ruin him, you don't have more power.'

He scratched the tip of his nose. 'I've told you everything, son.'

He reached out to pat my shoulder and I backed away.

'No, I don't think so,' I said. 'When you returned from talking to him you looked shellshocked. Not like someone who'd negotiated a compromise. Hoffman reminded *you* about something, didn't he?'

No answer.

'What's he holding over you, Bill?'

He stepped further into the ramp.

'First things first,' he said. 'My offer.'

'First answer my question?'

'These things are irrelevant!'

'Honesty's irrelevant? Oh, I forgot, the truth is relative.'

'Truth is *justice*! Getting into irrelevant areas that bring about injustice is *deceitful*!'

This old man, he plays ten . . .

'All right,' I said. 'You're entitled to your privacy.'

I looked at Robin. She cocked her head very slightly, toward the cavern.

'Goodbye, Bill.'

He held me back. 'Please! Everything in due time! Please be patient!'

His crinkled chin shook so hard his teeth knocked. 'I'll tell you everything when the time's right, but first I must have your commitment. I believe I've earned it! What I'm offering you would enrich your lives!'

'We can't give you an answer just like that.'

He climbed further up the ramp. 'Meaning you think I'm mad and your answer is no.'

'Let's get back and clear our heads. You, too. Pam needs to know you're safe.'

'No, no, this isn't right, son. Leaving an old man in the lurch after I've . . . flayed my soul open for you!'

'I'm sorry—'

He clutched my arm. '*Why not just agree?* You're young, robust, so many years ahead of you! Think of what you can do with all that wealth.' His eyes brightened. 'Perhaps *you* could figure out a way to save Aruk! Think of the meaning *that* would bring to your lives! What else *is* there to life but finding some kind of meaning?'

I removed his fingers from my arm. The record in the game room had caught. The old man playing ten, over and over . . .

'I was wrong,' he said, behind me. 'You're not the compassionate boy I thought you were.'

'I'm not a boy,' I said. 'And I'm not your son.'

The retort bursting out of me, the same way it had out of Dennis Laurent.

The look on his face . . . I *felt* like a bad son.

A maddening man.

Mad or on the brink of it.

'No, you're not,' he whispered. 'Indeed, you're not.'

Robin took my hand and we both left the ramp. Moreland watched us, not budging.

After we'd gone a few steps, he turned his back on us.

Robin stopped, tears in her eyes.

'Bill,' she said, just as sound came from the top of the ramp.

Moreland looked up and almost lost his balance.

Another noise – hollow, metallic – came from above, just as he straightened.

Then rapid, muffled footsteps.

Two figures in black rain slickers barreled down the ramp. One grabbed Moreland. The other stopped for a fraction of a second, then came toward us.

Glossy wet slickers, galoshes. All that rubber buffed brighter by moisture.

Like giant seals.

Anders Haygood splashed water on us as he waved the automatic.

36

His heavy face was calm, the lower half shadowed by stubble. Wide mouth set, gray eyes as dead as pebbles.

'Against the wall.' Practiced boredom. Ex-cop's familiarity with rousting suspects.

He frisked me, then Robin. She gave out a high-pitched sound of surprise. Not reacting was agonizing.

From where I was standing I could see Tom Creedman with his grip on Moreland. From the way his fingers hooked, it must have hurt, but Moreland wasn't showing it. Staring at Creedman, as if trying to snag his eyes. Creedman's face was rain specked and sweating, his gun jammed against Moreland's rib cage.

'The boys from Maryland,' I said. 'Off on a South Seas lark.'

Creedman's black mustache arced in surprise. Haygood flipped me around with a surprisingly light touch. His cleft chin looked rough enough to hone a blade.

I smiled. 'Why'd you pull me over, officer?'

A muscle in his cheek jumped.

He put his gun against my heart and chucked Robin's chin. His hand dropped lazily onto her chest. Brushing. Squeezing.

Robin's eyes closed. Haygood continued to touch her, studying me.

I looked at Creedman. The water rolling off the top of his hat and into his eyes. He flinched, and Haygood finally let go of Robin.

'Never met a cannibal before,' I said. 'Who did the surgery? Or was it both of you?'

'Fuck off,' said Creedman.

Haygood said, 'Chill,' but it was unclear who he was addressing.

Creedman frowned but shut up.

The rain, louder; they'd opened some kind of hatch aboveground. Found the tunnel with the help of all the doors I'd had to leave open. The slab sticking out of the laboratory floor.

They'd probably climbed down and walked some distance before figuring out where it led. Unable to broach the webbed door, they'd retraced their steps, made it over the wall, and come in from the other end.

The rain blocked out the music from the game room. I could still hear the nagging drone of the generator.

'The boys from Maryland,' I repeated. 'Reporter buys information from cop on a murder case, gets them both fired. Reporter finds a job with Stasher-Layman and procures cop a position there, too. Must be a close friendship.'

Creedman wanted to say something, but a look from Haygood silenced him. Haygood the pro . . . he kept his gun steady while exmaining the cavern with all the passion of a camera.

'You've done lots of cute things for the company,' I said, 'so now you get a sun-and-fun assignment. But does the home office have any idea you handled it by replicating the murder that got you into trouble in the first place? Slicing up women and pretending to *eat* them? Or maybe you *didn't* pretend. You did say you were a gourment cook, Tom.'

'What is this?' said Haygood. 'A bomb shelter or something?'

'If I know about Maryland, don't you think others do?'

Creedman looked at Haygood.

Haygood continued to inspect the cavern.

'What they don't know,' I said, 'is the part of it that's wishful thinking, Tom. Telling me it was a rape-murder when it wasn't. A few problems in the *potency* area?'

Creedman turned red and tightened his grip on Moreland.

Haygood repeated, 'A bomb shelter?'

'Japanese supply tunnel,' said Moreland. 'My little sanctuary.'

Keeping his eyes away from the game room.

'What do you have down here?'

'Old furniture, clothes, a few books.'

'Let's take a look.'

'There's nothing interesting, Anders.'

'Let's take a look, anyway.' Haygood waved us forward with the gun and told Creedman: 'Bring him over.'

Creedman poked Moreland and the old man tripped forward.

'You two, out,' said Haygood, when they'd passed. He looked down the narrow opening and frowned. 'Don't surprise me, doctor. You go in front, Tom. Anything happens, kill the girl.'

Creedman didn't argue. I'd have pegged him as the one in charge. Class snobbery. Haygood's police experience gave him the edge.

I thought back to the day we'd arrived. Haygood on the dock, butchering the shark with quiet authority.

Haygood and Skip Amalfi.

Was Skip just a cover, allowing Haygood to come across as the aimless beachbum? All along, Haygood's attitude toward him had been a mixture of patience and contempt. Watching, amused, as Skip peed on the sand. Remaining in the background as Skip harangued the villagers.

Tolerating him the way you tolerate a dull sibling.

Skip, stupid enough to get sucked into a fantasy of running a resort. The dream probably planted by Haygood.

Skip peeing in front of women . . . Had he also been involved in the cannibal murders? Probably not; too unstable.

But he *had* served his purpose the night of Betty Aguilar's killing: fishing on the docks, as Haygood knew he did most every night. There to hear Bernardo Rijks's cries of alarm, rushing over to subdue Ben.

Haygood and Creedman had murdered both girls. First AnneMarie Valdos on the beach, a rehearsal for Betty and setting up Ben. And the stimulus to local unrest that had justified the blockade.

Then, Betty in Victory Park – what had they used to lure her? Dope? Money? One last fling before motherhood?

Cutting her throat and carrying out the mutilation. Drawing Ben out with a bogus emergency call, then choking him out, pouring vodka down his throat, and positioning him with the corpse.

An ex-cop would know how to pull off a perfect choke hold.

An ex-cop would know about positioning corpses.

The park because it was secluded and a common spot for partying. And because Rijks the insomniac walked by every night.

Even if Rijks hadn't heard the moans, he could have been led to it by a night-strolling Creedman. Not as neat, but no reason for anyone to catch on.

Because Ben came from trash and Betty had been promiscuous.

Ben lying asleep on the carnage. An absurd alibi.

Skip's outrage, genuine. Hostile to Moreland because his father resented the old man, he'd eagerly whipped up the villagers' anger.

Framing Ben had killed three birds with one stone: damaging Moreland irreparably, getting rid of his protégé, and causing another deep rip in Aruk's social fabric.

Hastening the exodus from the island.

Hoffman's and Stasher-Layman's war of attrition. Perhaps Hoffman had decided to speed things up after coming face to face with the old man, his stubbornness . . .

Believing Moreland cared about the island, when all he really wanted was a few years of peace for the *kids*.

Moreland willing to do anything to prevent Hoffman from finding out about the kids. Willing to let Aruk die, buying time.

The two of them circling like wrestlers, waiting for an opening.

Still, the same thing bothered me: if Moreland had that kind of power over Hoffman, why not bargain harder?

Creedman stepped in front of me. 'Stay back.' The thin mustache was beaded with perspiration.

'Sure, Tom. But when this is over, share some gourmet recipes with me. How about *girl* bourguignon?'

Creedman's nostrils opened. From behind, Haygood cleared his throat and Creedman grabbed Moreland and cuffed him through the passage. Then he turned sideways and squeezed in himself. When he was several paces ahead of us, Haygood cupped Robin's buttock, squeezed, and shoved.

'Go, babe.'

Then the heel of his hand hit me in the lower back.

We filed out. When the passage widened, Creedman stopped and Haygood herded us into the center. The dead eyes shifted as he heard something.

Music from the game room. The broken record removed. Something new asserting itself above the generator.

The wheels on the bus go round and round . . .

'What the . . .?' said Creedman.

The game room was less than thirty feet away, the door partially open.

Haygood said, 'What's with the music?'

'I like music,' said Moreland. 'As I said, it's my refuge.'

'Kiddie music?' said Creedman. 'You *are* one buggy old fart.' His eyes brightened: 'Do you bring little girls down here to play?'

Moreland blinked. 'Hardly.'

'*Hardly*,' Creedman imitated. 'Maybe you bring kiddies down here to play *doctor*.'

The doors on the bus go open and shut . . .

'Projection,' said Moreland.

'What's that?'

'A Freudian term. Projecting one's own impulses onto someone else. That's what you just did, Tom.'

'Oh, fuck off, you self-righteous bag of shit.' To us: 'Bet you didn't know Dr *Bill* here was once the ace pussy-hound of the U.S. Navy. Big-time stud, chased everything in a skirt, the younger the better. Remember those days, Dr *Bill*? Chasing and bagging, dark meat, light meat, *any* kind of meat? Just couldn't control your pecker, could you? Drove poor *Mrs* Bill to one-way surfing.'

Moreland said nothing, did nothing. That blank look . . .

'Turned herself to shark chum,' said Creedman, 'because Dr *Bill* here couldn't stop playing doctor with the local pussy. Nice advantage, that M.D. Knock some little thing up, do your own abortion—'

'Unlike you,' I said. 'Assault with a dead weapon.'

Creedman snarled. Haygood clicked his tongue and said, 'Check out all these doors.'

'Maybe *you* should,' said Creedman. 'You're the expert.'

Haygood shrugged and pushed Robin, Moreland, and me close together. Backing away, he said, 'Not the stomach, the head,' and Creedman raised his gun till it was half a foot from Robin's right eye.

'Any problems,' he said, 'I want to see her brains on the wall.'

He stepped back some more, pausing a few feet from the entrance to the latrine, then flattening himself against the wall the way cops do and inching toward the opening, gun first.

Waiting. Looking back at us. Waiting some more.

He peeked in. Took a long, slow look.

The broad face puzzled.

Moving to the next door, just as carefully.

'Wait,' I said. 'It's rigged – that door and the others. He's got it booby-trapped.'

Haygood turned.

'He *is* nuts,' I said. 'Stockpiling food and clothes and survival gear, preparing for the end of the world. I'd let you blow yourself up, but he's rigged enough explosives to turn us all into soup.'

'That so?' said Haygood.

'Tell him, Bill.'

'Nonsense,' said Moreland. 'Utter nonsense.'

Haygood thought a while. 'What doors are you saying are rigged?'

'That one for sure,' I said. 'The room where the music's coming from has a package of dynamite hooked up to the record player. The cable runs into another room. Connected to a generator – listen.'

The drone.

'He's got it set up so if the record arm's lifted, boom. There are probably other traps, too, but that's the one he showed us.'

'Ridiculous,' said Moreland. 'Go take a look, Anders.'

'How about *you* go in there,' Haygood told him. 'Turn off the music while I watch you.'

Moreland blinked. 'I'd rather not.'

'Why not?'

'Because it's silly,' said Moreland.

'Come over here,' said Haygood.

Moreland ignored him.

'Come over here, *piss*ant.'

Moreland closed his eyes and moved his lips silently.

Creedman took hold of his shirt and yanked him forward. 'Move, you crazy asshole!'

Moreland passed within Haygood's reach and Haygood got behind him.

'Go,' he said, shoving the old man.

Moreland stumbled and stopped. 'I'd rather not.'

'Go or I'll kill you, sir.'

'I'd rather—'

'Okay,' said Haygood, smiling at me. 'Thanks for the tip, doc. What else should we know about?'

'I wish I knew.'

The driver on the bus says, 'Move on back . . .'

'Fucking maniac,' said Creedman. 'Let's shoot all of them right now and get the hell out of here, Anders.'

'I don't think so,' said Haygood.

Ordered by his bosses to keep Moreland alive. Till the insurance policy was found . . . Hoffman going along with the stalemate for thirty years, willing to wait a while longer.

Thirty years of silence from Moreland had convinced him the paradise needle had been forgotten. So he'd felt safe in refocusing his energies on Aruk. Wanting to destroy the island, depopulate it, rebuild it in his own image.

Moreland claimed it was simply greed, but I doubted it.

I visualized Hoffman at a D.C. power lunch with the brothers from Stasher-Layman. 'Soft money' changing hands, a discussion of potential sites for a multibillion-dollar project, with Hoffman getting a chunk of the profits.

Storing human garbage along with plutonium and cobalt and strontium.

The need for an isolated spot. A remote place with no political constituency.

Hoffman smiling and coming up with one.

Finding out that Moreland still lived on Aruk, but that the doctor was unable or unwilling to reverse the island's economic problems. The population sliding, the welfare checks coming in regularly; what little commerce there was, dependent upon the Navy base.

Send in the advance team: Creedman, Haygood, the Pickers. Probably others. The goal: hasten the decline and isolate Moreland so that the old man would sell out cheap.

Then Moreland starts writing letters, and the team's told to speed things up.

Creedman and Haygood coming up with a grisly touch – perverse mastery over the case that had ruined their careers. A side benefit: slaking their own hatred for women.

The team . . . Lyman Picker's plane crash an accident or had his big mouth offended the higher-ups?

Haygood, living on Harry Amalfi's airfield, had been in a perfect position to mess with the plane.

Creedman . . . the crash had taken place just after Robin and I finished drinking with him outside the restaurant. Creedman and

Jacqui had both gone inside the restaurant, but after the explosion only Jacqui had come out.

Creedman not bothering because he'd *known.*

Someone else had known, too: Jo, opting out at the last minute. Opting out of the base dinner, too, to plant the roaches. And now she was up there with Pam . . .

'Okay, let's get out of here,' said Haygood, pointing back to the rear ramp.

'Those boxes in the tunnel,' said Creedman. 'There could be something important in them.'

'They could also be rigged. We'll check it out later.'

'I opened a few boxes,' I said. 'All I saw was food and drugs and bottled water. Like I said, he's planning for Armaggedon.'

'Stop being so helpful,' said Creedman. 'It won't do you any good.'

Haygood said, 'Come on, folks. Out.' He might have been guiding a tour.

He turned his back on the music room and began to herd us forward.

'Actually,' I said. 'He does have some kids down here.'

A strangled noise rose from Moreland's throat.

Haygood stopped. 'That so?'

'Right in there.' I pointed to one of the sleeping areas. Haygood's eyes followed. 'Want to see?'

Before he could answer, I shouted, *'Kids! Kids! Kids!'*

Creedman cursed and Haygood's hand tightened around his gun. But he stayed calm and kept his eyes on the sleeping-room entrance.

Nothing happened. Haygood smiled. 'Very funny, sir. Onward.'

Then a small white face appeared in the doorway to the music room. Two others.

Three, four, five, six. All of them, openmouthed and wide-eyed with wonder.

Except the blind one. He was making quick little circles with his hands.

Lesions and scars bright as strip-joint neon.

Haygood's calm finally shaken.

Creedman's face lost its color. 'Oh, shit,' he said, and took his eyes off me. I hit him hard under his nose, grabbed for his gun as he went down, but missed. Shoving Robin out of the way, I threw myself on top of him.

Haygood wheeled around. The soft people began croaking and rasping, looking at Moreland, moaning that burn-victim moan.

Moreland ran toward them. Haygood aimed his gun at the old man's back. The soft people kept coming and Haygood's bafflement gave way to revulsion and fear as he stepped back.

I had Creedman's gun now and was punching blindly at his face.

Haygood charged Moreland, shoved him to the floor, kicked at his head, aimed at me. The soft people were between us. I crouched low. They kept coming at Haygood and he struck out at them wildly as they cowered and moaned. Retreating closer to the door he believed was rigged to blow, he stopped. Trapped, confused.

Brassy hair visible above the throng. I pointed Creedman's gun at it.

But I was an easy target, too, and he raised his gun arm high while fending off the soft people with his free hand.

I shifted sharply to the right, trying to stay clear of the soft people so they wouldn't be caught in the middle.

Haygood lost sight of me, as he shoved and circled.

Moreland got to his feet, hurled himself at Haygood.

Haygood turned reflexively at the movement and fired. Moreland's left arm turned red and he fell.

The people converged upon his prone form. Haygood looked for me, but I was behind him.

I shot him five times.

His black slicker exploded. He stood there for a second. Collapsed.

The soft people were all over Moreland, croaking and moaning as he bled.

Robin was shouting my name and pointing.

Creedman trying to get up, holding his face. Blood gushed through his fingers. One eye was swollen shut and his nose was already blackening.

I put the gun to his forehead. He sank back down.

Robin pressed herself against the wall, staring at me. All the blood.

Moreland struggled to stand, the wounded arm dangling, dripping, the other arm trying to shield the soft people.

They were entranced by Haygood's corpse. Gray skin, eyes really dead now, dull and empty as the shark's. Gaping mouth leaking pink vomitus.

Blood spread from under him, settling in the crevices of the stone floor.

I'd turned him into a sieve.

I felt big as a building, sick to my stomach.

I'd never owned a firearm, never imagined killing anyone.

Robin, being there to see it.

37

Moreland's blood took me away from those thoughts. His sleeve was dyed crimson, and red drops hit the floor with a soft plunk.

He seemed unaware, kept trying to calm his kids.

As Robin ran to him, he said, 'It's all right, dear. Right through the muscle – the latissimus – and I'm leaking not spurting, so the brachial artery's been spared. Probably the basilic vein . . . I'll be fine. Get me a clean shirt from the basket in there and I'll staunch it.'

He smiled down at the smaller of the men who'd met us at the end of the tunnel. 'A little booboo, Eddie. Daddy's going to be just fine. Go help Gordon.' Pointing to the blind man who was up against a wall, grimacing and threshing the air.

'Go, Eddie. Tell him everything's okay.'

The little hunchback obeyed. Robin came back with a plaid shirt and Moreland pressed it against his arm. Smiling at me, he said, 'Wonderful bluff. We're a good team.'

One of the soft women looked at Haygood's body and started to whimper.

'Bad *man*,' said Moreland. 'Bad, bad *man*. All *gone*, Sally. He'll *never* come back.'

Creedman gasped. His face was ballooning. I yanked him to his feet.

'Let's get out of here,' said Robin.

'There's still Jo to consider,' I said. 'Where is she, Tom?'

Creedman stared at me. More shock than defiance, and his eyes were glassy. Had I hit him that hard?

I repeated the question. He cried out in pain, held his head, started to go loose. When I saw his eyes roll back, I propped him up.

Moreland had managed to quiet the soft people and was guiding them back into the game room. Despite the wound he looked revitalized.

'Play some more music, kids. How do the *daddies* on the bus go?'

Silence.

'Come on, now: "The daddies on the bus go . . ."'

'Ee ee ee.'

'Right! *Read read read* – you should read, too. It'll make you smart – go get some books down, Jimmy. Give everyone a book. I'll be right back.'

He smiled, closed the game room door, bolted it.

From inside, the music resumed.

'All right,' he said, eyes full of fear.

'Is there another way out besides the two ramps?' I said.

'I'm afraid not.'

'So either way, we could be walking into something.'

'But we're trapped down here, too,' said Robin. 'The longer we stay down, the more dangerous it gets, and you're still bleeding, Bill.'

'I'll be fine, dear.'

'Taking the rear ramp,' I said, 'will lead us into the forest and zero visibility, so I vote for the tunnel.'

Moreland didn't argue.

I shook Creedman back to consciousness. Holding him by the scruff, I pushed him past the smaller rooms and into the large entry cavern. His weight dragged. The hand I'd pummeled him with was beginning to throb.

'Stay behind me,' I told Robin and Moreland. 'If she's waiting for us at the hatch, Mr Gourmet here will be her first course.'

The return trip seemed a lot quicker, Moreland maintaining a good pace despite his age and his injury. Silent, no attempts to convince us of anything.

The one time our eyes met, his begged.

To let go? Forget about the things he hadn't revealed?

Creedman was limp with dejection, but conscious. He tried to get me to do all the work, and I had to shove him every other step. The silence of the tunnel emptied my head, until I thought of Haygood, perforated.

Remembering what he'd done to AnneMarie and Betty helped . . . the shark, the molding of bleached white jaws nailed over the door.

Trophies. I didn't want one.

Fifty feet from the hatch, I ordered Creedman to stay silent. His face was so bloated that his eyes could barely open, and his nose leaked filmy, blood-streaked mucus.

We reached the astroturfed steps and the open hatch. The lab above was a square yellow sun.

Someone had turned the lights on.

No choice but to go on. Motioning Moreland and Robin back, I propelled Creedman up, one step at a time. His rain boots squeaked but he kept quiet. Then, as we approached the top, he began to struggle.

A sharp jab of the gun in his back stopped him.

Three more steps. We waited.

Quiet from above.

Two more steps. One.

No sign of Jo.

We were in.

The room was just as we'd left it. Except for the doorway to the front office.

A man sat there, bound to a chair, gagged.

Thin, scraggly gray beard, spiked hair.

Carl Sleet. The gardener whose voice had drawn Ben to the park.

His eyes zoomed to Creedman, pupils constricted. His fingers flexed below wrists secured to the chair legs with plastic ties. The kind policemen used. Had Haygood taken care of him first?

But no: Creedman looked as confused as I was.

I stood there trying to figure out what to do next.

Jo's face appeared in the doorway, hands up. No weapon.

'Don't shoot,' she said cheerfully. 'Now, how about I move *my* scumbag out of the way so you can get *your* scumbag through.'

Her gun sat atop the books on Moreland's desk, well out of reach.

She produced something out of nowhere and held it up.

White card in a black leatherette holder, next to a silver badge. Some sort of government seal on the card, but I was too far away to read the small print.

'Where're Robin and Dr Moreland?' she said.

'Waiting for me to give them the okay.'

'I heard shots. Anyone actually hit?'

'Moreland was wounded.'

'I heard six shots. One, then five more.'

I said nothing. She laughed and waved the card. 'Don't worry, it's genuine. Except for the name.'

I stepped closer.

Department of Defense, a numbered division that meant nothing to me. JANE MARCIA BENDIG, SENIOR INVESTIGATOR.

I stood there, gripping Creedman. Wishing I had three more arms and a weapon for each.

'Look, I can understand your being wary,' she said. 'But if I wanted to shoot you, you'd be dead. I *am* a crack shot.'

I didn't respond.

'Okay,' she said. 'I can get in big trouble for this, but would giving you my gun make you feel better?'

'Maybe.'

'Suit yourself.' She stepped back and I managed to keep my gun on Creedman and pocket hers.

'Happy?' she said.

My laugh scared me. 'Ecstatic.'

'Okay, you're the guy in charge now. Why don't you give your friends the word.'

Moreland and Robin came up.

Jo said, 'Looks like that arm needs attention, doctor.'

'I'm fine.'

'Doesn't look fine to me.'

'You're not a physician.'

Carl Sleet made a noise.

'Put a lid on it,' she said, and Sleet obeyed.

Moreland said, *'Carl?'*

'Carl's been naughty,' said Jo. 'Pilfering petty cash, tools, your old surgical kit. Putting cockroaches in people's rooms. When he thinks no one's looking he tends to skulk around places he shouldn't be. I've had my eye on him for some time. Tonight, instead of leaving with the other members of the staff, he stayed in one of the storage sheds. Thought *he* was watching *me*.'

She smiled.

'After I dropped Pam off, I went back and watched him some more. Did you know that you hum when you're bored, Carl? Not advisable when skulking.'

Sleet writhed in the chair.

She turned to me. 'When you and Robin showed up at the bug zoo, he was off in the bushes, watching you. After you went in, he waited then made a call from the lab phone, right here. His pals got over in a jiff – probably waiting down the road, outside the gates. They left him here to stand watch, went into the lab, were gone for a long time, and came back. Then they headed for the walls, and that was the last I saw of them. I decided to take Carl's place. I'd like my gun now, please. I have others in my room, but like I said, I could get in real big trouble.'

I hesitated.

'Pretty please?' she said, in a harder voice.

I handed her the automatic.

'Thanks. I'll take custody of your scumbag now. Producing more plastic ties.

I gave her Creedman, and she bound his wrists behind him and moved him closer to Carl Sleet.

'Carl,' said Moreland, sadly.

Sleet refused to look at him.

'Okay,' said Jo, 'let's get these losers locked up and see to that arm.

'After all these years, Carl,' said Moreland.

'All these years, Carl's been bearing a grudge against you, doc. Or at least that's his excuse – I'm sure the money they paid him didn't hurt.'

'A grudge?' said Moreland.

Sleet still avoided looking at him.

Jo said, 'Something about a cousin who saw a monster and died of a heart attack. Carl says you told the guy he was crazy instead of giving him heart medication.'

'That's not true. His arteries were clogged. Highly advanced athero—'

'You don't have to convince me.' Freeing Sleet's limbs from the chair, she stood him up, placed him face to the wall, and flipped Creedman around in the same position.

'Did Sleet say anything about calling Ben to the park?' I said.

'No.'

I summarized Ben's alibi.

'Well,' she said, 'I'm sure old Carl will be forthcoming when he finds out what it's like to be charged with multiple murder.'

Creedman stiffened, and she said, 'Watch it. Can I assume some of the five shots went into Haygood?'

'All five,' I said.

'Dead? Or did you leave him to bleed down there?'

'Dead.'

'Nothing worse than a bad cop,' she said. 'Even before he got busted in Maryland he was a suspect in some burglaries. He and Mr Creedman have been doing bad things for a long time.'

'Who pays the bills?' I said. 'Stasher-Layman?'

'You won't find their name on any checks. All cash. Mr Creedman here is the bursar. Haygood's really dead, huh?'

Big smile for a split second, then it was gone. Slip of professionalism. Something personal.

Haygood monkeying with the plane.

'Your husband—'

'He wasn't my husband. Though we did have a . . . relationship.'

'Was he also—'

'He was a botanist, just like he said. Keeping me company.'

She frisked Creedman. 'I tried to talk him out of going up in that heap. Traveling with me was always tough for him – okay, let's put these morons somewhere safe and see to that arm. Does the tunnel lead all the way into the forest?'

'Yes,' said Moreland.

'What do you keep down there, Dr M.?'

Moreland didn't answer.

She frowned. 'C'mon, I'm one of the good guys.'

'It's a long story,' I said. 'It's a very long story.'

We moved Sleet and Creedman to the house, locking them in separate basement closets, and put Moreland on a sofa in the front room. Gladys ran in from the kitchen, stared at the bloody sleeve, and put her hand to her mouth.

'He's been shot but it's not serious,' said Jo. 'Tell Pam to bring her medical stuff.'

Gladys ran up the stairs, and Pam came rushing down seconds later, carrying a black bag.

Moreland waved at her from the couch. 'Hello, kitten.'

She supressed a cry, unsnapped the bag, and crouched next to him.

'Oh, Daddy.'

'I'm all right, kitten.'

Pulling scissors from the bag, she began cutting away at the sleeve.

'Clean through the lattisimus. No arterial . . .'

Jo hooked a finger at Robin and me.

As we left, Moreland called out my name.

I stopped.

'Thank you, Alex.' Another beseeching look.

Once in the living room, Jo took an armchair under Barbara Moreland's beautiful, sad face.

'Tell me what's down there,' said Jo.

We did.

She tried to maintain her composure, but each revelation knocked it looser. When we were through, she was pale. 'Unbelievable – six of them, down there all these years?'

'Locked up for their own good,' said Robin.

'Twilight Zone . . . unbelievable. Think he's crazy? I'm asking you professionally now.'

'Obsessive,' I said. 'And a hero of sorts. Everyone else went down on that plane.'

'That plane . . . they like plane crashes, don't they? . . . Must have somehow heard Defense was sending someone here and figured it was Ly. All he wanted to do was see the trees, bring some photos back for his pals. But they assumed *he* was the agent, me the tag-along – top of everything else, they're sexist pigs.'

Cold laugh.

'Six of them,' she said. 'Crazy . . . are they – is there any danger going down there?'

'They're harmless,' said Robin. 'But sick.'

She described some of their physical anomalies.

Jo said. 'And what did he call this toxic injection?'

'The "paradise needle."'

She repeated it. 'Talk about a Christmas gift. For years, we've been watching the financial angles, but this is *gorgeous* – Moreland actually kept records of the injections?'

'So he says.'

Her eyes sparkled. 'These . . . people. They're all retarded?'

'Yes,' I said.

'But not vegetables.'

'No. More like small children.'

'Any way they could testify in court?'

'I don't see how. Apart from mental incompetence, they can't speak. Damaged vocal chords.'

She winced. 'Still . . . just the visual impact – we can video them, get Moreland to list all their problems. A whole other line of evidence. Thank you, Dr M.'

'Are you after Hoffman?' I said. 'Or the entire Stasher-Layman organization?'

She smiled. 'Let's just say we've been working on this for a long time.'

'Major financial angle.'

'The kind of thing that raises everyone's taxes by a couple of bucks but the taxpayers never find out about . . . I've got to go down there and see them with my own eyes. Start documenting. I'm going upstairs to get my camera, then I'd appreciate it if one of you would take me back.'

'I wouldn't approach them without Moreland,' I said. 'Apart from what they just went through, they've got all sorts of physical problems – sensitivities.'

'Such as?'

'He mentioned sunlight, there may be others.'

'What does sunlight do to them?'

'Destroys their skin.'

'My flash isn't UV.'

'At the least, they'll panic when they see you. They've been down there so long, let's hold off till we're sure we can't hurt them.'

She thought. 'All right . . . but I've got to see this. If he's right about the arm only being a flesh wound, he should be able to take me himself.'

She tapped her leg very fast, checked her watch, and stood. 'Let's go see how he's doing.'

'His whole purpose in life all these years has been sheltering them,' said Robin. 'He's not going to use them.'

'I understand the man's got principles. But things change, you have to adapt.'

A strand of hair looped over one eye and she shoved it away. The gun was in her waistband. She ran a finger over the butt. 'Things change quickly.'

38

Moreland's arm was bandaged and it rested on his chest. A thermometer protruded from his mouth.

Pam read it. 'A hundred. Are you comfortable there, Daddy, or should we try to get you up to your bed?'

'This is fine, kitten.' He saw us. 'I used to call her that when she was little.'

Pam's look said it was another lost memory. She snapped her doctor's bag shut.

'How're we doing?' said Jo. I thought of how she'd waited upstairs, knowing we were down there with Creedman and Haygood.

Using us. But I'd just shot a man in the back, and there was no anger left in me.

'I'll survive,' said Moreland. He stole a glance at me.

Jo said, 'I know about what you've got down there, Dr Moreland. Whenever you're ready to show it to me.'

'He's not going anywhere,' said Pam.

'It's something of an emergency. A lot's at stake. Right, doctor?'

Moreland didn't answer.

'What are you talking about?' said Pam.

'It's complicated,' said Jo. 'I think I can help your father in a big way if he can help me.'

'What's going on, Daddy?'

Moreland held out a hand to her and grasped her fingers. 'She's right, it is complicated, kitten. I should get down there—'

'Down *where*?'

Moreland blinked.

Pam said, 'Who's she to tell you what to do, Daddy?'

No answer.

'Who are you, Jo?'

Jo flashed her badge.

Pam stared at it.

'Long story,' said Jo. 'Come with me for a sec.'

She put her arm around Pam just as she'd done a few hours ago. Pam shook her off angrily.

'I'm not leaving him alone.'

'It's . . . fine,' said Moreland. 'Thank you for taking care of me. Go with her. Please. For my sake.'

'I don't *understand*, Daddy.'

'Robin,' said Moreland, 'could you go along and help explain things?'

Robin said, 'Sure.'

'Why can't *you* tell me, Daddy?'

'I will, kitten, all in due time. But right now I need some rest. Go with them. Please, darling.'

The three women left and Moreland beckoned me closer. The rain was hitting the picture windows sharply, like buckshot on metal.

He stared up at me. Chewed his lip. Blinked. 'Your questions down there, about what Hoffman had over me . . . the things Creedman said about me down there. There's some truth to them.'

Moving with difficulty, he faced the back of the sofa.

'I was a different man back then, Alex. Women – *having* them – meant so much to me.'

Forcing himself to face me, he said, 'I've made mistakes. Big ones.'

'I know. Dennis thinks the man who died at sea was his father, but he's wrong.'

He tried to speak, couldn't.

'I'm not judging you, Bill.'

Though the room was dim, I could see dark spots on the white couch. Spots of his blood. His eyes were sunken and dry.

'When did you figure it out?'

'You paid for Dennis's schooling – Ben's too, but Ben gave you something in return. And you got upset about Dennis and Pam getting close. So upset you spoke to Jacqui about it and she called Dennis off. I didn't think you were a racist. Then, after what Creedman said, it made sense. It must have been hard since Pam came back.'

'Oh,' he said, more exhalation than word. 'As a father, I'm a disgrace. They've both turned out better than I deserve. I sent Pamela away because I didn't – couldn't cope after Barbara died.'

Propping himself up.

'No, that's not all of it. I sent her away because of the guilt.'

'About Jacqui?'

'And the others. Many others. I *did* serve as my own abortionist. Barbara had never been a happy woman, I made her miserable.'

He sank back down again.

'The bastard was right, I *was* a repugnant lecher. Lecher with surgical training . . . but Jacqui refused to terminate . . . Barbara's death made me realize . . . how could I hope to raise a daughter?'

'And you already had kids.'

He closed his eyes. 'I put the needle in their arms . . . my life since then's been a quest for redemption, but I doubt I'm redeemable . . . Jacqui was such a *beautiful* thing. Barely eighteen, but mature. I was always . . . hungry – not that it's an excuse, but Barbara was . . . a *lady*. She had . . . different drives.'

A woman alone on the sand, the day before she died.

'It was the baby that drove her to it,' he said. 'The fact that I'd actually let it get that far.'

'How did she find out?'

'Someone told her.'

'Hoffman?'

'Had to be. He and Barbara were chums – bridge partners. A young man paying her attention.'

'So Barbara went along with his cheating.'

He smiled. 'I suppose she can be forgiven that tiny revenge.'

'Did their playing go beyond bridge?'

'I truly don't know – anything's possible. But as I said, Barbara wasn't inclined to the physical . . . toward the end, she hated me fiercely. And she always liked *him* – found his interest in cuisine and tailoring *charming*.'

'Then why did he tell her about Jacqui?'

'To wound me. After our dinner at the base, we spoke of several things. Including the fact that he'd seen Barbara in Honolulu the day before she died. *He* took the picture I showed you. I'd never known. It was mailed from her hotel, compliments of the manager, I'd always thought it a courtesy.'

'Did she go to Honolulu to be with him?'

'He claimed not, that their running into each other was a coincidence. At the hotel bar, he was there on Navy business. Maybe it's true, Barbara did like to drink . . . he told her about Jacqui and Dennis, she cried on his shoulder about my whore and my little bastard. *Shattered*, was his exact word. Then he smiled – *that* smile.'

'But how did *he* find out?'

'Back in those days, I was less than discreet – discretion wasn't part of being a first-rate cocksman. So Hoffman or a member of his staff could easily have heard something, or even seen something. There was an empty hangar on the north end of the base. Little unused offices we officers used, to be with girls from the village. "Play rooms" we called them. Mattresses and liquor and portable radios for mood music. We still thought of ourselves as war heroes – entitled.'

'Did Hoffman bring girls there?'

'Not that I saw. His only lust is for power.'

'And when Jacqui gave birth to a fair-haired baby he figured it out.'

'A beautiful baby – a beautiful woman.'

'Was it only Aruk you fell in love with, Bill?'

He smiled. 'Jacqui and I – she's a very strong woman. Independent. Over the years we've reached an understanding. A fine friendship. I believe it's been good for both of us.'

Thinking of the oil over the mantel, I said, 'Strong – unlike your wife. Did Barbara have a history of depression?'

He nodded. 'She'd been chronically depressed for years, taken shock treatment several times. In fact, the trip to Hawaii was for her to consult yet another psychiatrist. But she never showed up for her appointment. Probably spent her time drinking with Hoffman instead. He sensed her vulnerability, told her what I'd done, and the next morning she walked into the ocean.'

Some of his weight shifted onto the wounded arm and his breath caught. I helped him find a comfortable position.

'So you see, that's the hold he has over me: keeping it secret from Pam. I killed her mother and so did he. In that sense we *are* partners. Rams locking horns, just as you said. Beautiful analogy, my friend – are you offended by my thinking of you as a friend?'

'No, Bill.'

'All these years, I've yearned to expose him. Convinced myself the reason I haven't done it is the kids' safety. Then, tonight, you began asking questions and I was forced to confront reality. I acquiesced because I knew it would ruin Pam. I sent her away because I was overwhelmed and guilty, but also because I didn't want her here on the chance that she and Dennis . . . so what happens? She comes back. And it starts . . .' He grabbed my arm and held tight. 'What do I do? There's no escape.'

'Tell her.'

'How can I?'

'In due time you'll be able to.'

'Men have mistreated her because I abandoned her! She'll despise me!'

'Give her some credit, Bill. She loves you, wants to get closer to you. Being unable to is the biggest source of her pain.'

He covered his face. 'It never ends, does it?'

'She loves you,' I repeated. 'Once she realizes the good things you've done, gets to really know you, she may be willing to pay the price.'

'The price,' he said weakly. 'Everything has its price . . . the microeconomics of existence.'

He looked up at me. 'Is there anything *else* you need to know?'

'Not unless there's something else you want to tell me.'

Long silence. The eyes closed. His lips moved.

Incoherent mumbles.

'What's that, Bill?'

'Terrible things,' he said, barely louder. 'Time deceives.'

'You've made mistakes,' I said, 'but you've also done good.' Ever the shrink.

His face contorted and I took his cold, limp hand.

'Bill?'

'Terrible things,' he repeated.

Then he did sleep.

39

It was a big beautiful room in a big beautiful hotel. One glass wall looked out to white beach and furious surf. Yesterday, I'd seen dolphins leaping.

The three walls were koa panels so densely figured they seemed to tell a story. Crystal chandeliers hung above black granite floors. Up in front was a banquet table laden with papayas and mangoes, bananas and grapes, and thick, wet wedges of the kind of orange-yellow, honey-sweet pineapple you get only when you harvest it ripe.

Sterling silver coffeepots were set every six feet, their shine blue-white.

Other tables, too, round, seating ten, interspersed around the hall. Hundreds of men and a few women, eating and drinking coffee, and listening.

Robin and I watched it on TV, from a suite upstairs. Room service and suntan lotion and every newspaper and magazine we could get our hands on.

'Here he goes,' she said.

Hoffman stood up at the center of the big table, dressed in a mocha suit, white shirt and yellow tie.

A banner at his back.

He talked, paused for applause, smiled.

The banner said: PACIFIC RIM PROGRESS: A NEW DAWN.

Another one-liner. Laughter.

He continued talking and smiling and pausing for applause.

Then he stopped and only smiled.

Something changed in his eyes. A shutter-snap flicker of confusion.

If I hadn't been looking for it, I probably wouldn't have noticed.

If I hadn't been looking for it, I wouldn't have been tuned to C-Span.

The camera left him and swung to the back of the room.

A tall, gaunt old man in a brand-new charcoal-gray suit walked toward the front.

Next to him walked a woman I'd known first as Jo Picker, then as Jane Bendig, official-looking in a navy-blue suit and high-necked white blouse. Fox the last three days she'd worked nearly twenty-four hours a day. The easy part: using Tom Creedman's computer to send bogus messages by e-mail. The hard part: convincing Moreland he could redeem himself.

The doctors and psychologists at the medical center had helped some. Examining the kids with care and compassion, assuring the old man they were clinicians, not technocrats.

Jane shared her grief with him, talked numbers, morality, absolution.

Eventually, she just wore him down.

Now he walked ahead of her.

Behind the two of them, six men in blue suits flanked a massive black thing, like pallbearers.

Black thing with legs, a shuffling variant of the circus horse.

Stirring and confusion at the other tables, too.

Moreland and Jo kept marching. The black cloth seemed to float in midair.

Some men next to Hoffman began to move, but other men stopped them.

Zoom on Hoffman's face, still smiling.

He mouthed something – an order – to a man standing behind him, but the man had been restrained.

Moreland reached Hoffman.

Hoffman started to speak, smiled instead.

Someone shouted, 'What's going on?' and that seemed to shake Hoffman out of it.

'I'm sorry, ladies and gentlemen, this man's quite disturbed and he's been harassing me for quite a—'

The men in blue suits flicked their wrists, and the black cloth seemed to fly away.

Six soft, misshapen people stood there, hands at their side, placid as milk-sated babies. Ruined skin highlighted mercilessly by the chandelier. The doctors at the medical center had established that only UV was a threat. The black sheet protecting them from the stares of gawkers.

Gasps from the room.

The blind one began bouncing and waving his hands, staring up at the light with empty sockets.

'My God!' said someone.

A glass dropped on the granite and shattered.

Two blue-suited men took hold of Hoffman's arms.

Moreland said, 'My name is Woodrow Wilson Moreland. I'm a doctor. I have a story to tell.'

Hoffman stopped smiling.

40

A few days later, on the plane back to L.A., it hit me. First-class flight, seats like club chairs, the Defense Department's generosity allowing Spike's crate a seat of its own.

Dinner had been salmon stuffed with sole mousse. I'd indulged in half a bottle of Chablis and fallen asleep. Robin had finished only a third of a glass, but she'd drifted off too. Now her head was heavy on my blanketed shoulder.

Sweet sleep, but I came out of it thinking about Haygood – who he'd been as a child. Was there a mother out there who'd mourn him?

Stupid thoughts, but inevitable. I tried to shake myself out of it, thinking of the good I'd been part of.

Ben freed. Some limited hope for Aruk.

The 'kids' liberated and well cared for.

Moreland hospitalized, too, and evaluated. No Alzheimer's, no obscure neurological disease, just an exhausted old man.

I'd visited him an hour before we left. He hadn't told Pam or Dennis yet.

Holding back. His entire life, after the paradise needle, a struggle against impulse.

Heroism thrust upon him, he'd reinvented himself.

A thirty-year transformation, from a cruel womanizer to the patron saint of Aruk.

But yet he felt guilty.

Other sins?

Things for which there was no atonement?

As I'd left his hospital room, he'd called out, 'Time deceives.'

The same thing he'd told me as he bled on the white couch.

Another confession?

Well, that's it. Is there anything else you need to know?

Cold hands . . . still afraid.

Not unless there's something else you want to tell me.

A long silence before he'd closed his eyes and mumbled.

Terrible things . . . Time deceives.

Offering himself to me – defenses down, his world unraveling.

The first time, I'd comforted him instead of pursuing it. The second time, I'd just kept walking.

Not wanting to know?

Terrible things.

Time's deceit.

His unique *brand* of deceit. Presenting a veiled truth while changing time and context.

Telling me about cannibal cargo cults because he suspected AnneMarie's death had been part of a money-driven conspiracy.

Recounting the nuclear blast because he'd been part of another technological horror.

Discussing Joseph Cristobal's vision and 'A. Tutalo' because he yearned to unload the secret of his kids.

And something else.

The first case he'd discussed with me, moments after we'd met.

Discussing in great detail, but unable to locate the file.

Because there'd never been a file?

The catwoman.

A 'lovely lady . . . sweet nature . . . clean habits.' Thirty years old, her mother was morose . . .

Abused and humiliated by a philandering husband – forced to watch him make love to another woman.

The husband dead, years later. Eaten away by lung cancer.

A ravaged chest . . .

I'm all right, kitten.

Kitten, kitten . . . I used to call her that when she was little.

Pam not remembering.

Sent away too young to remember anything.

But *Moreland* remembered everything.

He'd exiled her to the best schools, turned her into an orphan who'd become a woman demeaned by men.

Marrying a philandering abuser. Turning off sexually.

Humiliated . . . had she, too, watched her husband rut with a lover?

Those sad eyes. Driven to depression. To the brink of suicide, she'd admitted to Robin.

So fragile, her therapist searched for family support, located and phoned Moreland.

To Pam's surprise, he flew to Philadelphia. Offered a shoulder to cry on – and more?

Had she told him the details of the humiliation?

Or had he assigned one of his lawyers to find out the facts?

Little kitten . . . pouring her heart out to Daddy.

The truth torturing Daddy. Because of his guilt about sending her away.

Guilt about having once been exactly the kind of man who hurt her.

A few days later, the philandering husband dies in a freak accident.

Falling barbell. Ravaged chest.

And 'kitten' returns to her birthplace.

Is there anything else you need to know?

Not unless there's something else you want to tell me.

Had Moreland stalked the young surgeon? Or had he hired

someone to make things right? He was a wealthy man with the means to arrange things. The obsessive's talent for rationalizing extreme measures . . .

The barbell hovering over that arrogant chest . . .

The man who'd hurt his 'kitten' so deeply.

Or maybe it *had* been an accident and I was letting things get away from me.

Terrible things, he'd said.

Had to be . . .

I'd never know.

Did I care?

At that moment, I did. Maybe one day I wouldn't.

Robin's breath reached my nostrils, hot, tinged with coffee and wine.

A pretty, dark-haired flight attendant smiled as she walked down the aisle.

'Comfy, doctor?'

'Fine, thanks.'

'Going home?'

'Yup.'

'Well, that's nice – unless you'd rather still be on vacation.'

'No,' I said. 'I'm ready to get back to reality.'